I0523129

AMERICA
Túwaqachi

The Saga of an American Family

By

P.J. Parker

First published 2017
Paperback ISBN- 978-0-9986856-0-1
Copyright © P.J. Parker, 2017

Edited by Hayley German Fisher

Cover Design by P.J. Parker

Author Portfolio: https://about.me/author_pjparker

Dedication

To a woman of profound and unconditional love:

Aileen Bernice Cecily (née Dennes) Hardaker
1914–2014

Every family deserves an Aunty Aileen.

Fourth Morning of the Seventh Moon

There were no stars, only the darkness and an arctic chill that had intensified since the first thin, blood-red stripes of sunrise shimmered on the ocean's horizon.

The morning was, as I remember, brutally cold and dim. Flurries of flakes, then sleet, followed by storming snow, enveloped our small flotilla of makeshift rafts and reed canoes. We had fared well on the many weeks of the crossing—holding our course to the east, a little to the north. But on this day, we were tossed by mounting swells. We attempted to stay close to the other crafts within the escalating churn and crash of breaking waves; the whipping, numbing bite of wind and spray; the shattering menace of jagged, blue ice that tumbled through the water about us.

The men sat upright, my father included, their eyelids squeezed tight shut—frozen shut, the elders would later insist. Their fur long coats were encrusted with ice, thrashed by the brunt of the weather as they pulled crude wooden paddles through the surge.

The women huddled beneath hides of mammoth, slathered in warming fat, exposing their faces only now and then to cry out, their shrill voices a beacon to our brothers and sisters hidden by the increasing deluge.

I, too, crouched under the heavy skins at my father's side, gripping firmly to the warmth and flexing sinewy strength of his legs—unafraid because of it.

And in that bitter, turbulent darkness, with the new day attempting to dawn, the promise of our future echoed through my mind and we pushed on toward our Family's place of *Emergence* into the New World . . . the Fourth World.

–First Light, Son of Great White Bear

Do you not recognize me?

Másaw, the Keeper of this story, his face dark red, creased heavily by time and perhaps by some great sadness, drew back on an ornate feathered pipe that had been in his possession for longer than even he could recall. The pungent smoke drifted about him as he surveyed those gathered at his fire to hear the tale he had promised to tell. His hair was coarse and thick, jet black with no hint of gray, his braided ponytail intertwined by leather strips of bison and caribou. It draped over his shoulder and across a vest of colored porcupine quills. His left hand, twisted by age, lay in his lap, but his right—the one that held the pipe to his lips—was still strong and firm. It was filled with memories of gripping the manes of wild ponies, of loosing arrows to kill his enemies, of caressing the cheeks of those he had loved and somehow lost. Black marks were etched across the back of this hand, their significance known only to him and one other.

He slipped the pipe from his mouth and studied the carving along its red-soapstone stem. He tapped the spent tobacco from the pipe's head, replaced it with a pinch of leaves from his pouch, and relit it with a smoldering twig from the fire. Only then did he begin the story that had taken a lifetime to commit to memory.

"Trickster Coyote, in any of his many guises, may or may not let the revelation of truth come our way." Másaw's storyteller voice, deep and melodic, blended with the wind-ruffled leaves above and the crackling fire, whose brightness pulled him from the darkness.

"The formation of this planet. The separating waltz of the continents. The construction and destruction of the first lands, or *worlds*. And the eventual creation by beaver or beetle or muskrat, or perhaps tectonic movement, of that which would one day be named *America*. These stories have been told and retold with the certainty of the spider hole woven into the center of any well-made blanket. Yet likewise with the agreed-upon uncertainty of which direction the wind blows above the valiant warrior's lodge.

"Vagueness leaves wandering paw prints along the dry creek bed of man's first appearance on this ancient landscape. Some believe that tribesmen took many generations to cross the broad, temporary land bridge of Beringia from Asia to America's northwest. But when? Why? And, indeed, what of the evidence of civilization scattered far across the continent, which long predates their theory? Ask Trickster Coyote and he may well tell you such an account of *Emergence*. Or he may suggest the story of Raven, who found our forefathers in a clamshell on the beach at Naikun, where they entered a world peopled by birds and beasts of terrifying size and power. Other times, he may whisper the details of Sky Woman's descent to Earth. Or he may lick his lips slyly, letting his tongue slap back into his mouth before allowing that man was placed on the prairies, in the woodlands, and on the edge of the Blue Pond, by the Creator—as a child of the varied and beautiful land that is his Mother, and as a brother of the animals that are his equal in every way."

Másaw puffed attentively as those before him nodded in wonder. He was silent, the story that had taken millennia to evolve even now in no hurry to be told. And then the words came once more.

"Many truths resonate within the echoing howls of Coyote's tales, though some are designed to distract and contradict, to force us to follow his gaze toward the hope of the new moon, and to find the song within our own hearts before we might possess any real understanding of this noble land and the paths its people have taken.

"So, my children, come close and listen well, if you desire to know some of that which is true. With words and thoughts garnered from rock, tree, song, and wampum, diary, manuscript, and memory, I shall convey one family's journey through history. Perhaps permitting the gusting wisps of smoke and legend to move between the passages, to reveal what came before the existence of this land and Our People, and recognize that which even the Trickster would only ever dare to allude.

"As the great oak looms overhead and the woodland sounds soften the darkness about us, allow my words to ignite your thoughts and imagination, to draw them through the fire and into the far-reaching depths of time, to where those who came before us first set foot on the land that is our Mother—to the place where the legend of America and our family begins."

Túwaqachi, the World Complete (15,999 BC)

"Father?"

"Yes, First Light?"

But the boy was suddenly distracted. He moved with a slow confidence across the low tufting grasses of the tundra, crouching to touch the caribou imprint left in a drift of snow. It was still fresh and crisp. Rising to his full height—almost to his father's elbow—he sniffed at the breeze and scanned the horizon. His gaze fell upon the vast escarpment of ice. It appeared close enough to touch but was further than any in his family had yet journeyed from the inlet where their canoes had landed the previous Thaw. Obviously impossible to climb, the dazzling white arc encompassed First Light's world to the north, east, and south. It left only the icy ocean to the west open for his dreams to escape and enter. And yet higher still, beyond those frozen cliffs to the southeast rose Two Brothers, two mountains, of such brilliance and height they commanded the respect of all who lived under their morning shadow. Indeed, they were Gods.

The sharp musty scent of caribou cut into First Light's nostrils. He smiled, knowing his skill had brought them downwind of their prey. *Food!* Too many weeks had passed during the Freeze when meat was scarce. The salted stocks in the village pits were near empty, and the sea life was swimming far beyond the breakers—farther than was safe to set traps or netting. First Light's stomach ached from hunger, but knowing he would soon make his first kill and become an asset to the family at the age of seven Thaws kept him cheerful and alert. He stepped across a rivulet that carried the melting snows to the nearby coast, and sank onto a thatch of yellow grass. He grinned at his father, who squatted beside him.

"Father, how many sleeps until the Spiders return to our village?" The boy sat attentively as Great White Bear's eyes crinkled and his mouth spread into a broad smile that revealed strong teeth—whiter even than the bank of snow at his back. Rolling his weight forward so his knees crunched deep into the pebbles, Great White Bear cupped his hands in the stream and lifted fresh, freezing water to his lips. He held out his hands to his son, and the boy leaned over his father's life-scarred fingers and drank.

"Both the Spider Clan and the Walrus Clan will be amongst us soon, when the sun rising between the shoulders of our Two Brothers falls directly upon the Shaman's Stone."

"And will Rainbow Cloud be with them?"

"We shall see," Great White Bear whispered, chucking the youngster under the chin. "Now, best we track down your caribou before the daylight dims."

First Light stood, feeling for the blade within his pouch. Smaller than the palm of his hand, it fit easily into his grip. He ensured the razor-sharp cutting edge faced away from his fingers that bore the scars of practice. His father, who was twenty-five Thaws in age, carried a similar tool—though it was the strength of his hands and the swiftness of his feet that had provided meals throughout the seasons of near starvation, on the tundra in both this world and the previous. Great White Bear's skills had earned him the right to make important decisions within the combined families.

The two followed the scent as it grew thick, and Great White Bear fell back to let his son make any choices—correct or not. Both knew that skills must be honed for a young man to survive with a future Clan of his own.

They scurried low and swift through coarse grasses, jumped streams and boulders, scrambled across dunes of ice, until First Light finally threw himself against a bank of mottled gray snow. He dragged himself up to its peak and peered over the top. Through wafting flakes, he saw the magnificence of the caribou, his heart beating rapidly as he surveyed the size of the herd, felt the presence of his father several paces behind him. The mature caribou were large—much larger, stronger, and faster than any man. Hunting parties would follow herds for weeks, just as he and his father had done, becoming one with their brothers, watching for any sign of weakness or age, or slowness with calf or injury. Only then would there be the hope of a kill. Beyond the farthest bull, his antlers jerking left and right as he sniffed suspiciously at the wind, several mastodons lumbered. They ripped at sodden grasses, lifting and shoving the mulch into their gaping mouths. First Light lay patiently as the sun rose toward the top of the sky. And then he saw it. The small calf he had been spying on for several weeks, still wobbly beside its mother. It limped from a deformity of the leg. Nevertheless, it was brawnier than First Light himself.

Despite the chill of the day, sweat coursed down First Light's neck and back to saturate his skins. His breathing picked up as the mother caribou stepped toward him to drink from the brook, nudging her feeble offspring to follow. She bellowed, and First Light's grip tightened on his blade. He silently thanked Mother Earth and brother caribou, and asked that he and his weapon might be worthy, that the Spirit of the calf might once more inhabit the flesh of life and inform others that he was an honorable hunter.

Great White Bear rested his chin on his fists, almost smiling as he watched.

And then he let out a sudden gasp of dread.

But it was too late.

First Light scurried over the dune. He collided with the lame calf and scraped his blade across its neck, cutting deftly though an artery. The animal's bawl spluttered to a stop.

In the same instant, a saber-toothed cat sprang high from her hiding spot in the grasses. Her enormous curved teeth glinted in the icy brightness. Caribou bucked and mastodon trumpeted as the cat leapt over the boy, knocking him with her rear paws. She clenched her forelegs and claws around the cow, no more than an arm span away.

No sooner had the cat's teeth ripped into the caribou than Great White Bear leapt from the top of the dune with a warrior's speed. He grasped his son and the slaughtered calf and tumbled away from the great cat. They dropped abruptly into a shallow ditch.

Caribou scattered in all directions, kicking ice and mud into the air. "Do not move, my son. Do not make a noise or the cat will take us both." His whisper was almost inaudible.

First Light detected the cat's movement at the far edge of his vision—long teeth thrusting repeatedly into the meat of the caribou, ripping chunks of flesh from the bone. But still he stared into the eyes of his father, past the flared nostrils of the calf he had killed. Emotions rippled across his face—thrill that he had made his first kill, fear that a predator ate within an arm's length of where he lay, and pride that he had achieved something remarkable in the sight of his father. Tears filled his eyes, but he knew his father would recognize they were of accomplishment rather than fear. He smiled, and so did Great White Bear, with the sound of tearing flesh close to their ears.

Father and son remained tight within each other's embrace as the cat feasted. Now and then she cast a wandering gaze toward them, purring and snarling with a deep rumble. First Light's back was soon numbed by a trickle of melting ice and the full weight of his father pinning him down. But nothing could diminish the warmth of true happiness. When the herd of caribou had long disappeared and the cat had finally dragged a leg of the carcass back to her litter, First Light's father helped him up and together they hefted the calf onto the bank. Great White Bear fell back on his haunches, beaming in elated exhaustion. Then he handed to his son his own stone tool—a dependable blade that had been with him during many great hunts. First Light accepted it in awe—noting the sharpness of its cutting edge and how the blue-black obsidian sparkled, reflecting the clouds overhead. He placed it carefully in the leather pouch at his waist and lowered his head in acknowledgement of the one he respected without reserve. Then he gripped the calf by the back legs and held them close to his chest. His father lifted the remainder of the carcass and draped it across the shoulders of his son—the hunter.

The kill was heavy, but sinewy strength and determination kept First Light's back straight and shoulders broad. There was still value in the remains of the cat's kill, so Great White Bear deftly skinned the carcass with seven strokes of his long blade. He filled the hide with chunks of meat and some of the sweeter morsels the cat had missed. Great White Bear carefully cut out the half-eaten heart, for the Shaman would find knowledge within the grooves made by the saber teeth. He hefted the freshly butchered package over his shoulder, the caribou's two rear legs, still plump and full, thrusting high above his hooded coat. First Light surveyed the tundra from the top of the dune. The mastodons once again stood lazily, eating their fill, but the only sign of the caribou was a rising vapor to the north.

It took much longer than First Light had anticipated to walk across the tundra back to the village. The sun dipped to rest on the westerly ocean before them. They trod methodically, skirting the single grove of spruce where brother sloth hung from the middle branches. At more than three times the height of Great White Bear and six times that of First Light, the languid beast would never seek to cause them harm. Still it was wise to stay clear of his far-reaching arms. The sloth screeched some kind of distant, echoing acknowledgement, and First Light sensed his brother knew what he had achieved on this day.

* * * *

The village of First Light's people, Our People, stood where a river fed into the ocean. Waves crashed along the stony beach. Fish traps swayed—empty—in the current. Large granite cliffs rose high above the two lodges. Between the buildings was the area of the Great Fire, and on the shore the Shaman's Stone stood high. The rays of the afternoon sun highlighted its slender serrated silhouette. Around the village, hides were slung across scraping frames, and a few small fish hung over a fire pit, fresh tundra grasses smoking below them. The bleached remains of shellfish, oysters, crabs, and caribou from the previous season were piled high for whenever they might be needed. Five men were readying their blades for the Thaw hunts, and they stood when they saw Great White Bear and First Light approaching. Circling Eagle, without doubt the family's most prolific hunter even before he'd reached his seventeenth Thaw, thrust both hands into the sky and sang loudly of the new hunter. First Light, despite his burden, pushed himself a little taller as he strode past the group toward the nearest shelter. He was no longer a child, but one of the men he had long admired.

The shelters, much longer than they were wide, stood the height of two men. Sun-dried mastodon skins stretched tight across bowed frames, were tied securely at a peaked ridge that ran the full length of each lodge. Sods of earth were piled upon the sides of the largest, where yellow and orange grasses sprouted. Two great tusks marked the single opening to the lodge in which Great White Bear and his family lived with ten other adults and their children.

Great White Bear held the opening skins high, and First Light stepped through the doorway and down the three steps to the warmth of the woolly-mammoth-layered floor of the inside pit. As always, he felt he had been welcomed into the belly of a large, protective beast. To his left and right the ribs and tusks of ancient elephants curved to the top of the ceiling, crossing at its apex and intertwined by sinew and leather lacing. Between these supports an intricate progression of sun-bleached mammoth skull, pelvis, and femur created a solid insulating barrier to the outside elements—made permanently waterproof by the outer skins and turf. When he was much younger, First Light had often attempted to count the skulls—each one taller and wider than he could then reach. The Shaman had assured him there were more skulls in each lodge than sunrises during the Thaw.

The brothers and sisters of the Great White Bear Clan gathered in the first smoky room stopped their chores and stood, holding hands open and high as they took up the chant started by Circling Eagle. The emotion within First Light's chest seemed almost unbearable, and his cheeks ached from smiling. At the partitioning skin to the second and final room, he turned to his father for reassurance. Great White Bear simply smiled, pulling back the hide and motioning for his son to enter.

The space was brightly lit, as always. Scenes of successful hunts and miraculous stories from his family's past were painted upon the coarse skin of an ancient mystical animal that all but covered the rear wall of the lodge. First Light, and indeed everyone in the village, had spent many an evening in front of this history, listening to their oldest brothers. One brother was as old as forty Thaws and forty Freezes, and it was said not only had he lived most of his life in the Third World, but he had actually been born before the destruction of the Second. He'd been one of the few who still possessed the song in his heart, and so was spared. First Light's gaze followed the history as it circled the hide, his focus resting on the depiction of the end of the Second World—our Mother teetering off balance, mountains plunging into the oceans, and the vastness of ice spreading across her swollen belly.

The picture's magic was made stronger by the soft melodic humming in the room.

First Light's mother, Little Pebble, kneeled on the far side of the central fire. Smoldering mammoth bones glowed red within the shallow pit before her. To First Light, she was the most beautiful woman in any world, her hair long and shining, braided now with leather and shells. Her garments were of soft caribou, rubbed and polished translucent. Around her neck hung a string of pearls, interspersed by the teeth of arctic fox.

Little Pebble had been preparing for her son's arrival all day—knowing he would return as a man. She beamed at Great White Bear as he stepped around her, running his fingers through her hair before taking his seat at her right, slightly behind. The firelight made her eyes dazzle as she hummed the tune she always said had been within her heart since before she was born. Then she held her arms wide and beckoned for her son, the man, to approach. First Light shuffled around the fire, kneeled, and dropped his head and torso to lower the calf from his shoulders onto the wide cutting rock next to the fire. His entire body ached, but without the weight of the kill he felt suddenly lightheaded and had to bite his lower lip to stop anxious tears from welling. Little Pebble smiled and touched him gently on the hand.

For many, many heartbeats, First Light watched her expertly use her cutting blades and scrapers to loosen the hide. Once removed, she handed it to a young girl called White Cloud—also seven Thaws old, and gifted by another family in the previous world to be joined with him. She blushed when First Light caught her gaze. She would now be required to prove the success of her training by tanning the skin and presenting it to him by the new moon. Little Pebble continued her work, cutting across the muscles to produce cleanly separated chunks, knowing that to carve along the thread of sinew and flesh would make it tough and less palatable. She piled the meat upon the edge of the stone and placed the lungs, heart, liver, and kidneys in a container of tanned hide, the brain in a treasured wooden bowl.

When all was complete, Little Pebble held her hands high and let out a soulful note. Four of our sisters took away the cutting stone and the calf. First Light leaned toward his mother, and she touched his forehead and ran her fingers across his cheeks, the blood of the kill leaving honorable marks upon his skin.

* * * *

Feasting, singing, and stories of the hunt lifted the village into the evening. When the celebrations had mellowed into a thoughtfulness that huddled around the embers of the communal fire—drifting on the low moaning chant of the Shaman—First Light made his way alone down to the beach. The dark glow of the midnight sun hung at the horizon's edge. It skimmed effortlessly toward the icy eastern escarpment. But the high moon lit the pebbled shoreline and breaking waves with a light almost as brilliant as the brightest of Thaw days. The crashing of water continued, as always, audible from everywhere First Light had ever known. However, this time it was different. He was a man now—the first to cross into adulthood in this new world. He lowered himself onto the pebbles and leaned against the Shaman's Stone, feeling its power at his back. The energy and heat of the monolith's magic seemed to flow within him. He was not tired when the sun began to shine its earliest yellow hues onto the breakers farthest from the shore. He glanced up to see the top of the sacred stone bathed in amber, then stood to watch our Father rise majestically between the shoulders of the Two Brothers. Their shadows fell across the unfathomable distance of tundra that separated them from the village. Soon the light shone directly into First Light's eyes, and a familiar silhouette shimmered toward him in the glare. It had the profile of Great White Bear, but even so, First Light knew instantly it was not he.

Rainbow Cloud strode forward like a hunting cat with the same strength of height and broad shoulders, the same rolling gait as First Light's father. They were indeed the same man, split in two at birth, so the family might be rewarded by twice the skill in hunting each brother possessed.

* * * *

"The animal kills will be meager during the Thaw. We must look to the ocean if we are to survive the next ice." The Shaman, Night of Thunder, spoke confidently as he held high the caribou heart so all could see the grooves ripped in its side. The lodge fire sparked and the antlers the Shaman wore on his head cast a shadow across the ceiling. First Light gasped in awe.

"But the caribou grow strong and plentiful," Rainbow Cloud said. "Did not my brother's son become a man only yesterday amongst the rumble of a mighty herd?" He grinned and clapped Great White Bear and First Light on their shoulders.

Night of Thunder squinted, turning the heart and running a finger down the leftmost groove. "They grow abundant and healthy, from the succulence of the tundra's herb grasses and from the fresh waters that emanate from the east. I fear they are too strong—not only for our hunters, skilled as they are, but for the others that prey on this valley's inhabitants."

Great White Bear stepped toward the Shaman. "It is true what you see, wise man. In the last weeks of the hunt, I saw only two animals that could be felled by a man. One was my son's first kill. The other was prey to the saber-tooth." The men in the room shifted uncomfortably, murmuring to each other. First Light strained to hear what they said.

Circling Eagle pulled the long blade from his side and held it toward the fire. "Do you suggest, Shaman, that we and the great cats will starve during the next Thaw and Freeze because the caribou are too strong?"

The Shaman held out his hand, took the blade from Circling Eagle, and cleaved the caribou heart in two. "I read this flesh and say what it forebodes. It suggests not that the cats will starve, but that brother caribou will not be their first choice of prey."

A shiver coursed down First Light's spine.

* * * *

The combined brothers of the Great White Bear, Walrus, and Spider Clans set out across the tundra. Their breath crystallized in the chill of a sharp Thaw morning to fly back and sting their eyes and cheeks. First Light strode a few paces ahead of Great White Bear and Rainbow Cloud, but stayed close enough to be part of their conversation.

"It is good to be with you once more, my brother. I have missed your company during the length of this Freeze."

"And I have missed yours, Rainbow Cloud, though it seems the Freeze grows ever shorter, even in this new world."

"It is as you say. The waters of the great pond also encroach upon this new land just as they did in the last. We chose a place for our lodges by the southern rim of this valley, only to have them swamped by a tide during the time of endless night. It may have been a tide usual to this new land, but our wise men do not believe so."

Great White Bear nodded. "The changes in our Mother are quickening."

First Light said, "I have kept watch of brother sloth. He ventures farther and farther from his grove during the twilight, only to lumber back to its safety by day. I think he is searching for a new home."

Both Great White Bear and Rainbow Cloud smiled at the interjection before appearing to realize its import. They caught each other's gaze then looked out at the thirty or so men of the hunting party fanned out around them. The brothers of each Clan mixed freely with the others to share knowledge of stealth and skill.

First Light now concentrated on his own vital chore. As he'd been the last to note the location of the caribou, it was his charge to lead the family to them. The bellow of mastodon—normally the herd's docile companions—echoed across the tundra but gave no hint of direction. The party passed through a graveyard of those ancient beasts, where thousands of skulls, ribs, and bones littered a broad, shallow basin in the plain. It smelled of the sweet purple grasses they favored. In silence the hunters moved through this holy place. They skirted the sun-bleached remains of past generations, stared in awe at complete skeletons reclining in the slushy frozen mud. Some were still covered in thick, sagging skin, with tufting patches of coarse hair draped across rib cages and clinging to skulls. Deep pits that once were eyes seemed to follow the men as they went. When they reached the far side of the graveyard, they dropped to their knees and ran their gloved hands across the earth, lifting mud, ice, and sod to smear their faces and hooded long coats. First Light smoothed the ooze across his cheeks and broad nose. He slathered it over his thick lips, under his chin, and across his forehead. Sticky and invigorating, the mud immediately began to tighten the pores of his face. The smell of it melded with his own and he knew, now more than ever, that he and his four-legged brothers were equal in every way. Each possessed the same simple quest—to survive.

A remote vapor glinted against the glacial backdrop.

"There," he indicated in a hard-learned wail, passed down through his family. It sounded like a far-off walrus resting lazily on the rocks. The Clansmen took up the call as they too saw the haze rising to the northeast. The tender slaps of affirmation from Rainbow Cloud and Great White Bear made him grin as he doubled his pace to keep up with their increasing stride. They ran to the beach, along the pebbled grade, before rushing through a freezing torrent that poured from the tundra into the sea. Rainbow Cloud yanked First Light up on to his back, and the men separated, sloshing up several tributaries and crawling onto grassed embankments. They pulled themselves across the frozen tundra, and their bodies became one with their Mother, smothered in the scent of both her and their brothers.

Then they were still.

* * * *

The heat from his father and uncle kept First Light warm throughout the chill of their first night out in the open. They huddled close, talking in whispers, their bodies vibrating in silent chuckles at Rainbow Cloud's stories. Finally, First Light fell into a light doze, the arm of his uncle cuddling him close in sleep as Great White Bear took the first watch.

He woke long before he was due and lay in silent contemplation with his father. They studied the vast herd of animals resting less than a handful of ragged ice dunes from their position.

"We will sleep amongst our brothers within the next three high suns. Then surely we will know them, and which will provide for our family," Great White Bear whispered.

"But Father, what of the Shaman's message to look to the ocean for our stores? Will not the Spirits be angry that we have ignored their wisdom?"

Great White Bear looked at him thoughtfully. "Your mother and our sisters are capable of wielding the tools of the sea. Their skills are more attuned than ours with that task. We in turn must do as we know—use our talent to hunt and capture our brother, whose duty it is to help us in our quest."

First Light took his watch between the bulks of the two sleeping men, turning from one to the other as they slept. Their cheeks, their chins, their every breath and flutter of eyelid was identical. First Light touched his own face—a face he would never clearly see—and wondered if he resembled them at all. In his gut, he knew he did.

To the north, the tundra turned to a panorama of undulating snowfields punctuated by jagged rocky outcrops reminiscent of the Shaman's Stone. The steaming bodies of the caribou lay, their heavy breath and snore blanketing the landscape. One or two of the stronger males shuffled warily at the herd's edge with their own watchful gazes.

All three men were awake when the lead cow bellowed her wakeup call. One by one the three-thousand-strong herd stood and lifted their tails to empty full bladders. The cacophony of awakening bawls rose almost as high as the sulfur scented vapor of the animals' morning ritual. Rainbow Cloud elbowed his brother, chuckling over the perils of yellow ice.

First Light spent much of the morning crouched in silence, watching the caribou eat their fill, rub contentedly against one another, rest among the dunes, and do that which made their lives complete. Great White Bear tore a fistful of salted eel from a slender carcass deep within his rucksack and passed it to him. First Light rolled onto his back, and the impossibly blue sky took up his vision as the smell of the surrounding herd filled his nostrils. He savored the briny, chewiness of the dried sea creature.

"Tell me of your journey since the last hunt," First Light said to Rainbow Cloud. He slipped off a glove to poke at a piece of eel skin stuck between his molars.

"It is a wide land that I have seen, First Light. My Clan of the Walrus walked many moons to the south, where the great white ice wall falls into the ocean."

"Did you climb to the top?"

"We tried! But there was no foothold—not even the slightest crevice to stick a boot. The cliffs are sheer. Straight up! Much higher than our strongest athlete could throw a line."

"What do you think is at its peak?"

"That I do not know, my young man. But I can tell you gusting breezes threw clouds of flurry over its edge, and with it seemed to fall an acrid stench and a howling trumpet of beasts I have neither heard nor dreamed of, in either this world or the last."

First Light held Rainbow Cloud's gaze. "Not caribou or mastodon?"

"Louder than both. Their deep rumble made the very ground shake, and their shrieking could signify nothing good."

A cow and her calf sloshed through a nearby brook. First Light was glad of the distraction and watched them cross to the other side.

"And what of the ocean itself?" Great White Bear muttered under his breath as he, too, kept close watch on the cow and calf.

"Ah, my brother, it appears impassable. The curve of the coast can be seen to run for many weeks' travel to the south. Lofty ramparts of boulder and ice are thrashed by waves almost half as tall. Our craft would never survive were we to hug the land. We might fare better on a deeper sea course, but there is no guarantee we would find another valley as verdant as this."

"It is true that our destiny and heart song brought us here."

"It is true."

* * * *

And it was true that by the third full rising of the sun, the hunting party was surrounded and accepted by the herd of caribou. The enormous animals roamed freely amongst the men, whose own movements were slow or nonexistent. The Clans were not the remotest threat to the healthy mature caribou. Even a fit calf could outrun an attack from many directions by the swiftest of hunters. *Our brothers are superior in all respects*, thought First Light, admiring their size and strength. He knew, as all those men did, that the grunting kick of a hoof could kill a man instantly. Any impact, intentional or not, could bruise or break bones enough to cause a man's death. Even the Shaman's strongest medicine could not heal it.

"And yet our brothers are gentle. They mean no harm to the worthy hunter," First Light whispered. His father's welcome arm reached across his shoulders to pull him close.

*   *   *   *

The sun skimmed the horizon and rose to the top of the sky for the fifth time during the hunt. The Clansmen were beginning the day that would be drawn upon the Family History skin. It would be burned into First Light's memory until the very moment his own heart stopped beating.

Huddled in the center of the herd, the men of the Clans of Great White Bear, Walrus, and Spider were one with their brothers. There had been no sign of weak or frail caribou. All were healthy and strong. First Light sensed the concern amongst his fellow hunters, but still they watched with vigilance for any changes. Undoubtedly the Spirits would favor them for their alertness and present those animals whose destiny coincided with their own.

There was a distant rumble; felt more than heard. The caribou lifted their heads to bellow, nudging at those dozing amongst the tufting grasses. They swished their heads side to side, unsure which way to move.

To the east, a haze of powdered snow puffed into the air. The muffled din grew louder as the haze pushed toward them.

Suddenly, a massive bull careened through the caribou. It rushed up the dune and thumped heavily between Great White Bear and Rainbow Cloud, only to lose its footing and slide down the icy slope behind them. The two men rolled out of the way, but even First Light knew this was only the beginning of a disaster unforeseen by the Shaman. He scuttled down to his father and fell awkwardly against his chest as another bull and two cows leapt over the top of the dune and trod within a finger's length of their prone bodies. The noise was now deafening. The caribou were spooked, stomping first one way then the other in escalating panic. A saber-tooth. Perhaps a pride of saber-tooths.

First Light reached for Rainbow Cloud, and his gut wrenched at seeing his uncle's bruised and bloodied face before he was thrust back by the force of several animals rushing between them. The other Clan members were indiscernible, scattered across the dunes by the terror of the stampede, their yells indistinct beneath the deafening rumble.

Great White Bear yanked at his son, and then they were on their feet running along the lower ground between two ice dunes. Enormous caribou ran on either side of them, and First Light felt only horror as even his father was dwarfed by the beasts that ran twice as fast—even three times—as he and his father could ever hope to.

Great White Bear yelled something repeatedly, but First Light could not understand.

Ahead of them the higher dunes abruptly changed direction, and the caribou lurched and stumbled, their legs buckling beneath them. Choking from the stench of fear, First Light felt strong hands thrust under his armpits, fingers digging into his ribs, lifting him up, throwing him brutally between two beasts toward the top of the curved embankment. He tumbled through the air, catching a momentary glimpse of the three-thousand strong stampede that churned the landscape in every direction, before being blinded by the mud, slush, and stones flung against him with bruising force.

He landed haphazardly against the ice, scraping the skin from his forehead and cheeks and finally coming to rest on his back, his vision filled by the mud-flung, mottled blue of the early Thaw sky above.

He could not move—did not want to move.

The horrendous noise, the horrid crunch and grind of the stampede continued in the rifts around him, but all he saw was the blue sky. At some point, he became aware of his finger twitching of its own accord, but then it stopped.

Eventually the caribou slowed and settled until the only sound was the crash of far off waves and the meandering tread of nearby beasts.

The sun slipped to the horizon.

First Light's vision blurred, sensing he would not see his father or uncle again in this world.

And then he was still.

* * * *

Knuckles brushed against First Light's forehead, then a palm caressed his cheek. Dark eyes peered into his—searching—before he was lifted from the ground and slung over a shoulder. The earth bobbed swiftly, his arms slapping against the back of a mammoth-hide long-coat.

He watched the heavy fur boots below run from slush and tundra to pebbled beach, and then they stopped. First Light was shrugged off and lowered to the ground, where Circling Eagle gazed into his eyes. He rubbed First Light's arms, legs, and torso, blowing warm, moist air across his face and deep into his lungs.

First Light's body convulsed, his skin suddenly burning, and he retched onto the ground beside him. Circling Eagle held him secure until he was finished, until the shaking subsided and the youngest man of the family was calm and quiet.

* * * *

The Shaman crouched on the ground before the Great Fire of the village. A mammoth skull—elaborately decorated with red ocher—had been dragged out from the second lodge and now stood beside him. He caressed its sides, its cheek. The blazing fire lit the skull's depths, reflecting within its cavernous interior to highlight the reddened sockets, which contained wisdom far older than Our People. The Shaman's chanting was low and monotone, punctuated by the rhythmic crash of waves upon the nearby shore.

Our brothers and sisters sat in silence at the very edge of the fire's light, behind them only the chilled darkness and the remote rumbling purr of the great cats, who watched their every move but refused to approach the flames of man's only true power.

First Light kneeled beside Little Pebble, both their faces flushed with sadness but dry of eye in respect of the great men they honored. First Light looked around the family circle as the Shaman's chant scraped across his heart. White Cloud huddled with another young girl, their heads bowed almost to the ground. Circling Eagle stood solid but forlorn, staring at the glowing skull, clenching his fists. Beside him stood Dark Hair, who's belly swelled with the child of Rainbow Cloud. "*Perfect*," Rainbow Cloud would say of her. "*Wide hips for the bearing of many great warriors. A glorious, round belly that becomes only more beautiful as our family grows. And a voluptuous posterior that indicates a full and healthy life.*" Rainbow Cloud would laugh, in adoration. "*She has the body of Mother Earth herself*," he would gloat, smiling at Great White Bear who, First Light knew, felt the same way about Little Pebble.

First Light focused upon the bodies laid out before the Great Fire.

Great White Bear.

Rainbow Cloud.

Great White Bear had delivered First Light to safety during the stampede, and Rainbow Cloud had led several Clansmen to the security of a rocky outcrop. Then both brothers had been taken by the Spirits.

The two hunters lay in a shallow trench scratched into the permafrost. The ceremony was entering its seventh twilight as the families surrendered the brothers to Túwaqachi. They were the first. The Fourth World was now complete.

The bottom of the grave had been covered with charcoal from the Great Fire, sprinkled with a thin layer of grainy white limestone, then a rich depth of red ocher transported from the previous world. The men lay upon the foundation, side by side, each a mirror image of the other. They wore clothes of finely crafted caribou, decorated with more than six thousand ivory beads. Their hair cascaded freely from beneath fur caps encircled by arctic fox teeth, and carved ornaments adorned their foreheads. Their arms—strong biceps bedecked by ivory bracelets—were folded over their pelvises. Two tusks arced protectively on either side of the brothers.

The Shaman bent over them now, the low moaning chant barely falling from his lips as he tenderly sifted another layer of red ocher across their bodies.

First Light walked past the blaze toward his father and uncle. At the side of the pit, he felt the hand of the Shaman fall heavily upon his shoulder. Night of Thunder stared into his soul, his eyes wide, reflecting the fire, the sorrow, and the thankfulness of the tribe that the Spirits had spared the other Clansmen. First Light placed his hand upon that of the Shaman.

"My father and uncle are ready for their journey."

The wise man nodded.

First Light kneeled at the head of the burial pit. From his cloak he pulled two figurines that he and the village men had fashioned from an ancient mammoth tusk. They were smooth and solid within his grip, the symbols of greatness honed and polished by all. Carefully, First Light urged the Great Walrus figurine beneath his uncle's shoulder blade. Then, pressing his cheek against his father's ocher-dusted chest, he pushed the sculpted Great White Bear deep under the earthly body that shared its name.

The sun dipped below the westerly ocean.

The Great Fire sparked and cracked.

The ceremonial chant grew louder, lifting up into the air.

And above them, the Northern Lights streaked across the sky. Green fluorescent ribbons of brilliance shot from one end of the valley to the other.

First Light turned to follow their course, catching the gaze of his mother and Circling Eagle, the new leader of the Great White Bear Clan. The lights brightened the tundra and the far-off glacier, shrouding the distant shoulders of the two majestic mountains to the southeast. Their slopes glowed beneath the aurora.

"Our brothers are showing us the way," Circling Eagle muttered at his ear.

"And we will follow them," First Light said.

Glacial Horizons (15,976 BC)

Our brothers are showing us the way, so indicated the symbols of the Family History.

"And we will follow them," recited Rearing Mammoth, son of First Light.

His fingers traced the twenty-two pictograms circling from this historic decision until they touched upon the portion of blank skin, still free from the burning charcoal stick of the Shaman.

The hunter in him knew his own story would one day be seared into this heritage.

At fourteen, Rearing Mammoth was strong and healthy, possessing the same lithe muscular physique as his father. His straight dark hair was chopped at the shoulder. The slant of his nose and the sparkle of his eyes was reminiscent of White Cloud, his mother, but he was without doubt the son of First Light—the revered provider who had kept the Clan safe from the claw and fang of the ever-present saber-tooths until his passing, the previous season, at the respectable age of thirty Thaws.

Rearing Mammoth strode through the inner rooms of the lodge. He lifted the skin at the entrance, grabbed hold of one of the weathered tusks, and pulled himself up the steps to the snow-covered gravel outside. Striding across the central village clearing, he shielded his eyes from the intense sunlight reflecting off the fissured glacial walls rising vertically above the village. The escarpment was a dazzling, blinding white, except where cracks in the ice exposed a deep blue-gray. If he peered into those cracks, he could see another world behind the translucent walls: shifting shadows, Spirits captured and frozen into Mother Earth herself.

Several young ones were attempting to scale it. One boy clung much higher than the others, but still had no hope of reaching the top, at least eight hundred times higher without any sign of foothold.

"Whoa!" yelled Rearing Mammoth, reaching up to grab the boy, who was little more than an arm's length above him.

Tusk laughed and squirmed in his older brother's grip. "Put me down, put me down!"

"Not until you tell me your secret for climbing so high."

"I have magic boots, sewn by the Shaman."

"By the Spirits of the caribou, so you do!" Rearing Mammoth chuckled, tugging off one of Tusk's boots to expose a small pink foot.

"Mama, Mama!" the younger screamed.

Rearing Mammoth lifted Tusk high, throwing him up above his head before catching him securely in his arms. Together they fell to the ground in a giggling heap.

"Should you not be with the other men, Rearing Mammoth?" White Cloud asked, a tender scolding, turning from her work at the nearby smoking pit.

Rearing Mammoth threw her a smile, which he knew reminded her of his father and so always brought her happiness. She was right, though. He reached into his pouch and extracted the blade his father had received from Great White Bear, and in turn had handed down to him. Its edge was sharp. Its depths were black, tinged by the sparkle of an even darker hue. It reflected Rearing Mammoth's wide, blinking eye, and the clouds that billowed behind him. He replaced the blade in his pouch and stood.

"I love you, little brother," he whispered, rubbing his nose against Tusk's. "I love you, Mama," he shouted before running in the direction of the men.

Snow crunched beneath his feet as he ran through the familiar boulders of ice and rock that surrounded the village. He skimmed the broad slush stream that snaked away from a glacial cave, then scaled the gentle rise of a hillock covered with the tufting grasses of the tundra. In the distance, past the snow-mottled yellow and orange landscape, he could see the crests of waves. Legend assured him the ocean was encroaching into his family's shrinking world. White Cloud and many others were certain their Mother was pushing them toward their intended path.

Rearing Mammoth joined the men amongst the scattered clusters of monolithic rocks, where they were searching for stones and blades of value in the midst of the shattered debris.

"I have the hard stone," he shouted. The men looked up to see him pull the slab from its satchel and hold it up to the Two Brothers, rising majestically above the escarpment, dwarfing even the glacial rim that towered over their lives. Their peaks disappeared into the sky.

He placed the slab reverently upon the ground before the men and crouched beside Red Star, the youngest man at nine Thaws old. Red Star held his own stone high, black and smooth, then brought it down solidly and smashed it onto the slab. The single clap of agate against agate echoed through the grove and out onto the tundra, a unique sound only man could create. Our Mother might send many rocks cascading from a slope; our brothers might kick stones in their meandering. But only man could strike a single rock against another, one solitary time. Rearing Mammoth gazed out to where caribou and mastodon grazed with musk ox and yak. As usual they were undisturbed by their smaller brothers' activity.

Red Star slammed his stone against the slab a second time, amid the impatient murmurs of a few of the men. Rearing Mammoth caught his gaze and nodded in reassurance. Red Star then struck the slab a third time, and one side of his stone shattered and broke off. Satisfied, he held up the shard, gently testing the sharpened edge with the pad of his finger.

"Well done. The first blade of the season," Rearing Mammoth said.

The youngest man smirked as he shuffled aside so the next, Sundance, could try his skill. But before the later could get into position, another Clansman pushed his way to the front of the group, knocking both Red Star and Sundance to the ground. There was a scuffle before the interloper lifted his rock high, daring any to approach, then brought it swiftly down against the hard stone.

Rearing Mammoth watched with narrowed eyes. Something would need to be done.

* * * *

The fire in the lodge smoldered as it seared the chunks of meat and fish upon its hot stones. Billowing smoke filled the top of the space and darkened the uppermost ribs and skulls that sheltered the families within. It made Rearing Mammoth's eyes water, so he grabbed the entrance hide and rippled it to draw in the welcome cool twilight air. His torso was bare in the heat of the lodge, covered in a glistening sweat. The outside fires blazed, tended by the youngest men, lighting the dozen lodges that huddled close to their protection. In the muted light beyond was the ever-present glint of carnivorous eyes.

Muttering to himself, Rearing Mammoth let the flap fall closed and ambled toward the corner he shared with his brother. Young Tusk was sucking on a caribou bone his mother had cracked for him, and Rearing Mammoth lay flat on his back beside him to observe his brother's determination in extracting every last morsel of marrow.

Sundance shuffled over to join them and settled in close to Rearing Mammoth on the woolly flooring so that both shared the same view up between Tusk's arms and straight into his mouth. Teeth gnawed up and down the bone. A small finger was stuck into the shattered end and then sucked vigorously.

"I heard what you said," Sundance murmured.

"What?" Rearing Mammoth asked. "I have said nothing."

"I agree with you. I agree with what you said."

Tusk raised an eyebrow, flipped the bone, and attacked the cartilage.

"But I have not yet earned the right to make such statements. I have said nothing."

"Rearing Mammoth, you are the direct descendent of the Great White Bear after whom our Clan is named. You are the son of the first to become a man in Túwaqachi."

"We are all children of Mother Earth and equal in her design."

"Yes," Sundance said. "But you will one day be our leader. Even the most ancient amongst us agrees. I am willing to follow you now. I am willing to hear what you say."

"Mama," Tusk said, holding up the bone. White Cloud took it and with a single thwack of her grinding stone split it down the center.

Tusk's eyes bulged in delight as he grasped the shattered pieces. He stuck the ends of both portions quickly into his mouth.

Rearing Mammoth chuckled, then turned to Sundance to murmur in hushed whispers. White Cloud continued her work at the fire, but the two men of fourteen Thaws had no doubt she would catch every word.

"Our Clan has grown too large," Rearing Mammoth said. "We are losing our sense of family. The stories and songs of Our People indicate the number of Clan members should be no more than the number of fingers and toes of its greatest warrior. Fewer and we would not survive the tundra. But more only invites internal conflict."

The lodge was filled with the gentle snores of the very old and the quiet conversations and muted laughter of those finishing their evening meal. A young woman called Many Caribou was singing to a gathering of girls—something about collecting herbs to use when smoking fish. Rearing Mammoth rolled onto his side, propping himself up on his elbow to watch her. White Cloud caught him looking and gave him a knowing smile.

"Nearly one hundred brothers and sisters reside in our camp," he told Sundance. "Our Clan is swollen with others who have followed their heart song to this new world, and by the Spirits who bless us with abundant strong children."

Sundance nodded in silence. Tusk slurped at the marrow-flavored spit that dribbled down his chin.

Rearing Mammoth lowered himself back down. "Aggression has grown amongst the men." His words were slightly muffled in the long curls of brown hair that sprung thickly from the wool hide beneath them. "They vie for superiority in the simplest of everyday chores. Take the striking of the first blades this morning."

"But that is natural," Sundance said. "There are leaders. And there are those who choose to follow."

"I agree, my brother. But our tundra grows smaller with each tidal moon. There is no longer ample space for our families to separate and follow our own paths around the necessary circle of the seasons. Instead we endure an unhealthy closeness through both Freeze and Thaw that can breed only discontent. The natural leaders are unable to lead in their turn."

"The increasing size of our Clan has been of benefit to keep the cats at bay," White Cloud said.

"Yes. But we cannot continue living under the threat of these carnivores. And we cannot continue living in this diminishing valley."

White Cloud scooted away from the fire to rest against the partitioning wall. She pulled Tusk into her arms. "Your father once followed brother sloth deep into the ice corridors south of our village."

"Brother sloth!" Sundance exclaimed. "He must be old as the tundra itself, yet we've seen neither him nor the short-faced bears for many Thaws."

"Do you believe the cats have taken them?" Rearing Mammoth asked his mother.

"No more than I believe the cats are responsible for the diminishing numbers of caribou," she said.

After a lengthy silence, Sundance turned back to his companion. "Rearing Mammoth?"

"I believe brother sloth has found a way out of the valley. Up onto the glacier that creeps between the shoulders of the Two Brothers. There, we too may find the space we need to live as intended. It is time for us to move on—to leave the tundra."

Tusk's eyes grew wide. His mouth fell open, and his chubby hands—still gripping the now marrowless bones—dropped into his lap.

* * * *

Rearing Mammoth and Sundance were less than half a moon's walk south of the village. They would have progressed farther except for the short stride of Tusk, who was determined to go with them on their adventure. The elders had concluded it would be good experience for the young boy of five Thaws, for he had much to learn in the few short seasons before his impending manhood.

The three of them had followed the line of the glacier, hugging close to its base when it was lit by the yellow-blue rays of morning. When the midday sun slipped behind the southern rim, throwing the lower ice cliffs into dark shadow, they arced further out into the open tundra. None of them wished to be surprised by the glint of fang or a deep rumbling purr. They trudged on, picking at tundra herbs and stuffing them into their pockets and satchels to supplement the dried fish White Cloud had bundled for them. Even Tusk was burdened with a pack half his size. Nonetheless, Rearing Mammoth knew his little brother did not mind, happy that the contents included several cracked bones specially for him.

Well before the sun had dipped on their fifteenth day of walking, they selected a high rocky outcrop on which to spend the twilight. It had the safety of several hundred paces of clear tundra in all directions, as well as a broad, flat top surrounded by chunky shards of rock that would afford shelter from the chilly evening winds. Rearing Mammoth and Sundance ripped at dried grasses, foraged through scattered bones, and tossed everything flammable they could find up into the center of the shelter for Tusk to assemble into his first fire—an important step in the making of a man. The boy piled the material, then searched his pack for the flint his mother had entrusted to him. Rearing Mammoth ached from suppressing the continual urge to intervene—to push Tusk aside and light the fire himself—acutely aware of the sun's rapidly diminishing glow and the dangers posed by any night without fire.

When Tusk finally coaxed the fire into life he let out a scream of enthusiasm as the flames flared suddenly high. The men laughed, clapping arms around each other's shoulders as the boy did a dance of achievement.

The three of them sat close, chewed on fish and herbs, and shared a bladder of melted ice. Tusk's fire would keep them safe and warm, along with Rearing Mammoth's cloak—another treasured gift from his father that easily engulfed them all, protecting them from the glacial wind.

* * * *

Rearing Mammoth was woken by Sundance shoving at his shoulder.

"Wake up, my brothers," he whispered, urgent.

Rearing Mammoth and Tusk jolted from their slumber. Instinctively they threw themselves against the rocky parapet beside their companion. The musky stench of cat filled their nostrils.

The rumble of the beast resonated all around them.

Sundance held up a single finger, then a second, then a third. Rearing Mammoth closed his eyes, listening to the tread of paws and the deep snarling purrs on the other side of the stone. He held up four fingers and then reached for his blade. Sundance gripped his hunting blade and a smoldering bone from the fire.

Tusk grabbed a serrated scraping stone in his shaking hands. His eyes were wild.

One large cat bounded up the side of the outcrop to stand in full view on an overhanging boulder. She stared down at them, inside their protective enclosure, tilting her head from side to side. Her scarred yellow-brown coat was immaculately groomed, but the long tufting hair of her snout was matted with the bright red smear of uncongealed blood from a recent kill. Her upper lip curved over the top of foot-long saber teeth. They were yellowed and smattered with blood and hanging threads of sinew. One had had its razor-sharp tip snapped off. Rumbling breath stunk of decayed caribou. She stepped from boulder to boulder as if to survey her catch from every angle before settling on the original stone. There she reclined in the rays of the new day's sun.

Many moments passed.

"Do you still sense the other cats?" Rearing Mammoth murmured out the corner of his mouth.

Tusk gave a single shake of his head, keeping his gaze on the beast above them, as she grooming herself.

"Do they slumber around our camp?" Sundance asked. "Or have they returned to the lair while this one guards their next meal?"

"We won't know until we crest these boulders and run down amongst them to make our escape."

"You believe we can outrun them?" Tusk asked incredulously. The cat stopped her preening to stare directly at him. A pink tongue flicked out to wet a paw, and the paw stroked the full length of a protruding tooth.

Rearing Mammoth felt his young brother shudder and press in closer to his side. "If we stay here, we die."

"Why has she not slaughtered us already?" Sundance asked.

"She will keep us fresh for her pride's feast tonight, perhaps as easy fare for her litter to kill."

Tears welled in Tusk's eyes. "I cannot run faster than her." Any one of the beast's muscled legs was longer and stronger than the boy's entire body. The three were silent, until in the slightest of whispers, but with the determination of the Great White Bear, he said, "You must go without me."

Rearing Mammoth brushed his thumb over his brother's cheeks to push away the tears. "Nonsense, Tusk. Look at her. She is fat and has a belly full of meat that weighs her down." The boy stared at her with uncertainty. "Have you ever trapped the tiny vole that scuttles through the skulls of our lodge?"

"No. He is small and tricky."

Rearing Mammoth leaned down to press his nose against Tusk's. "And so are you, my brother. So are you." With their noses still touching, the elder could see the confidence growing in the eyes of the younger.

"Look, she is drowsy," Sundance muttered. "Now is the time."

Rearing Mammoth nodded. "We must run and not turn back. Leave our packs. Go straight for the cliffs. The smaller clefts in the wall may provide safety from the larger cats. If one of us falls . . ." Rearing Mammoth squeezed the hands of both his companions. "Go!"

The three sprang up and leapt over boulders and down opposite rock covered slopes of the outcropping. The cat dived for the spot where they had been. She turned and snarled, scattering their packs and satchels across the ground and still-glowing embers of the fire. Then she pounced once more up onto the surrounding boulders and down the edge of the rocky outcrop in pursuit.

The other cats were gone, returned to their lair. Tusk shot over a hillock and down into a long sunken rift that weaved its way toward the glacier. Sundance skirted a rise that ran parallel to the one Rearing Mammoth pounded along with all his might. A blur of yellow-brown fur darted between them and then dropped out of view, hidden by a grass-tufted hillock.

She was after Tusk, and anger filled Rearing Mammoth's heart. He let out a mighty yell that tore from the bottom of his gut. It resonated across the tundra and seemed to propel him ever faster.

Ahead of him the cat crested a mound, her face covered in fresh blood. She let out a howling gut-wrenching roar, flicking her head and pawing violently at her cheek, before making a run for Rearing Mammoth.

Rearing Mammoth ran parallel with the cliffs, over ridge after ridge, the cat popping in and out of view as he headed closer to the safety of the glacier. He was seventy paces or so from his goal when Tusk bounded from the rift and threw himself into an ice crevice small enough for a vole. The cat was racing through the grasses, still flicking her head, close enough Rearing Mammoth could see the bloody gash that left a strip of the upper lip dangling beside her saber.

Sundance stumbled in full view of the cat before launching himself into the same impossibly slim crevice Tusk had entered. Rearing Mammoth took advantage of the cat's distraction and changed direction to head for another fissure. Blood pounded through his heart and head, and his lungs burned and ached. His muscles felt like they could fail at any moment. The cat loomed behind him, but he dared not look. A fissure was three breaths ahead. He did not even know if he would fit. Using the last fragments of energy left in his legs, he jumped. His feet left the ground and his arms shielded his face as his body flew into the crevice and skidded roughly across the jagged ice. He rolled as he slid, and the beast slammed into the fractured opening in the glacier. The edges cracked as the cat twisted and squirmed at the entrance. Ice crunched and shattered as it clawed and snarled, less than half a body's length from where he lay. She smashed her head against the ice with an excruciating roar that echoed through the fissure. The gash in the beast's mouth smeared red across the ice walls—flicking clots from its whiskers as it fought. Something long and bloody flew toward Rearing Mammoth and bounced to a stop at his feet. Tusk's serrated scraping stone, with pieces of the cat's fur-covered lip still stuck to its edge. Rearing Mammoth picked it up in awe.

* * * *

Rearing Mammoth, Sundance, and Tusk scuttled sideways through corridors of blue ice as wide as one man or thinner. Along the way they passed clearings that could have held their entire village. Sometimes they could see the sky, sometimes they crawled beneath low hanging, dripping blue ice ledges and scrambled through caves that echoed their every grunting movement. In honor of his great deed, Tusk lead the way, though he readily accepted subtle tips from Rearing Mammoth. They were heading south and were never more than a few arms' lengths from the front face of the glacier.

Before midday they had passed a few slim crevices that allowed them to peer out at the open tundra. There was no sign of the cats, which reassured them especially as the crevices grew wider. By the time the sun had risen to its full height, the crevices they passed on their route were wide enough for the largest of mastodons to enter. Rearing Mammoth's directions to Tusk became more precise, as their passageway splintered into many. Tunnels, caves, and corridors struck straight into the depths of the glacier, all of which would offer good hiding places if the cats returned.

They spent that night in a small ice cave with an entrance so tight Rearing Mammoth and Sundance had to remove their hooded jackets to squeeze through. First Light's cloak remained with their abandoned packs on the outcropping where they'd camped, and Rearing Mammoth swore he would recover it on their return. But the confines of the cave with a small fire provided enough warmth to make them sweat in its closeness. The herbs they'd gathered just outside the glacier's edge were no match for their lost dried fish and caribou, but they made a pungent wad that—once chewed and chewed and chewed—could be swallowed to satisfy otherwise empty stomachs. The three chattered long after they should have been asleep. Tusk told the story of his confrontation with the cat, and the men urged him on, willing to hear even the minutest detail for the tenth and eleventh time. Finally, they lay in a huddle, staring up at the dull blue glow of the ice above, the remnants of adrenaline flowing through their veins and promising the deepest of dream-filled sleeps.

* * * *

"Caribou!" Rearing Mammoth yelled to his companions. He was hunkered down in the center of a broad clearing, and Tusk and Sundance ran quickly through the passageway to catch up. He removed a glove and ran his bare hand across the snow-covered ground. The imprint of caribou was still precise, without erosion. "At least fifty were in this clearing this morning."

"Are there any in poor health?" Sundance asked, inspecting the hoofprints.

Rearing Mammoth crawled close to the ground, fingers tracing, eyes searching, nose sniffing the heady aroma of his brother. Tusk followed his brother's every move.

"Here!" Sundance shouted

Tusk and Rearing Mammoth scuttled over to view a print that dragged through the snow for at least three of Sundance's hand-lengths. A matching print lay several steps ahead, and several steps beyond that. The herd was heading into a wide passage that cut deep into the glacier's face. Tusk ran to follow the dragging print toward the entrance, then stopped abruptly. His body stiffened, and he pulled the scraping stone from his jacket. Rearing Mammoth and Sundance drew their blades, their senses heightened for threat.

Tusk looked back to them and jerked his head toward the side of the clearing. He ran low, almost on all fours, along the snow, gravel, and ice toward a protective crevice. The two men trusted his instincts and followed, throwing themselves against the ground to slide in beside him. Inside was a bunker that allowed Tusk to stand and stare out the horizontal crevice into the clearing while the other two squatted beside him. Rearing Mammoth smelled the distinctive odor of cat.

"They have tracked us?"

"I doubt it, little brother. The scent of caribou is far stronger than ours in this place and would have covered our trail. They wouldn't even smell Sundance." He smirked.

The first cat sprung through the clearing and straight into the deeper glacial passage in search of the caribou. Three more followed. A fourth entered the space, stopping to sniff at the hoofprinted ground. It prowled in a small circle, squinting at the edges of the area, sniffing at the windless, chilled air.

"One day we will be able to defend ourselves against you, my brother," Rearing Mammoth muttered beneath his breath.

The cat glanced in their direction before heading after the leaders of its pride.

"Do we follow them?"

"Yes, as closely as we dare. They may rob us of supper tonight, but we must follow our gentler brothers and find a way out of the valley."

Tusk held up his scraping stone. "We will escape this valley and have caribou in our bellies. Perhaps even a feast of cat!"

Rearing Mammoth smiled as he ruffled the youngster's hair. "All in good time little brother." The three scrambled from their hole, dusted the powdered snow from their jackets and set off after their brothers.

The passage led to another large clearing that ran for several hundred foot falls to the south before turning east and then north into an even broader ice field. The cats lurked in the distance, so the three kept low against the ground and close to the edge of the ice cliff. As they crept around the ice floe, each glimpse through a crevice revealed the inside of the glacier had collapsed in upon itself. Though from the outside the glacial horizon appeared intact and impossibly high to scale, inside the structure had buckled and sunk to form a manageable grade. The slope likely hid many dangerous ravines beneath snow and thin ice, but Rearing Mammoth was sure it would lead to the top of the glacier, many days' journey to the north. A short distance up the incline were the silhouettes of many caribou. Higher still, a solitary mammoth plodded slowly through the wind and snow.

And above them all rose the Two Brothers, appearing almost as one from this direction. They signified the entrance to the greater part of Túwaqachi, or so Rearing Mammoth hoped.

No, he knew.

He was certain.

* * * *

Rearing Mammoth let out a whoop, whoop, whooping call that tore eastward between the shoulders of the Two Brothers who had dominated the Great White Bear Clan's existence for more than a generation. The Clanspeople stood around him as he lifted his arms high, fingers spread wide. The vibrato of his voice reached a crescendo that matched the strength and achievement of his scouting party's discovery.

"Magnificent," White Cloud uttered as she surveyed more land in one glance than she had known in all of her dreams.

Tusk pressed against her leg, holding her hand in a firm grip.

The glacial terrain spread north, east, and south for a journey of many, many moons—no, Thaws. Gorges and canyons cut deep scars that twisted and splintered across the ice into a distant blur. Splotches of brittle grassy herbage grew from exposed rock, and the strangest of stunted ancient trees clung to raw cliff faces or stood proudly upon islands of black granite that seemed to float upon the icescape. Free-flowing rivers and streams skimmed and ate into ice valleys before cascading down crystalline cliffs chiseled from frozen water. Herds of caribou, mastodon, mammoth, yak, and many other smaller mammals smudged the whiteness.

But it was none of this that made Rearing Mammoth's heart sing so loudly.

For ahead of them all, glistening upon the farthest horizon, possibly farther than any would travel in their own lifetime, was a shimmering strip of green fertile land, punctuated by a range of verdant peaks, no doubt thrust up long before even their own two snow-covered brothers were a thought in their mother's design. And within his heart he knew the distance promised abundant food and freedom for the generations to come.

Ice (15,958 BC)

Dancing Bird placed a single stone on the cairn that marked his Clan's arrival at the green horizon. Men lifted their wives and children high upon their shoulders. Many hands, large and small, piled rocks and pebbles one upon the other or jiggled them into tight crevices near the upper most reaches of the commemorative structure. Tusk's good humor grew more boisterous as he let his wife slip from his shoulders down into his arms. The whole family rejoiced with bouts of singing, laughing, and dancing.

Dancing Bird's friends, Musk Ox and Bear, lifted him to balance upon their shoulders. With his calves held steady in their grip, he placed a stone for his father and another for his mother. For a moment, he stared past the top of the cairn out across the vast frozen landscape he and his friends had been traversing their entire lives. Filling his lungs with frigid air, he let out a whoop, whoop, whooping call in echo of the one emanated by Rearing Mammoth almost eighteen Thaws ago. Only a few moons older than his father had been at the beginning of the *Ice*, Dancing Bird felt great sorrow that they were unable to stand on this new land together. He filled his lungs once more to send an oath, a promise, to the ears of his ancestors. "You and I are of one blood, my fathers, my mothers. We are the blood of the Great White Bear, and through it and the honesty of the song in our hearts we will continue our journey together."

Bear and Musk Ox released their grip on Dancing Bird and he jumped to the ground, landing lightly upon the grass that spread from the cairn to the glacier's edge. It felt strange to settle on the moist, brown-green carpet—not as soft as mammoth hide. He pulled off his moccasins to feel it beneath bare feet. Still cold and wet, it was so different from the gravel, ice, and patchy herbage he was accustomed to. It felt good.

Musk Ox sat and pulled off his boots as well, followed by Bear. Bear locked beefy arms around his friends' necks to wrestle them both flat against the grass. Triumphant, he let them go, and the three lay on the embankment, mesmerized by the cairn, the green valleys and peaks in the new land, and the desolate icescape they could now leave behind. Toward the distant north and south, the first fires of their fellow Clans sparked to life in the waning light. They, too, had reached the fertile land. A gusting breeze brought the smell of roasting fish down from the first makeshift camp in this new terrain. Bear ambled toward the heady aroma, Musk Ox plodding at his heels.

"Leave at least one fish for me!" Dancing Bird called after them, watching as they weaved through the valuable piles of bones and skins that had been dragged along their frozen trail.

The ice had once appeared so full of color—myriad tints and hues from the blue-white of new snow drifts to the scarlet ice dunes of sunset. Now it seemed only dull and gray.

Tusk squatted beside him, cradling his baby son in his arms. He ran a hand over the turf with a satisfied sigh, but then he, too, stared out at the ice. A ripple of sorrow crossed Tusk's face, and Dancing Bird knew his uncle was thinking of Rearing Mammoth, Many Caribou, and the others who had not survived the treacherous journey to reach this place.

"It is no good for the Clan to see you beaten in a fight, Bird," Tusk muttered out the side of his mouth.

"But look at the size of him!" Dancing Bird shouted, waving toward Bear.

"If ever you are to lead, you will need more than just physical strength. Sometimes strategy is more potent in defeating our adversaries, or surviving in our world." He pulled his infant son closer to his chest and pressed his lips against the ruffle of black hair covering his small head.

Bird studied his uncle's face. Deep lines scattered from the corners of his eyes. The skin of his jaw clung tight against the bone—like the dried mammoth hide stretched across the ribs of a lodge. His mouth, usually spread in a congenial smile, was downturned. At twenty-three Thaws, Tusk was not much older than Dancing Bird, yet the younger knew how much his uncle had endured to ensure both the

Clan's and Dancing Bird's survival. Tusk had readily taken on the role of parent when Dancing Bird was orphaned—had taught him to be a man when he was barely a man himself.

"The sun may drop below the horizon tonight," Dancing Bird said.

Tusk gave a slight nod. He lay down on his back, balancing his son upon his abdomen.

"Tell me the story again," Dancing Bird said after a long silence, as the sun seemed to hover above the ice. A lump welled in the back of his throat.

Tusk turned to hold the young man's gaze.

"No. You tell it to me. It is as much your story as mine."

Dancing Bird licked his lips and cleared this throat.

* * * *

The early morning sunshine shot up the ice-covered valley. It glinted off the backs of slumbering mastodon, reflected between the antlers of caribou. Our lodges had stood upon a frozen precipice for several moons as Our People dared go no further into the valley. Our Shaman, our wise men, and our ancient matriarchs would not risk the lives of Our People. The valley's sides were steep and prone to falling rock and ice, the lower reaches covered from edge to edge by a swiftly moving glacier. It was ravaged by crevice and fissure that scouts determined too wide to traverse, too deep to survive any fall. The glacier was fed by grinding rapids of ice, half melted, but compacting and refreezing into a glacial river that rumbled and scraped down the full length of the valley. Clanspeople stuffed their ears with mammoth hair to stifle the sound.

Towering above the head of the valley and at four scattered points along its northern rim were vast dams of thick translucent ice. Fractured and cracked, they barely held back a freezing bluish slush that could flood the landscape within days. Our men and women argued day after day about the dangers of following the valley; the Shaman burned the bones of caribou, mastodon, and mammoth. He sang over the ashes of our ancients that had perished as Our People waited upon the precipice. But still, even he had no answer other than that we must wait.

"Do you think I have failed my brothers and sisters?" asked Rearing Mammoth.

Many Caribou stayed quiet until Rearing Mammoth reached over and rubbed the bulge that was their unborn child.

"We are alive, my husband. Our Mother has led us here for her own reasons."

Rearing Mammoth contemplated her words. "Yet brother caribou is willing to risk his life to traverse the valley—and it is he who we must follow. Thousands pass our encampment each month to climb down onto the ice and head into the new day's sun. We watch them travel off into the distance, foraging upon the land Our Mother has provided."

"Yes, but we are not our brother. Perhaps we are more aware of the danger than he."

"Or more scared of what the future may hold," said Rearing Mammoth.

"No, I do not believe that is so."

"Then what?" he asked.

"Perhaps it is because brother caribou's family numbers are uncountable and we, by comparison, are so few." Many Caribou walked away from the precipice back toward the lodge. Her husband followed close behind.

"Do you think we overvalue our own lives? The survival of our own family?"

Many Caribou held his hand to her belly once more, to feel the child that jumped and kicked like a dancing bird.

* * * *

In the distance, an approaching rumble. Rearing Mammoth awoke from a deep slumber. He flicked his eyelids open as the growl reached a deafening high-pitched screech of ice against ice. He tightened his embrace of Many Caribou just as their bodies were flung sideways, into the bruising skulls of the lodge wall. All around them, bones rattled and skins shook. Someone screamed. Rearing Mammoth staggered to his feet only to be thrown back down onto the wooly hide. The entire lodge lurched, and the far end collapsed as Our People scrambled from its dark, smoky interior. Rearing Mammoth pulled Many Caribou into his arms, ignoring the streaking pain where a shard of lodge-bone had cut into his shoulder. Together they stumbled from the shelter. Out in the open, with nothing to protect them but their faith in the millions of stars above, the earth beneath tilted and twisted. Clanspeople faltered, sprawling onto the icy gravel around the Great Fire. Rearing Mammoth thudded to the ground with his wife on top of him—secure, he prayed, within his arms.

The undulating landscape jerked to a bone-jarring stop.

The grate of grinding ice splintered into silence, pulling the breath from Our People.

Silence.

No one made the slightest movement or sound—still as their brothers and sisters, muted in terror in the valley below. There was only the imagined echo of ears flicking, nostrils flaring, hooves and padded feet solid upon the ice to detect the direction of impending danger. The sky had turned an early-morning magenta, slashed by a deep red gash. In the distance, birds took flight.

And then a resolute crack cut the silence.

"Back from the edge!" Rearing Mammoth yelled.

The ground swelled and then began to disintegrate. The lodges and Great Fire buckled and tumbled with rock and ice into the precipice. Many Caribou's brow knitted in determination as they scuttled and clawed their way across the frozen ground away from the abyss.

On the far side of the valley, a deep fissure split haphazardly down the side of the lucent, frozen wall of water. A second cut stretched open in jolts—enormous slabs of ice breaking away to balance perilously along the dam's lip before crashing into the valley. A third fracture appeared, and then a fourth. Chunks of ice twice the size of the mightiest mastodon jettisoned from the middle of the dam, followed by a gushing, freezing sludge. The beasts upon the valley floor scattered with no mind for direction as the world crashed down around them. They stumbled into crevasses, on top of each other, trampling their smaller brothers in the stampede. A pride of fleeing cats was crushed in the smothering white clouds of churning snow and ice. The larger mammals lumbered on, in turn submerged beneath a tumbling wave of glacial slurry.

Rearing Mammoth's heart pounded, a pulsing ache within his skull, and then the second dam collapsed. With no cracks, no splits or crevices, the ice face simply slid out into the gorge, and the enormous bulk of slush and debris behind it cascaded down into the valley below the remnants of the village.

The Great White Bear Clan seemed to gasp as one.

"The torrent of ice!" someone screamed.

"Our brothers!"

Above the churn and noise, Rearing Mammoth shouted to the Shaman, "How far will the tide go?" He kept his arms and legs wrapped tight around Many Caribou, his large hands and forearms protecting their unborn child.

The Shaman gazed into the distance at the rolling crest of the white tide, the scream and trumpet of his brothers, as it swept toward the east horizon. Finally, he held his hands to his face and let out a howl that cut deep into the heart song of all still alive to hear it.

* * * *

Rearing Mammoth and young Tusk hunkered down on a large, half-submerged rock that jutted out over the edge of the precipice.

"The valley floor no longer moves" Tusk said.

"I still hear a minor rumbling. I doubt this ice river will ever be completely stopped."

They eased onto their stomachs and crawled up to the rim of the rock. Tusk peered over the edge, letting both arms dangle into the void. Rearing Mammoth stared across to the far side of the valley.

"Now that the sludge has all but emptied, you can almost see through the dams that are still intact."

"The one just there must be quite thin," Tusk said. "It appears almost blue." A bird swooped down behind the dam. Its silhouette was blurry through the ice.

The two men rolled onto their backs, and the sun shone on their faces. Rearing Mammoth elbowed Tusk in the side with a chuckle.

"This is your first Thaw as a man, my brother. You will soon need a wife."

Tusk flushed. Though he was proud to have gained the honor of manhood, at eight Thaws he knew he had many skills to learn from his brothers and sisters before thinking of a family of his own. "Perhaps in four or five Thaws."

"Still, you must be on the lookout for a future mate. The other Clans will congregate here now that the dams have emptied. Perhaps you will meet someone who makes your heart sing."

"Is that when we will tread into the valley to continue our journey?"

"We will wait another moon, at least. The quake and flood have left no life to support us during the many hundreds of days it will take to traverse. There are still greater herds of caribou and mammoth migrating toward this valley. We will allow them ahead of us to set the pace. They, as well as we, need the herb grasses to survive."

"Do you think the fish that jump up the rivers will have survived?"

"I am certain there are rainbow brothers as plentiful as ice drifts and snowflakes."

* * * *

Dancing Bird paused his storytelling when Tusk's wife, Like Blue Skies, brought them a basket of roasted fish. The flakes of watery flesh tasted succulent with the strangely aromatic herbage from this vibrant new landscape.

"We discovered a small plant with a tuberous, sweet-tasting root," said Little Blue Skies. "But I'm afraid Musk Ox and Bear devoured the last of it from the kitchen fires. I will be sure to hide some from them tomorrow."

Dancing Bird nodded in amused appreciation that he had received any food at all, despite his friends. After eating his fill, he gave his fingers one final lick then lay back down on the grass and soil, surprisingly warm opposite the cool twilight breeze.

Tusk finished the last of his fish as Like Blue Skies held their child to her breast. He cuddled into her and they watched until their baby breathed deep in sleep. He motioned for his nephew to join them, and Dancing Bird scrambled over to lay his head on his uncle's shoulder.

"Please continue," Tusk whispered. "I wish to hear more of my brother."

So Dancing Bird continued their story.

* * * *

Our People had journeyed for many moons and still the ice valley did not end. On either side, great white mountains soared high above the clouds. Valleys hung between each of the peaks, and smaller glaciers peered over their edges. Now and then chunks of ice crashed down the steep embankments. Rivers cascaded into our world.

We needn't have feared for lack of food. The river and streams that cut their course across the top of the glacier, or pooled in large finger lakes, held fish and water herbs in abundance. The sides of the valley were strewn with crevices and rocky outcrops covered in patchy grasses and other fodder. During these months, Our People consumed more game than ever from brothers caribou, mammoth, sloth, and bear, as the meat was preserved just below the slow flow of ice.

Our gentle four-legged brothers led our migration without worry, for there had been no sign of the great cats for many moons.

* * * *

By the time the next Thaw was almost passed, the Clan had reached a broadening of the valley such that they could only imagine the northern rim. The verdant horizon to the east somehow glowed a stronger emerald.

We had erected two lodges in an ice canyon in time for the Freeze, and the Spider and Walrus Clans had established their lodges close by. The Sundance Clan and Brown Bear Clan—*whoever heard of a Brown Bear?*—were within three days' walk. The echoing clap of a single stone against another told us that at least one more Clan had lodged somewhere farther behind us. The valley swirled with flurries of sleet and snow. The sky was an iridescent white blanket that allowed no sun or starlight through.

"We have more than enough food to last until the Thaw, but I discovered more patches of herbage in the next canyon to boost our supplies." Many Caribou smiled as she unrolled the old wooly sleeping hides in the smoky confines of the lodge. "I will gladly barter them with the Spider women for one of their fine skins."

Rearing Mammoth pulled off wet boots to warm his feet at the central fire. His wiggling toes caught the attention of Dancing Bird, who lay chirping and gurgling in a basket nearby. "Yes, this may be the last we see of them before the coming blizzards. If the weather is as fierce as last Freeze, we dare not wander from this canyon. Our four-legged brothers, too, will be searching for shelter. I would prefer you take one of the younger men, perhaps Black Rain, if you forage away from the village."

"Nonsense! He would only cause me misery, wondering why he had been assigned such a menial duty. No predators have stalked us since we entered this valley, and I will stay well clear of our gentler brothers."

Mammoth sat up cross-legged in front of the fire, interlacing his fingers with his toes, feeling the heat that lessened the ache of many months of trekking and hunting. He stared past the flickering flames to the basket where Dancing Bird lay. "Yes, of course."

* * * *

Dancing Bird suddenly bolted upright from his cuddle with Tusk and ran toward the monumental cairn. He peered up at the stones he had placed for Rearing Mammoth and Many Caribou, and then out at the desolation where they had been lost. His throat constricted until he felt he could not breathe.

He felt his uncle's approach behind him.

"Why?" he asked through gritted teeth, as the wind whistled around the top of the cairn. "Why must these stories be about death?"

Tusk stepped closer until the fishy sweetness of his breath wafted across Dancing Bird's shoulder. The younger listened to his uncle's rhythmic breathing, allowing his own to match the slow comforting pace.

"I, too, was angry. It hardly seems fair that such a fine hunter and a skilled forager should be taken from us. For many Thaws, I refused to accept this fact of life: that we survive by only the grace of our Mother and our predator brothers. That we are powerless to define our own future. Why should we be at the mercy of the elements? Why should we be prey to animals far stronger than we will ever be? Though I was surrounded by our Clan, I never felt more alone than when my brother was taken away."

Dancing Bird turned and the two men held each other's gaze. Then Tusk gave Like Blue Skies a reassuring nod and she carried their son to the warmth of the closest makeshift lodge.

Staring after his wife and child, he murmured, "I endured those Thaws only because of you, Bird. You gave me a reason to survive and perhaps—I'm not certain—but perhaps there is more. Gradually, we will make sense of the things that happened. They will make us stronger in some way. So, no, I do not believe the stories of Our People are about death at all. They are about life. About our journey toward something much greater than we know." He gave Dancing Bird a squeeze on the shoulder. "Now, finish our story."

* * * *

The valley was filled with the glow typical of early Freeze. The sun shone deep in the south—so far south it was not visible from our lodges. Great shadows stretched for lengths of hundreds of days' walk across the valley. They ended in a thin white luminous horizon that separated the earth from the pale blue, cloudless sky.

Rearing Mammoth sat with several other hunters by the second lodge, reviewing the quality of their blades and scrapers. Most were damaged or blunted from overuse. A handful of the larger blades could be restruck to make smaller—much smaller—cutting tools. But none of their weapons were worthy of dissecting a large animal, were any to be slaughtered the following season. They would need to source new tools, but the few masses of stone that drifted upon the moving landscape were either too hard to splinter or so soft they crumbled.

Still, Rearing Mammoth managed a smile as Many Caribou passed by on her way out of the village. He watched as she headed toward the canyon's entrance and the plain outside. She moved quickly through the chill, her great coat flapping around her ankles, a large empty basket hooked to her waistband and a smaller fur-lined one attached to her back with strips of hide. Two small arms stretched up out of that basket to grab at her braided hair.

The short period of daylight passed slowly in the village, marked only by the scraping of hides, the strengthening of lodges, and the smell of roasting meats that promised to stop the rumbling of stomachs by dusk. Propping a large tusk against the side of the second shelter, Rearing Mammoth surveyed the sky—a pale, pale blue that would shortly turn blue-black. He walked briskly out into the icescape to peer east, straining to see Many Caribou and Dancing Bird before again looking to the sky. Darkness was stealing in from the edges.

Cupping his hands to his mouth, Rearing Mammoth let out the call of his namesake toward the village. The bellow was modulated low, a request for his brother to join him. Within heartbeats Tusk was at his side and they were running through the twilight toward the neighboring ice canyon.

The canyon floor was deep with powdered snow. Along the edge were the footprints left by the Clanswomen as they'd collected herbage over the last several weeks. To one side, the tracks of mastodon pressed heavily into snow and gravel. The prints ambled down a crystalline alley that ended in a warm spring.

Tusk ran his bare hand over an imprint then lifted his fingers to his nose. "It came through this morning. Not long after dawn. Yet there is no sign of the beast's return."

Rearing Mammoth hunkered down to touch the fresh prints from Many Caribou's moccasins. "She waited here a long time, many heartbeats, growing agitated before proceeding toward the spring."

Before he'd even finished speaking he was running down the alley with Tusk at his heels. The passage snaked left and right. Great chunks of ice had been sheered from the walls, and in the tighter turns, hundreds of overlapping footprints showed where the huge animal had panicked in the narrowing confines.

"There is no way out for such a large beast!" Rearing Mammoth yelled as they passed a section of wall slashed and gored by broken tusks.

Many Caribou's prints trailed over those of the mastodon, oblivious to the state of the beast somewhere ahead of her. Rearing Mammoth took off at a dead run, knowing instinctively where his wife had stopped, had listened, and then had moved on. He bit his tongue, cursing himself for not having shared his own skills with her. All about him were signs of a beast that was very, very afraid, and just as dangerous.

A sink hole opened up and Rearing Mammoth leapt across it. Tusk followed but fell against the far side, chest slamming into the ice, legs dangling into the pit.

"Keep going!" Tusk yelled. "I'm fine—keep going!"

Rearing Mammoth hurdled down the crystalline alley.

* * * *

Dancing Bird bit his lower lip to stop it trembling. "I still do not understand the ending of this story. What happened?" he asked.

"I do not know," Tusk said.

"Are we supposed to know?"

"I'm not certain. Perhaps parts of our life story are better unknown."

Dancing Bird looked up at the brilliance of the stars, seeking some sign from his father and mother, some direction for hope to follow, for the song in his heart was almost inaudible.

Then he felt the arm of the warrior, the uncle who had saved him from death. It wrapped around his shoulders and pulled him close. "After I pulled myself up out of the pit, my chest and legs were badly bruised, so that I could barely walk or even breathe as I limped toward the spring. There was no sound. No bellow of mastodon or shout of warrior.

"Eventually I came to the dead end at the spring and was shocked by what I saw. For what I saw was nothing.

"Snow whipped through the tight walls of the canyon. But there was no spring. No mastodon. No brother or sister. The floor was powder, free of prints of any kind. It dipped precariously toward the center of the space, and I slipped. My arms floundered as I sank up to my chin in the snow dust. With no foothold, all my weight fell on my arms that somehow clung to the ice rimming the canyon. I kicked and yelled and struggled, but all that came of it was exhaustion.

"I rested my cheek against the ice and screamed for Mammoth and Caribou. And that is when I saw you, Bird. Your basket balanced on a ledge halfway up the side of the canyon, as if thrown there by a warrior's strength or a mother's determination—we will never know which.

"The sky above turned black, the flurries whipping in a suffocating whirlpool. The hide of my gloves would not hold, so I flung them off one at a time and dug numb fingers and nails into the ice. Any movement below my chest seemed to suck me deeper into the drift, and so I used only my arms, elbows, fingers, and chin to scrape out of the powder, one finger's length at a time. With my frozen, raw, and bloody fingers, I finally reached up for your basket and pulled it down to hug against my chest.

"You were silent, but awake. You did not cry. And in your eyes I saw that you trusted me.

"I held you tight beneath my coat and stared once more around the space. Even my own footprints and all evidence of my floundering were gone—as if I had never been there at all."

And that was all there was.

Dancing Bird circled the cairn that marked his family's migration from ice to abundance. He placed his hands upon it and peered again at the stones he had placed for his mother and father. And for himself. They shone in the twilight, the minerals twinkling. He thought about the small stones they used to make their blades and cutters and scrapers, and he wondered . . . Was there a stronger stone? A stronger, more powerful stone that would protect them—not only against their larger brothers, but also the world in which they must survive?

And then, deep in his thoughts, Dancing Bird stared up into the verdant mountains.

Vision Quest (15,383 BC)

Distant Thunder crawled from the sage-smudged womb of Mother Earth, the residual heat of the grandfathers pluming around him. Rising to his full height outside the sweat lodge, his mind was clear, his vision crisp, his senses heightened. His skin glistened with perspiration from days of purification within the confines of sapling, hide, and ceremony. His stomach growled from fasting, and yet he felt no hunger. The naked flesh of his chest and arms pricked with the reminder of the long winter just passed, and yet he felt no cold. The Shaman approached from the nearby alter, the skull of mammoth held high upon a stick behind him, the blades and feathers of their ancestors scattered across the sacred mound of soil. Neither said a word nor made the slightest noise as the elder lifted the ancestral cloak of caribou onto Distant Thunder's shoulders. The heavy skin folded about his body, covering all but his bare feet from the chilling bite of the northwesterly wind.

And then, deep in his thoughts, Distant Thunder stared up into the verdant mountains.

Whip-poor-wills called from the surrounding darkness. Fireflies circled the trunks of ancient trees. The breeze smelled of moist and succulent pine.

Distant Thunder walked alone through groves of trees, pushing branches and twigs from his path. The subtle flex of sapling pressed against his flesh, not to scratch or hinder, but willing to bend to the progress of the seeker.

He followed the trails of those who had arrived on this mountain long before his own family, crossed logs over ravines, waded fords of cascading rivers, climbed rocks to higher ground. He scaled the side of the mountain, past caves and through woods, over fields open to the night sky, then back into the darkness of wood.

He knew he had arrived, even before he saw it. A gentle wind caressed his neck, and sister hummingbird hovered only a breath away. She stared at him as if curious, determining his courage and virtue. She turned her head to and fro. He extended a hand from beneath the cloak, and the hummingbird flitted around it before darting through the undergrowth and into a clearing. That was his destination. Distant Thunder crawled low beneath bough and brush to follow.

Dense foliage embraced the clearing. No trail or track cut through it. The grass was lush and green, spongy and welcoming beneath his feet, between his toes. The hummingbird had disappeared, but Distant Thunder knew his guide would not desert him—that she would always be near as his quest continued. The clearing was still, except for the twinkling of the stars above—the sparkling pinpoints of brother bear, brother caribou.

In the dark of night, Distant Thunder absorbed the beauty and energy of this sacred place. He knew his brothers watched him from the shadows, but they would cause him no harm if he were true. He walked around the space, collecting large stones. These he placed in a circle, three paces in diameter, in the middle of the clearing. He crawled back into the woods and returned with branches, cones, and leaves to spread over the grass inside the stone circle. Digging deep into the pouch of his cloak, Distant Thunder extracted three items, and then walked one final time around the circumference of the stones, clockwise. In the direction west he kneeled and placed the black obsidian blade of Great White Bear. In the direction north he placed the revered scraping tool of Tusk the Cat Killer. In the direction east he placed the sacred stone of Dancing Bird, whose power had been hidden by the blizzards of legend and time. When he reached the southern edge, he lifted the cloak of First Light from his shoulders and it fell to the ground at his bare feet.

And then he entered the circle as he had entered the world.

He sat down in respectful silence and observed all that surrounded him throughout the long sleepless night.

With the rise of the new day's sun, the hummingbird appeared again. She flitted back and forth inside the circle of stone, hovered before his face, then darted off toward the north.

Intellect and wisdom, Distant Thunder thought to himself. The legend of young Tusk, drawn upon the skin of his family's history, had long been engrained in his mind—had become part of his very being.

The sun rose to its highest point, directly above the clearing, then fell below the canopy line and plunged the clearing into night again. The stars were blotted out by storm clouds. Rain fell upon the clearing, yet Distant Thunder remained dry within the circle, within his thoughts and prayers.

His lids were heavy in the morning, when next the hummingbird flapped her gentle breeze against his face. He forced his eyes open, stretched his back, and gazed intently to assure his guide he had not fallen asleep during his quest. Then she darted off over his head toward the south.

Innocence and compassion, Distant Thunder thought. The story of First Light; the lessons he learned for us all; the future that, perhaps, he foresaw.

Distant Thunder's stomach snarled with hunger. He bent in pain before forcing his body upright once more. He held his breath as spasm after spasm tore through his abdomen, making him slick with sweat. He clenched his teeth and prayed.

He felt the cloak of First Light at the southern edge behind him, the innocence and compassion it embodied, the magic it possessed.

The sun set once more, and Distant Thunder sat alone in darkness.

His stomach would not cease its complaining rumble.

His entire body ached from sitting so still. His mouth was dry. His tongue had started to swell.

His view of the circle and the universe had become hazy.

And then the woods around the clearing exploded into noise— loud, deafening—as his brothers went about their lives, fighting for their own survival, perching upon the branches and in the protection of the foliage and their homes. Little brother yellow jacket hopped from one branch to another, and the racket was harsh and horrendous. Firefly buzzed by a leaf, its song piercing and painful. Distant Thunder pressed his hands to his ears, but nothing could dampen the sound. The dark of the wood plunged into a blackness he had never before seen, it swirled around him, the intense noise of life moving in motion with branch, twig and leaf. The stars cartwheeled across the sky, faster and faster, spinning Distant Thunder within their suffocating grip. The stones of the circle also turned about him as he crouched upon the grass.

He dared not close his eyes.

Gradually, the universe slowed into stillness and silence once more, so dark he could not see his upheld hand before him, not even when he touched his nose to ensure he was still there. He waited, barely breathing, his body defined only by the painful pulse running through it.

When the new day dawned, Distant Thunder saw sunlight creep over the blades of grass before his eyes, touching his nose. The excruciating ache had slowly urged him forward through the darkness until he was bent, his shoulders upon his knees, his legs crossed beneath his chest. But still he had seen through the night without sleep.

The breeze of the hummingbird was above him.

Distant Thunder turned his head to see his friend and then painfully righted himself. His hands pressed deep into the grass, shaking with the exertion.

The hummingbird hovered patiently.

Distant Thunder gazed at her through bloodshot eyes, unable to follow her movement as she darted to and fro. He held out his hand, and she hovered above it for just a moment before speeding off over the obsidian blade of Great White Bear in the direction west.

Introspection, Distant Thunder thought as he stared not at the blade, but within himself. This time he did not notice the day, or the night, or the day that followed as he searched deep within his heart for his own song and where it would lead him and his future family.

When he at last became aware of his surroundings, he did not know whether it was day or night, dark or light. His vision and mind were blurred, his body nothing more than a collection of aches to let him know he was still alive. When the tears came, he supposed it was sudden, unexpected, but they had lain close to the surface for a very long time, held within him and his family for countless generations. His first sob in that quiet space frightened him, but it was quickly followed by more. It grew loud and uninhibited within the embrace of Mother Earth. He clenched his fists, pressing them to his face, his eyes squeezed shut as the cries of death and longing, hope, past and future, passed through him and out of him.

"For whom do you cry, my son?" the Great Spirit asked.

Distant Thunder recognized the enormous bulk of brother bear at the edge of the circle, direction east. *Illumination*. He came and sat before him, and the Spirit was great within the circle, taking up almost all of the space. It set a heavy paw against Distant Thunder's bare foot.

"I do not know, Great Spirit."

"Yes, you do," the Great Spirit said.

"I cry for our family. For our brothers and sisters, our mothers and fathers, our sons and daughters. For I see that we are all one. We are all connected. We are a part of the same world, the same destiny."

The Great Spirit leaned in closer. The warrior, at fifteen, was small in comparison. "And what else did you see, my son?"

Distant Thunder felt the ache and shudder of sorrow in his heart.

"I saw the Great Twins. I saw them fall."

"Great White Bear and Rainbow Cloud?"

"No," Thunder said, the word catching in his throat.

"No," the Great Spirit echoed, softly, gently.

The Great Spirit pressed its paw more firmly against Distant Thunder's sole. Its heat crept through him, until it warmed his body and spirit.

"Can you guide me, Great Spirit? Will you tell me what I must do?"

The embodiment of Spirit leaned down, the bear snout and breath hot against Distant Thunder's face. "Already you possess the power within you to become great, if only you would use it. You must sharpen your awareness, always, as you would a hunting blade. You must keep your family sheltered and fed, for they have a very, very long trail to walk. Your family, my son, the Clan of the Great White Bear, plays a part in the history and destiny of this world, Túwaqachi. Where that destiny leads is solely up to you and those who follow in your footsteps. Those who follow the truth of their heart song. Only then will they truly survive. And only then is survival of true value."

The Great Spirit dissolved into darkness and brother bear lumbered from the circle, pushing through the undergrowth and into the wood.

Distant Thunder pressed his face into the lush grass to smell the sage, cedar, and pine. Then he lifted his face from Mother Earth and called, "I pray to the four directions. Hear me. I thank you for these gifts, for without them we could not live. Grandmother, you have shared with me your wisdom, and I thank you for this gift. Grandfather, you have shared with me your strength, and I thank you for this gift."

When the sun next shone, it warmed his back, giving him energy. Distant Thunder rose to his feet for the first time in many days. He shuffled to the south of the circle and lifted the cloak of First Light up onto his shoulders. He pulled it tight around his body, shivering as the comfort of his family surrounded him. He moved around the circle, collecting the blade of Great White Bear and the scraping tool of Tusk the Cat Killer and placed them carefully into his pouch for future generations. As he kneeled to retrieve the sacred stone of Dancing Bird, Thunder noted how it shone, how his reflection shimmered along its length, sharper even than Great White Bear's blade. He caught a glint of light off a stone in the circle he'd laid out that first dark night. And then another flash of light off another stone. A jolt of energy coursed through him as he saw that all the stones in the circle he had created were of the same dazzling glassiness, the same magical substance as the stone of Dancing Bird.

He picked one up, and its shattered edge was undoubtedly sharper than any blade he had ever known or heard of. Perhaps the magic of Dancing Bird's discovery could again be realized.

P.J. Parker

The Story of Beaver (14,194 BC)

Beaver sat upon the hillock, high above his family's lodge by the lake, taking in the last rays of a long summer day. He had loved this place since he had become a man—it reminded him of the special site of his Vision Quest, and he often came to give thanks to the Great Spirit for all that was good in the life of his family.

From here he could see his world.

The vast grass plain before him was home to countless caribou, mastodon, mammoth, and bison. The lumbering beasts were fat and healthy and lived long lives, and the more ancient and frail ones followed their duty to succumb to the blades of their smaller brothers.

Here they were safe from the saber-toothed cats and dire wolves, who rarely visited from their dens in the surrounding hills.

Far to the north, the glaciers looked miniscule between the rugged mountain ranges—small icy spots on a horizon seldom visited. The noise of calving was faint at this distance, but on almost any summer evening Beaver could discern the toppling of ice into the finger lakes, scraped into the plain floor by the retreating giants.

On his lap Beaver held the stone he'd been working on for most of the afternoon. It had grown too dark to keep working, but he'd struck two blades of good quality. Their long, tapered tips glinted in the last rays of the day. He observed them proudly, laying side by side upon a hide, surrounded by the scattered shards of many weeks of failed attempts. The blades would see his family fed well through the remaining summer and coming winter.

It was time for Beaver to collect his tools and return to the lodge for food and company, love and laughter. But first he would wait for the Home Star to shine bright. First to appear were the sparkling pinpoints of the two youngest wolves, followed by their three older brothers—the eldest with his dog. Opposite them reclined the two grizzly bears, luminous in the dark blue night sky. They pointed toward the star that did not move. The Home Star. Beaver was thankful that his brothers had been placed in the sky by Trickster Coyote. Together they had given his family direction on where they had come from and where they were going.

With care, he wrapped his blades in the swatch of caribou hide. Then, picking up the last dark, glassy-blue stone, he walked contentedly down the hillock to the lodge.

Fluted Stone (12,500 BC)

The body of the bear lay sprawled across blood-soaked gravel and grass. Blazing Sun and the other hunters walked around the carcass in awe of its size. Dark Moon paced from one outstretched, blood-caked paw, past the enormous chest, past the arm—which itself was as long as Dark Moon was tall—before he stopped near the still-warm snout and stared into its milky-white eyes in search of his brother's soul.

"As tall as three warriors standing atop one other," he said incredulously. "Almost as massive as brother mammoth." The beast's soft belly had been ripped open, meat and offal torn savagely, blood still glistening fresh.

"Dire wolves," Blazing Sun muttered. "Far stronger than all of us combined, yet even this beast never stood a chance." He pointed toward the tufts of gory, gray fur caught between the bear's teeth. "Our brother put up a fight. He may have had the speed to run down any prey, but not the agility to protect himself from a vicious attack by many wolves at once."

"Have you ever seen a bear this size?" Dark Moon asked as he climbed up onto the chest of the carcass.

Blazing Sun joined him atop the beast, gripping his younger brother's shoulder to steady himself. "Our father's father told stories of such large brothers and sisters, but it seems they have become rare. Many animals drawn upon our Family History no longer graze about us."

"You mean they roam farther along the plains? In the mountains?"

"Perhaps. Or perhaps they have served their purpose, to be replaced by others whose story is yet to be told."

Moon bent to brush his hand tenderly over the bear's glossy brown fur. "Do you think our family could disappear, too, Sun?"

Blazing Sun smiled and shook his head, "Not if we bring the remains of our brother back to the lodges before the dire wolves return. We will show him the respect they did not."

The two men stepped down and extracted cutting blades from their satchels. Blazing Sun assigned each of the hunters to different parts of the beast, watching as they cut through the thick skin. They gripped the pelt with an aching, sinewy strength to slowly urge it from the flesh. It would take two at least to carry the pelt back to the village.

"This will make many fine coats and blankets. Our sisters will be pleased." Blazing Sun gazed up toward his namesake, shielding his eyes from the glare as he determined the length of daylight still remaining. "Moon, come. We will take the skin now and return to this site with the rest of the Clan before the sun drops halfway to the horizon. We will need all hands. Runs Like Wind, please oversee the cutting and scraping."

With great effort, the rolled skin was placed upon the shoulders of Sun and Moon, but before they could take a step, a howl echoed across the grasslands. The men turned, expecting the threat of dire wolves, from which their only prospect would be to scatter and run, hoping the predators' interest would be held by the remains of the bear.

But what they saw was, quite possibly, more dangerous.

The brothers threw the hide to the ground. Blazing Sun's heartbeat quickened, his warrior instincts coursing through his veins.

In the distance was a troop of thirty or more men. They were tall and wide-shouldered, their skin ruddier than Sun had known of any Clan. There was confidence in their movement. Their sticks and blades reflected the afternoon sunlight.

"I do not recognize them," Moon said.

One of the visitors waved in apparent friendship, but he was physically taut—prepared for swift action.

Blazing Sun motioned with the slightest of hand movements, catching the attention of his men. They tightened their grips on their blades—muscles tensing under the stretch of caribou vests and buckskin leggings. Blazing Sun lifted his hand to his mouth and let out the call of the Great White Bear Clan.

The growl reverberated across the plains.

The strangers stopped several hundred paces away as their leader issued directions. Then, as one, they turned toward the hunters clustered around the corpse of the bear and laid their blades and sticks upon the ground. Only then did they continue through the swaying grasses.

"Be wary," Blazing Sun whispered to those at his back.

"You, the hunters of the Great White Bear!" shouted the leader. "We have followed your stories across this vast land for generations."

The ache in Blazing Sun's every muscle raked deeper, ready for attack, hoping for friendship.

The leader held out his arms, hands open, fingers extended. When he came within the arc of a hunting blade he stopped, holding the gaze of Blazing Sun. His skin glowed. His long, dark hair blew free about his shoulders. His nose was straight and proud, his lips thin, and his eyes full of life and song.

Blazing Sun stepped forward. "I am Blazing Sun of the Great White Bear Clan, descended from First Light, himself the heir of our Clan's origin in this new world." He cast his blade upon the sagebrush beside the discarded hide and extended his hand.

The two men gripped one another's forearms in solid greeting.

"My brother, I am named Fluted Stone, and we are of The People."

Their grip tightened, the warmth and strength of friendship flowing through it.

* * * *

The hunters of Great White Bear and The People crossed the plains up into the foothills, carrying upon their shoulders the meat and bone and precious organs of their fallen brother. They skirted the herds of mammoth and caribou as they made their way. Bison walked leisurely from their path, intent on tearing the sage from about their feet, chewing it indolently as they stared at the far-off horizon. A lone, ancient mastodon ambled in the eddying waters of a pond, drinking and splashing contentedly.

"I have never seen such a beast," Fluted Stone said.

Blazing Sun nodded. "We, too, have seen very few as we follow the great herds' migration. The brother we carry on our backs is one we have not seen in many generations."

The group mirrored the course of the stream, which meandered from the foothills around the rim of the plain.

"Our village," Sun said, motioning to where the stream cascaded from a shallow draw between two hillocks. Five shelters were scattered about the edge of the waterway—stick and pelt, bone and grass. Pine embraced the lodges in shadow and scent.

The villagers stopped their labors and welcomed their brothers and the strangers that walked amongst them. The Shaman raised his rattle high, singing loud to the sky for the bounty they carried. He rejoiced for their visitors.

The hunters placed the bear at the Shaman's feet. All gathered around the tender mounds of flesh and life, intrigued by its size and also by The People in their midst.

Beautiful Leaf caught the gaze of Fluted Stone and smiled shyly.

"What do you see, Shaman?" Blazing Sun asked.

The Shaman, vast in age, stretched his arms high to the sky and closed his eyes. "I see the silhouette of our elder brother, the big man with the big feet and hairy body who lives in the shade of the forests to the north. He speaks of change, and that change will be good. He speaks of a natural knowledge and skill, and that is why he has sent our brothers that stand beside us now—that they may drink from this stream, eat from this meat, hear our stories, and share their own."

Blazing Sun turned to Fluted Stone and nodded, almost imperceptibly.

"This is a time of change," the Shaman repeated. "This is a time of enormous power."

* * * *

The celebration of new friendship lasted long into the night, under a spangled banner of stars that slowly etched across the sky. The sparkling points of Wolf and Grizzly slunk leisurely until they shone over the village—the eye of Grizzly shining brighter than at any other time of year. Fluted Stone sat beside Blazing Sun in the comfort of lush grass. He held a chunk of raw bear and told his story, capturing the imaginations of all who lingered nearby in between satisfying mouthfuls of the succulent, bloody meat. Beautiful Leaf listened for many heartbeats before she hesitantly retired to the lodge closest the stream.

"My heart song tells me I may soon be one with the Great White Bear Clan," Fluted Stone whispered to Blazing Sun.

"Indeed," Sun murmured happily. "We would gladly have you as our brother." He wiped the back of his hand across his mouth. "Our Clans should meet, on the new moon, where the stream falls into the finger lake. Our sisters have much knowledge to share of the insects, herbs, and gourds that inhabit these hills and plains. And I am certain men and women from both our Clans would benefit from a closer acquaintance."

Fluted Stone winked. "Yes," he said before rising suddenly to his feet. Sun stood with him, aware of the danger.

A shadow passed through the dark of night, beyond the glow of the lodge's fires.

Blazing Sun lifted his hand and all fell silent, listening to the rustle of brush as an enormous beast lurked close but out of sight. The hunters of the Great White Bear Clan pulled out their blades, The People reached for their sticks.

A gigantic head emerged into the edge of the firelight, matted gray wool hanging from gaunt cheeks and earflaps, eyes blinking hazel over curving tusks, each one taller than any hunter in the Clan. A fat, wrinkled trunk, scarred and ancient, swung slowly, almost touching the ground at its feet.

"Mammoth," Dark Moon breathed. The villagers watched and waited, not daring to stir panic, as the beast scrutinized them from the scrub.

"It is the matriarch of the herd," the Shaman said. He stepped between the men and the beast. "She has been visiting in the dead of night while your party has been on the hunt. She is questioning, but I do not yet know what."

The matriarch stared for several heartbeats, sniffed at the air, and then turned from the light to lumber off into the dark, back to her herd on the plains below.

"We will have to move," Blazing Sun said. "We have no defenses here against such a beast, if we have garnered her interest."

Fluted Stone gripped Sun's elbow.

"My men will help yours keep watch for the remainder of our time here. But perhaps there is another story I should tell you before the new day comes."

Blazing Sun raised an eyebrow.

"Juniper!" shouted Fluted Stone. "Bring me the cores from your knapsack."

The hunter brought his sack and lifted out two cores of shimmering, glassy-blue obsidian. Fluted Stone hunkered down in front of the fire to gouge a pit in the embers with a cooking stick. He placed the cores in the hollow and covered them with the charred, glowing remnants of intense heat.

"These will be ready before two settings of the sun."

* * * *

Blazing Sun stared incredulously. "You can kill a beast without laying your hands upon it—a healthy, mature beast at a distance?"

"Yes." Fluted Stone placed his stick into Sun's hands.

It was about three feet long. The mainshaft was wood, honed very straight. The end was hollowed out and entwined tightly with gut of caribou to secure a foreshaft of mammoth bone.

The split end of the bone held a fluted, obsidian stone of remarkable beauty and craftsmanship. Longer and more refined than any handheld blade of the Great White Bear, the point was tapered toward the end. Percussion scars along the sides made it exceedingly sharp and strong.

"It is a dart, a spear." Fluted Stone guided Blazing Sun so he held the spear lengthwise above his shoulder. "Hold it like this to throw. Or like this"—he moved Sun's arms and hands to change his grip upon the spear—"to jab and deliver a death blow at close range."

"But surely it would only bounce off of mammoth or caribou," Dark Moon said, taking the spear to feel its weight.

"Each large animal is different, and that you will come to know. Go ahead and throw the spear." Fluted Stone gestured toward a chunk of bear that had been hung from a branch. "For mammoth, it is best to aim for the lungs, where the hide is thinnest and the ribs are rounded, allowing the point to slide past them, deep into the animal's interior. Higher up, the hide is very thick and the bones of the rib, flat. The spear would deflect, and the wounded animal would defend itself."

Dark Moon threw the spear. It shivered through the air and sliced into the bear's flesh.

"Now place hide over the meat," Fluted stone directed one of his men. "Three layers . . . four."

Blazing Sun accepted the spear from Moon, lined up his aim and threw it with all his might. Again, the weapon was true, cutting through four layers of hide, through flesh and embedding itself in the tree behind.

"My men and I have killed grown mammoth bulls from a distance of up to thirty paces."

The Shaman watched in silence, extracting the teeth from the mandible of the bear and placing them in the pouch that hung from his neck. "It is as the big footed man in the forest foretold," he said. "We have been delivered great power."

Blazing Sun nodded.

The men practiced with the spears all day and the next, and listened to the words of The People long after the sun went down.

* * * *

The matriarch of the mammoth visited the village each night—preceded by the signaling twilight twitter and insect calls of the men that kept watch along the trail. She peered from the dark toward the light of the fire and the people who gathered around it. Each time, the villagers stopped their carousing and held still and silent, waiting to see what she would do.

On the second night, the Shaman held her gaze, daring to walk to the edge of the light until the mustiness of her scent filled his nostrils and he could see his own face reflected in her hazel eyes. When she retreated into the dark, the Shaman returned to his stone to contemplate her actions.

* * * *

The two obsidian cores were removed from the embers and set beside the stream to cool. After supper was concluded and the matriarch had paid her visit, the Clanspeople gathered to learn from Fluted Stone.

He sat on the trunk of a lazy tree, and Beautiful Leaf placed a thick hide across his knees to protect him from the cutting sharpness of the rock. Juniper handed him the hammer stone, a chunk of soft limestone the size of his fist. Fluted Stone hit the stone against the leading edge of the core and struck off a glassy blue shard, the length and thickness of a man's hand. Another hit sheared off another shard onto the protective hide. After several minutes, he'd created more than a dozen blades.

The men muttered in awe at the effect that cooking had on the obsidian's structure and fracturing.

"Next we make it as flat as possible." With gentle taps of the hammer stone, Fluted Stone shaved off humps and ridges, smoothing the sides so it was symmetrical in his grip.

In the distance, mammoth trumpeted and shrieked in fright. There was a rush of movement and then all was silent again. The villagers waited, then returned their attention to Fluted Stone. The Shaman walked to the edge of the light, staring out into the night.

Fluted Stone picked up a carved stick of antler and showed the hunters how to thin, notch, and flute the blade, wiping at his brow as the heat of night fell. "This weapon must be used nobly amongst our brothers. Take pride in your work and do it well."

Fluted Stone nurtured, flaked, and honed the blade into a thing of magnificence before passing it around.

Blazing Sun turned it over in his hand, taking care to not cut himself on the sharp edges and tip.

"It is truly beautiful," he said, meeting Fluted Stone's gaze.

"Please accept it, and my story, as our gift to you."

Again a blast of terror trumpeted from the plains below. The noise of unsettled movement carried toward them, followed by shrieking and whimpering wails.

"The matriarch will return a second time tonight," the Shaman said.

And she did.

Her large head, tusks, and trunk loomed out of the jet black as she dared to fully enter firelight. The brothers and sisters of the Clan scuttled to the far side of the fire, weapons drawn, but the Shaman stayed, peering into the eyes and mind of the ancient one.

The matriarch lifted her trunk high and bellowed loud into the space, stomping her left foot into the dirt and sage and kicking up a cloud of dust.

The Shaman returned with a chant that modulated in time with the swinging of her trunk. When he finished, he turned toward the villagers, his body silhouetted by the mammoth's bulk. He appeared troubled.

"She must lead her herd from the plains. She must lead them toward their future, their destiny. It is this way." The Shaman motioned directly through the village, beside the course of the stream.

The matriarch turned and walked off into the black night.

"They must leave right now."

* * * *

The heavy footfalls of several score of mammoth reverberated throughout the darkness, their trumpeting wails pushing closer and closer to the Great White Bear Clan and their visitors.

"Quickly," Blazing Sun ordered. "Collect our tools, the cutting blades and stones. Moon, pull the Family History from the wall of our lodge. I am entrusting its care to you. My sisters—Beautiful Leaf— salvage whatever food stores you can. We must move to the far side of the stream immediately."

Fluted Stone directed his people to help, and ordered chaos engulfed the village. Clanspeople scurried from lodge to lodge, from pit and food cache, through the ambling current of the shallow stream to the safety of the far side. They passed tools, skins, and baskets of seeds, fruit, roots, and dried insect larvae, hand to hand across the water.

But then the matriarch entered the fire's glow and without hesitation lumbered straight into the village. She swung her trunk and lifted it high to trumpet the way to the herd.

"To the other bank!" Blazing Sun yelled. "Drop what you carry! Run!"

Several more mammoths appeared, hesitating but a moment before they trod heavily through the village.

Blazing Sun manhandled his people into the water, pushing them toward safety. They rushed, then huddled on the far side of the stream in a shallow indentation of the cliff face. When all were safe, he grabbed the Shaman's gnarled hand, helping him balance the tools and sacred artifacts of his trade. They stumbled through the rocky stream to the far side. Fluted Stone extended his hand and pulled them up the pebbled embankment where they pressed themselves against the cliff face with the rest of the Clanspeople.

More mammoth stumbled into the village, bypassing the fire and the lodges as if not wanting to disturb their smaller brothers' homes. Dozen by dozen, hundreds of the great beasts kicked up a choking dust, filling the draw with their heady smell and deafening noise. A young calf, his wool still short and patchy, was frightened by the fire and recklessly kicked through it, spreading logs and flame. He squealed when a grown male pushed him with his trunk, onward into the darkness, to carry on up into the higher gulch.

Blazing Sun tensed, his awareness heightened beside Fluted Stone and Dark Moon. Their hunting senses tingled, and Fluted Stone pressed a spear into Blazing Sun's hands.

"You sense it, my brother?"

Blazing Sun nodded. "The stench. They are closing in." He wrapped his fingers around the shaft and flexed his arm muscles, ready for defense. The herd hastened their pace, their trumpeting more urgent.

The pack of dire wolves struck swiftly and savagely from many directions at once. They raced up the streambed, and along the trail to attack the last of the trailing mammoth. Shrieking resounded as several dogs attacked a calf. The mammoth stomped and twisted to protect their own—knocking and crushing the flimsy lodges, scattering the debris left behind by the Clan. Loose bones and skulls, sticks and furs were kicked, shattered, and trampled. Then the wolves struck the defending bull, their greedy and dirty mouths biting into the soft underbelly, snapping at tender folds of flesh.

The Clans pressed together on the far side of the stream, holding each other tight, the men before the women and children with spears and blades at the ready.

Three mammoth sloshed across the water and up onto the embankment past the Clan, to escape the tooth and claw of wolf. They turned back and forth in confusion, blaring, their trunks and tusks careening and slashing. A lone wolf chased one mammoth toward the Clan, before both animals slammed into the cliff face. The mammoth slipped, then toppled, rolling down the slope into the stream. A tusk snapped off in the tumble, and blood poured from the tender base of the ivory stump. He staggered back onto his feet to follow the matriarch's course, the wolf continuing pursuit.

Blazing Sun was the first to throw his spear, and it pierced the chest of a wolf bounding toward the Clan. Immediately the animal dropped to the ground, dead.

Another Clansman launched a spear to wound a second, and it yelped in pain and splashed about in the bloody, cascading water of the stream.

Blazing Sun ran down and pulled his spear from the wolf he had slaughtered. He skirted the cumbersome movements of terrified mammoth, and went in to kill the wounded dog. It bit and snapped in agonized anger before lunging awkwardly toward him. With both hands, Blazing Sun jabbed the spear into the animal's face, then again into its neck and side. The blade became lodged between two ribs, and the foreshaft snapped under the animal's weight. Blazing Sun was thrown down into the current, and the wolf, twice his bulk, lunged at him again, its mouth a dripping bloody mess. It slammed its paws into Blazing Sun's chest, dug its claws through his open caribou vest and deep into his flesh. Half submerged beneath the dog's weight, Sun strained to hold the wolf's jaws from his throat as its foul breath heaved in his face.

Abruptly, the dire wolf was thrown sideways into the water. It writhed and thrashed and then, with an urgent shudder, it stopped dead, the spear of Fluted Stone sticking from its gut.

Fluted Stone gripped Blazing Sun's bicep and bloody vest and dragged him through the water and up onto the rocky shore. They ran up the incline just as another mammoth careened through the waters and up over the bank, its giant pads crunching through rocks and pebbles, the low swing of a tusk flinging stones into the huddle of Clanspeople against the cliff face before it rushed once more into the stream.

More spears flew, hefted by the skilled hunters of The People. Each met its mark, and dire wolves dropped to the ground to be trampled by the stampede.

The wooly beasts maintained their rush, destroying all semblance of village and wolf as they disappeared into the night and toward their destiny.

The dust was heavy and thick, lit from within by the fragments of lodges now fully aflame.

* * * *

Blazing Sun and the Clanspeople waded back across the stream, their spirits low. Their homes and possessions were razed. The remains of the bear lay trampled into useless shreds, along with the mush that once was dire wolves.

"At least we have our tools and blades," Moon said, holding the Family History close to his body. "And we now have the fluted stone." He squinted thoughtfully. "We must start rebuilding our food cache for the coming winter immediately."

Blazing Sun wrapped his arm around Moon's shoulders. "We are all safe, my brother, and that is all that matters."

Fluted Stone bent to trace the imprint of mammoth with his fingers. "The People will gladly share our cache with your Clan, Blazing Sun. We will work together to ensure each other's survival."

"Thank you, my brother."

The Shaman sent a howling chant into the night before dropping to his knees and shaking his rattle.

From the night came the visage of the matriarch, lit by the remnants of their fire. She sent a blast from her trumpet toward her herd then lowered her head to peer at the Shaman. The old man stood, daring to stroke her trunk and one great curved tusk. For many heartbeats, he pressed his hand upon the ivory, feeling its strength and determination. And gratitude.

"She is here for us now," the Shaman said with certainty. "She has returned to ensure our survival. To be our first."

The spear with its fluted stone burned hot in Blazing Sun's grip.

He tipped his head toward the matriarch, in honor and appreciation.

Many Hands (8135 BC)

"We must treat with respect our world and all upon it. Túwaqachi is not inherited from our ancestors; it has been loaned to us by our children." Dusk Runner's voice was imbued with the magic that had made him Shaman of the Clan.

Many Hands listened, looking out at the swaying sage grass, cascading rivulets, shallow lakes, and uncountable bison as far as the eye could see, many generations roaming together as one.

"Our brothers are plenty, and we may easily take as many as we please."

"That is true, Many Hands, but we must honor them. If they disappear, then so do we—for our circle will be broken. Though our skill and knowledge is great, our lives are fragile—little more than the crystalline breath of a buffalo in the wintertime, or the flash of a firefly in the night."

Many Hands nodded, understanding. "The Clans will arrive over the coming days for the autumn hunt," he said.

"I sense the Spirits will recognize and reward the song we have lived by." The Shaman hesitated before taking his eyes from the bison to focus on Many Hands. "How fairs One-Tree Rock?"

Many Hands's brow wrinkled. "He has been flogged and all his belongings confiscated."

The Shaman nodded. "One-Tree Rock knew the consequences. To undertake an individual hunt so soon before the group venture has long been forbidden. All our Clans rely on this time of cooperation, to build their meat, hide, and pemmican supplies for the coming winter." The subtle movement of the bison across the sway of sagebrush appeared as a gentle ripple of brown on yellow and green. "If our brothers had been scared from this meeting place, the group hunt's honor and success might have been compromised." Dusk Runner placed his hands upon Many Hands's shoulders. "We must all work as one, Many Hands, and never place the desires of one over the needs of the greater family. This has been told in the legends of your forefathers, as far back and farther than Great White Bear himself. But do not fret," the Shaman said in a gentle manner used only with those who truly knew him. "One-Tree Rock will learn his lesson and become an asset to our Clan once more. And he too shall share in the abundance of the coming hunt."

In the smudge of distance, the last of the previous month's storm clouds pressed over the edge of the horizon. A jagged bolt of lightning coursed from the cloud onto the far plains. The Shaman counted under his breath. He reached seventeen before the low rumble of thunder vibrated the air around them.

"We have seen the last of this season's rains," he said. "Let the hunt begin."

* * * *

The Wolf and Coyote Clans were first to arrive at the encampment of the Great White Bear. They swiftly and efficiently erected temporary lodges beside the brightly painted, conical, stick-and-hide constructions of their hosts. The following days saw the arrival of the Clans of Whip-poor-will, Beaver, Rock, Grizzly, Cloud, White Dear, and The People. All built shelters or settled their hides under the broad protective canopies of trees and rocky ledges. By the evening of the twelfth sun, almost three hundred and twenty Clanspeople congregated around the fires scattered along the shallow-edged arroyo.

The Shamans gathered amongst the boulders along the ridge above the makeshift village. They twisted twigs and grass into effigies of bison, pierced by the symbolic stick spears of the hunter, and placed them in a shallow basin beneath a cairn constructed of rocks from each family's home site. Sweet-smelling smoke wafted and eddied as they shared the sacred pipe. Chanting and singing drifted through the days and long into the nights, following the smoke from their fire into the sky.

Many Hands walked with the leaders of the kindred Clans, observing the collaboration of their brothers and sisters, knowing it was a sign of their prosperity. Men and women bartered and traded chert and obsidian, herbs and seeds, blades and blankets, meats and berries. Some sat shucking pine cones open, flicking the nuts from amongst the woody leaves. One basket was already full enough to last a family two or three nutritious years. Others were learning the essentials of percussive foraging—the skilled tapping of wood to determine hollows and the hiding places of succulent grubs. Still others were weaving the pelts of white mice into what would be a fine cloak.

"Our sisters give us much to be thankful for," Many Hands said.

The men nodded in agreement.

Black-Footed Crow of the Beaver Clan said, "Indeed, many moons have seen our only sustenance gathered by our women. They are wise, and without their work we would perish."

The sagest matriarchs had assumed control of the kitchen fires. They prepared and roasted raccoon, deer, and rabbit on the open flames. Tubers and roots crisped on the hot stones. Sweet prairie turnips lay washed upon a hide, ready to be eaten crunching-raw. Many Hands and the other leaders continued along the dusty slope of the arroyo, downward to the lower plain behind the hillocks. In the increasing gloom of twilight, they passed the history of bones that lay embedded in the sandy walls of the gulch.

"The beasts of legend," Many Hands said as a few of the leaders ran their fingers along the smooth curve of a large deteriorated tusk. "Our Shaman, Dusk Runner, possesses the ochre-colored skull of one such forgotten beast."

"It must give him strong magic," Black-Footed Crow said in admiration.

The bottom of the arroyo spilled out onto an expanse of flat, open dirt. The cliffs rose high on either side. Toward the twilight moon, fires blazed, silhouetting men and boys toiling to reconstruct and strengthen the deep-blood kettle before the evening's supper— ready for the new day and hunt.

One-Tree Rock was sweating and grunting as he hauled a log up and over a mound of animal skulls and ancient carcasses that had solidified into a stony barricade. A boy at his heels dragged a twiggy clump of brush that he thrust into a gap in the kettle wall. Many Hands could see One-Tree's self-respect was no longer diminished but growing strong once more with the physical labor. One-Tree nodded in deference to his leader as they passed.

The deep-blood kettle was almost a hundred paces in diameter, arcing out from the base of the cliff into the plain and back again. Scattered about its interior were the discarded bones of the previous years' hunt. All would be used to strengthen the kettle for the activities of the coming day.

"The kettle is almost secure," Black-Footed Crow noted. "But I suspect in the next year we may have to increase its size. More Clans have followed our stories. They, too, would benefit from the group Autumn Hunt."

Many Hands looked up to the bluff. For a moment, he thought he saw the slinking shadow of old man coyote, who had taught the Clans the secret of the deep-blood kettle. But then he recognized Dusk Runner and the other Shamans, each holding flaming torches. From the edge of the bluff they peered down into the hungry maw of the kettle. Dusk Runner called out to those below, then threw his torch high. It sailed, spinning, through the air, then landed with a sparking thud in the middle of the kettle. Dusk Runner pressed his fingers to his temples and sang out into the night for the bison to come. His intonations were pleased and thankful, his words honorable toward the bison that would give themselves in the new day. One of the Shamans unwrapped folds of caribou skin to expose the Pipe of the Hunt to the night sky. It was stuffed and lit and passed around their circle. Then, as one, the Shamans sang out in prayer.

* * * *

One-Tree Rock had been chosen to call in the bison, but his transgression had moved the honor back to Many Hands as the most skilled hunter.

On the day of the hunt, Many Hands rose long before the sun. He stepped out into the chill of the morning, his thick fingers tying on his caribou vest. Then he tugged his breechcloth over his belt and re-knotted the bandannas securing the buckskin leggings at his knees. Neither he nor anyone else would eat or drink on this morning. All were silent as he made his way through the cluster of shelters to the edge of the hillock where the broad landscape of bison opened up before him.

The Shamans waited patiently at the Medicine Pole—carved from a tree by Dusk Runner when he first chose this site for the Clan's summer base. A painted bison skull sat upon the top, with fresh sagebrush thrust into its nose and eye sockets. It bore the scorch marks of previous ceremonial sage-burning. The Shamans chanted as Many Hands came near, and Dusk Runner reached into his satchel to present Many Hands two offerings—a small flute made from antler, and a small spear tipped with a grooved stone. Many Hands hung them from a branch on the Medicine Pole.

Another satchel at Dusk Runner's feet twisted and growled. He squatted and reached inside to grab the small animal by the neck, motioning for Many Hands to join him. The Shaman lifted a rock and brought it down upon the skull of the wolf-like animal in his grip. Then he dismembered the carcass, revealing the gut and vital organs to the rising sun. He wiped his thumb across the heart, liver, and spleen—all still pumping and quivering—and leaned forward to smear the marks of a noble hunter upon Many Hands's forehead, cheeks, and chin.

The hunter rose to his full height, and the Shamans placed upon him the bison robe and headdress. The skull, with its benevolent face and small dark horns, was heavy above Many Hands's shoulders, the trailing fur-covered hide weighty even for his warrior musculature. The hide smelled ancient and musty, though the beast had lived only five autumns previous. The inside of the skin was wrinkled, dried layers flaking off to cover his face and clothing in a fine animal dust.

The sweat of night still clung to him, the musky stench of the previous day's work filling his nostrils. Crouching low, he scampered down the arroyo onto the plain, alone, leaving his fellow hunters behind him to make their way to the sage brush gauntlet. He lay low in the grass, using the raw strength of his fingers to pull his weight through the sage, through the dirt, closer to the bison. The great skin dragged behind him. The sun was rising quickly, the sky a cloudless, cold iridescent blue. He came to a ditch in the plain, scattered with the dried dung of bison. Peering out at the animals ahead of him, he crumbled the desiccated dung in his hands then rolled decisively in the dust, wiping it across his vest and spreading it over his bare, hairless chest and about his armpits. Wherever he sensed his own sweat, his own smell, he smeared handfuls of dust so he would be indistinguishable from his brothers. He felt giddy from their scent, happy he was one with them, that he was the same as them.

Through the early morning, he crept ever closer to his brothers, their munching, belching, and farting growing ever louder. When he reached the outer edge of the herd, he rose up and swayed the hide back and forth in the tall grasses until the bison noticed and became intrigued. Many Hands was small beside them. He hoped they would think him a calf, a stranded youngster that might need protection. He bobbed up and down, ensuring he caught their eye, before shuffling toward the walled course created by the Clans. He prayed to the Great Spirit, happy and determined when he saw the bison were following.

The course was a long V-shaped funnel of strategically placed brush, logs, and rocks spreading out into the plain. It led up the steep incline of an arroyo and to the dead-end precipice of the bluff— directly above the deep-blood kettle.

Many Hands moved faster and faster, daring to bawl in feigned distress, thankful his larger brothers answered his call by meandering protectively after him. The bison were so numerous as to be uncountable, but this season the Clan would need fewer than thirty to secure their winter and ensure their survival.

His legs ached as he nudged ever closer to the course, shuffling low and praying to the Great Spirit, and to the Spirits of the animals behind him. Though his method was of trickery, gleaned from the ploys of Trickster Coyote, he was certain his brothers were aware of the deceit and knew they had been chosen for the higher purpose of their small brothers' continuance. And in return the Clans would pray for their brothers' souls, so they would know without doubt their deaths were honorable, and they would once again inhabit the flesh of their brethren to live upon the fertile plains.

Many Hands soon sensed his fellow Clanspeople hovering on either side of the course, hidden behind rock, tree, and log, behind bush and under skin. When he estimated thirty or so bison were within the chute, the Clanspeople stood and shouted, waving their arms, their spears and clubs, flapping their robes and skins as the bison passed them by.

The herd panicked, kicking up a churning dust and running up the course. Many Hands darted left and right, avoiding the bruising knock of knee, the killing kick and stomp of hoof. He ran sideways, dodging, ducking, and weaving between the heavy bulks. He caught the gaze of One-Tree Rock from behind a clump of sage and called upon the strength of Dancing Bird, the agility of Tusk the Cat Killer, the dedication of First Light, and the calmness of Beaver as he ran toward him.

The Clanspeople yelled louder, and the herd stampeded faster, up through the drive, up into the gauntlet. Many Hands threw himself over the wall of sage brush, and the crack of skull upon skull was loud as he and One-Tree Rock tumbled to the ground. Each wrapped his arms around the other to minimize the impact, and they rolled to a halt within the hovering dust and stench of bison.

They jumped up to shout at the spooked herd, and the bison thumped up the steep incline of the arroyo toward the bluff. The first ones saw the edge and tried to stop, but they were pushed over the precipice by the forward thrust of their frightened brothers. Bison charged blindly over the top of the cliff and tumbled into the deep-blood kettle far below.

Within the maw of the kettle, the Shamans ran amongst their animal brothers with spear and fluted stone where needed. Dusk Runner scurried from beast to beast, gazing into their eyes, whispering prayers into their ears, placing his hands upon their great chests and feeling for remnant signs of life. He ensured all passed peacefully and quickly to the higher hunting grounds they had earned by their sacrifice.

A single bison bull, the last in the gauntlet, reached the precipice and skidded to a halt before the drop. He turned upon the warriors behind him.

"Let him go," Many Hands said. "We have all that we need. It is not his time or his destiny." The bull careened down the slope, through the choking cloud of hanging dust as the warriors scattered from his path.

* * * *

"Thirty-seven bison in total," Dusk Runner called from the center of the kettle. "All died valiantly. All will speak of our integrity and return to inhabit the flesh of their coming generations."

Many Hands leapt over the side of the kettle with One-Tree Rock beside him. The buzz of jubilation coursed through the crowd around the kill site. The chant of the Shaman filled the cauldron as the warriors worked to skin and dissect. Many Hands reached into the mouth of a bison and sliced his cutting blade through the farthest reach of its tongue. A second cut along the underbelly saw the tongue slip free from its gaping mouth.

He called out to One-Tree Rock, "My brother, share this delicacy with me."

One-Tree was honored that he had been forgiven. The two men leaned against the carcass as each, in turn, took hefty bites from the plump length of flesh. The meat was soft and bloody, vital and life-giving. All the Clanspeople were crowded into the kettle, savoring the sweetness of the still-warm tongues, the raw tenderness of the fresh hump meat, or the succulent semi-digested vegetal contents of stomachs and intestines.

The Shamans gathered beside the carcass of a large cow and deftly sliced their blades up under her rib cage to extract the moist, warm liver. Dusk Runner held it high, fresh blood running down his forearm as he sang loud.

The feast and preparation of the bison continued for many days. The people worked hard to skin the hides, to smash the skulls and extract the brains, to lay out sinew to dry for making strong thread. They collected horns to be fashioned into spoons and cups. They melted marrow from bones and smoked strips of meat into jerky. They roasted leg meat and loins, pounded them with tallow and bone marrow into pemmican. And they lit fires around the perimeter of the deep-blood kettle to keep predators at bay.

By the end of the tenth day, only piles of burnt bones remained.

* * * *

Many Hands presented each Clan chief with a bison tail for use as a sweat lodge whip. "Thank you," he said. "And may each of you carry the flowering stick of success back to your villages."

Many Hands looked proudly upon his Clan as the visiting Clans departed. Three valiant warriors from The People, Cloud, and Beaver Clans had chosen to stay amongst the Great White Bear—their hearts entangled with three sisters of the Clan. Likewise, two of Bear's youngest men had followed their hearts to Whip-poor-will and Beaver. Several boys also changed Clans, to learn from a charismatic hunter or follow an elder brother who had found his heart song. The Beaver's skill in fishing the great river to the southeast attracted recruits from all of the attending Clans. Many Hands smiled. "Our yearly gatherings with our brothers, and the success of the trading and group hunt shall be long celebrated. But perhaps . . ."

"Perhaps what?" the Shaman asked, a gleam in his eye.

"We should commemorate our gathering place—celebrate our friendship in a place of permanence that all can be proud of. We should build something. Something magnificent."

P.J. Parker

Do you understand the meaning of the soil beneath your feet? (1302 BC)

"I am the eldest son of Bright Eyes, the beautiful woman with the long dark hair, created from plant, dew, and warmth, directly descended from the Clan of the Great White Bear. The wife of Ambling Waters, a seeder and nurturer of woodland crops, the mother of Hope, Faith, and myself—Moon River.

"The valley of our generation is green and lush, covered in parkland of oak, hickory, walnut, pecan, mulberry, and hackberry. Bear, deer, and white-tailed jackrabbits scurry beneath the protective canopy of the majestic magnolia. Braided streams and bayous echo the call of cormorants, ducks, geese, and pelicans. The slow-moving waters are fat with bass and crappie, blue gill, crawfish, and whiskered mudfish. One arm of the greatest waterway—after which I am named—twists and turns across the floodplains and into our valley to hold and protect our place of meeting.

"Each year of my life, our Clan has joined others at this bend in the river. We arrive a single moon before the sunrise that the Shaman calls the summer solstice, and we leave three moons later, at the time of equinox when the leaves begin to turn.

"I tell you a story of when I was a man of seventeen summers, respected in battles against the Shaved Heads and Sheep Eaters of the north, and celebrated as a buffalo-caller with my distant brothers of the Finger Cutters. But it is my labors at this bend in this river of which I am most proud."

* * * *

The basket of soil was heavy in my arms—the rough weave of reed pressing into my skin, creating a marked pattern over my naked chest and abdomen as I trudged across the terrain toward the point.

"The summer heat has settled in," I noted, wiping at the sweat that slicked my arms and shoulders. I only managed to rub a black smudge across my flesh. The men and boys with me each lumbered with a basket or sack of earth, and we were covered in the dust and soil of our origin. We barely looked like the great warriors and hunters we were. It made me smile, but oh, how I ached. Still, my morale was high and my heart song strong as I carried the load with my brothers.

"We should jump in the river before our next batch," Choctaw grunted, slipping and then steadying himself.

"You are always the first to suggest that, our man of the river. But indeed, I will be glad to cool down in the current." Our brothers murmured in agreement, and the idea quickly spread along all who hiked the trail. Our tread increased in speed.

My thighs ached as we climbed from the riverbank up onto the bluff, but my heart swelled to see what many different Clans had created in this place.

The first curved ridge was the height of a warrior, thick with swaying chaparral. Through a passage and fifty paces beyond lay a second ridge, upon which stood a dozen houses of cane thatch and daub, with fires smoking beside them, abundant squash-laden vines spilling about them. Young boys ran in excited circles as we passed. Women worked, even as young girls looked up from their sewing and scraping and drying. The passage cut through the second ridge to a third, a fourth, a fifth, a sixth, each crested by lodges and shelters of families and Clans from the outer districts. There were hundreds— soon to swell to thousands—of makeshift dwellings for the approaching weeks of trade and ceremony.

"We will complete the Flying Bird long before the equinox," Choctaw said, hurrying to walk beside me.

"The Great Spirit will be pleased to see that it flies with his sun and moon through the seasons." I stopped just inside the sixth ridge, and those who followed filed before me from the broad passage. The inner ridge curved around us to encompass the large plaza, the enormous concentric semicircles of our ceremonial mounds open to the bluff and the view of the rising sun.

"Drop your baskets. We will rest for a moment before continuing," I called out, placing my own basket at my feet and rubbing at the ache in my shoulder.

At the center of the plaza is a large, circular construction of stick and grass. At almost fifty paces in diameter, the Meeting Lodge easily holds two hundred of the Big Men who keep their Clans fed and clothed, their warriors trained, and their sisters skilled. The Big Men who keep their families alive.

Leading out from this lodge are five paths that cut through the outer rings to the outside land. They symbolize the paths traveled by all who come each year, and the journeys we all must eventually take. Just outside the lodge stands the Medicine Pole—the strongest Medicine Pole anywhere along the flow of the Moon River, from the Great Lakes of Shining Waters in the north to the crash of waves in the south. Shamans from hundreds of Clans and tribes and groups have touched it with their magic, painted it with their chants, adorned it with their sacred ancestral effigies. It is marked and etched with symbols of valor, integrity, and honor. It is hung with skulls of bison, deer, caribou, and one bulbous skull of frightening proportions smudged bright red ochre. All skulls face east—away from the westerly direction of evil and death.

Vacant sockets stare into the future.

Hoisting my basket up onto my shoulder, I motioned for the men to follow. They got to their feet and started the final leg of labor along the main ceremonial axis that led west toward the Flying Bird.

"Moon River!"

My name echoed across the plaza, and I turned to see my brother Hope running toward me. His feet were swift, his stride strong, but something in his manner troubled me. I motioned for Choctaw to take my stead in directing the men to the top of the Flying Bird mound, and I walked quickly toward my young brother.

"Moon River!" Hope yelled again. "Come. We have received word of the Shaved Heads." The Shaved Heads had long caused skirmishes in the north, ruthlessly pushing other Clans from the lands of their own birthright—their stories. Hope turned on his heel to run back the way he'd come.

"Choctaw!" I yelled, motioning briskly and taking off after Hope.

Choctaw threw his soil basket to the ground, leaving the men in bewilderment as he followed my boot tracks across the ridges and out past the unfinished rings of the complex.

My mother, Bright Eyes, stood at the entrance of her lodge upon the edge of the most ancient ring, the little bundle of my sister in her arms. With a grave look, she nudged open the skin, and Choctaw and I followed Hope past her into the shelter's dark confines.

"We have received tidings from scouts," said my father, Ambling Waters, "sent by the approaching Big Men, that the Shaved Heads are following their Clan's journey to this place. The tall, fierce ones carry weapons of war."

The ancient men inside the lodge muttered their concern. The smoky interior seemed suddenly heavy, the central fire sparking and sending silhouettes swaying against the walls. Bright Eyes sat with Faith held securely in her grip. I could not help but see and feel her distress.

"How many days distant?" I asked.

"All Clans will arrive here within three. The Shaved Heads within four."

"The Summer Solstice."

Ambling Waters nodded. "Our friends are walking into the unwanted path of war."

I stood and paced, finally stopping in the darkest recess of the lodge, my hand upon the honed branch that rose from the outer wall to the center of the grassy, cone-shaped roof above us. The tremble of anger grew within me. My grip on the branch tightened. "This is a place of ceremony and trade, a place of friendship, of worship. It will be filled with women and children, whose destiny lies in the future, not mired in the horrors of war with the tall ones."

My gaze fell upon Choctaw, covered in the black soil of our creation, the Flying Bird. Then I looked to Hope—only recently a man, and one who had never known war. My heart ached. I hit my fist into the branch then stepped back to the fire, hunkering down to gaze into its colors.

"We must ready ourselves for the arriving Clans," I said. "The Big Men are to be brought immediately to the central Meeting Lodge that we may make our plans before the Shaved Heads arrive. But first . . ." My heart song resonated within the fire as it sparked and spat. The flame smelled of oak and hickory. The clay cooking stones glowed bright. I could make out the fingerprints of both my mother and younger brother in the handmade rocks. "But first, we must finish the Flying Bird."

*　*　*　*

The days leading up to the solstice were long. I was thankful for their length, as all who arrived at the Flying Bird Complex swelled the ranks of those lugging soil. Four hundred or more Clanspeople formed a human chain from the riverbank, up the side of the bluff, through the rings, past the Medicine Pole, and along the concourse to the base of the Bird. Twoscore of men worked on the ceremonial mound itself, hoisting the heavy baskets of soil up the steep slope to their brothers at its crest. We worked day and night.

The Shamans supervised the placement of the soil, patting it down with bare foot and prayer, stomping it with song and dedication.

The past months had seen the Bird rise to the height of twelve men, with a wingspan of over two hundred and fifty of my own paces. In the days before the arrival of the Shaved Heads, the mound was enlarged and sculpted. The figure grew strong and bold.

I ran barefooted up the mound to the group of Shamans huddled at its crown.

"The form is almost complete," said our Shaman, Born In The Rain. "Perhaps one thousand baskets more and we will be ready to place the tufting grasses."

By the third day, over fifteen hundred brothers and sisters of the trading Clans were uprooting clumps of sage and chaparral from the surrounding forests and pastures, collecting handfuls of pale purple coneflower, prairie parsley, downy phlox and blue-eyed grass, bluestem and sneezeweed, ragweed and goldenrod.

"Integration of beauty and brotherhood is important," said one Shaman overseeing the placement of grasses. And I saw what he said was true as the mound turned from raw sculpted soil into an entity carpeted with the life of our Mother. The Flying Bird had become part of our Mother's body—a child of man, nurtured within the grass-covered womb.

* * * *

The Bird was complete.

All Clans had arrived, with several hundred shelters pitched on the ridges, in the wooded pastures, or scattered along the bluff.

The Big Men sat within the circular Meeting Lodge at the center of the complex. The heaviness of worry crowded in the space. Smoke hung low above heads bent in quiet whispers.

When the last had entered, I pushed myself to my feet and cleared my throat.

"The Shaved Heads have followed the course of the Clans from the north. Some come by merchant trail, but most have cast their canoes down the waters of the Moon River."

Wounded Ridge rose beside me, the painted fringe of his jacket hanging to below his knees. "Our People are tired from the pilgrimage. We have few weapons, for most of our burden has been items of trade."

"We can defend the bluff above the river," White Bones said. "But the land beyond the rings is open and exposed—there is little in the way of physical protection."

Stream That Comes From The Ground made his way through the others to stand before the fire's glow. He was massive, perhaps as tall as the Shaved Heads, at nearly seven feet. He wore a robe of bison, and the dark skin of his forearms was heavily scarred by hunting and battle. "We are not stuck on a piece of land. We need not stay here." His voice boomed within the lodge, and a murmur rippled through the crowd.

I stepped around the fire and stopped at the giant's side, my eyes level with the broadness of his shoulders. "It is true. We could scatter like leaves on the wind. We could retreat and hide, to fight our

85

own battles as best we know how. But what of our wares? Our ceremonies? Our reasons for communing here in the first place? It is true we are not stuck to this soil, we could go at any time, but we have built something here. This soil has meaning."

I looked around the room.

"Do we know the number of warriors who approach?" asked Stream That Comes From The Ground.

"Varying reports say between seventy and one hundred."

"Too many for one Clan to handle," Stream said. "But if we stand united, we are superior."

Wounded Ridge folded his arms, the fringes of his sleeves flinging about his legs. "But what of our women and children, Moon River? There is nowhere for them to hide. The women might be adept at thinning the forest into parkland through brushfires, or selecting and cross-breeding wild plants to produce hardy and abundant food supplies, but they have no skills of war."

My thoughts turned to my own mother and baby sister.

But then all the words of those who had spoken fell together.

* * * *

On the day of the summer solstice, when the sun finally dropped below the horizon, the land was thrown into an inky blackness below a thick cover of cloud that hid the stars. The rings of the mound complex were invisible in the dark, all signs of shelter and life hidden in the gloom.

Except for one small glimmer of light.

High on the bluff, a fire smoldered and flickered before the Medicine Pole, errant flames leaping out into the night with the smallest gust of breeze from across the flood plains.

A Shaman's chant drifted about the plaza, lifted by the flames to soar off the bluff and over the waters. The voice was tired and frail.

I stood atop the edge of the central ring, my eyes open but discerning nothing as I stared out into the night.

Ten spears lay at my right foot—an eleventh in my hand— ready.

I sensed the warriors beside me by only the heat radiating from their bodies, the whisper of their controlled breathing.

We waited, listening to the prayer from the center of the plaza, ready for any movement or noise not our own.

A warbler called from the rushes on the far side of the bayou. A signal from our scouts.

The canoes of the Shaved Heads were nearing.

The beat of my heart was strong and slow. Waiting. Ready.

A wood-pewee chirped. Her mate answered. A second signal.

The Shaved Heads were climbing the bluff, homing in on the fire and the sound of sacred prayer.

The smudge of dark shadows ran from the rim of the cliff and fanned out across the plaza to surround the lodge.

The Shaman's voice grew strong as another voice joined him from the Meeting Lodge to sing praise into the sky.

A water thrush called several times from its nest… then again… a single time.

Eighty-six warriors per the signals from the scouts.

The shadows carried bows, to cast their spears and darts across great distance.

I looked to the cloud cover, high above the undetectable concentric rings of soil. The sky was so dark it was as if the moon and stars had been swallowed by the unknown, but my eyes were adjusting, spotting shadow upon shadow, limber silhouettes crouching, huddling, and sprinting with stealth across a grand space they had no knowledge of. They were closing in on the two singing Shamans.

Even when the first fearsome Shaved Head stepped into the meager glow, the song of the Shamans held strong.

The Shaved Head spoke angry words that echoed through the night. He held his bowed dart before him—the sharp point glinting in the face of Born In The Rain.

The Shamans's song changed into a high-pitched staccato emanating from deep within them.

I echoed the call.

And then, two great plumes rose behind me as our sisters set bonfires alight. The flame jumped from torch to torch around the outer ring of the complex, casting deep shadows of our warriors across the plaza and against the clouds above.

A second call and the next ring was torched—flames leaping along rows of kindling until they reached the edge of the bluff.

I sensed the bravery of the Shaved Heads, but I also sensed their fear and wonder as they stood, still, within the embrace of the fiery ring.

Flames shot around the third outer ring, then jumped to the next one in, before blazing rapidly back and forth around the curves of the remaining central rings. It was a wall of flame, left open only to the bluff and floodplains toward the Moon River in the distance.

Our fifteen hundred Clanspeople stood proudly atop the ridges of the inner rings, behind the torches and kindling, showing our unity, our determination and might. To the tall ones, it would appear that Our People walked within the fire. The women used blankets to make the flames do their bidding. The men held their spears high, their yell filling the cauldron with a deafening and awful noise.

The Shaman repeated his staccato, boldly facing the warrior before him, and again I echoed his call.

Flames cascaded from the two bonfires at my back down onto the main concourse, flaring along the grand axis toward the enormous Flying Bird Mound.

The mound burst suddenly, explosively, into a blaze of kindling soaked in fat and grease.

At the same instant, the solstice moon broached the horizon in the east.

The moon was large—a bleeding orange-red—appearing as though an outstretched hand could pluck it from the sky. It lit up the plains and reflected off the Moon River. It turned the waterway into a bloody ribbon that snaked across the landscape.

The clouds reflected the low-slung moon as well as the six rings of fire—a semi-circular gash against the darkening crimson night sky.

To the west, toward death, the light-shimmering reflection of the Flying Bird against the clouds quivered and cast its wings to glide through the night sky—soaring above those who had called it into the world.

Still the Shaved Heads stood their ground, but in the blazing light of fire and moon they bowed their heads in honor of our magic.

There would be no bloodshed on this soil. Not on this night.

I called to my brothers—those who stood with me, and those who stood before me.

"United we stand!" I roared against the growl of the fire. "There will be peace amongst our brothers, that we may live as was intended upon the abundance of our Mother. On this solstice, on this sacred soil of Túwaqachi, below the wings of the Great Eagle Spirit, our union stands strong and tall!"

The Three Sisters (250 BC)

Hohokam may tell you he is descended from the first Clan to cross the icy sea upon reed and raft, to fight the animals of legend upon the land of Túwaqachi, to marry into Clans of repute and valor, to be stolen as children in the night by warriors, to be taught their ways, to gather within the fire and songs of the colorful Flying Bird that united them all. He may tell you of his Clan's journey along the trails and waterways of trade and warfare over mountain and across plain, from wetlands to dry, from sea to shining sea. He may sing they left their breath wherever they placed their feet upon the soil, to join with an ever-growing web of family whose heart song will always be that of the Great White Bear Clan—the family whose past and future are entwined with the fate of the Great Twins.

* * * *

Hohokam stacked baskets of maize and decorated pottery onto his litter. He secured them with ropes, tying the knots just as his father had taught him long ago, giving the loops the extra hitch his mother had advised was best. When all was set, he turned to the People of the Highlands that had gathered to see him off. All wore faces of amity, with a tinge of sadness at his leaving.

"Goodbye," Hohokam said as he touched hands, gripped forearms, and nodded in thoughtful appreciation. "I will tell your stories to my Clan and I may return to visit at the first signs of spring."

Hohokam gave a single salute then lifted the mainstay of the litter up onto his shoulder and pulled it slowly behind him. He trudged across gravel and grass amongst the scattered pit houses, smiling at those that he passed. The magnificent ponderosa that cradled the village in its mountain clearing soon swallowed him—trunks of orange bark heavily scarred by age, branches stretching above him, the trail deep with generations of cones and needles. The air was crisp with the smell of pine, sometimes like vanilla, Hohokam thought. There was no sound of bird or animal, only the gentle whistle of the mountain breeze. It was soft against his skin.

He was glad to be on his journey home, but happy he had established trade with the People of the Highlands. He'd learned how they harvested maize and tilled the clearings for their crops of plants no longer wild. Their careful prayer and collection of seed had yielded heads of corn much longer and fatter than he had seen before.

The moon had been high upon his arrival in their village almost four moons ago. The time-to-plant wind had just begun to blow, the grass had turned green, and the mesquite in the surrounding valleys had been yellow with flowers. He had followed the women into the forest, observing as they scattered and dropped their seeds into holes and told the worms to leave them alone.

At night, he had sat in their pit houses, listening to their stories of agriculture. Some stories crossed with those of his own Clan's heritage. Often the teller would pause, the smoke and smell of supper hovering close, to take note of the crickets' song. The music of the crops, the women had called it. It was the crickets that told them when to bring in the harvest, Hohokam recalled as he imitated his very small brother. His chirps drifted through the trees to keep him company on the trail.

It was at least a moon's walk home, and the wooden mainstay dug into his shoulder, rubbing and blistering his palms and hardening the callouses of his fingers. But he did not mind. The strength of the seed he towed would help them in the years to come, and the beauty and worth of the traded pottery would see his family well fed through the coming season. Perhaps his endeavors would catch the attention of the Shaman, under whom he desperately wished to train—to learn the ways of nature, the movement of his brothers, and the knowledge of the powers all about them. To one day become a Shaman himself.

The shaded ponderosa gradually fell behind him, and he stepped into the rising heat of the desert floor, toward his people and the Place of Snakes.

* * * *

Hohokam lay asleep, curled up in the dirt next to his litter. The night had been hot, so he had stripped off his clothing and bunched it beneath him as padding against the rocks and stones. The sun was rising. He could feel its warmth on the bottoms of his bare feet, but still he kept his eyes closed, wishing he could remember the dream that had kept him company through the night. It had been a towering cliff face, dotted with brightly lit holes. He rolled onto his back and yawned, rubbing at the ache in his shoulder and wondering if he should remain just a little while longer.

The sharp end of a stick prodded the muscled flesh covering his ribs.

He grabbed the blade from beside his vest, reeling into a low crouch, eyes and mouth wide, looking all around. The sunshine blinded him, but the booming laughter left him chuckling.

"Best you put on your breechcloth, little brother, before coyote takes back what he gave you." Darkwater held out his hand to lift the younger from his squat.

Hohokam got to his feet and slapped an arm around his brother's shoulders.

"I have missed you, Darkwater. But how did you know of my arrival?"

"The wind told me so, little Hoohoogum," he said, picking up the sweat-soaked vest and sniffing at it before throwing it to his brother.

Hohokam smiled, pulling on the vest. "Come, see what I have traded," he said, nodding toward the litter as he donned his breechcloth.

"This Highland pottery is distinctive—much different from our red-on-buff designs." Darkwater crouched to caress the stonework. "They are beautiful, Hoohoogum. They will trade well. And the seed?"

"I will tell you as we go," Hohokam said, reaching for his rawhide pouch of pemmican and offering some to his brother.

After they had eaten, they ensured that the litter and its contents were secure. Darkwater grinned when he saw the extra hitch in each of the knots. "You do the memory of our mother proud, little

Hoohoogum. I will take the load for a while, as I see your shoulder pains you. You can take it again as we near the Place of Snakes."

Hohokam slung both their satchels about his neck and was thankful for the lighter weight. The sun had fully breached the horizon and cast long shadows across the desert before them—red and orange, fading into the shimmering blue haze of the far-off horizon, many days distant. What was once desolate wasteland was crossed with several hundred manmade canals, some no wider than a footstep, others more than sixteen paces in width. To walk the edge of every canal, Hohokam guessed, would take more time than a moon.

Darkwater lurched, dragging the litter behind him. "Urgh! No wonder you are hunched over, little brother."

By midmorning they had reached the first canal. It sliced a line across the desert at least a day's walk in either direction. It was only just wider than his shoulders, but still Hohokam jumped into the deep trench as Darkwater pulled the litter over the gap. It was cool in the canal, the water eddying around his knees as he reached up to guide the litter above. Then he kicked his foot into the hard clay and secured a hold to climb out.

Patches of purple, red, green, and gold amaranth spread far, kept luscious with the water from the canals. Soon they came upon Clanspeople, bent low to water the plants while others tilled the soil.

As the brothers approached the Place of Snakes—a rambling settlement of perhaps six hundred adobe lodges strewn amongst the pastures and canals—Hohokam could not help but shake his head in newfound disbelief at the fields of undersized squash, limp beans, and ragged cornstalks with ears no larger than his thumb, frail in comparison to those he'd helped cultivate in the Highland forests, despite the water and attentiveness.

When the orange adobe of their home came into view, Darkwater dropped the mainstay onto the ground. He rubbed his arm from the exertion, twisting and stretching to work out the knots in his muscles. He sat at the edge of a shallow canal, shucking off his moccasins to cool his feet in the mud and slow trickle of water.

Hohokam sat beside him and removed his own boots to share the relief from the dry heat of the day. "I will tell you a story from the

Highlands," he said, and his voice trembled at the very thought of the legend and its power. The magic that was now his to tell others.

Darkwater leaned back onto his elbows and cocked his head, intrigued.

"Sky Woman was pregnant when she fell through the hole in the sky to the land on which we live. Once upon Túwaqachi, she gave birth to a daughter who grew into a beautiful young woman. Both mother and daughter were very happy. When the time was right and the west wind blew through her, this beautiful young woman also became pregnant with twin boys."

Hohokam and Darkwater shared a knowing smile—the quickest flicker of the mouth and crinkle about the eyes only a close brother would recognize.

"Sadly, the young woman died with the birth of her sons, and so Sky Woman buried her within the soil of this new world. From this ceremonial mound of earth, the Three Sisters grew. They provided food for the twins, and food for all of Our People, wherever they traveled. Together the Three Sisters, as companions, continue to grow strong and flourish, ensuring the survival of those they wish to serve. Separated, they are lonely and sad, unable to carry out their purpose."

"And who are these Three Sisters, little Hoohoogum?" Darkwater asked.

"They are Corn, Bean, and Squash."

They gazed at the corn growing across the canal from where they sat. Early in the day's journey, they had passed many crops of beans. And on the far side of the Place of Snakes, far from any stands of corn or bean, Black Rattler and his Clan grew vast tracts of squash. In between the Three Sisters were fields of cotton, tobacco, and pigweed.

Later that evening, Hohokam stood in the middle of an adobe lodge at the center of the Place of Snakes. More than one hundred family members crowded into the space, sitting knee-to-knee on grass mats, leaning forward, straining to hear.

"The Three Sisters are companions who should never be separated," he said. "Sister Bean, for the highest yield, requires tall poles for her vines to climb. She depends upon the height of Sister Corn's stalks to lift her up. In turn, she enriches the soil at Sister Corn's feet. These two thrive as they assist each other. The more Sister Bean enriches the soil, the higher Sister Corn grows, and the more pods Sister Bean produces, the more she enriches the soil, and so on.

"But it is Sister Squash who completes the Three. She stays close to the ground—spreading her vines far, embracing her taller sisters. Her broad leaves cover and protect the soil, keeping it moist for Sister Bean, keeping weeds at bay and providing shade for the shallow roots of Sister Corn. Her spiky tendrils are a painful warning to any predator of her siblings.

"The strength of one strengthens another, which strengthens another, which strengthens another, in a continual cycle. Supported by the others, all three flourish."

Hohokam reached into the basket at his feet and pulled out a dried ear of Sister Corn from the Highlands—as long and as thick as his forearm.

An excited murmur ran through the room.

Hohokam said no more as he gazed about the lodge. He caught his brother's eye—a glimmer of Bear pride crossing Darkwater's face—before he looked to the Shaman standing in the shadowed corner of the lodge. There was no word, or nod, or signal, yet Hohokam knew what the wise man was thinking. It made him happy.

P.J. Parker

Great House Made of Dawn (828 AD)

Chaco accompanied the Shaman, Friend of the Snake, along the ragged gash of their home canyon. He was eager to learn all he could. Though still in the dark of early morning, they had no need for torch as they knew the trail and the canyon well—the looming sandstone walls, the scrubby, meandering arroyo. Both men were the age of eighteen summers, and their lives were woven together—one a man of constructing ceremony, the other a man of ceremonial construction. They were silent as they trod, for Chaco knew the Shaman's thoughts must be his own. Friend of the Snake tilted his head to contemplate the last of the stars above and sniff at the wind. Chaco sniffed as well, detecting the fragrance of the juniper that grew on the mesa above them. He could also smell coyote, perhaps skunk.

When they reached the canyon's entrance—a deep slash cutting through the mesa out onto the desert plateau—the first slivers of dull red dawn were skimming the horizon. Between the east and west mesas stood the Banded Butte, rising from the desert floor to twice the height of the surrounding escarpments. The bands of history wound horizontally around it, from base to majestic, flat-topped summit.

The uppermost band blazed a bright crimson, the first sacred point on the land to be touched by each new day.

As he followed close on the Shaman's footsteps, bare feet leaving little trace upon the trail, Chaco watched the crimson radiance drip down the sides of the butte, as if it were melting from the world of night into the one of light. The lower rings, shadowy black, gently bruised into a deep purple, then red. The top of the butte flared a bright orange as the sun climbed in the east. Then the burnished glow etched its way down, band by band, story by story, devouring the crimson of early morning. When Chaco and Friend of the Snake stepped onto the ramp at its base, the Banded Butte was the brightest point in a vast landscape yet to awaken.

They stared up, mesmerized, until their trance was broken by a roadrunner scuttling from grass to cactus and disappearing into scrub.

"Come, Chaco," Friend of the Snake murmured with a wave of his hand. The Shaman strode up the rampart with Chaco at his side. The glare of dawn blinded them, so with upheld hands, they made their way up the butte until the trail was no more than a vertical slit in the stone. Chaco pulled off his moccasins and pushed them into his satchel. The Shaman pressed both hands and one bare foot against either side of the crevice, then flexed all his muscles to urge himself vertically up the crevice. His flute fell out of his satchel, and Chaco picked it up and slipped it into his own pack.

"I have it," Chaco said, starting the ascent. The day burned on as they climbed—fingers and toes, elbows and palms. Every part of Chaco's body ached from the exertion.

When they were halfway up the side of the butte, the Shaman lodged himself in the tight confines of the fissure and gazed out at the surrounding world. Chaco followed his lead.

"The world seems very young," Chaco mused.

"And yet she is immeasurably old," Friend of the Snake said.

The earth and scrub were now fully alight, the long shadows shortening as the two watched from their lookout.

"I am certain today will be the solstice of summer," the Shaman said. "But only the Sun Dagger will say for certain."

Chaco nodded. "My men will reconfirm the center line of the Great House at noon and measure the angle of the sun above the horizontal. It will be good to validate the construction's alignment against the solstice."

The Shaman turned to him. "We shall see." He put his hand to his mouth and let out a yelping staccato that filled the big sky around them. "Hi-yi-yi-yi-yi-yi-yi-yi-yi," he called to the new day. When the echoes of welcome faded, he said. "Race you to the top, my brother of the Bear!"

The two men moved as one—arms and legs stretching, fingers grappling, the pads of bare feet and toes pushing against stone and into the cracks of the vertical climb. Soon they were out on the open southern face of the butte, confident as they pulled themselves up the raw stone, loose pebbles and shards of rock falling from their footholds. Friend of the Snake took the lead, but it was Chaco who first tumbled over the upper rim onto the ceremonial shelf of the Banded Butte. He rose to his feet and extended his arm to help the Shaman. They stood together before three monolithic slabs that leaned askew against the overhanging rock face, which rose to the top of the butte high above them.

The sun was almost at its zenith.

Chaco pulled the flute from his pack and handed it to the Shaman before squatting beside a rock at the edge of the precipice. The stone's surface was carved with a rectangle and what appeared to be a rattler. The images had long been smoothed and made indistinct by generations of respect. He ran his finger along one shallow groove. Before him lay the scattered remnants of a signal fire.

Friend of the Snake strode reverently toward the three slabs of ancient rock. Dwarfed by their sheer size, he ran his hands over them, feeling their heat, then ducked to crawl beneath their lean. The wise man sat in the shadows before a carved spiral in the wall of the butte. Chaco's eyes followed the curve of the coiled calendar, from its center, around the nine and a half turns to its final end.

Is it the end, or merely the middle? he pondered.

Its shape and significance reminded him of his family's history skin, whose pictures and stories spiraled through the generations of the Great White Bear, from its center toward the hide's frayed edges.

To the left of the carved spiral on the cliff face, a second, smaller spiral spun off, only just hidden in the shadow of slab. The Shaman sat in silent prayer for many moments, the sun blazing down against the three stones that shaded him. Friend of the Snake lifted the flute to his lips, placed his fingers over its holes, and began to play the song from his heart. The resonance was rich and warm, deep and melodic. It wafted about the slabs and across the rocky shelf.

And then Chaco saw it.

The Sun Dagger appeared on the rock face directly above the Shaman's shadowed head. It dazzled within the shade as the sunlight slipped through a gap in the overhead slabs. The dagger cut slowly down the rock, slicing through the very center of the etched spiral.

"The middle of time," Chaco whispered to himself.

Friend of the Snake placed his hand to the light of the Sun Dagger then ran his palm down the length of its blade—feeling its power. He touched his palm to his forehead before dropping his head in prayer.

* * * *

"The story you hold within you is very important, Chaco," Friend of the Snake said as they walked along the roadway back into the canyon. "For your story holds the design of the Great House Made of Dawn. And through your telling, it will be built."

They passed the prairie dogs, whose own settlement of holes and bunkers spanned either side of the road. Chaco knew well that his project was sacred to many, that it was the center of their religious and economic universe. Indeed, all roads, including the one on which they walked, like a starburst, coursed from the Great House in straight lines across desert and mesa, over causeways and up steps cut into rugged rock. Toward the Monumental Valley in the west, toward the Place of Snakes in the south, and toward the Cliff Peoples of the north, the roads cut unerring routes to trade and unity.

They turned onto the road that traversed the canyon from end to end—straight and shallow, sometimes more than ten paces in width. It ran past the scatter of outlying villages surrounding the Great House, edged by carefully placed stones.

Up ahead, a cloud of dust stirred. Twoscore men hauled trunks of spruce and fir behind them. The branches had been stripped, but still the trees drove deep grooves into the surface of the road as they were dragged.

"This path will need to be scraped again by the end of the moon," Chaco muttered.

"How many trees have been secured for the construction?" the Shaman asked.

"Several hundred lie in the shadows of the Threatening Rock, ready for the beams of the upper floors and roofs. Several thousand more will be required by the time the fourth and fifth stories are built."

"It must soon be time for me to choose posts for the next kiva," said Friend of the Snake. "I surmise we need at least one for every thirty apartments in the Great House. Already we have eight, but it appears we are ready for the ninth."

"You are correct, Shaman. We have plans for the ninth ceremonial room and shall begin digging the pit in the coming days, now that the spine of the Great House has surely been aligned to the summer solstice."

The early afternoon sun beat down upon them as they walked the remaining length of the canyon.

At first, as always, the Great House appeared part of the canyon wall that rose behind it. Built from the same stone, the Great House was as much a part of the landscape as the people whose sweat and toil had pulled it from the earth.

The full-scale of the building became evident only when they were almost upon it. The sides of the canyon fell away as the walls of the Great House rose from the ground. Fields of squash, corn, bean, and tobacco grew before it, and the southern wall ran east to west, following the daily course of the sun. The wall was solid and much higher than a man could jump or reach. So far it had only a single door. The larger structure rose behind it like a stepped butte.

Chaco pushed open the door, and it swung effortlessly upon well-greased hinges.

To one side, his men had marked the spine of the building, perpendicular to the front wall and aligned with the sun of the summer solstice. Rocks and pegs and ropes stretched north, toward the rear. To the other side, the first section of the Great House had been nearly completed. The apartments curved around the enormous court, and stepped back and up, above the ceremonial space. The outer edge of the immense arc rose to five stories, with finely crafted stone and masonry, T-shaped doorways, and ladders climbing from one level to the next.

In his mind, within the story that filled his heart, Chaco could see the completed Great House curving in its vast semicircular form—

embracing two ceremonial courts, the terraced apartments and open roof spaces facing the sun, observing and measuring its course through the heavens, documenting the seasons and solstices, worshipping the Father that had impregnated Mother Earth to give them life.

Beautiful town, he thought to himself, the pride of the story swelling his heart.

Friend of the Snake passed through the opening behind him. He slapped his shoulder in friendship before walking briskly across the court toward the main kiva of the Great House Made of Dawn. It would be a night of ceremony and dance.

"Come see me at moonrise," said the Shaman as he swung his feet down onto a ladder and descended into the shadowy darkness of the sacred kiva.

A man called Rain Shadow approached from a mound of rubble at the building's spine.

"The alignment is exact. Has the solstice been confirmed?"

Chaco nodded with a satisfied grin. "We should complete the spine separating the two ceremonial courts within two moons, and I have promised the Shaman another kiva."

They walked toward the central wall in mid construction, and Chaco noted the work, ensuring it followed his story. Two dozen men were cutting and chiseling raw blocks of sandstone and smoothing any rough ridges, lifting and pushing them into place along the building's spine. Others hauled baskets of rubble up ladders to the higher levels of wooden scaffolding. They packed it between the honed masonry walls to form a strong and insulating core that would keep rooms cool in the high sun of summer and retain the warming heat in the low-slung light of winter.

Three of Chaco's most celebrated masons cut and shaped smaller sandstone pieces to decorate the outside of the structural wall. Each created a distinct design influenced by their heart song.

All had a place in the house they were constructing.

All held a symbolism of strength that would last into the distant future.

Chaco joined the workers placing rubble into the core of the central wall until it was solid—with no room for even the sharpest blade to slide into any gap.

Some time later, Chaco finally slumped into the shade, pressing his back against the cool wall and splaying his legs across the dirt. He guzzled water from a hollowed-out gourd, and it was sweet against the dryness of his mouth. Children played on the far side of the court, running with dogs and kicking a ball. Clanspeople sat on the shaded terrace roofs of their apartments, readying food for the evening's feast, weaving baskets, and cutting turquoise jewelry and beads.

"Turquoise," Chaco said thoughtfully.

Rain Shadow sat beside him, grabbed the gourd, and held it to his lips. Then he poured the vessel over his head and let the water stream over his face and his long, plaited hair.

"Do you know why we can build this Great House, Rain Shadow?"

"Because you have the story within you, my brother."

Chaco smiled. "That is but a small part of the legend."

One by one the other men stopped to listen. They leaned against the wall or hunkered down in its shadow to drink from their own jugs of water.

"You all know well that the storerooms cresting our House are brimming with the maize from our forefathers' Place of Snakes. When our brothers produce more than their people can consume, they bring it to the trade fairs at this meeting place."

"I have been to the Place of Snakes as a child," said Towering Clouds of Thunder. "They, too, have built towns of great size over the generations, but nothing that compares to this beautiful House."

"For we have turquoise, my brother." Chaco swelled with pride, recalling when he worked as a young boy in the mines with his father. "In times of abundance, the Clans bring to trade and barter their vegetables, their dried meat, their corn, beans, squash, and tobacco. But it is the sacred blue stone that holds its value always. For when the sun refuses to shine, or the brush dams are arid and the Three Sisters are overcome by sadness, it is the blue stone that brings the Clans to this place—that they may trade it back for the abundance of our stores, that they may share in the wealth of produce we have secured for them."

Chaco looked upon several families in the highest apartments of the House. They reclined on their terraces, some in the cool shade, others rejoicing in the last rays of the afternoon. Their hands were worn. Not from tilling the fields, or hunting pronghorn or elk, but from shaping turquoise into valuable beads, stringing them onto lengths of sinew for bracelets and necklaces.

"This Great House and the surrounding villages will shelter many thousands of people—far too many for the canyon and mesas above to feed. It is the blue stone that is the phenomenon behind our civilization. The blue stone is what allows us to live in this place, to construct such a magnificent wonder, and to dream of futures without fear of starvation."

The men sat contentedly in the lengthening shadows. Torches were lit, and doors and windows glowed against the sandstone. Drifts of smoke from kitchen fires wafted the scent of rabbit, snake, and fox across the plaza. The sweet smell of fire-charred corn filled the space, and Chaco's workmen rose as the stars appeared.

"How goes your training with the Shaman?" asked Rain Shadow as he stood to leave.

Chaco gave his friend a knowing nod but said nothing.

Soon the moon appeared.

* * * *

Chaco descended the ladder into the kiva. The wood of the rungs was smooth against his bare feet as he left the torch-lit night of festivities in the ceremonial court for the smoky darkness of the underworld. His belly was full and warm with corn and rabbit.

"It is not only this House that is made of dawn," whispered Friend of the Snake as Chaco placed his feet upon the sacred dirt floor. "This part of Túwaqachi is itself made of dawn. It is made of pollen and rain."

Chaco sat on a bench that curved around the edge of the large circular space, and listened attentively. Friend of the Snake squatted before the kiva's shallow round navel, his face and outstretched arms hovering over it, feeling the gentle wind of *Emergence* blow through him. Then he rose and walked to the edge of the kiva, where he removed the necklace of turquoise and silver from his neck and placed it in a niche in the northern curve of the space.

"I saw the Great House in its entirety today," Chaco said. "My story revealed itself to me as I stood at its very center."

Friend of the Snake leaned forward, his elbows on his knees, his hands clasped together.

"The completed structure will encompass more than six hundred apartments and at least forty kivas. The two largest kivas will lie at the head of the two ceremonial courts, and each will be twice the size of this one."

The two men gazed around the smoky space, and they were pleased.

"Together we will venture to the place of trees to choose the central beams," Chaco said. "The trunks must be much larger and stronger than any we have hauled so far."

The Shaman nodded. "Without doubt, these walls will be sanctuary and home for well over one thousand of our brothers and sisters, and their children, with the story you tell."

"It will be a strong community."

Friend of the Snake turned to the flicker of flame emanating from the central firebox. "The changing population of trade swells our families with each season, and I foresee other great houses will be built along the length of our canyon."

"Do the secrets of the kiva tell you how many?" Chaco asked.

The Shaman reached into the wall niche for his necklace and held it between himself and the fire. The silver and turquoise reflected slivers of light in the ambient darkness that embraced them. Hanging from one of its silver links was a small copper bell and a single macaw feather. The Shaman stared into the stones then pulled the flute from his belt and held it to his lips. But he played not a note as he saw something in the stones. He set the flute at his side, paying it no mind as it rolled across the bench and onto the floor at his feet.

"What do you see, Shaman?" Chaco asked.

The Shaman stepped to the center of the kiva, where he fell to his knees in front of the navel of *Emergence*. Then he turned to Chaco and smiled. "Kokopelli will play many tunes upon his magical flute as he visits our villages on his mischievous journey. His back will be hunched from wondrous song and legend, seed and fertility. His music will embrace times of great prosperity and happiness, generations of trade, and a richness of culture and creativity that will reach into the heart songs of many. Our stores of grain and coffers of turquoise will be filled to their brim many times over, ensuring a long and satisfied life for generations to come."

His voice cracked, and he pressed his hands into the dirt as he peered into the kiva's navel. Then, without warning, he rose and strode toward the ladder to leave. With his foot upon the lowest rung, he stopped. "There are secrets of the kiva I may not tell even you, Chaco. Not until I place the rattle of the Shaman in your hands. Know only that our immediate future is secure and good, but it will not always be so. A time will come for the hole to be punched through the bottom of the bowl, as it is placed over the face of our dead—over the face of our civilization."

The Shaman stepped up and into the night.

Alone in the dark, Chaco gazed at the ladder that led up through the smoke hole and out of the sacred space.

Through the hole, he could see the spark of a single star, shining bright.

P.J. Parker

Creators of Tall Buildings; Ancestors of the Peaceful People (1209 AD)

Hopituh Shi-nu-mu shuffled about the central navel of the kiva, deep in prayer. The firebox cast his shadow around the broad curve of wall, and along the great beams that held the wooden ceiling high above. He stopped at the niche in the northern curve to peer at the turquoise bead within, and then looked up through the smoke hole toward the spark of a single star, shining bright in the very early morning. He pressed the painted prayer stick against his chest, its plume of eagle feathers quivering with each slow beat of his heart.

Since the death of his father, White Bluff, the previous year, Hopi had earned the positions of Shaman, of Sun Watcher, and of Inside Chief. Hopi was well versed in his responsibilities to his people. But now his heartbeat was erratic, slowing and quickening, for the prophesied time was approaching.

He passed the white shell in the eastern niche, then the red bead in the southern. He stopped by the western curve and closed his eyes, holding the prayer stick to his forehead. Inside the niche was a wedge of iridescent blue turquoise, and its power seemed to steady the rhythm of his heart. Hopi squinted up through the smoke hole again. From this angle, he could see only the immense curvature of overhanging sandstone that sheltered the Clan's Cliff House beneath the verdant mesa above.

The morning passed into afternoon and yet Hopi continued to pace the sacred space. Only when the sun had passed its zenith and shone through the smoke hole to light the turquoise bead did he hunker down on the polished floor, hold the prayer stick before him, and sing loud. The song resonated within the kiva. It sparked the four sacred stones of Spider Woman and billowed out the hole with the smoke from the firebox. His song drifted up amongst the dwellings that huddled in the cavernous contour of the cliff face.

* * * *

Hopi emerged from the kiva onto the plaza level of the Cliff House. The sun was rolling across the sky toward the far side of the narrow canyon, its rays reaching under the sandstone overhang to paint the massive recess of rock a vibrant yellow. He stood a moment to breath in the air. After the staleness of smoke that had held him for almost three days in his trance of prayer, the sweet smell of spruce, intermingled with pinon and sagebrush, invigorated him. He shuddered to realize he was once again amongst the living—far from the bugs of the underworld. He took several deep breaths, filling his lungs, exulting in the breeze that wrapped around him. As he stretched, he peered down at the pine trees clustered along the lower levels of the canyon, just beneath the House and broad slabs of cliff. Nettles, cones, and branches grew thick in the canopy, the myriad greens, yellows, and browns providing safety to many of Hopi's smaller brothers. Nests clung to almost every branch, but all had been discarded and forgotten many moons ago. There was no sign of his feathered brothers, and eventually he conceded that, despite his prayers, they might never return. Far below, the canyon floor was mottled shadow, rippling with the movement of the spruce. There was a trickle of water in the riverbed. *The reservoirs are not yet dry,* he thought.

"Hopi! Welcome back," called a voice from above.

He held a hand to his brow against the sun and scanned the stone dwellings of the Cliff House stretching several stories above. Fox Walks Well was climbing down to greet him, causing a flurry amongst the turkeys that huddled on the ledges. They squawked and gobbled as Hopi's young brother jumped from a ladder amongst them. Clanswomen were scattered along the terraces, grinding corn, weaving, adding wood to their fires, and cutting the tender meats of rabbit and rodent to toss into simmering pots. Raked piles of drying corn kernels—black, red, white, and yellow—dotted almost every spare surface of roof terrace.

Hopi's stomach growled as he climbed the nearest ladder to meet his brother.

The two clasped forearms, but were quickly interrupted by their sister, Yellow Snake Who Rattles, running toward them. At thirteen, Yellow Snake was a beautiful woman the two brothers were proud to call sister. She wore a brightly colored skirt and shawl, a necklace of turquoise, and her hair swept up into squash blossoms on either side of her head. The features of her face were delicately drawn, but she shared the handsome pride of the Great White Bear Clan with her brothers. She carried a bowl of corn stew, almost spilling it as she flung her arm around her eldest brother's waist.

"Thank you, Yellow Snake," Hopi said as he accepted the bowl. He started shoveling the spicy stew into his mouth, and the three crouched in the shadows of the overhanging rock. Around them the spruce swayed amongst the chatter of domesticity.

"You have been in the Spirit world for many days," Yellow Snake said. "Much longer than any previous time. I had feared you would not cross the rainbow back to our world, but then I heard your song and knew you would soon return. Is the stew all right?"

Hopi smiled and nodded.

"How is the situation outside our house, Fox?"

Fox Walks Well had been appointed Outside Chief. Whereas Hopi was responsible for all that occurred within the village—deciding all important matters, greeting each new sun with prayer, drawing up the calendar of events, designating the times of planting and rites of puberty, and translating the meanings of Vision Quests—Fox Walks Well was responsible for all outside matters, such as guarding the agriculture, hunting grounds, turquoise, salt beds, and water resources. He also constructed defenses against unfriendly tribes and coordinated with the peaceful Clans that inhabited the cliff dwellings in the surrounding canyons.

"More refugees arrive every day, my brother. The Badger Clan continues to expand their Spruce Tree House in the next canyon to make room for more of their kindred as they arrive. They say the Place of Snakes is almost totally abandoned, its canals holding only dust, the Three Sisters unable to grow despite their combined strengths."

Hopi nodded. "And the Great House Made of Dawn?"

"Its apartments, too, have begun to empty, with very few new families securing a home there. I fear it will be desolate before we are blessed with children of our own."

Hopi muttered to himself, and both Fox and Yellow Snake raised their eyebrows in question. He wiped at the stew on his cheek and licked it from his lips and fingers. "They once were noble cities and economies, but both are joined to the productivity of the lands along these great roads." Hopi's eyes changed hue as his thoughts darkened. "Without the continuous flow of trade, the Clans cannot support such large houses." He stared out into the higher spruce branches for signs of birdlife. "In the end, when the rains are few and the stores of maize are low, one cannot eat turquoise."

"But the rains still come," Yellow Snake said. "Intermittently."

"And they will assist life for those smaller family groups that choose to stay on the soil of their children. But the Horned Water Serpent seems to have abandoned us. The rains and the seasons have become unpredictable. Our calendars are no longer aligned with the fertility of Mother Earth and the masculine strength of Father Sun." Hopi handed the empty bowl to Yellow Snake with a thankful smile. "Come, Fox. Show me the state of our reservoirs, for I dreamed of them during my prayers."

* * * *

Fox and Hopi climbed down from the Cliff House and walked the length of the canyon beneath the canopy of spruce, following the trickle of the waterway. The ground was soggy beneath their moccasins, and Hopi was thankful for that.

"Have there been any more skirmishes?" he asked as they approached the first dam.

"A band attempted to ransack the House of Many Windows two nights past, but it was easily handled by our brothers there. Peace was made and food gladly shared. The band has now continued on their journey north."

"It is true then that our brothers still seek their place in this world. We can only hope they will find it."

A swift with black and white wings darted through the air. It flew ahead of them, close to the ground, and disappeared into dense undergrowth.

"A good sign," Fox said.

"A sign," Hopi muttered.

The first and second brush reservoirs were each over half full, but the third was no more than a muddy puddle that spread the width of the canyon. Two boys stood in the middle with baskets full of silt. They prodded and dug at the messy ground, hoisting it into their baskets. Drag marks scraped the site toward the broad, low dam of twig and brush. Silt had been thrown onto the wall and patted down to strengthen it for better times.

"The reservoirs have been lower," Fox noted with a shrug.

Hopi nodded.

Their path turned toward a steep, twisting trail of steps cut into the side of the canyon, leading to the top of the mesa. Fox and Hopi climbed quickly, familiar with the almost two thousand steps and handholds of the track since the time they could first walk. Hopi caught the vista of their Cliff House between the sway of spruce and the curve of rock. The immense construction held its own majesty amongst the beauty of the nature that made their world. Within several heartbeats, they reached the top of the mesa and the full brilliance of afternoon sun. Hopi pulled at his breechcloth, tightened the knot at his hip, and brushed at the dust that covered his legs from the climb. He clasped the satchel at his waist that held his Corn Mother.

The mesa was not as lush as when they were children. But still the broad, flat escarpment was covered from edge to edge by the Three Sisters, growing in the waffle pattern of fields with a handful of seeps and springs scattered in between. Hundreds of Clanspeople tended the crops. They hauled baskets of water, tilled the sandy soil, plucked weeds, guided Sister Squash's vines across the earth, and weaved Sister Bean's tendrils to the upper reaches of Sister Corn's stalks. Children clamored around a rambling growth of prickly pear, using wooden tweezers to extract the thorny, succulent fruit. The older wise women, their backs bent low, gave directions to those who required it.

"What troubles you, Hopi?" Fox asked, his voice a whisper. "You have said nothing all afternoon of your time in the underworld.

Yet I know it is all you have thought of since you climbed back into ours."

Hopi embraced him. His muscled arms, grown strong from prayer and conflict, wrapped around the shoulders of the warrior. As Hopituh Shi-nu-mu pressed his cheek to his brother's, his vision blurred.

"What is it, Hopi?" Fox asked quietly, unafraid of his elder brother's emotions, despite the positions each held within their Clan.

Hopi stepped back, firmly clasping Fox's shoulders. He was silent for many moments, studying his brother's face. "We will soon be split, Fox—never to see one another again. But more than that . . . Our time in this place is coming to an end." He kept his back to those tilling the fields. "Soon we must all leave that which we have built, and never return. The world we have created will no longer exist. This is what I have seen as I prayed before the navel of our kiva."

"Is it because the Horned Water Serpent has deserted us, that the rains are no longer dependable?"

Hopi shook his head. "No. Nor is it because of those who invade our mesa in hope of ejecting us from the wealth of this land. It is simply time to go, to continue our promised migration, so we are ready for the next world. That is all I can say."

Fox and Hopi held each other's gaze.

"As the Outside Chief," Hope whispered, "you are aware of the sacred tablets held within the walls of our kiva."

Fox nodded, keeping his arm about his brother's shoulders as they walked the mesa's rim.

"The tablets hold more value than our personal goals or relationships—indeed, more significance than our own family story. The two tablets, entrusted to our Clan before the Great White Bear entered Túwaqachi, must complete their journey. And it is you who must take them."

"Then the foreseen time approaches?"

"Yes, it—"

"Outside Chief! Fox Walks Well!" The call echoed across the mesa. From the north, several scouts of the Bear, Spider and Badger Clans ran toward them with bow and arrow in hand. All in the fields stopped their work, their faces cut by wonder and confusion, and perhaps fear.

"Outside Chief, Inside Chief," Spirit Warrior called, pushing through the corn toward the edge of the mesa. He gave a deep-throated whistle that alerted all across the farmland. The call was taken up by others, and the same whistle echoed through the crops, tumbling over the massive escarpments of sandstone, down the twisting stretches of canyon and into the thousands of rooms of the many houses perched amongst the cliffs below the mesa.

Fox and Hopi stared past the scouts, toward the north. Though the distance was far and strained the eyes, they could see the movement of cornstalk was unnatural. The hum of the wind seemed to drop, allowing them to recognize the advance of danger.

Hopi yelled his own sign, the high staccato of brotherhood, urging the women and children down off the mesa as quickly as they could go. Men threw their baskets to the ground and picked up shovels and hoes as weapons. Though they were people of peace and wanted nothing more than the simple happiness of family, they would do whatever was required to maintain their survival.

An arrow thudded into the chest of White-Tailed Deer, no more than two paces from the chiefs. He dropped his spade and fell to the ground.

Several more arrows struck the dirt at their feet, and Spirit Warrior held up his bow and gazed down the length of the arrow, past its blade and into the surrounding foliage of the Three Sisters. With no weapons other than their bare hands, Fox and Hopi dropped into a crouch, feet spread wide, arms extended, ready to pounce in any direction. Hopi kept his eyes upon Spirit Warrior, who stood tall, scanning the horizon, his nostrils flaring slightly, his line of sight equal with the height of the corn.

Spirit jerked to his right and shot an arrow into the corn, where a guttural howl of death was returned. Then his gaze flicked to the left, and without hesitation Hopi launched himself into the green and yellow stalks.

His feet dug into the earth, sending him blindly through the growth until his shoulder smacked solidly into muscle and bone. He tumbled to the soil, entangled with the skilled strength of a mighty warrior—the flash of painted face and dark hair, the breath of one who had eaten raw snake. The back of a clenched fist slapped against the side of Hopi's head as the two rolled. The rigid stalks of Sister Corn blocked them and Hopi grabbed the warrior's arm and twisted it behind his back. An indignant yell filled his ears, and the warrior threw his weight into Hopi's side, slamming an angry fist against his chest and another against his throat. The cutting edge of a blade glinted for but a second before Hopi kicked it to the ground. It skidded across the soil, and Sister Squash hid it beneath her broad leaves, her thorns scratching and cutting as she did her best to assist.

Fox thudded into the dirt, wrestling with a second warrior, alongside Hopi and his rival. Elbows and knees connected with prone stomachs and cracked into ribs. Blood flicked as a punch landed against Hopi's eye, and it swelled instantly, making it almost impossible to see. He ducked as Fox and his foe flew over him to his other side, only to lurch back so that all four fought in a tumbling mess. Hopi's attacker threw Fox to the ground and pounced upon him. A blade slashed through the air, followed by a deep grunt and an arc of blood that sprayed higher than Sister Corn.

Hopi staggered to his feet, but was shoved sideways by the other warrior, out onto open rock. The two gripped each other, punching and rolling over sandstone until they hit the canyon rim. Hopi cracked his skull against the stone. Bloodied knuckles smashed repeatedly into his face as he summoned all his energy to his feet and knees. With a mighty kick, he catapulted the warrior over him to slam flat against the rock face behind him. But the warrior came for him again, and together they stumbled and tripped off the ledge, falling several body-lengths onto a slim, brittle shelf.

Hopi's breath caught in his throat. His body ached—every muscle, every bone, every thought. Still he recoiled to his feet as the warrior leered toward him, a blade in his hand. Hopi turned and hopped quickly down several of the steps he'd known his entire life, his moccasins squeaking against the stone. The warrior followed, and Hopi urged him on with gestures and taunting calls. Down and around the cliff face they went. When Hopi reached the shallow tread before a difficult kickback, he deftly twisted himself around and onto the security of the lower toehold. The warrior attempted the same maneuver, but his footing was wrong and he lost his grip and surety. His fingers grappled and scraped against the rough stone, and Hopi arched backward as the warrior made a grab for him.

The warrior fell down into the depths of the canyon, into the highest branches of a spruce, with an angry shriek that stopped abruptly with an echoing crack.

Hopi did not bother even to look. Instead he leapt back up the cliff steps and ran back to the corn. Spirit Warrior turned a slow circle, his bow with arrow poised and ready, scanning for further signs of threat.

Fat, dark clouds filled the sky, and thunder rumbled in the distance.

It would rain soon.

Fox stumbled from the wall of crops, his chest heaving, his eyes still searching, his every muscle tensed and his body covered with sweat and dirt. And blood.

The three men glanced from one to the other and then out across the land. Spirit lifted his chin and motioned toward the farthest reaches of the mesa.

"They are leaving," he muttered.

For several moments they stood in silence as others of their Clan emerged from the corn. All were bloody and bruised. All but one was alive.

White-Tailed Deer lay crumpled at their feet, his dead eyes gazing toward a future that no longer existed.

* * * *

Tall thunderheads rolled over the mesa, throwing it into dark shadow. Heavy rain fell, slashing at the mature crops, coursing across the plateau and over the sandstone rim, cascading down into the canyons that meandered through the verdant landscape. The wide rock overhang held the rain off the ancient homes of the Cliff House, protecting them as well as the granaries and stores from the worst of the torrential weather.

Torches lit each of the structures, pulling them from the gloom. The brightest point was marked by a dozen torches clustered around the podium on which White-Tailed Deer lay. The bowl of life had been placed over his face, its base perforated by an irregular hole to allow his Spirit to escape.

For three days, his life had been celebrated and his passing mourned. Now the Clan had withdrawn, to allow his wife, Gentle Stream, to say her goodbyes. Hopituh Shi-nu-mu held both their hands as he softly spoke the sacred words. Then he placed Gentle Stream's hand upon that of White-Tailed Deer before he left their circle. He stood for several moments, just outside the glow of the torches, as Gentle Stream kneeled at her husband's side and whispered into his ear. Hopi did not know what words a wife would whisper. Perhaps one day he would, but not yet.

At the farthest end of the plaza, Yellow Snake Who Rattles sat watching him. He held up his hand toward the shadows. She nodded and disappeared inside her apartment.

He turned to climb down the ladder into the kiva, but his attention was drawn by the curtain of water falling outside the Cliff House. The dark cascade of rain reflected the torch-lit House in ghostly perspective. The massive sandstone buildings climbing the inside of the cliff were brilliant in their detail, but without any sign of family or life. Hopi looked up at the terraces and apartment doors and windows, where he was relieved to see a score of his Clanspeople completing the last of their daily chores. But in the mirroring fall of water, they were gone. Not even his own likeness looked back.

Hopi touched his tender, bruised eye, then grabbed the top of the ladder to climb down from the Fourth World, Túwaqachi, into the humbling darkness of the kiva.

*　*　*　*

His feet had not yet touched the bottom of the ladder when he began chanting. The patriarchs of the Clan sat in silence, listening to the words that could be spoken only here—here, where the first Three Worlds converged at the bottom of the rainbow leading up to the Fourth. Though their faces were in shadow, Hopi knew them by where and how they sat, the humility of their bearing, how they held their hands—most still youthful, all worn by toil, some scarred by battle,

115

one etched by revered black marks. They passed a pipe around the circle. It glowed in the darkness and filled the space with muskiness. When it was handed to Hopi, he stopped his song long enough to draw deeply from it. He held the smoke within him, allowing it to calm him and make his coming statements vital and true. As the smoke eddied from his nostrils, he studied the carvings along the pipe's soapstone stem. The Great Spirit stared back at him through the eyes of Brother Bear. He passed the pipe, then stood before the kiva's altar. His hands rested naturally upon the two powerful slabs that had lain there for longer than his own lifetime, or his father's or grandfather's.

He reached into the satchel at his waist and pulled out his Corn Mother. He placed her upon the gray marble of the two sacred tablets—a marble that existed not in this world, nor even the Third or Second. A reddish cloud blossomed through the web of mottled gray stone, crossed by marks cut into it before time had begun. Hopi ensured the four-kernelled tip of the perfect ear of corn—his Corn Mother—was centered upon the sacred red bloom.

His words reverberated around the darkness to all who had gathered to hear.

"My Corn Mother was laid beside me on the day of my birth, sharing the first twenty days of my existence in the darkness and protection of our universal parents. She was with me when the fine white cornmeal was brushed upon my skin, and again when the ashes of cedar were rubbed across my flesh to ready me for the world I was about to enter."

Hopi lifted his Corn Mother and passed her above his head four times.

"My name is Hopituh Shi-nu-mu," he said. "I am living a long life, with nineteen summers already passed. I am strong and I am healthy. I am productive and am doing what I have promised.

"You were with me, Corn Mother, on the day I was delivered from the Dark into the world of Light. You have borne witness that I am who I say I am, and that what I speak is true. I belong to this family and I belong to this earth as I follow the Road of Life."

Reverently, he replaced her upon the slabs of marble. For many deep breaths he said nothing, allowing his thoughts to thicken and gain strength from the energy of the sacred tablets, from the kiva itself.

"Over the past few seasons, we have seen others encroach upon the lands we occupy. We could stay here and protect ourselves; we could fight for what we have built. But that is not the way of Our People, and it is not our destiny. So, too, do the earth and sky seem to wish us farewell from this place. The winter snows and summer rains defy the calendars of the past millennia, rendering unpredictable the bounty of our Three Sisters. The knowledge of Shamans past no longer holds true, as the world is rapidly changing. Though the Horned Serpent appears to taunt us, he merely urges our family to continue our journey.

"It is time for us to complete our promised divine migration. The Clan of the Great White Bear will take the most important steps of its intended story and heart song."

The Clanspeople held their reverent silence, but Hopi could feel their thoughts. He picked up the first of the ancient tablets and ran his fingers across the indented glyphs.

"The time was long ago when the original four Clans were given their Guardianships and scattered in the four directions, to find their own way and prove their trust. We are the People of Earth. We are the color of the Earth—red. This stone tablet with its red bloom was entrusted to us, that we might learn the teachings of the earth: the plants that grow from its soil and rock and how best to grow them, the herbs that cause death and those that promote life. We have been true to our Guardianship. We are ready for the four Clans to merge again as one. We are ready to share our knowledge.

"The yellow Clan was given Guardianship of the Wind, securing their sacred tablets in the high mountains on the opposite side of our Mother. They were entrusted to learn of the sky, and breath. How to take the wind into themselves for spiritual advancement.

"To the black Clan was given Guardianship of the Water, that they might learn the ways of this humble yet most powerful of all elements.

"To the white Clan was given Guardianship of Fire, that they might understand it and share its secrets, at the time when all four Clans merge in the New World."

Hopituh Shi-nu-mu turned the tablet over, then placed it once more upon the altar with the second stone and his Corn Mother.

For a moment, he faltered, a sharp pain thumping in the bruised flesh of his eye and cheek. He pressed a hand to his face, but it did little to relieve the ache.

"The last steps of our four migrations will not be easy. I have seen within the navel of the kiva that our coming generations will suffer much hardship and turmoil. The flute of Kokopelli will seldom play. The four Clans will come together, but not all have completed their lessons, and one has lost the tablets entrusted to them so long ago."

Hopi noticed his brother's hands gripped tight to his knees. He knew that his younger brother was anxious. And that he would miss him.

"On which road should our divine migration take us?" Fox asked.

Hopi walked to the far side of the kiva and gazed down into the navel.

"Our journey across Túwaqachi has always been written in the stars—designated by their placement in the heavens by Trickster Coyote. Peer into the night sky and you will see the starburst of roads that join the Place of Snakes with its myriad canals, the Great House of Dawn and its outlying villages in the Canyon of Chaco, and even our own Houses that cling to the underside of cliffs cut into this verdant mesa. Follow the map in the sky, keep the door in the top of your heads open, and your migration will lead you to the center of the world, the middle of nowhere, the three sacred mesas that define our migration's end. There you will be surrounded by your enemies but also by the four sacred mountains that will keep your water jar full and your people safe."

"You speak as though you will not be with us, my brother," Fox said softly, the pain evident in the crack of his voice.

Hopi held up his hand. He clenched his fist to stop it's shaking. "Our Clan is closer to home than any other of our brothers, Fox. As Outside Chief, you will lead our family and our name to the Third Mesa at the center of the world. It will be up to our Bear Clan to welcome those who follow, to ensure they have pursued their heart song, completed the purification of the four migrations, and learned their lessons well. You will secure the two sacred tablets upon the Third Mesa."

"And you, brother?" Fox asked, his voice humble in the sacred space.

Hopi went to sit beside his brother. "There is more yet to my personal migration and what can be done in the name and Spirit of the Great White Bear. Though you will hold our destiny in the center of the world, I will bring our name and our stories to the east—to join with our kindred brothers of the Moon River, with the vast power of the mighty City of the Sun and beyond.

"The other Clans will soon arrive. The greatest times of our family are before us. And so are the darkest."

City of the Sun (1322 AD)

Thunderbird ascended on the heady currents of air that bore her high above the vast landscape of Túwaqachi. She stretched her broad wings, the heat lifting her through the silence, her glossy brown feathers shimmering in the sunlight.

She passed Eagle, his tail feathers kissed by Sun, as he returned to those below with the promise of their prayers and thanks.

And still she circled higher into the heavens.

She thrust back her wings, the clap of thunder resounding in her wake, the freshness of sky against her face, Túwaqachi fully revealed beneath her.

Thunderbird had known the four cardinal directions of this land for millennia, had flown through its Rocky Mountains to the west, skimmed its Great Lakes to the north, scoured its beaches to the east, hunted along its bayous and swamps to the south. She had learned and kept its secrets to herself.

She had seen the large beasts of time come and go.

She had observed the *Emergence* of humankind, followed their migration across the tundra, across the ice, across plains and deserts and through woods. She had watched them assemble lodges, build mounds and wonders as much a part of this natural world as they. She surmised there were one hundred million of them now, sharing her world—almost as many as there were bison upon the plains.

And it pleased her.

A break in the clouds revealed the long sinuous thread of the Moon River—the Father of Waters—plaiting down the heart of Túwaqachi, the maze of other mighty rivers joining its journey to the ocean in the south. Dotted along its course were the thousands of villages and ceremonial mounds of mankind, linked by trail, trade, and economy. By serpent, corn, and river.

At the center of this web, near the joining of the Big Muddy and the Moon, stood the most daunting construction of mounds and lodges. At times they housed over twenty thousand people, with many more in the neighboring fields and woods. And yet even this creation appeared part of the land from which it had emerged.

Thunderbird swooped down, wings held back, and the clouds dispersed in her wake as the City of the Sun came into view.

Hundreds of mounds spread wide across both sides of the river, encircled by daub and thatch dwellings. The low-hanging sunrise stretched their shadows across the plain.

An armada of canoes lined the riverbanks.

On the western perimeter of the City of the Sun, a large ring of cedar posts caught the sunlight, casting shadows to mark the season of harvest and ritual.

Before the immense earthen island at the center of the city, tens of thousands of people chanted and danced in honor of the snake, to the rhythm of drums, rattles, and flutes. They were strong and healthy, their bellies full with deer, turtle, frog, and squirrel.

They were happy.

On a plateau halfway up the great mound stood men and women of ceremony and religion. And above them, atop the climb of one hundred and fifty-six steps, stood the Birdman.

He was tall and red of skin, his face tattooed and his eyes blackened, with beaded forelocks and earspools pierced with feathers. A mask atop his head bore the noble features of Eagle, and a plate of shimmering mica and copper covered his chest. He wore a heavy cape of colorful plumage and stood upon a blanket of shells. With his feet spread wide and his arms outstretched, he sang into the sky, worshipping not the sun but the power behind it—the future it would reveal.

Thunderbird could see he was a generous man, and that generosity channeled the power from the heavens to his people upon the earth.

She swooped low across the crowded plaza and circled the city to mirror the movement of their ceremonial dance. The power of the Birdman and the stories of Brother Bear were strong here. But she did not linger. Instead, she thrust her wings back with the resounding crack of thunder and shot up into the clouds, high above the people and the City of the Sun, high above the world they all shared.

Clouds (1492 AD)

Clouds sailed across the great pond from the haze of the
rising sun toward Túwaqachi. They gathered in tall thunderheads.

P.J. Parker

The Child of the Sun; The Silent Enemy (1541 AD)

Cahokia and his men had spent the last moon burying the dead of the outlying villages that now stood empty above the river bluffs. The plague that rampaged through the first village had been a shock, but by the fifth he felt only numbness and uncertainty. Entire Clans lay dead in their lodges and in the shallows of the bayous, their flesh disfigured by rash, scabs, and deep, pitted scars. Bulbous bumps stretched their skin and ripped, seeping dark pus. Some carcasses were no longer recognizable as people he had once known. The foul stink of disease stained the very soil. It scratched into his nostrils as an uncomfortable itch, tightening his throat until he felt he would choke on the small amount of food he had been able to swallow.

Standing upon the monumental mound at the village center, Cahokia's view stretched five days' walk to the north and five to the south along the floodplains of the Moon River. The great waterway twisted across the landscape as it always had, but now he feared it carried something new within its muddy depths. To the north, the sky was a heavy black haze from villages they had torched once the rites had been completed. Far to the south he thought he could determine the kitchen-fire smoke of his own town eddying upon the breeze. He stared at the drift, hoping it meant his people were safe. Between the mound and the waterway below, his men continued in their duties. Many were emotional, despondent, all heavy footed from weeks of torment and lack of sleep. These men were hunters, foragers, farmers, and warriors. None had known such hardship as this.

Creek approached him from what had once been the lodge of the village chief.

"The Shaman is saying the last of his prayers for these people," he said quietly. "The relics of Chief Black Fish and his entourage have been laid. The heads of his four sons, warriors who showed much bravery both in life and in this Black Death, have been respectfully separated from their bodies and positioned around their father, that they may represent the four cardinal points and assist their Clan in finding their way to the next world."

Cahokia nodded. "The scouts?" he asked.

Creek hesitated. "There is no word yet from home. We can only wish this pestilence has not reached them."

One by one, several lodges skirting the plaza near the mound burst into flame as Cahokia's men ran from one to the next, igniting the thatch with torches. The granary popped and sparked as it was consumed, black smoke billowing into the sky.

"We will burn the fields and dugouts before this day is done. We must leave no trace of the disease that resides here. Perhaps one day the mounds will again be habitable."

Cahokia felt a deep ache in his chest. He held his hand to his mouth to stifle a cough. With a shudder, he spat up an acrid bile.

"Chief Cahokia?"

Cahokia cleared his throat and spat again. "It is nothing, Creek. Just the smoke."

Both men fell silent when they heard the song of the Shaman. No Man Hunting stood before the Chief's Lodge, an enormous structure that dominated the top of the mound. From his pouch he tossed a handful of leaves, twigs, and dust into the meager fire he had built. It spluttered and flashed. He twisted a stick into its flames and then touched the torch to either side of the lodge door before throwing it high into the roof thatch. The flame quickly took hold, licking around the building, chunks of daub melting from the walls, rifts of fiery thatch dropping to expose burning posts and beams beneath. No Man Hunting stepped back, toward Cahokia and Creek. The roof of the Chief's Lodge collapsed in upon itself with a cacophony of groans and bangs. Stick and thatch and daub toppled into a ferociously blazing heap.

The smell of burning flesh was sickening.

No Man Hunting's face was dark and haggard, his posture hunched and weary, the wrinkles of his cheeks more pronounced after all he had seen. Closing his eyes, he took a deep breath. "We are to return to our own people immediately. No matter what we might see on the way, we must ignore it and move without deviance to those still alive."

"But it is our duty to care for the souls of our brothers," Creek said.

No Man Hunting held his gaze. "First we must ensure the safety of the living. Our brothers and sisters. And our children." The Shaman swallowed heavily, trembling. "The dead will understand, and we shall return to them. But if . . . If we are unable to return . . . then brother coyote and Old Man River will take the burden."

Cahokia pulled his cape of feathers tight about his body.

* * * *

Seventy-five men trudged along the muddy trail by the edge of the river, with Cahokia and No Man Hunting in the lead, and Creek amongst the last. The only sound was the churning of the waterway and the incessant whacking of red-crested woodpeckers.

They passed the dead of smaller villages, scattered across the dirt and grassy riverbanks. They scanned for signs of life, but there were none. No Man Hunting wore a stony expression Cahokia had never seen upon him before.

Their path led through a narrow ravine and out onto an open field where scattered huts faced a ceremonial mound no higher than a warrior's shoulder. One side of the mound had been ripped open to the rich black soil beneath. Two smokeless fires still glowed but would soon extinguish. Cahokia stopped at the edge of the village, waving his men on ahead of him with a nod or reassuring touch upon the shoulder as they passed. At the end of the line, Creek stopped at his side to survey the desolation. The misshapen remains of people lay about, and yet the huts stood soundly as if nothing had occurred at all. A young woman was curled up by a fire, her hair long and beautiful, but her flesh was blackened, scabbed and disfigured by the disease that had killed her.

"How could the Great Spirit allow this to happen?" Creek asked. "Have we really been so untrue to the songs in our hearts as to deserve this end?"

Cahokia placed his arm around Creek's shoulders; they were cool and clammy to the touch.

At the rustle of dried grass they fell silent, searching for its origin. Creek freed an arrow from his quiver and placed its notched end against the string of his bow.

Cahokia lifted his finger to his lips, looking from lodge to lodge. He pointed toward the hut nearest the river and the two of them crept carefully toward it. Cahokia crouched beside a body and peered into the dark interior of the hut. Seeing nothing, he crawled inside. It was pitch black, but as his eyes adjusted he caught the edge of a silhouette at the far side of the hut.

"Hello," he said softly. He held out a hand, and the small silhouette grabbed his thumb. "It's all right. You can trust me," he whispered. "I'm here to help you."

The little one—a young boy—threw himself at Cahokia, wrapping his arms around him and pushing his face into his chest. He sobbed loud in the gloom of the hut, gripping hard to Cahokia's cloak. Cahokia returned the embrace, rubbing the boy's smooth back.

"Shhh," he said, rocking the boy. "It will be okay, my little man." Cahokia closed his eyes, hoping what he said was true. He lifted the boy into his arms and crawled back out into the sunny field. The boy was naked, his skin free of scabs or rash. His hair was long and unkempt, his body trembling violently as he whimpered.

Creek checked the other huts then joined Cahokia to jog the trail, through a wooded copse into a field that cascaded to the river's edge. Cahokia sank into the lush grass with the boy, and Creek hunkered down at their side. They stayed quiet and still until the boy's trembling subsided.

Creek pulled the boy into his own lap. "What is your name, little one?" he asked, lowering his head to catch the boy's gaze.

"Tallahassee," he said. "I am seven summers."

The men nodded.

Tallahassee looked up, eyes wild, back toward his village and then deep into the woods.

"You are okay now. We will look after you," Creek said.

"But the monsters!"

Cahokia caught Creek's gaze. "There are no monsters here, Tallahassee," Cahokia said.

"There are," the boy said. "I saw them. Great beasts with six legs and two heads. The front head was long and fearsome, with large eyes. The back head was covered by a shining mask that clanked and scraped as it moved about. They carried sticks that spewed fire and made noise like the Thunderbird."

"Did these monsters hurt your people?" Cahokia asked.

"They came out of the woods and we were afraid. They took the freshwater pearls from our ceremonial mound, and then disappeared. It was then my people were overcome with the red spots." The boy's eyes glazed over, and his trembling began anew. Creek pulled the boy close to his chest, his concerned eyes on Cahokia.

*　*　*　*

It was a moonless dark when Cahokia and the others reached their village. The fires burned low, Clanspeople sitting around them at their supper, but with none of the singing or chatter that normally accompanied the evening meal. All turned toward them when the group entered the clearing, though no one stood in welcome.

The night was interrupted by coughing and spluttering, the smell of sickness evident amongst the lodges. The men returned to their brothers and sisters, sitting silently about the fire to cuddle their wives and children. Creek lumbered toward the kitchen fire with Tallahassee clinging tight to his back. He placed the boy onto the dirt and then grabbed two heads of charred corn from the cooking stones. The boy ate hungrily under his watchful gaze.

No Man Hunting and Cahokia remained at the edge of the fire's glow, surveying their people. None showed the dreaded red spots, but all were weak and tired. Cahokia searched amongst the fires for his sister, Sky Full of Stars. His jaw tensed when he could not find her, and he left the Shaman's side and strode across the plaza toward the lodge upon the highest mound.

He hesitated at the entrance, listening with silent dread to a long bout of coughing from within. Then he pulled the hide to the side and entered. Sky Full of Stars lay crumpled by the fire, holding her hands toward the smoking heat. Cahokia went to her side and pulled her into his lap. She felt very cold, and he rubbed her arms to warm them. She managed a smile.

"What is wrong, my darling sister," he asked.

"Cahokia," she said before another attack of coughing sent her convulsing in his arms.

"Do not speak," he whispered, brushing his cheek across her forehead. "Have you eaten?"

She nodded.

He reach for a skin and pulled it and his feathered cloak around his little sister. He smoothed her hair, running his fingers through its length. Then he nudged another log onto the fire with his foot and rubbed her back until she fell into a shallow, fitful slumber. All through the night he held her by the fire and, though he was weary, he dared not sleep. Instead he studied his sister's face, the same noble flat forehead as their mother, and wished the elder was still here to help them.

Whenever Sky coughed, he cuddled her more tightly and held a gourd of water to her lips. When the entrance hide was rimmed by the light of the new day's sun, Sky Full of Stars was burning within his embrace. He urged her from her sleep to drink a mouthful of broth brought in by one of the old women. His legs were numb from sitting, but still he stayed, not wanting to disturb her as she slept once more.

For three days, he maintained his vigil, allowing himself to doze only when she had gone a time without coughing and her skin was no longer hot to the touch.

He awoke abruptly to Creek's hand upon his shoulder, unable to suppress a hacking cough as he wiped the sleep from his eyes. Creek jerked his head toward the lodge entrance. Seeing that his sister breathed and slept soundly, Chief Cahokia gently slid from beneath her and laid her down upon the skins. He rose awkwardly to his feet, stretching his legs and back as he shuffled out of the lodge and into the light of Father Sun. Creek led him to the fire and pushed a wooden bowl into his hands.

"We must all keep up our strength, my brother." He sat patiently as Cahokia scooped the food into his mouth. The quiet village was disrupted only now and then by the sounds of sickness.

"Come, the Shaman needs to talk with you."

No Man Hunting's lodge was small, with a low roof that allowed only sitting inside, to keep humble all who entered. A single skin covered the dirt floor from edge to edge, and a hole cut in its center defined the fire pit where embers glowed almost black. The Shaman glanced up from the fire as the men entered, eyebrows raised.

"My sister fares well. I am certain she will survive."

No Man Hunting nodded, and his shoulders relaxed. "We have lost Trail Runner and his wife, Sweet Flower."

Cahokia's heart sank.

"I fear there are more who will not last this moon. Even the sweat lodge is of no help in purifying the weak. It only makes them weaker still."

The Shaman threw a handful of herbs into the fire. It flared as he shared his cup of Black Drink—a bitter, frothy, dark liquid.

"Tallahassee shows no sign of cough or fever," Creek said as he handed the cup to Cahokia. "Though he says he was amongst the first in his village to be struck with the disease. The fever and spots quickly overcame all of his village so none were left to care for the sick. It was but a handful of days before all but Tallahassee were dead."

"These monsters the boy spoke of," Cahokia said. "We have heard these tales before. But surely they cannot be true. They must be designed to keep children from wandering off alone in the woods."

The Shaman's gaze remained unfocused on the fire. His eyes reflected the flames, though were otherwise dead. "Yes," he said. "We have heard variations from the trading Clans in the south and east. They are woven into the same fireside stories as the large canoes pulled across the blue pond by clouds." No Man Hunting rubbed at his face, looking weary and lost. "Every legend has, at its core, a basis of truth. An attempt to explain the unexplainable. I can only surmise that these beasts do exist, and they have finally encroached upon the valley of the Moon River."

Creek shivered in the heat of the lodge. "There have been no scouts or tradesmen from the Land of Flowers in the east for almost three moons. Do you think . . ."

"I do not know."

"What do we know, Shaman?" Cahokia asked.

"We know many Clans no longer exist, and any stories they have told us must be taken as our own so they are not forgotten." The Shaman tossed a sprig of sage onto his fire, and the lodge filled with sweet-smelling vapors. "All Clans, though our names and bloodlines are many, are linked to the kindred Spirit of the Great White Bear. We are connected to each other by the stronger bonds of nature that have always existed in the sacred world: Eagle Clan to Thrush Clan, Bear to Forest, Field to Mountain, Beaver to River. It is these lines of familial connection that will allow our many Clans to survive. Together we are obligated to ensure the knowledge and rituals of our brothers and sisters endure—no matter what the future may bring."

Again the Shaman rubbed at his face, exhausted.

"The universe itself is woven with these closely knit Clan clusters. But our families are also connected with Clans opposite in nature: Sky and Earth, Land and Water, Left and Right. The whole of Our People are made up of the two sides which, when joined together, have much power.

"Just as the Great White Bear Clan once joined with The People, their opposites, to share the power of their cooperation, we must now also join our opposites, even those who may once have been our enemies. Only then will we become one and survive the approaching clouds—the unquestionable merging of the four Clans."

Cahokia considered the Shaman's words. "We will head north," he finally said. "We will follow the river upstream to where it is fresh and not muddied by the diseases that have come. There we will join with our brothers who live on the shores of Gitchigoomie and the other Great Lakes, far from this pestilence. And these beasts."

The Shaman agreed. "You are chief and we will do as you say." No Man Hunting placed his hand on Cahokia's and stared into his eyes, then turned quickly away as if he did not want to see him. "You need to rest," he said, his gaze again locked on the depths of the glowing embers. "Creek will take the lead to ensure all is ready."

* * * *

Cahokia crossed the central clearing between the Shaman's lodge and his own hut. Deep within his lungs he felt the rasp of a cough, but he suppressed it—not wanting his people to think him weakened. He ran to the outskirts of the village and into the surrounding wood. When he was certain he was alone, he convulsed with the cough. It wracked his entire body, and he doubled over to gag and vomit in the grass. A slick sweat covered him, steeping his buckskin. Leaning against a tree, he threw up a second time, tears stinging his eyes and his muscles exhausted.

He wiped at his mouth and saw his hand was covered in blood.

* * * *

Holding the entrance skin wide, Cahokia ducked and entered his lodge. Two girls were attending to Sky Full of Stars, who was propped up by the fire. She smiled at her elder brother and he nodded appreciably, noting the color in her cheeks, the light in her eyes. He sat silently as the girls combed Sky's hair and braided it with beads.

"You look better," he said after the girls had finished their task and left.

"Mmmm. I still ache, but the fever has broken and I was able to eat a little pemmican just now."

"That's good," he said quietly. "Sky, I . . . I need you to be strong."

She tilted her head quizzically.

"Before the moon has waned, we will be journeying upstream. No matter what happens to me, to any of us, I need you to promise me you will complete the journey." He reached for a bow and a quiver of arrows and pressed them into her hands. His tattooed forearms trembled.

"What do you mean?"

"You must make it to the waters downstream from Gitchigoomie, and the strength of the confederacy of tribes that reside amongst the finger lakes. You are my only sibling and you must survive. Promise me."

She nodded, uncertain and concerned.

* * * *

The moon was low in the early morning sky. It glinted off the ripple of water as the people of Cahokia packed their belongings into the flotilla of canoes and barges lining the banks of the bayou. All had partaken of the Black Drink to purify and make them strong for the journey—whatever it might bring.

Three women—the last of the Blue Jay Clan—had joined them the previous evening. They told stories of the beasts that brought unease to all. And so, the people were ready for conflict, most with weapons at their sides. But their chief knew they hoped it would not come to pass.

The first barges, brimming with baskets of corn, dried fish, and persimmon bread, were pushed into the current as Cahokia and Sky Full of Stars stepped into their canoe. Creek, No Man Hunting, and Cahokia's most trusted warriors joined them. All the men were painted ochre, accentuating their tattooed bodies, and adorned with quills of many colors. Feathered shields sheltered the oarsmen on either side. Adjusting the headband of cuckoo plumes upon his head, Chief Cahokia took his place beneath the canopy at the rear of the canoe. He gripped his bow and blade, his gaze rarely leaving Sky Full of Stars, sitting at his feet.

The armada, over two hundred canoes and barges strong, cruised the meandering bayous, keeping clear of the main flow of the Moon River and its dangerous current. Only rarely did they venture onto the river itself, rowing close to shore before slipping again into the gentler riffle of the waterways along the floodplains beside it.

The sun was glaring, and the water shimmered crisp and unreal when Cahokia heard the first call from the canoes at the fore. He craned his neck to see upstream. Men stood in their canoes, waving and pointing toward the eastern shore.

A dozen fearsome beasts stood upon a promontory. The sun glinted on the masks upon their back heads, and their front heads jerked violently, mouths chomping, nostrils flaring.

One rose high upon its rear legs, its front legs scratching at the air. It let out a high-pitched noise from its nostrils, and then all took off at a gallop along the top of the headland, their silhouettes cast against the heavens.

"Sky Dogs," No Man Hunting muttered in awe. He held his hands to his face and began a deep-throated lament.

"They run as fast as elk," Creek said.

Cahokia sat staunchly, his eyes on the beasts as they ran down onto the bank and mirrored their course along the river. Still, Cahokia and his people held their bearing to the north.

One beast shouted and brandished a stick above its head. Fire shot from it into the sky, and thunder rumbled across the waters.

Farther ahead, an uncountable number of beasts sauntered on the beach. Men stood enslaved within their shadows, linked together by chains and collars. Broods of large black dogs snapped and bit angrily.

Two of the beasts shot their sticks in quick succession from the shore. A warrior in Cahokia's canoe dropped suddenly, his chest and face a bloody mess.

Cahokia gripped Sky's shoulders and urged her down low, beneath the rim of their vessel where she would not be seen.

Thunder rumbled again, and another warrior toppled.

Chief Cahokia stood and called to his people, "Take the canoes to the far side of the Moon. Perhaps these beasts cannot cross the current. I will keep my course to distract them."

The canoes turned into the swift waters of the Moon River to make the difficult crossing.

"Jackrabbit! Steer closer to my barge. Take my sister with you," Cahokia said, and Jackrabbit nudged his small fishing canoe against Cahokia's. "Sky! Go with Jackrabbit. Remember your promise. You must make it to the finger lakes."

Sky Full of Stars opened her mouth to object, but then she only nodded, tears welling in her eyes as she got to her feet. She held out her arms to hug her brother, but he turned away as a fit of coughing wracked his body, bloody red vomit spewing into the water. She grabbed his arm and pressed her face into the feathers of his cloak.

"Please go," he said quietly.

He held her hand as she stepped up on the edge of the canoe and climbed over to the other.

The sky erupted with thunder again, and Jackrabbit jerked cruelly backward. He peered down in wonder at his ripped-open chest before the blood drained from his face and he collapsed into the muddy waters of our past and future. His canoe rolled with him, filling with water. The hands of many warriors reached out but failed to secure it before it started to sink. It was all Cahokia could do to pull Sky back into his own canoe, but his weakened state sent him tumbling over the edge. Creek lurched to grab his chief and Sky and thrust them down onto the wooden floor of their vessel.

In the tumult, the canoe had drifted toward the shore, and the beasts were splashing in the reedy shallows about them. Thunder struck, and three more warriors shuddered and slumped against the shoulders of their brothers, spraying the craft with blood.

Men ran down to the canoe amongst the two-headed beasts. They overcame Cahokia, Sky, No Man Hunting, and Creek, and next Cahokia knew they were upon the beach, with beasts looming high, stomping their hooves and snorting noisily.

Some of the men in chains were recognizable as brothers from the east, their faces sad and sorry.

He watched one beast in awe as its rear metal-covered head rose and dismounted, landing on the ground.

A man, Cahokia thought, staring at him and then at the muscled animal beside him. The man removed the shiny mask, and he had the countenance of a white ghost, what the people called a *booger*, with a hairy face.

He spoke to one of the chained men, and his words were choppy and strange. "*Hablarás mis palabras.*"

The chain around the man's neck was caked in blackened blood. He spoke to the man beside him, and he to the next man in the line—an emaciated warrior from the Land of Flowers—and so on until the last man stepped forward.

"Before you is the Child of the Sun. From where he comes all obey him. They offer him tributes and seek his friendship. They rejoice to see him, and as a token of their love and obedience, all give him riches from their countries to show their esteem. He comes in peace and amity, for he loves us all."

The booger with the hairy face stared at Chief Cahokia without emotion. He smelled putrid, like the disease, and his eyes were yellow—shot with blood and deceit.

"If you are indeed the Child of the Sun," Cahokia said, "then dry up the great Moon River and perhaps I will believe you. But I know in my heart what you say is a lie. Our People are strong and we will not bend to the wishes of an enslaver such as you." Cahokia spat at his feet—a blood-flecked globule of saliva.

Several others dismounted from their steeds, and a heavy stone hand slapped Cahokia across the face. No Man Hunting was pushed to the ground and then all three men were dragged up the beach and tied to willows.

Cahokia's lungs ached, and a blackened, bloody bile smeared his lips and chin.

Sky Full of Stars screamed as she was dragged into the undergrowth by two of the boogers.

Cahokia yelled, "No!" But his sister was gone.

The boogers threw kindling to the ground at the captives' feet, and one held a torch high, but he was stopped by the raised hand of the man who had spoken—the Child of the Sun. No Man Hunting moaned a prayer chant into the sky—the same prayer he had sung on the mound for the village dead. The Child of the Sun approached Creek, studying his stature, prodding the tattoos on his powerful chest. Then he stepped over to Cahokia. Again he spoke, and the message was passed from man to man along the chain of slavery.

"The Child of the Sun seeks only the soft yellow rock. Tell him where it is, and he will love you and your people."

Cahokia's anger shook his body more than his sickness ever had. He convulsed with a suppressed cough, and the man before him smiled. The Child of the Sun barked orders and a gang of large war dogs was brought down onto the beach on lengths of chain held tight by men. Still the dogs dug at the ground and lunged, snarled and frothed.

The man pointed to Creek, and the dogs were upon him.

Creek, the warrior, uttered no sound as he held himself rigid against the tree. He shuddered and seized as the dogs bit into him, ripping and tearing at his living flesh.

The Child of the Sun held Cahokia's gaze, and it was met with silent determination and pride.

The Child of the Sun barked again, and the men pulled the dogs back from Creek's limp, bloody carcass. They tossed their torches onto the kindling.

* * * *

Sky Full of Stars lay sprawled upon a muddy patch of grass, her clothes ripped and splattered by the dirt that had been thrust upon them. Boogers stood, laughing and adjusting their long blades and armor, distracted from the one who lay weakened in the muck by their own high spirits.

The smell of burning flesh lingered heavy in the air.

The boogers called to the others on the beach to join them, and in the clamor Sky scuttled backwards into the undergrowth. Then she staggered to her feet and ran, trees and shrubs reaching out to scratch and cut. Her moccasins were gone, her feet were bloody, but she ran as fast and as silently as she could.

Darkness came.

Echoes through the wood said the boogers were following her. She smudged herself with the scent of the soil and her brothers and hid in a log.

The boogers passed by with pigs that grunted and sniffed at the ground. The animals plowed their snouts into the dirt around her hiding place, but they did not find her.

P.J. Parker

We the People . . . The People of the Long House (1562 AD)

The forest trail crested the ridge amongst a sprawling grove of hawthorn, sassafras, sycamore, tamarack, and buckeye. The large stand of trees appeared incongruous after the dense vale of hickory, with its dappled shadows and woodland grasses that huddled between slabs of moss-covered granite. Yet here all the trees grew together with their brother hickory—their individual stories and seed migration leading them to this place of confederacy. They spread down into the valleys on either side of the ridge, their many colors mingling between the shimmering waters of the Great Lakes to the north and the finger lakes to the south.

Handsome Stream stopped to catch his breath beneath the shelter of the grove, leaning against a sassafras as he dug a stone out of his moccasin. He was making the journey in good time, having begun the run at the break of dawn. With a hand to his brow he squinted up through the branches toward the sun, almost at its meridian. Despite the cool air, his body was hot and slicked by perspiration, his moccasins and beaded loincloth more than adequate attire for the grueling course.

Etched across his bare chest and upper arm were the lines of his lineage—the tattooed silhouette of brother bear. Twenty scratches of claw cut down his left arm to mark his age.

His long, dark hair had fallen free of its loose braids. Deftly he twisted and knotted it at his back then wiped at the sweat on his forehead. Ensuring his message stick was still tied securely to his belt, he set out once more along the trail.

Handsome Stream ran the trail with a warrior's speed, his feet barely touching the earth that had routed messengers between the

People of the Five Nations for generations. He was proud to be in the league of men entrusted to carry the message sticks. The one he held had already traveled from the People of the Great Flint in the east to those of the Standing Stone. It had traversed the trails high above the shores of the Great Lake to his own People of the Hills, and coursed around the northernmost fringe of the finger lakes to the People of the Great Swamp, where he had been stationed. For almost three days the message stick had followed the course of the sun and moon along the connecting trail as it cut through the otherwise rugged terrain.

That morning, before sunrise, the call of woodcock and warbler and the screech of horned owl had alerted Handsome Stream of the approach of Moose in the Water. Moose had entered the village stockade and placed the message stick into the hands of the chief before retrieving it and running back toward the gate, handing it off to Handsome Stream, who was already at full speed. The message stick, with its seven notches and dangling string of thirteen purple and white shells of wampum, was within the stockade for no more than a breath of woodland air before it was on the trail again to its final nation.

Less than a handful of valleys and ridges were left between Handsome Stream and The People of the Great Hill on the western fringe of the confederacy, but still he did not slow. He passed signs of bobcat and bear, lynx and fox, wolf and deer, his stride confident as he took the dips and curves and hillocks and ledges. There had been no others on the trail throughout that morning, though he was aware of the calls of nature that followed his route—aware they sped far ahead of him to alert the People of his approach. The People of the Great Hill protected the western door of the Five Nations' symbolic Longhouse. They would know of his arrival long before he got there.

The trail led into a broad wooded valley, cutting a course straight and true alongside a brook. Then the wood changed to cultivated pasture, the Three Sisters growing strong, men and women looking up from their work to ponder Handsome Stream's message. The children dropped their tools to run at his heels, but few could match his pace. Handsome Stream veered off the main trail to sprint up the steep incline toward the top of the southern ridge with a growing crowd behind him.

They ran around the great hill and into a vast clearing, dominated by an intimidating row of palisades that surrounded the village lodges. Handsome Stream's position as messenger had allowed him to visit all the major villages of the Five Nations, and most were similar in construction and fortification. But the scale of the village of the People of the Great Hill always struck awe and respect into his heart.

He loosened the message stick from his belt and gripped it as he sidled through the main gate, not much wider than a man's shoulders. His followers crowded around the gate, only able to enter one at a time. Two dozen longhouses were scattered within the stockade. Handsome Stream ran along the closest house, the sign of Turtle above its doorway. In sixty full-speed strides he reached its end, where builders were extending it further—setting trunks into the ground and interweaving them with saplings, lashed together by bark twine.

One of the daughters must be bringing a new husband home to the Longhouse of the Turtle, Handsome Stream surmised with a thoughtful smile. He passed a second longhouse, the sign of Sandpiper above its porch, before running into the central ceremonial square and across the flattened expanse toward the Longhouse of the Chief of the People of the Great Hill. The symbol of Wolf hung proudly above its entrance.

Coyote is Dancing slinked by and pointed to the slanting stick that signified the longhouse was empty and that no one who was not of the Wolf could enter.

Handsome Stream came to a breathless stop.

The crowd surged into the yard behind him as silently as they could, intent on hearing his words.

"I have a message stick for Chief Yellow Corn." His chest heaved as he held out the stick to convey urgency.

Coyote smiled. "I see your hair still curls like the blonde, booger fishermen who smoke their catch on the seashores to the east."

Handsome Stream looked around before settling his gaze back on Coyote. "Where is Chief Yellow Corn?"

"He knows of your journey and asked me to meet you here." Coyote leaned forward, peering closely. "It is true what they say. Your eyes reflect the color of the sky." He sneered, revealing pointed canines, and held out his hand. "You may give the message stick to me."

Pulling the stick and its wampum close to his chest, Handsome Stream glared at Coyote is Dancing. His brow furrowed in growing distrust.

Coyote rolled his eyes. "Chief Yellow Corn is on the lake. He asked that you meet him where the fish jump up the falls."

Handsome Stream turned on the ball of his foot and ran across the yard. The young men and boys again followed his course, determined to compare their speed to his.

Handsome Stream followed the trail down through the wooded parkland and onto the cultivated floodplain, where baskets were piled high with squash and bean, and farmers shucked the husks off long ears of sun-kissed corn. The plain dipped and then he was surrounded by dense fields of the Brother of the Three Sisters—tobacco. The crop was still green but already possessed a pungent magic that melded with the scent of earth. The path narrowed through a ravine toward the edge of the lake then opened up to sand that squelched beneath the swift tread of moccasins. Waves crashed upon the beach, and Handsome Stream shielded his eyes from the dazzle of water to make out the fishing party ahead. Canoes clustered close to the shore where a river surged into the lake. Men cast nets into the water, and large fish flapped on the ends of upheld spears.

Chief Yellow Corn stood within a large corral built in the flow of the river, surrounded by a score of muskies. The great chief and another man thrust their hands into the water, hefted an enormous fish, and threw it up onto the bank. The silvery-green muskie was the size of a young man—it would stand up to Handsome Stream's chest, at least. It flapped around upon the stony bank, its mouth gulping at the air, its glassy eyes shining bright in the afternoon light.

Another muskie flew through the air to land and flap beside it.

Chief Yellow Corn saw Handsome Stream standing there, but he was in no hurry to shirk his duties in the fishing expedition. He remained in the water until all of the muskies were flailing on the banks and being bundled into cornhusk baskets.

"We have been expecting you, Handsome Stream," he bellowed as he strode up onto the shore to admire the catch. He held out his hand toward the messenger.

Handsome Stream passed him the message stick, and the chief ran a finger along its length, stopping at each of the seven notches.

"Seven days," he muttered. "Very well, then." Chief Yellow Corn tossed the stick back to Stream then wrapped his arm around the messenger's shoulders to lead him back toward the village. "You will stay in our village, now that all have received the message for the Central Council Fire. You are more than welcome in our party as we make our way to the meeting."

"Thank you, Chief Yellow Corn."

They climbed from the beach and into the first tobacco field. "You have matured into a fine young man, Handsome Stream. It would be an honor if any of my granddaughters should happen to catch your eye. Genesee has uncommon beauty and intelligence, don't you think?"

Stream smiled and nodded. "It may yet come to pass that a child of the Bear shall share the Longhouse of the Wolf, but . . ."

"But you fear for your mother's loneliness."

Stream nodded.

"Sky Full of Stars is yet a beautiful woman. I know her hardship, but you are testament to her good nature and strength—her resilience. She, too, is welcome in the Longhouse of the Wolf."

Handsome Stream was thoughtful for the remainder of the trail.

* * * *

Genesee stood tall at the entrance of the longhouse beneath the shade of its porch. Her dress of deerskin was elaborately quilled and beaded, and shells hung from her ears, wrists, and neck. Her hair fell to well below her waist and shone with bear grease and fragrant woodland oils. Handsome Stream, whose thoughts had long been captured, could not help but dream of her beauty whenever he slept, or even when he didn't.

As he crossed the ceremonial square of the village with Chief Yellow Corn, he knew Genesee studied him just as he studied her.

"It appears your minds are already as one," Yellow Corn whispered. He seemed pleased he had correctly guessed the object of his granddaughter's affection.

"Grandfather," Genesee said in welcome to the chief before turning to Handsome Stream. Her gaze flicked to his bare chest before returning to his face. "It was cold here last night," she said, holding up a buckskin shirt. "I made this for you."

Stream accepted the shirt without taking his eyes from her face. "Thank you. It's beautiful."

Chief Yellow Corn was already entering the longhouse. "You will eat at our fire this evening, Handsome Stream. I will see you then." And with that, he disappeared inside, leaving Stream and Genesee alone.

* * * *

It was almost twilight, the last rays of sun piercing low through the trunks of the stockade and throwing striped purple shadows across the village. The dust of his journey had been washed from Handsome Stream's skin, and he wore the new shirt of supple hide. His hair had been oiled and twisted to hang down his back with a decorated comb of antler to hold it in place. He walked into the Longhouse of the Wolf—with Genesee's hand in his. Neither of the two could hide their smiles, whose meaning all could easily discern. Handsome Stream held the entrance flap open so the granddaughter of Chief Yellow Corn could enter and lead the way.

The first apartment of the longhouse was lit by the fire in the middle of the broad central aisle. The flickering orange and yellow light reached across the squat, skin-covered platforms on either side of the aisle, reflecting off the possessions of the two families that shared its warmth. Genesee ensured Stream knew each of the women and their families. He in turn thanked the women for allowing him passage through their home and nodded respectfully toward their husbands.

They walked around the fire with its pot of turtle and white fish simmering amongst the hot rocks, then followed the central aisle and stepped beyond the separating skin into the second apartment. It, too, housed two families—both homes with their privacy skins wide open.

Stream peered in at the shelves, brimming with winter clothing, bundles of beaver pelts, ropes, and nets. Braids of corn and sacks of food—peppers, squash, and herbs—hung from the beams up high.

Handsome Stream already knew all in the village by sight and most by name and occupation, but he happily accepted Genesee's formal introductions as they continued through apartment after apartment.

Stream reached for the skin covering the entrance to the next, perhaps the tenth apartment, but Genesee placed her hand on his. Her eyes shone in the firelight, and she gave Stream a minute nod and a smile that he readily savored. Together they pulled back the painted deer hide and stepped into the principal room of the longhouse. The walls were lined with woven matting and furs. Shelves and hooks held fishing spears and nets, hunting bows and arrows, bird traps and herb baskets, and the netted sticks for the game of tewaaraton. Several hides were tied between beams and posts, revealing the History of the Wolf to all who entered. A muskie lay sizzling upon the cooking stones, its sweet aroma mingling with that of corn ears charring in their husks.

Chief Yellow Corn sat on one platform, and on the other Autumn Moon Shadow was directing her daughter and granddaughters in the making of the evening meal. As matriarch of the Longhouse of the Wolf, Autumn Moon Shadow was the source of all who lived within its walls. She was the direct lineage of Wolf and, as such, was the keeper of its culture. She alone was responsible for defining and maintaining the integrity and value of all aspects of her Clan. She was also of the highest rank in the family. Her husband, Chief Yellow Corn, was chief only by her nomination.

"Handsome Stream, come sit by my fire that I may see your face as we talk," she said.

Stream sat on a mat between the fire and platform before the matriarch. Genesee sat beside her grandmother.

"Chief Yellow Corn tells me you lead an exemplary life. You know what is well and what is not."

"I am what my own mother has made me, and has allowed me to determine for myself," Stream said.

Coyote is Dancing slunk into the apartment and up onto the platform with Chief Yellow Corn. He spoke to him in quiet, snapping whispers.

"You are a messenger for the Five Nations," the matriarch continued, "but do you know what the message was that you carried here today?"

"Yes, it was to announce the Central Council Fire in the coming days."

Autumn Moon Shadow raised her eyebrows.

Stream uncrossed his legs and stretched them out before him. "The meeting is being held at your request, Autumn Moon Shadow. The bark-eaters from the north have encroached on the Vale of the Three Falls. They kill beaver and steal pelts that are not of their hunting grounds."

Autumn Moon Shadow nodded, seemingly pleased he was aware of this important issue. She stepped down into the aisle and bent over the muskie to prod it with a cooking stick, then motioned for Genesee and another of her offspring to pull it from the fire. Satisfied, she kneeled beside Handsome Stream on the cornhusk matting.

"Undoubtedly any connection between the Wolf and the Bear would increase both our families' strength and story," she said. "But in you, there are more complex ties to the universal family—of that I am certain. Tell me, Handsome Stream, of these bark-eaters. The *Adirondacks*. The enemy who call our Five Nations *Iroquois*— rattlesnakes ready to deliver the death bite. What do you think should be done about their raids on our hunting grounds?"

Stream was silent, aware both Chief Yellow Corn and Coyote is Dancing had stopped their own whispered conversation. Genesee stared at him in concern, and Autumn Moon Shadow seemed to scrutinize the slightest flicker across his face. Her authority could deny any relationship between Bear and Wolf. He held the matriarch's gaze, noting the same flame and intensity he had seen in Genesee. Without a word, he looked up to a bundle of tewaaraton sticks on a shelf, and then back into the hazel depths of Autumn Moon Shadow's eyes.

For a moment, the matriarch was still. Then her mouth spread into a wide grin that made her cheeks round and her eyes crinkle. She nodded.

"Good. Now we eat the fish," she said happily.

* * * *

Lake Onondaga shimmered in the early afternoon light. Stream and Genesee had been walking for three days on the trail, amongst the People of the Great Hill. They had been joined by the People of the Great Swamp on the second day. Stream was happy to take the Five Nations' trail at such a leisurely pace, welcoming the time with Genesee but also the conversations with Chief Yellow Corn and the other men. He noted the turns of the trail, attuned to any nuance that would make his next message run more efficient. At least two thousand were making the pilgrimage toward the Central Council Fire from the west, and as many would be coming from the east.

As they established camps upon the shores and within the forest, Handsome Stream took his leave, his fingertips reluctant to withdraw from Genesee's for even a short time. Promising to return to her before nightfall, he continued on alone, up into the hills of his nation. His brothers and sisters hurried to and fro with gifts and supplies, finishing their chores before the Central Council Fire could begin. He strode through the entrance of the stockade and passed a score of longhouses until he was at the very rear of the village he had called his own since birth. The timber and bark house he shared with his mother was nowhere near as imposing as the longhouses. Indeed it was little more than a wooden dome with no length at all.

Sky Full of Stars had never married. She cherished her son, but without a daughter her house would never grow. Stream stopped before the doorway and placed his hand upon his heart—upon the tattoo that curved across his chest and matched the image of Bear that crested the porch. Then he pulled aside the entrance skin and stepped in.

Sky Full of Stars looked up from her fire. She was unable to contain a laugh as she ran to embrace him. "I see the warbler was truthful when he said you had confirmed your love. Is she here?" Sky Full of Stars peered around Stream and out the entrance, then back into his face. "Let me look at you," she said, placing her hands on his shoulders and standing high upon her toes. "Yes, it is true."

Stream laughed, pulling his mother in tight. "It is Genesee, mother—the granddaughter of Autumn Moon Shadow and Chief Yellow Corn."

"Wonderful, wonderful."

They held each other in the dim house and listened to the pop and crack of the fire. When Stream finally pulled away, though his words went unspoken, she nodded in understanding.

"My darling, you are a man and you must do as a man does. The hearth of the Wolf will keep you warm. And within your body, and the bodies of your sons and daughters, the blood of the Bear Clan will flow."

"But what of you mother? I cannot leave you here alone."

Sky Full of Stars gave a slight smile and shook her head. "I am not of this place and yet these are my people. We are all connected, we are all one. It does not matter whether my home is here above Lake Onondaga or upon the Great Hill of the Western Door—for both are within the same Longhouse of our civilization. I will stay here, Handsome Stream, with my memories, but also with the knowledge that I will see my own grandchildren grow strong and tall, and I will ensure they know our songs."

* * * *

The Central Council Fire blazed upon the shore of Lake Onondaga, beneath the great Tree of Peace. The majestic pine was the height of forty men, the spiral growth of its branches, needles and cones reflecting the spiral of life toward the whorling star-spangled sky. At the very top of the tree, so high no one could see, was perched the Eagle that Sees Far. Her wings were spread wide, her talons grasping the five arrows of the Five Nations.

About the fire sat the peace chiefs and Big Men representing each family of each Clan, of each of the Five Nations of the confederacy—seventy in all. Handsome Stream hunkered down at the edge of the fire's glow, behind the other men of the People of the Hills. Though all were equal within the light of this flame, Handsome Stream had never spoken at any meeting. He had thought it right that the agenda be run by those of larger longhouses. But one day, with the joining of the Bear with the strength of the Wolf, it might give him cause and confidence to speak his mind.

Farther along the shoreline was the flicker of a smaller fire where a thicket of wood stepped all the way into the water. Within its illumination stood the five war chiefs, intent on listening to the council proceedings.

And farther still were the hundreds of fires of those who had converged on this place of meeting. Not even a whisper bounced across the water from those who awaited the outcome of the council.

For many heartbeats, only the crack of the Central Council Fire and the chirp of a single cricket disturbed the thoughts of those who peered into the flames, until there came the movement of many men from the wood. They stepped into the light, one by one, holding the wampum of stories and meetings past. Morning Star Blackbird, a mighty warrior known and respected by all, emerged with his arms outstretched, holding the wampum of Hiawatha—follower of the Great Peacemaker and founder of the confederacy.

"We are the *Haudenosaunee*," Morning Star Blackbird called as he walked around the fire. "We are the People of the Longhouse." The wampum was made of several thousand beads, the high contrast of white whelk shell symbols beaded against a background of purple quahog clam shell that shone in the light. The symbols' placement embodied the Five Nations, strung together on a white band without beginning or end—the common thread of unity, representing all time, now and forever.

Morning Star Blackbird placed the wampum of Hiawatha reverently before the fire. Then, cupping hand to his mouth, he called the trilling song of his namesake.

Next to step from the shadows was Atotarho—the first among equals, the Chief of the People of the Hills, the Keeper of the Central Fire, the protector of wampum. He took his seat upon a mossy stone slab beneath the Tree of Peace. Atotarho was a giant of a man, powerful of build and features. His arms and legs were bare, but a wolf-skin mantle covered his shoulders and a tunic of soft fur wrapped about his waist. His moccasins were ornately quilled with colors, and on his head he wore a soft band of deerskin covered in the plumage of small birds. His hair was tied into many braids twisted and quilled to appear as snakes. Though his countenance was at first glance quite fearsome, Handsome Stream felt no doubt of his kindness and wisdom.

Atotarho beheld the flames as Morning Star Blackbird addressed each of the Five Nations, from east of the fire to the west.

"You, the *Kanien'kehá:ka,* People of the Great Flint, who sit under the shadow of the Great Tree, whose roots sink deep into the earth and whose branches spread wide—you are the first nation, nearest the rising of the sun, for you are warlike and mighty.

"You, the *Onayotekaono,* People of Standing Stone, who recline against the Everlasting Stone, emblem of wisdom that cannot be moved—you are the second nation, for you always give wise counsel.

"You, the *Onöñda'gega',* People of the Hills, who dwell here at the foot of these Great Hills—you are the third nation, for you— *we,*" he added with a respectful nod, "are greatly gifted in speech.

"You, the *Guyohkohnyoh,* People of the Great Swamp, who live in the Open Country and possess much wisdom—you are the fourth nation, for you understand best the arts of raising corn, squash, and beans, and of building houses.

"You, the *Onondowahgah,* People of the Great Hill, who dwell in the Dark Forest nearer the setting sun—you are the fifth nation, for your superior cunning in hunting.

"As Five Nations united, we have a common interest and no foe shall subdue us. We shall protect the feeble bushes, the fishermen of the southern rivers and eastern seashores. We form alliance and friendship with our brothers across the plains to protect us all from the coming storm. For we know without our alliance we shall be enslaved, perhaps annihilated. We may perish under the war-storm, our names no longer remembered by good men nor repeated in dance and song. Brothers, these are the words of Hiawatha. This is what he said."

Blackbird retreated into the congregation and sat upon the ground—one equal amongst all others.

Chief Yellow Corn stood and cleared his throat. "You all are aware the bark-eaters encroach on the beaver grounds. They steal the pelts that keep our families warm, and whose bartering fills our bellies with bison meat from the big game hunters of the plains."

"They should stay north of the Great Lakes," Coyote is Dancing said with a snarl. "We do not pilfer their fishing grounds, and they have plenty of beaver in their own rivers."

"Agreed," said a chief from the east. "They have refused alliance and now they show their intentions against us."

Deep into the night, Handsome Stream listened to men talk amongst themselves as others stood before the fire to give their opinions. Coyote is Dancing made his way around the circle one man at a time, whispering into their ears and holding their gazes until they nodded in agreement. Coyote dragged himself low across the grass to Handsome Stream, but held his gaze only less than a moment before turning up his nose in distrust and edging around him to the next warrior. After a time came words of anger as tempers began to flare and the name of war was on the tips of men's tongues. Handsome Stream said nothing. Though he knew confrontation would allow them to show their courage and strength and fulfill their duty toward their families, he felt a heavy sorrow press against his heart as Atotarho spoke the outcome of the council.

War.

A satisfied growl emanated from the far side of the pack.

Atotarho gave a single nod and Morning Star Blackbird stood and walked through the night toward the grove of the five war chiefs. Stream strained to hear their conversation but knew the chiefs could not act upon the council findings without approval from the highest power of the Five Nations. Blackbird resumed his position at the Council Fire, and all waited as the five war chiefs headed toward the main encampment—toward the matriarchs of the longhouses—toward the mothers of all children.

From across the water, Stream could just make out Autumn Moon Shadow and the other matriarchs. He was certain Sky Full of Stars was amongst them and glad that she was. The echoes of whispered conversation rippled across Onondaga. Soon all were nodding in agreement, perhaps a little sadly, and the war chiefs returned from the mothers and entered the glow of the Central Council Fire. They stood with their backs to the flame, facing Atotarho upon his moss-covered slab. Chief Broken Tree, the most revered, spoke for them all.

"It is in the nature of men to be warriors. It is our duty to protect our families, to use our might to right wrongs, to bravely wear the heron plume on the battlefield when it is needed to ensure peace." Coyote is Dancing and several men pumped their fists and whooped loudly. Chief Broken Tree stood in silence until the ruckus subsided. "But women are our connection to Mother Earth, and they know the hearts of men better than men. They create and care for the future of the nation and its culture—its children. It is true men cannot always clearly see the path to peace, but a woman knows it is she who must bury her loved ones, the babes she bore and suckled and fed and taught. Only she would clearly see and know whether any war was worth its reprehensible cost.

"Hiawatha passed the laws of the Peacemaker to us to ensure our survival. But it is *Jikohnsaseh*, Peace Queen and Mother of Nations whose words come to us with clarity, directly through the Mothers of our Clans." Chief Broken Tree turned to stare through the flames of the council fire.

"Handsome Stream! Stand!"

All in the clearing looked to him, and he hesitated before rising to his full height. He took a deep breath and held it.

"The Clan Mothers have forbidden us to go to war," said Chief Broken Tree. "However, the Mother of the Wolf has endorsed your recommendation."

Handsome Stream slowly released the breath from his lungs as he surveyed the crowd. He was one with these men and respected their thoughts. With the acknowledgement from Autumn Moon Shadow, he realized his own solution, though dangerous and with probable loss of much life, was more optimal than all-out war.

Stream cleared his throat. "We wish to assert the Vale of the Three Falls as a hunting ground of the Five Nations," he said. "We will send a messenger to the Adirondacks to select a thousand of their mightiest warriors. A thousand of our own will meet them on the central field of the vale. And there, between its falls, we shall compete in tewaaraton to settle the dispute."

* * * *

Handsome Stream sat cross-legged, in the middle of his mother's house, barefoot and shirtless with only a wrap of beaver hide tied at his waist. He was covered in sweat, and Sky Full of Stars and Genesee sat on either side, readying him for tewaaraton. They spoke only to each other, ignoring his suppressed winces and grunts. Sky Full of Stars twisted a dozen strands of his hair together then ran her clenched fingers up their full length to his scalp. She rolled the braid around her finger then yanked it from his head. Stream barely flinched, but his fists clamped harder upon his knees. Genesee did the same on the other side of his head, then dropped the braid she'd ripped out into the growing pile beside her. By the time Autumn Moon Shadow came and kneeled before him, the back and most of the sides were plucked of hair.

"Men will want to go to war, even the little war of tewaaraton," she said with a smile as she rolled a length of hair around her forefinger and wrenched it from above Handsome Stream's forehead. He clenched his jaw.

Tuft by tuft they pulled out his hair until only a small square remained upon the crown. They weaved it into three short braids and decorated it with colored porcupine quills and beads. Sky Full of Stars tied on a heron plume.

"For your honor and courage, my son. May you never need the chant, or rattle of the Medicine Man."

* * * *

The Adirondacks had accepted the challenge, and one thousand of their greatest warriors were strutting back and forth on the far ridge of the verdant canyon. They brandished their bent sticks and hollered insults across the vale.

Handsome Stream stood with the thousand chosen to play for the People of the Longhouse. All were plucked and barefooted, their flesh protected only by the ritual of song and dance, paint and charcoal, the honor of tattoos and decorated breechcloths.

Chief Broken Tree stood before them. "I have met with the war chief of the bark-eaters and the rules have been decided," he called. "There will be one ball. The bark-eaters' goal is the cliff face beneath the highest waterfall. Our goal is the rim of the middle falls. The canyon and all its tributaries shall be the sole hunting grounds of the Nation placing the first goal. There are no other rules."

The vale was a wide, snaking canyon crowded by ancient cedar, hemlock, and maple with only a handful of open fields scattered throughout. Not an ideal arena for tewaaraton. Trees as old as Stream's family story grew so tall they occluded any view of the river and falls themselves, though their roar could be heard anywhere. Stream had never entered this valley, but he had been told the middle falls were so wondrous they made the sun stop at midday.

As the men shook their fists and returned the chants of the bark-eaters, Stream flexed his playing stick then upended it to inspect the netted head for the tenth time. His stick was half his height; a treasured possession he had cut, split, heated, and bent himself. Its head was larger than his hand—a circle of bent wood netted by pliable deer gut. Satisfied, he let out a whoop and waved the stick above his head.

"I will offer you a wager," Coyote is Dancing snarled from behind him. He was shorter and more sinewy than Stream, and the shaft of his tewaaraton stick was smeared with blood from the fresh ceremonial cuts down the side of his torso. He was agitated, excited.

"Your proposal?" Stream asked.

"I, too, wish to join the Longhouse of the Wolf. Though Chief Yellow Corn may hear my words, it is Genesee whom I wish would invite me in."

Stream scrutinized him. "Why would I risk my happiness for you?"

Coyote sneered. "Because your blood is not pure. You are not worthy of the Wolf Clan or of Genesee. We should have gone to war and wiped from this land those who refuse to accept a Great Peace. If we lose this valley, it will be your fault."

Stream's grip on the stick tightened, his knuckles turning crimson. "You speak with unjust arrogance. But we will win, Coyote. That I assure you."

Chief Broken Tree stood at the edge of the bluff, the wooden tewaaraton ball in his hand. He called out to the war chief on the far side of the canyon, his message reciprocated by a threatening, taunting staccato. Then he threw the ball high into the air toward a central field of the gaping, evergreen gorge.

The ball had hardly left his grip when a mighty roar emanated from both sides of the canyon. The war cries of two thousand warriors reverberated across the vale with a clash. Then all scuttled down the sides of the valley, slipping and sliding through dirt and grass, amongst bush and trunk, keeping tight their holds on their sticks and all the while hollering insults toward the enemy. The two masses encroached on the open field where the ball had thudded into the grass, running toward each other with such venom that flesh knocked hard into flesh and sticks bashed brutally into backs and legs and faces. The game quickly became little more than a heaving, tight mass of warriors, refusing to budge in either direction.

Handsome Stream was somewhere in the middle, with no knowledge of where the ball might be. He was pressed between brother and bark-eater, their deafening shouts in his ears. An elbow jabbed into the side of his chest and he returned it with a thrust of his stick. The whole mass moved suddenly sideways several paces, and Stream almost tripped over the rubble of men beneath his feet—the awkward pressure of foot upon stomach, chest, face, then grass once more. He thought he saw the silhouette of the ball by his feet and grabbed for it with the netting of his stick, but the mass lurched again in the other direction.

"Iroquois!" a bark-eater spat at him, so close his words and teeth scraped across Stream's cheek.

Stream tried to turn, flexing his muscles and urging his arms above the shoulders of those around him.

"Meat-eater," shouted another, managing to free his own arm and punch Stream firmly in the face. In return Stream delivered a hefty blow that cracked the man's nose and spread blood across his face, and another that sent him down crumbling beneath the melee toward certain pain and broken bones.

Again the crowd staggered.

"Ball," someone yelled. Then another took up the call, and then another.

A wave of warriors clambered over those that had fallen. They crawled across one another, attempting to stand, fists and sticks punching and whacking. Several men piled upon Handsome Stream, and a bruising knee landed hard into his groin. A bloody hand gripped tight about his neck, but he shrugged and rolled then deftly thrust the end of his stick into the largest of the men who had tackled him. He heard ribs crack.

The horde moved no more than three or four paces from where the ball had landed.

For three days and three nights the warriors neither gained nor lost any viable ground.

By the fourth day, Handsome Stream's entire body ached. His muscles seemed frozen in their clenched position, his arm linked with a brother's in support, his bare feet pushing deep into the mud. His toes spasmed and cramped but he did not dare relax, fearing to even expel a whole breath in case the crush would prevent him from taking another. A warrior two shoulders to Stream's left was unconscious, possibly dead, his face pale and head limp, his body kept upright by the constant squeeze of warrior against warrior.

Then came a guttural scream from the center of the pack.

Stream looked up to see a bark-eater crawling from the melee up onto the shoulders of those around him, his stick held to his chest, the tewaaraton ball caught firmly in its net. Hands reached for him, sticks swung through the air at him, but he scrambled across the men, stumbling and rolling, and finally making his way to the edge and the open field. The mass became loose and shifting as the mire of warriors surged and split and scattered across the field.

At least a quarter of the men could no longer stand. They fell to the ground in exhausted heaps beside those killed in the crush. The remainder pursued the bark-eater with the ball. To protect him. To stop him.

Handsome Stream scrambled to the edge of the crowd and soon he was running through the wood with as many warriors as there were trees. The roar and rage was escalating as warriors struck out with their sticks, intent on maiming or rendering their enemy unconscious.

To kill. To kill.

Several times Stream caught sight of Coyote is Dancing on the far side of the wood, running parallel to his course, only losing sight of him when he was attacked or delayed by a bark-eater. Eventually

Stream's speed pushed him ahead of the pack. The bark-eater with the ball was less than a hundred paces ahead, and their goal of the upper falls was so close it filled the wood with its thunderous roar and spray.

Coyote sprinted up beside him and arced his stick to slam brutally into Stream's face. Stream faltered and fell, rolling as pounding feet passed him by, before recovering stride once more. He quickly passed those who had overtaken him until only Coyote and the bark-eater were ahead.

Coyote swung out his stick and tripped the Adirondack into a heap. Within a moment, Coyote had the ball in the net of his stick and turned on his heel back through the wood toward the convergence of friend and enemy. Stream turned with him.

"Coyote," Stream yelled. "I am here when you need me."

Coyote is Dancing kept up his pace through the warriors who only reeled in confusion at his direction. With stick or shoulder or fist, Stream knocked to the ground any who recognized the change in possession. Warriors were fighting and running in chaos, uncertain. Handsome Stream spotted an Adirondack who had caught on, and he scooped up a rock with his stick and flung it. It smacked the warrior in the head and he went down. Stream picked up rock after rock and launched them through the wood, increasing the confusion, knocking down random men. Coyote zigzagged, but his pace was slowing, more men were changing direction and gaining on him. He glanced sideways at Stream, then back over his shoulder, panic creeping into his face, sweat flying from his body.

"Handsome Stream," he finally yelped, an understanding resolving between them with unspoken words. Stream ran ahead of Coyote as a dozen bark-eaters were converging. "You are faster," Coyote yelled, and with that he swung his stick and flung the ball in Stream's direction. The wooden ball sailed through the trees, clipping leaf and branch. Stream raised his stick and caught the ball in his net then brought the stick in close to his body. He instantly doubled his pace, his footing sure as he ran through wood and clearing, jumping brook and marsh toward the middle falls. The melee of men fell farther behind with each stride, and a grass-covered clearing opened up around him.

Handsome Stream ran across the field faster than he had ever coursed the messenger trail. His body ached, his head thudded in pain, but the taunts of war were falling far behind. The river of the vale soon cascaded beside him, and the spray and mist from the middle falls rose high. He glanced over his shoulder, but the closest follower was well out of sight.

He stopped, heaving for breath, his muscles shaking, and with one final, jerking arc, he swung his stick and launched the ball out into the mist. It sailed across the top of the middle falls and into the sky above.

The sun blazed.

It stood still.

Trade (1584 AD)

River Maker stood amongst the trees, as one with the wood. The white-haired booger sat in the middle of a clearing, struggling to light his fire, his skin pale as his hair. A dozen traps were scattered on the ground, some cleaned and others still bloody with tufts of fur caught in their teeth. The evening twilight had eddied into dusk by the time the trapper's kindling sparked, and still River Maker observed him, unnoticed, from no more than five paces away.

The trapper hunkered down close to the flame, seemingly contented when it flared, then subdued. He stared at it, deep in thought, as the darkness settled over the forest. The fire became a dull ember glow before his outstretched hands. Several times he took a swig from a bladder. Only when he appeared satisfied by the heat did he break his reverie to pull a skinned carcass from his pack and place it within the coals.

Raccoon, thought River Maker.

The trapper turned it now and then, taking more swigs from his bladder.

The wood was quiet with no more sound than the buzz of insects and the far-off screech of a hoot owl searching for its own supper.

The raccoon sizzled, its sweet smell wafting through the clearing, and the trapper stabbed it deep with his knife. He smiled when the juices ran clear. He licked the blade, then he rattled through a rucksack and pulled out a dented metal plate for the roasted meat. He hummed as he flicked embers off the charred flesh with the point of his knife.

River Maker waited while the trapper sliced off a chunk of meat, placed it in his mouth and started to chew. Then, he reached out to a nearby twig and snapped it.

The trapper stopped, clasping his knife and looking around for the source of the disturbance.

River Maker stepped sideways, out of the shadow of his tree and into the glow of the fire. The trapper sat motionless as River Maker crept toward him. The two stared at one another, searching for intention. Then, River Maker crouched before the fire and gave the trapper a single friendly nod. He pulled a bundle of beaver pelts from his pack and placed them by the fire. He pushed them with his foot toward the trapper, who stared wide-eyed but continued to chew the lump of meat.

The trapper placed a hand upon the pelts.

"*Est-ce que c'est pour moi?*" he asked though shreds of raccoon. His face spread into a wide, toothless grin. He touched his fingertips to his chest. "*Je m'appelle Algernon.*"

Though the words were unknown, River Maker nodded.

The trapper chuckled, carved a chunk of raccoon, stabbed it with his blade, and held it toward River Maker.

P.J. Parker

Powhatan . . . A Chance of Brotherhood (1607 AD)

Waist deep in the eddying current of the Chesepiook, Arrow Feather had completed his morning bathing ritual and now called his prayers into the crisp blue sky. The river was freezing, despite it being the month of Great Corn. But this was of no concern to Arrow Feather as he sank further into the water, digging his toes into the sandy bottom, the last words of his song skipping across the swell that nudged against his stomach and rose to his chest and finally his chin. His prayers turned inwards and stopped only when he knew the Spirits were satisfied and he felt the friendly knock of a catfish against his elbow. Arrow rubbed the water from his eyes, smoothed back his thick black hair, and stared out over the waterway toward the haphazard settlement of buildings being constructed on the swampy promontory opposite his own camp.

"Why are these boogers so imprudent they build their homes in the bog?"

He stepped out of the water and sat upon the grass. The sun was warm on his skin and would soon dry him. As he readied his breakfast, he continued his watch across the water. From what he could tell, there were few men much older than his own twenty summers, but the majority were younger. There were no women, which was not a good sign. The village of the white man was mostly crude tents, but at its center stretched the wooden skeleton of a longhouse they were building from saplings cut from a nearby grove. They had begun to cover it with mud, though Arrow didn't understand why they did not use reed instead, as it better insulated against the winter winds and would not wash away with the first storm. He guessed he would see how the building would weather and if the white men would stay.

With a mouthful of pemmican, he glanced down at his body stretched across the grass. His skin was smooth and hairless, not so red as his brothers', but nowhere near as pallid as those over the river.

They had dug a triangular trench around their camp, and on this morning they were placing the first planks of a palisade, not much taller than any it was meant to protect. It would never compare to the stature of his own village of Werowocomoco which, unknown to the boogers, lay less than half a day's journey to the north on more solid ground.

More impressive than anything so far constructed on the swampland were the three large canoes the white men had arrived in. They were moored in the shallows of the bay, each large enough to hold thirty warriors. Large clouds had billowed above them, drawing them up the Chesepiook or so Arrow had been told. But now the billows were tied down against the upper deck, ruffling only in the stiffest wind from the great blue pond in the east. The vessels creaked and moaned in harmony with the ripple of water through the bayous, the tune of the breeze through stands of reed, the call of fowl flying overhead.

Arrow Feather was also new to this land of bays and waterways, having arrived only the previous summer. He had been readily welcomed into the Powhatan Confederacy on the shores of the Chesepiook when he was joined with Blossom of Black Cherry, the daughter of one of the lesser chiefs, Satchel of Blades. Arrow's native Clan was of high standing amongst the *Haudenosaunee* beside the finger lakes to the north and, though it was love and respect that had brought him south, any familial ties between the two confederacies were advantageous to all. It ensured continued trade and peace amongst the nations.

Adept at fishing and trapping, and strengthened by the lineage and stories of Bear, Arrow Feather had frequently traded pelts of beaver and deer with the booger trappers that wandered in the woodlands of his childhood and youth. All had been cautious, but friendly in nature, communicating mostly in unintelligible guttural tones, but each more than happy to trade him bells, knives, and kettles. He had learned many of their words and ways, and it was this experience that had prompted Paramount Chief Powhatan to personally assign Arrow Feather to his current scouting duty. The observance of large numbers of white men in one place was unusual, and the building of a permanent village was reason for wonder and opportunity—perhaps concern.

On three occasions white men had rowed smaller canoes to Arrow's side of the bay, talking hesitantly in a language more refined than the lone trappers of the north. One man—short and hairy of face—offered him some copper. In return he shared his supper of roast pumpkin and fish. On each venture, he was careful to learn a handful of their words: *ship, house, fort, church.* This last word caused them to drop to their knees, clasp their hands, and peer up into the sky. Arrow Feather mimicked their stance and they seemed pleased.

Warriors and merchants of the minor tribes, some from as far as the Falls, also visited the fledgling village. From Arrow's viewpoint, they appeared to be welcomed favorably. Their songs drifted across the bay long into the night, their silhouettes dancing before the flames. Only once were the voices of argument raised, and the thunder of fire sticks exploded into the night. But the disturbance, whatever its cause, quickly settled into apparent amity once more.

Arrow did not cross the water to the white man's village. He preferred the security of his distance, ready to report back to Chief Powhatan when summoned.

* * * *

"They do not understand the meaning of the soil beneath their feet."

Arrow Feather stood before Paramount Chief Powhatan and all the lesser chiefs of the confederacy in the main reed longhouse of Werowocomoco. He was barefoot, wearing only a deerskin apron over his loin and a thin strip of hide around his head. Behind the circle of powerful men sat their warriors, hunters, farmers, and fishermen, interspersed with the wisdom of women, including Blossom of Black Cherry. The smoky haze of tobacco and the central fire hung low above their heads.

"Though they have fire sticks and long blades, they are unaware of the power of the Three Sisters and appear not to possess even rudimentary skills in foraging or catching deer, fish, or fowl. They are afraid of brother bear."

Paramount Chief Powhatan rubbed at his chin, gazing deep into the flame. It was his brother, Chief Opechancanough, who asked, "Do the boogers not eat?"

"A cache of supplies from their big canoes is the main source of their sustenance. One young man—more of a man-child—came to my camp to offer a bowl of their food and a bladder of drink. The food was a mushy grain, liberally supplemented with maggots, both dead and alive. The drink was blood-colored and bitter. I spat it out."

"They eat maggots and drink blood?" Opechancanough shivered.

"It may not be by choice," Arrow said. "When I offered a smoked cheek of deer, my visitor fell upon it hungrily and with much happiness. Those in the village are also very welcoming of the local Clans, who sometimes barter food in return for the metal-wares and colored glass beads the boogers make in their furnace of fire."

The lesser chiefs nodded.

A muted silence settled over the longhouse. Arrow darted a glance at Blossom of Black Cherry, and she returned the tiniest nod, along with the loving curve of her lip. Arrow Feather felt her warmth fill him and could not help but stand a little taller, puff his chest out a little farther, and lift his chin ever so slightly.

"Within ten days, the large canoes lifted their clouds and skimmed down the Chesepiook and out of sight, leaving one hundred men to make their own way in the makeshift village. But without the supplies in the canoes, almost all were struck down by an idle sickness. Less than a handful were able even to stand or walk due to lack of nourishment. Certainly all would have perished had it not been for one of our hunting parties arriving with turkey and deer and corn to trade."

"We cannot be surprised," Chief Powhatan said. "It has always been the guardianship of the red man to know the teachings of the earth and the way of food, just as it was foretold that the white man would have guardianship of fire and learn its secrets."

The surrounding chiefs concurred.

Chief Powhatan said, "Though the white men have not yet found their footing in Túwaqachi, there is much we must learn from one other, as the unification of our two Clans has now undeniably begun. We shall share our knowledge of Mother Earth and they shall share their knowledge of fire. We will welcome our brothers with open arms, and our families will become one through trust, trade, and marriage."

"We shall have the power of the fire stick and the heated metal!" Opechancanough declared.

Chief Powhatan nodded, less certain. "And we gladly will share with them the power of our legacy."

* * * *

Arrow Feather was quick to slip his arm around his wife's waist as they left Paramount Chief Powhatan's longhouse. They walked briskly across the yard toward the single entrance of the village palisade, intent on losing themselves within the trails that ambled through the surrounding wood

"The people were pleased by your report, Arrow," Blossom of Black Cherry said with a smile. Her long hair fell about her bare, tattooed torso.

"And Chief Powhatan deciphered the meaning of the events quickly. A very wise—"

Arrow stopped in his tracks, pulling Blossom tight against him. A tewaaraton ball landed in the dirt before them and instinctively he slammed his bare foot upon it to stop its course.

Following close behind, naked children cartwheeled across the dirt and grass, legs and arms turning skyward. A young girl of eleven summers fell into a laughing heap at their feet.

"Matoaka, are you okay?" Blossom asked, kneeling to lift Chief Powhatan's favorite daughter off the ground.

Though young, Matoaka had already proven herself in the learning of her duties and the passion of her inquisitiveness.

"Arrow!" she yelled, throwing her arms around him. "You must tell me of the white men and their . . . and their . . ."

"*Fort*," Arrow suggested.

"Yes, *fort*," Matoaka said, rolling her tongue around the new word. "But not now, as I have important business." She laughed again, the high-trilling laughter of childhood, and then wheeled across the grass in pursuit of her playmates. Arrow nudged the wooden ball after them with the side of his foot.

"Little Pocahontas," he remarked as the girl frolicked with her friends.

"She is a child and children need time to play," Blossom said.

Arrow Feather turned toward Blossom and lowered his face to brush his cheek against hers. He whispered in her ear, and she, too, laughed the high-trilling laughter of childhood.

Then, holding tight to each other's hands, they ran from the village.

* * * *

The season turned from green to red, orange, and purple, leaves falling to camouflage well-worn trails. Bright cardinals flocked together to forage with sparrows, juncos, and goldfinches amongst the thickets.

Werowocomoco was being readied for a feast. Stag roasted above fire pits, corn and tubers charred in the heat of embers, sturgeon sizzled on the hot cooking rocks, and baskets brimmed with freshly plucked herbage, sunroots, cattails, ramps, and onions.

Arrow Feather rested against the trunk of a flowering dogwood with Blossom beside him, her head in his lap. Tenderly, he stroked her hair.

"The white men seem very slow to learn," Blossom said as she stripped the husk and silks from an ear of corn and threw it into the basket at her side.

Arrow nodded. "Beyond some ragged thatch construction, they have achieved little these last five moons and will not be ready for the coming winter. The recent report from their village is that most have died, with some abandoning their brothers to join with our own in the woodlands. Those who remain attempt to work the soil, but do so without any great result or willingness to learn. Indeed, they are disorganized with internal mistrust and fighting. Still, their main error is their choice of location, a breeding ground for the mosquitoes that give them the sleeping sickness. They make it worse by digging wells for freshwater that are soon sullied by the salt of the Chesepiook, and they bury their dead and heap their waste within steps of their homes."

"Did not Chief Powhatan offer them a better place for their village, where they could grow their own crops and build their furnace fires to bend the metal and melt the glass?"

"They refused to leave the promontory. Instead, they spread mistrust and strike out at the local tribes who have done no more than ensure their survival—as dwindling as it may be."

"In what way?" Blossom sat up beside her husband. She counted the number of ears left to shuck and tossed one to Arrow.

"Their stores of meal and maggots are slim. When they have little to trade, they attack the closer Clans, steal their supplies, kill our brothers without guilt, and burn their lodges. Then they wonder why they are attacked in retribution."

"Yet we continue to help them," Blossom said, furrowing her brow.

"They are our brothers, and brothers sometimes fight."

Blossom was not convinced. "They should submit to the wisdom and power of our confederacy."

"The men of Jamestowne—as they call their village, after their own great chief across the blue pond—are not yet aware of our confederacy and its power. They have dealt only with the smaller Clans on our periphery, with whom they have built an uneasy, sometimes volatile, relationship."

"There must be some way to create a Great Peace with these men, so that all may live as intended on this land."

Arrow Feather ripped the leaves from the maize and then reached for another. "Chief Powhatan has a plan toward that end, as the council have conceded it cannot be resolved by a game of stickball. With the cold winds of winter approaching, the rivers will soon be covered by cranes, ducks, geese, and swans from the north. Even the white men will not go hungry in a time of such plenty. But if they continue to encroach on our land and slay our brothers and steal from our sisters, then we shall reveal to them our true might. We will show them we have a command much greater than their own, custody over their very life or death, but we desire only to merge our families and share one another's knowledge."

"Would we not need the boogers to have one they looked up to amongst themselves in order to achieve that—a local leader whom they respected that could negotiate on their behalf?"

Arrow studied the ear of maize in his grip, the kernels of yellow, white, and blue clinging together upon the cob. "There is one who will rise to the occasion. A short, boisterous man with a hairy face by the name of Captain John Smith."

* * * *

Chief Opechancanough led over three hundred of the confederacy's three thousand warriors under the orders of his brother, Paramount Chief Powhatan. Arrow Feather was amongst their ranks and, along with a dozen others from various Clans who had been acquainted with the white men, would act as interpreter for the planned events. All were ready for battle, with fringed deerskin aprons and leggings tied securely, capes of otter and deer, heads and shoulders painted scarlet with nut oil and bloodroot, rawhide quivers of arrows, war clubs at their backs, and the feathered skins of birds—wings open—tied to the single length of hair on their otherwise plucked scalps.

Word had been secured that Captain Smith was fowling in the tributaries and marshes between Jamestowne and Werowocomoco. He apparently thought nothing of killing those who stood in his way or who would not readily barter for the needs of his own.

The warriors, all adept bowmen, split into groups. They crept through the woods, followed the snaking waterways, and trudged waist-deep in the marsh. When they located Smith's barge in the upper reaches of the Chickahamania, the calls of coot, heron, and chickadee echoed amongst the shadbush and rose mallow until all three hundred men hunkered in the shadows.

The barge came ashore, its occupants unaware of the force surrounding them. It pushed into the sandy bank and those aboard trod to land where they kindled a fire to broil a mallard. Smith was not amongst them. From hundreds of paces away, Arrow saw as his brothers walked brazenly into the clearing, bows drawn and arrows at the ready. The thunder of the white men's fire sticks shot into undergrowth and flesh, and arrows thudded into those about the fire. Seven of his brothers fell dead, along with the three boogers from the barge. Their supper smoldered in their fire.

One brother kneeled, holding his blade to the exposed throat of a white man, his ear close to the lips expelling their last breath. The warrior let out a call, and the force crept slowly through the marsh toward the higher reaches of the bayou.

Arrow was with those who first found Smith hacking his way through the undergrowth. The captain was quick to fire his stick, instantly killing two warriors, before pulling his guide, a man of the Falls, in front of him as a shield against the arrows of Chief Opechancanough's warriors. He took an arrow in his thigh and dragged his guide into the swamp where they sat submerged in the freezing water. Opechancanough let out a call, and all that remained of the three hundred warriors showed themselves along the banks, bows drawn and arrows pointed at the two wallowing in the shallows.

Arrow Feather showed little emotion as he gripped his bow. Their ruse was necessary to impinge on this murderous booger. The sun sank from the late afternoon sky until the bayou was no more than an inky black under a dull moon. And still Smith skulked in the water, holding his guide close with a blade tight against his chest, both of them gasping and shaking in the cold.

When the song in his heart told him it was time, Arrow stepped to the edge of the water. Smith had turned gray from the cold and only his eyes moved to settle upon Arrow and hold his stare. Warily, Arrow lowered his weapon and placed it upon the grass. Then he motioned with an outstretched hand for Smith to come ashore. When the booger refused, Arrow lowered himself onto his knees, clasped his hands together, and peered up into the night sky.

The first pinpricks of light from the seven brothers and their beautiful sister had begun to appear.

Arrow called, "Church!" Again he motioned for Smith to join him. "Church."

Smith was hesitant but finally threw his two small fire sticks ashore and waded toward the bank, pulling his guide with him. Unable to stand, they dragged themselves up onto solid ground on their knees.

Arrow reached out and placed his hand on Smith's shoulder. "Church," he said with a nod.

Smith's teeth chattered loud. Arrow Feather picked up his bow and arrow and tossed them out of reach, then squatted to rub the cold from Smith's arms, shoulders, and legs. He stripped off the captain's jacket and vest and massaged him more vigorously to warm the flesh, as another did the same for Smith's guide.

"I demand to be shown to your captain immediately," Smith barked indignantly.

"You will return with us," Arrow said in the white man's language, helping him awkwardly to his feet. "Your men have built a fire along the shore by their canoe."

Smith raised his eyebrows but said nothing more as Arrow Feather and another warrior took hold of his shoulders. They marched Smith and his guide through the wood.

Captain Smith stiffened as he was pushed into the clearing where his men lay dead. "You've slain my men with bows and arrows and push me near death with cold—" Smith stopped as a hundred arrows pointed toward him from only a few paces away. The tightening of the bows all at once created a screech that resonated around the clearing.

Chief Opechancanough stepped before him, an imposing figure with a broad scarlet-painted, tattooed chest, necklaces of copper and feathers. Snakes writhed and hissed through the holes of his stretched earlobes. The captain dropped to his knees and held his hands over his face, whimpering like a scared child.

"This is our captain," Arrow said. "Chief Opechancanough."

Captain Smith nodded as he peered cautiously through his spread fingers at the chief, then at the weapons aimed at him. He held up a hand and motioned toward his canoe. Arrow Feather walked to the vessel and studied the contents that lay strewn across its interior. He grabbed a satchel, and Smith nodded. Arrow Feather loosened the strings and peered inside, then rummaged through the contents before placing it beside Smith. The captain pulled his vest and jacket on, though they were still wet. Then he opened his satchel and pulled out a globe. He held it up toward Chief Opechancanough, his head lowered in supplication, muttering.

"Speak up, Captain Smith," Arrow said. "You know some of our words and we know many of yours. Speak your thoughts."

"A present . . . a compass for you, Captain," Smith said.

"He calls it a *compass*," Arrow translated.

"The roundness of the earth and skies, the sphere of the sun, moon, and stars," Smith continued, holding up the orb in one hand and reaching for the sky above with the other.

Chief Opechancanough looked down at the compass, and Arrow watched the needle inside fly with Smith's movements. Chief Opechancanough took the gift and stared at it while Arrow Feather translated. He went to touch the needle, but his finger was blocked by an invisible barrier. He tapped it—a hollow sound.

"The sun does chase the night round about the world continually," Smith went on, his head low.

The chief gazed intently at the needle and held it up toward the stars. "It holds true to the star of the northern cardinal of Túwaqachi," he said to Arrow. "But why does the booger not just look to the night sky?"

Captain Smith was still mumbling. "The greatness of the land and sea, the diversity of nations, the variety of complexions, and you we consider as our antipodes . . ."

"Captain Smith believes our Mother is round like a tewaaraton ball, Chief Opechancanough."

The chief chuckled, still turning the gift in his fingers. Then he turned to Arrow Feather. "Captain Smith uses words of eloquence, and his stance is of submission, but still I detect an air of abrasiveness, even without translation."

"He speaks with great pride—an underlying arrogance of superiority," Arrow whispered.

The chief nodded.

A yell of unbridled anger came from amongst the Powhatan warriors, and the men turned to see Lone Eagle Twilight pushing his way into the clearing. He threw himself upon Captain Smith and they tumbled, Lone Eagle's fists coming down on Smith's face and chest.

"This booger killed my son!" Lone Eagle yelled. "He killed my only son—my future!" His hands were quickly dripping with Smith's blood.

Chief Opechancanough stood stock-still, watching. Finally, he made a slight gesture and two warriors lifted Smith from beneath Lone Eagle, dragged him through the mud, and tied him to a tree. Smith struggled, shouting, even as arrows were once more drawn upon him.

Opechancanough strode over and placed his hand upon Lone Eagle's shoulder.

"Did you kill my brother's son?" he asked Smith in Powhatan.

"Did you kill my brethren's son?" Arrow Feather translated.

Smith held his head high.

"You and your brethren have killed many since you arrived," Arrow said. "And for what?"

Smith stared, defiant.

"We have shared our food with you, even when food was scarce. We wish only to trade with you. But, without doubt, we will kill you if you continue to kill our own."

Arrow Feather stepped back, out of the path of the hundred arrows trained upon the captive. Again, the screech of gut and sinew reverberated around the clearing as the bows were drawn tighter still.

Smith's arrogance dissipated until it was apparent he felt nothing but indignant fear.

Chief Opechancanough stepped between Smith and the gauntlet of arrows. He pressed the back of his hand to Smith's chest, touched the globe in his hand, then touched his own chest. "You gave me this globe," he said in English. "You gave me this star compass, and in return I will give you your life. Do you understand?"

Captain Smith nodded.

"Do you *truly* understand?" the chief asked.

"Yes."

* * * *

Arrow Feather and the bulk of his brothers made their way back to Werowocomoco before the rising of the new day's sun. Captain Smith, however, was led on a trek around the Powhatan Confederacy by the remainder of Chief Opechancanough's charge. For seven days, he was delivered to villages of increasing size, strength, vitality, and magnificence. Each successively compounded the insignificance of the struggling Jamestowne. He was led to the towns of the Youthtanunds, the Mattapanients, the Payankatanks, the Nantaughtacunds, and along the shores of Rappahannock to the Onawmanients and Patawomecks. The captain's reactions had been subdued, seemingly still holding himself in higher esteem and thus unable to be trusted to be their brother.

On the seventh night, he was escorted into the palisaded grandeur of Werowocomoco with warriors gripping his arms, bows and arrows still holding aim.

The central plaza was ablaze with light from the great central fire. The lodges, storehouses, and impenetrable palisades were bathed in light that reached far into the surrounding wood. Several hundred of Powhatan's bravest warriors stood staunchly around the fire—plucked and painted, decorated in feathers and beads, their blood-tinted torsos creating a circle about the small booger ushered into their midst.

Brutal hands released their hold and pushed Captain Smith toward the fire, where he stood in awe of the force that surrounded him.

Arrow Feather beheld him with a grim countenance, his tattooed shoulders hard against Susquehanna's and Tomahawk's. A reed mat was placed before the fire and Captain Smith was thrown down upon it.

The circle of warriors parted and the Shaman rushed toward him, yelling wildly and shaking his rattle. He was painted black from head to toe except his eyes, which were smears of white and red that reflected the fire's blaze. He was naked except for his apron and a crown of snake and weasel skins hung from his head. The skins flung about him as he stomped. Dream Wanderer screeched loud as three more of his kind ran into the circle, sprinkling coarsely ground meal around the central fire, enclosing the captain within its magic.

Captain Smith recoiled but was unable to look away, appearing even whiter and shorter than when he had entered Werowocomoco. Arrow Feather stepped from the circle to stand beside the captain, his position quickly consumed by his brothers.

"Rise," Arrow commanded.

The captain obeyed, his eyes on the Shaman and his men as they crouched behind the fire, seemingly within its flames.

Arrow and the warriors of Powhatan let out a deafening shout that reverberated from brother to brother, from fire to sky. A wooden platform was pushed into the circle. Paramount Chief Powhatan sat upon it. He wore a coat of raccoon skins, hundreds of brown and white tails hanging—a link to the spiritual powers of nature. He was flanked by two of his most trusted sister advisers, wearing deer hide skirts, long grease-shined hair, and bare chests as garishly red as the men's. A second line of men moved in behind the inner circle, and behind them the women of Werowocomoco.

Arrow pulled Captain Smith around the fire and urged him down upon the ground before Powhatan's platform. He then stood between the paramount chief and his guest. One of the matriarchs at Powhatan's side offered Smith water to wash his hands, and the other gave him feathers to dry them. Men and women filed before him presenting reed platters of roasted meat and vegetables, seared fish and corn, freshly picked cress and herbage, pots of sweet water.

Powhatan and his people were silent as the captain cautiously ate and drank his fill. Neither the paramount chief nor any other sampled the food. They merely observed.

Seeing that his guest had slowed, Powhatan gave a flick of his hand and the food was removed.

For many breaths of the night wind there was only an uncomfortable quiet, save for the crack and whistle of the fire.

Powhatan nodded to Arrow Feather.

Arrow turned to Smith. "What do you see, Captain Smith?"

Captain Smith was hesitant as he rose to his feet, wiping his hand against his breeches.

"I plainly see around me a great power, a great strength."

"And what else?"

The captain raised an eyebrow in question.

Arrow waited, but when no answer came he said, "Tell us of your land, Captain."

"We are a land of peace. We are a land of uncountable great towns filled with diverse peoples, governed by a chief who is himself very powerful. More powerful than any other upon this globe whose lands he has conquered by his august majesty. We possess hundreds of large canoes and mighty guns—immense fire sticks—that may destroy any town or people that our Great Chief James desires."

His speech and its translation were received with silence.

The captain went to continue, but Arrow Feather held up a hand. He looked to Powhatan, whose face was a mask of rage.

"Do your people still possess the two sacred tablets entrusted to you at the beginning of time—the words from the Creator that would guide you on the true path to your heart song?" Arrow asked.

The captain narrowed his eyes in confusion.

Arrow Feather pitied him. The captain's people had lost their way. It saddened him that the white man could not see his own brothers and sisters within the palisades of Werowocomoco. From the edge of his vision, Arrow noted the slightest of nods from the paramount chief and the swift movement of Chief Opechancanough from behind him.

"Is there nothing more you recognize in the people here with you in this space, upon this soil?"

Smith's mouth hung open, but no sound came.

Chief Opechancanough strode into the circle, a massive flat stone held high above his head. He slammed it down onto the grass before Captain Smith with an angry grunt that sent the captain lurching backward toward the central fire. The circle of warriors moved in toward him. Arrow Feather seized him roughly by the arm as other hands grabbed his feet and hoisted him above their shoulders. Smith flailed as he was passed roughly from one to another, tumbling and rolling on a sea of hands, shoulders and heads. He howled in despair, but his words were trivial beneath the noise of the gathering.

The captain was hurled to the ground at Arrow's side, and his head cracked against the stone placed by Chief Opechancanough, leaving a smear of blood. Many feet bore down heavily upon his legs, abdomen, chest and arms to stop his movement.

Chief Powhatan watched as warriors raised their clubs high. The captain cowered on the ground, a hand slipping free to uselessly cover his eyes to hide what was coming.

And then another set of hands touched his face.

Matoaka wrapped her arms around Captain Smith's head and placed her cheek against his. The captain jerked again, and Arrow stepped on his hair so his urgent movements would not hurt the young girl.

The crowd quieted.

Arrow crouched before Matoaka and whispered in Powhatan, "Remember, Matoaka, speak in English."

"Please, my father," she yelled, much louder than she needed to in the quiet of the crowd.

Smith's eyes twitched wildly at the sound of the girl's voice. He attempted to jerk his head again, and Arrow stomped his bare foot against Smith's bloody scalp, digging his toes hard into Smith's cheek to restrict any movement at all.

"Please hear me, father, for I think that the captain is a good man."

"Pocahontas!" Chief Powhatan shouted in mock-anger as he rose upon the platform.

"My father." Matoaka tightened her grip around Smith's head. "Though the captain may not see it, I know in my heart song that he is my brethren, that we are the same people."

Arrow placed his finger against his lips, and Matoaka nodded.

For interminable heartbeats, all listened to the miserable, frightened moan of Captain Smith's breathing.

Paramount Chief Powhatan stepped down to stand above his daughter and the man she protected. He pulled her up into his arms, tenderly nudging strands of hair from her face. Then he looked down at Smith, and the many warriors lessened the pressure of their feet on his prostrated body.

He spoke in Powhatan and Arrow translated.

"You are indeed a powerful man, that you need a little girl to save you where you are unable."

Smith turned his head upon the stone to see the chief and the naked child in his arms.

"Perhaps my daughter sees something I have not yet beheld. Could that be so, Captain?"

Smith looked at his blood on the rock, then up to the chief and Matoaka and finally to Arrow, with his thick curling lashes that surrounded eyes almost as blue as his own. Then his gaze went unfocused, Arrow thought perhaps to search for the heart song that must surely be somewhere within him.

* * * *

Blossom of Black Cherry pulled at her husband's hand as they strolled barefooted up the middle of a brook weaving through the woodland.

"Do you believe the ruse with Captain Smith worked?" she asked.

"I believe we have an ally in Jamestowne for as long as we are of use to him," Arrow said.

"Then you do not trust him?"

"Only as much as he trusts us."

The couple came to a pond and sank into it, holding each other tight in the swirling current.

"Chief Powhatan has taken the captain as his own son," Arrow said. "Smith is now known as Nantaquoud, in attempt to strengthen the bond."

Blossom was tentative. "Perhaps, soon, we will also have a son," she whispered.

Arrow touched his forehead to his wife's. "And hopefully our son will find true brotherhood with the sons of our white brothers."

Built on Smoke (1628 AD)

The plantation of Captain McMasters, One Hundred Oaks, covered an enviable eleven hundred and fifty acres along the western perimeter of Mulberry Island, Virginia. Despite its name, there were only two oaks that had not been cleared. The grand plantation home was a log and mud construction of four rooms—five if you counted the kitchen out the back. The tobacco barn was much larger. Both buildings looked tired and gray in the late evening light. They slouched on an eroded hillock to oversee the tobacco fields spreading down to the wharf on the waters of the Chickahominy. A dozen or more empty hogshead barrels lay scattered along the wharf, ready to be rolled up the hill to the barn.

Chauco dropped his hoe and pressed his hands to his back, stretching the ache of the day from his bones. He had been topping and priming the crop since well before sunup. His hands were stained brown and yellow from weeding and crushing cutworms. Beside him, a Negro named Abraham Johnson laughed and did the same. Abraham was a giant of a man, a full head taller than Chauco, and Chauco had never seen him without a smile on his face.

"Don't fail on me now, John," Abraham said to Chauco. "We still have to move the barrels up to the barn before we join our loved ones and take sup."

Chauco smirked.

Abraham called out to the other men in the field—all of them white—and all walked wearily toward the wharf, stretching and talking quietly. Abraham hummed. Chauco sang along, and the others took up the chorus.

The sun dropped quick below the wetland horizon, and Mulberry Island was cast with a violet light, soaked with the pervasive sweet smell of tobacco. A tavern ship lurked behind a distant island of rushes, sails furled, lanterns glimmering in the twilight and the shadows of men ambling about the deck. Despite the tavern's presence, the only sound was lapping water and the singing of the plantation hands.

The large wooden barrels on the dock were empty, but heavy. Chauco strained to push the first from the planks onto the potholed path leading up to the barn. Abraham rolled another barrel beside him.

"Why so happy," Chauco asked his friend.

"This is my seventh year of indenture, Mister John. Captain McMasters says to me today that I was twelve when I arrived at One Hundred Oaks, and after this season's crop I will be nineteen. I will be free of my bond. The captain has already set aside the fifty acres that will be mine by the coming spring."

"That is mighty, Mister Johnson."

"The goodness of my land may be too depleted from this year's crop to grow another of tobacco, but no matter. I plan to grow many acres of maize in this rich Virginian soil."

"You don't wish to return to your own land across the sea?"

Abraham shook his head, the glint in his eye dulling. "I have no family remaining there, and all I remember as a child is being afraid of the marauding, cannibal Imbangala. They enslaved our villages to make gold off the white man. My homeland means only slavery, or death. But here . . ." Abraham took in a deep breath of the sweet Virginia breeze, holding his barrel steady with his large, calloused hands. "Here in this land I will soon be free of my contract. It is here I may build my dream with Bessie." He gave the barrel a hearty push up the rise. When the men reached the barn, they positioned their load and then started the walk back for their next. "And you, my friend Mister John—Chauco—will you return to your people in the wood?"

"My parents, Arrow Feather and Blossom of Black Cherry, have journeyed to Orapax with my five brothers and the rest of the Powhatans. They are halfway to the Blue Ridge Mountains and far from the land taken by the white men. But my destiny is here with my wife and my child. It has always been the way of my people that the man joins the Clan and village of his wife."

Abraham nodded. "When does Matilda's contract expire?"

Chauco touched his thumb to each of his fingertips as he counted the years. "The original indenture was signed in England four summers ago. When Captain McMasters approved our union, he agreed I could reduce her time by lending my hand to the crops. But due to her being bedridden for several months after the birth of James, and now that we are to have a second child with the coming winter, it may still be two years before Matilda is unbound."

Abraham righted a barrel and waved for Chauco to take it. Then he grabbed another one for himself. "Perhaps the acres Captain McMasters assigns to you and Matilda will be near mine. Together we can grow our crops and maybe build a flour mill. I have seen a stone on my land that would do well for the grinding."

Chauco rolled his barrel up until it landed hard against the others by the barn.

Peering into the growing darkness toward the dock, Abraham counted the remaining barrels and sent four workers down to collect them. Then he grabbed the handle of the barn door and yanked it open so he and Chauco could enter. The pungency of the tobacco inside pressed heavy against them. It caused a tingling itch in Chauco's nose that would not abate no matter how much he rubbed at it. The ceiling was obscured by thousands of wilted tobacco leaves hung from lines crossing the width of the barn from one end clear to the other. The walls were likewise invisible—cloaked by sticks, lines, and open shelving draped with leaves, some still yellow, others that had turned a light tan.

"The leaves in the rear will be ready to strike by the morning," Abraham said, pointing to the tan ones. "I am certain the captain will agree."

They trod the length of the barn and Chauco listened carefully, knowing he would be responsible for reporting on crop stages once Abraham was free of his bond. They stepped lightly, for most of the floor, too, was strewn with leaves, laid out and covered with logs to press them flat and make them sweat in the heat of the barn. Abraham bent and pulled a leaf from beneath a log. It was large, dark, glossy, and moist. He gently pulled at the tobacco in his hands, stretching it as easily as the rubbed leather of a young doe.

"Almost the right amount of moisture," Abraham muttered. "These should be in case and ready to sort by the day of our Lord."

Chauco rubbed the leaf between his finger and thumb to feel the moisture. He held his fingers to his nose and sniffed. His nostrils tingled.

"No sign of mold," Chauco said.

"No, but we will leave the barn door ajar again tonight—"

A musket shot reverberated from somewhere near the barn.

They turned toward each other, then dashed for the door. The other bondsmen had just settled the barrels outside and looked around in confusion. Following Abraham's lead, they ran around the back of the barn, past the kitchen building and its garden, and down the slope toward the two cabins that housed Captain McMasters' eighteen bondspeople and their children.

The captain stood before the ramshackle buildings, the mouth of his musket lowered toward the dirt, his servants behind him. Chauco and Abraham came to a stop, their chests heaving from the run.

In the center of the lane, a white bondsman from another plantation cowered and cried. His master, Captain Jenkins, was beating him with a cane. The watching crowd flinched with each brutal thwack.

Abraham stepped over to his wife, Bessie, who was cradling Chauco's son. He wrapped his arms around her, and Chauco took James and pressed him against his breast, tight to his heart.

Captain Jenkins beat the young man—scarcely more than a boy—about the head and shoulders. His shirt had been torn and his back was etched with streaks of blood. His ear bled as he gripped his face, though it could not muffle the anguish of his cries.

"Come on, captain. You can stop that. You have him back now," Captain McMasters said.

"He's been nothing bar trouble since I bought him. Always running away." Captain Jenkins applied several more thwacks of his cane, and the boy collapsed onto his side. This seemed to incense Jenkins even more. He kicked the boy in the stomach, and then in the head. Then he sent a whack of his cane onto the boy's rump. It cut through his course breeches and snapped against raw flesh.

The boy was unconscious. Chauco thought that he might even be dead—a twisted, pathetic, pale carcass in the lane.

Captain McMasters fired his musket into the sky. "I must demand that you stop, Captain Jenkins. You are on my plantation and I will have no more of this cruelty."

Jenkins stopped, his face distorted and red with rage. He wiped the cane against his breeches, spitting in disgust at the boy lying still upon the dirt. He stretched out his fingers, wincing from holding his cane so tight. "Perhaps you want him," he said. "He still has four years to serve—or is it seven?" He sneered. "I'd gladly swap him for any of your Christians. But definitely not that half-breed." He waved toward Chauco. "Perhaps I'd even accept your Negro, but only if he contracts for another full seven-year term."

Chauco's heart thudded, and Bessie tightened her grip on Abraham with a grimace.

Captain McMasters let out an exasperated breath as he stared first at Jenkins, then at the boy, and then around at his own people. His gaze finally settled upon Abraham.

He hoisted his musket and pointed it squarely at Captain Jenkins.

"Get off One Hundred Oaks immediately and do not return, Captain. If the boy survives the night, tomorrow I will have my lead man bring to you twice what you paid for him."

Captain Jenkins turned on his heel and scurried down the lane toward his own plantation. "Nice doing business with you, Captain," he called over his shoulder.

* * * *

Abraham lifted the boy's broken body from the dirt and carried him into his cabin. He and Bessie pulled the rags from his body and checked for broken bones. His breathing was regular, but shallow. The fresh cane cuts crisscrossed his back and legs—a secondary layer over older, ropelike, purple welts that disfigured otherwise milky skin. Abraham ran a finger along each new laceration, scraping out the dirt and gravel before Bessie washed them with a stiff cloth dipped in boiling water. The boy only called out once as they tended to his wounds, but Bessie whispered in his ear the words of a mother and he seemed to fall into an even deeper unconsciousness.

"Looks like I got me my first son," Abraham said to Chauco, his usual happiness dented by worry.

Matilda arrived soon after the boy was wrapped in a blanket and placed on the slim, straw mattress Abraham and Bessie shared. Word had reached the kitchen of what had happened, and the mistress had excused Matilda earlier than usual to help with "the situation down the lane."

She nodded to Chauco with a concerned smile as she entered the cabin, then went straight to Bessie. They spoke quickly and quietly as they stood over the child, and Matilda ran the back of her hand across his forehead to feel for fever.

"The boy will live. We will make him strong," Chauco said, and Matilda squeezed his arm tenderly and took James from his grip.

She led the way out of the cabin to the side porch. The lane and the fields, the river and rushes were a deep purple under the rising moon. "We have to talk before supper," she said. With James cradled in one arm, she pushed the beaten boy's clothing into a wash bucket, and the water turned dark brown from the blood as she kneaded and squeezed. "I should be able to mend these before he needs them again," she muttered to herself.

Chauco kneeled beside his wife. He had never known another as beautiful as she—hair and eyes as black as raven, skin as white as summer clouds, a smile that made his heart sing. She allowed him to take James from the crook of her arm so she could work the breeches and shirt with both hands.

"Is something wrong?" Chauco asked. James reached for his father's face, small hands grasping at the smooth chin and thick lower lip.

For several minutes, Matilda kept at her chore. Then she stopped, pulled the dripping clothes from the bucket, and threw them hard as she could. They slapped against the porch railing and left a wet, bloody smear. Chauco pulled her into his arms, and her body, full with their second child, was cool against the heat of his own. He could see she wanted to cry but knew she wouldn't—not in the lane where others might see. He pressed his lips against her forehead.

"What is it?"

"The mistress says Captain McMasters will be traveling to Jamestowne within the next month. He has business with the legislature."

Chauco nodded. "The captain is a member of the House of Burgesses. You know he often attends the assembly. It is his responsibility."

Matilda shuddered and pressed her face into his chest. "The mistress says she cannot abide it here at One Hundred Oaks, or on Mulberry Island. She says Jamestowne is unworthy of being called a town in any way, especially with the increasing attacks by the . . ." The words seemed to catch in her throat. "By the smaller villages surrounding it. As a lady, she is used to the fineries of a town with a church and a store, with people who follow the word of our Lord. She intends to have children, but not until she is acquainted with a schoolmarm who has her own schoolhouse."

Chauco went still, dreading what he knew was coming.

"The Master has promised that, when he returns from Jamestowne, they will sail for Massachusetts Bay Colony where he will secure a house for her in Trimountaine. There is talk of renaming it Boston after the very town she was born in back in Lincolnshire, and she has already developed a fondness toward residing there."

Chauco pressed his cheek to the top of Matilda's head, feeling only the heartbeat of his wife and son against his own. He knew the mistress would bring Matilda with her—she was far too skilled to leave in this swampland. But he would be required there on Mulberry Island, to discharge her covenant as quickly as possible.

Chauco ran his tongue over his lips, swallowing several times to wet his throat so his voice would not crack when he spoke. "You will do well in the Bay Colony, Matilda," he said in no more than a whisper. "Within two years I will pay your bond and then you can return to Mulberry Island. Perhaps by then James will be able to read, and he can teach me."

Squeezing his family tight in his arms, Chauco stared off out into the darkening tobacco fields, then up into the sky where not a single star shone.

P.J. Parker

A Model of Christian Charity
(1647 AD)

James rode low on King as the stallion galloped at full speed along the trail coursing the length of the Boston Neck, from Roxbury Village out onto the fortified peninsula of the great Puritan city. He passed the earthen wall and wooden palisades and onto Colburn's Field. Eight men were swinging from the gallows beside the gates—burglars, pickpockets, murderers, and Catholics. To one side, the Charles River marshes were alive with fowl; to the other, merchant ships were moored in Gallows Bay.

He kicked his boots into King's flanks, gaining speed as he passed threescore gray planked homes and storehouses, Cole's Inn, and the imposing whitewashed church with its spire shadowing market square.

The two dozen pillories around the square were full bar one. Two church elders oversaw their charges, determined the men and women ensnared should receive their full punishment and that passers-by should pelt rocks, fruit, or insults at those who had disobeyed the laws of the church—the laws of the city. Rebecca and her husband, Abner, were held on opposite sides of the square. James guessed they'd been seen kissing on their back stoop again. Mister Scott hung limp from the trunk of an Oak, his arms stretched and tied to the branches, his naked back a mess of lash cuts—the penalty for sleeping late on the day of our Lord. Isaac Mather was a particularly sorry sight. He'd been pilloried more times than anyone else James knew. The scars of the branded *T* on each of his palms had healed—for his vice of thieving. But now he had a fresh one on his forehead—bloody, puckering, and ragged from his hairline down through one eyebrow.

There was a secondary burn where his left nostril should have been. The elder wielding the iron must have lost his grip.

Under the glare of the elders, James dared not pass without throwing an apple. It hit the pillory just beside Isaac's tattered ear, which had been nailed to the wood so often it was now no more than a bleeding stump on the side of his head. There was little doubt Boston would soon see Mister Isaac Mather swinging from the gallows above the bay.

Within minutes James had passed through the center of town and rounded the curve of Mill Pond toward the McMasters estate under the shadow of Milne Hill. The house with its shuttered windows was framed by several steep, shingled gables and a tall stone chimney, silhouetted against the hill behind it. The barn and corral to the rear were open and empty save for a dozen hens and a large sandy-colored sow that slept in the dust.

James jumped from King's back and passed the reins to the Negro houseboy without even a nod, before climbing the porch steps to the homestead.

"Ma?" he called as he strode into the main hall. "Ma!" he called up the stair.

Jemima pushed the kitchen door open a crack.

"Mistress McMasters been down in church all morning, Mister James."

James removed his buckle-trimmed hat and tightened the ribbon holding his hair back.

"Hungry?" Without waiting for an answer, Jemima turned to go back into her kitchen.

A goose lay on the kitchen bench, plucked and half stuffed. Onions and sweet potatoes were scattered across a baking tray. A plate of pole beans sat waiting to be stringed. James sat on a stool and grinned as Jemima handed him a well larded chunk of bread.

"What you smilin' at, Mister James?"

"Nothing, Jem . . . Nothing."

For all his twenty-one years, the kitchen had been the happiest room in the house for James. And Jemima had always been more of a ma to him than Mistress McMasters. Sometimes, as a child, he would sit for hours watching her work over the fire, preparing meals for the mistress and the others in the household. She would talk incessantly, but always with a smile in her heart and a keen ear for when she was called into the parlor.

He had often wondered if his own true mother would have been like Jemima, and deep-down knew that she would have. Though Mistress McMasters had taken him as her own when his ma and baby sister died in childbirth, it was Jemima who had cared for his every scraped knee and scolded him for any boyish outburst. She was just how a ma should be, and he loved her for it.

* * * *

In no real hurry to arrive at church for an afternoon of prayer and devotion, James trotted King down through Christopher Stanley's pasture and past a scattering of cattle before ambling along Boston's grandiose dockyards. Tall ships lined the wharves. Rows of barrels—stacked four and five high and heavy with rolled ropes of tobacco—waited to be hauled onto the ships for transport across the Atlantic to the home country. Wagons loaded with bales of cotton and crates of tea rocked back and forth while foremen cracked whips to ensure the white bondsmen and-boys did not slacken. The scene smelled thick with sweat, tobacco, sea air, and horse dung. Standing up in the stirrups, James marveled as one of the heavily laden tall ships was hauled back from the dock by a score of men and salt-encrusted lines. Men scurried as canvasses unfurled, and the wind made the sails bloom and pulled the ship out into the open waterway.

James wished for nothing more than to enroll on one of Captain McMasters' merchant ships and sail away on an adventure. After he completed his studies, of course. It seemed far more exciting than the mistress's wish for him to be a clergyman.

The toll of church bells echoed throughout the city, and James reluctantly nudged his knees into King's sides.

"C'mon boy, time to attend to duty."

He was one of the last to enter the church, the clang of the steeple bell still reverberating in unison with the creak of termite-ridden floorboards and parishioners settling onto uncomfortable seats. The intense stare of the pastor caught his attention from the pulpit, and he saw Mistress McMasters' bonnet up in the front pew, bent low over her prayer book. James took a seat at the rear with Matthew and Tobias Jefferson, men of equal age and piety. They shuffled along the bench to give him room.

The sermon crept across the afternoon. Words of brotherly affection, cast against the absolute depravity of man after the fall of Adam, were interspersed with hymns and prayers and reverent mutterings of *amen*. Pastor Calvin's interpretation of the bible reiterated the impossibility of salvation except for those few, the Elect, who were predestined to enter Heaven. James knew the words and ideology well. Four years at Harvard College had taught him that even good works could not bring on God's saving grace—unless you were one of the preordained. And though he did not yet feel it, his studies— and the cane the mistress used for more than just walking—might one day earn him grace, and inner peace, so that he, too, could be an avid crusader against sin.

* * * *

James sat with Mister Matthew Jefferson, a jug of beer, and good fellowship on the top of Milne Hill. The goose had been eaten for dinner with prayers of thanksgiving, the mistress had retired to the parlor to read her Bible, and Jemima had been left to clear the dining room, clean up the kitchen, and prepare for the next day's breakfast.

"Don't let me sniff no tobac on your breath when you return, Mister James," Jemima had warned him as he'd scuttled out the kitchen door.

James took a swig from the jug before handing it back to Matthew. He rolled onto his elbow in the dried grass and drew on his pipe. The sweet tobacco rolled around his tongue before curling out the side of his mouth. Below them, the lights of Boston blinked across pasture and road. The docks were ablaze with bonfires and lanterns as the work of the bondsmen continued through the night.

" 'Tis something to be proud of," he muttered, the pipe held firmly between his teeth.

Matthew wiped a drop of beer from his lips. "That it is, sir. Truly the Old Testament's 'City upon a Hill.' "

The men watched the city in the moonlight, swigging beer and puffing on their pipes. The gate that protected the peninsula had been closed, and beyond it were the lights of the lesser villages and homesteads scattered across the countryside.

"Tobias and I were thinking of starting our own town-building group," Matthew said. "We just need a few more good men, and some wives to be issued a parcel of land. Governor Winthrop says there's plenty of land for the taking. The woods and pastures just beyond"—he swept his arm toward the west— "aren't claimed yet."

"But those are the summer hunting grounds of the . . . of the red men." James looked down at his hands cradling his pipe. They were white, but there was more to his heritage than he had ever confided in his friend.

"Humph," Matthew said. "It is not summer now, and they're not using it. Governor Winthrop says it's unfettered and we may claim it as our own. We are, after all, the more advanced people—being white and Christian. Our rights supersede those of the heathens that lurk in the woods."

"Do you not believe all men are created equal in the eyes of God?"

"What in heavens are they teaching you up at Harvard, sir?"

"Nothing more than the purity of God's word," James said.

Matthew nodded. "And as both Pastor Calvin and Governor Winthrop explain, a man must know and adhere to God's word to have any rights at all. My mother taught me well to spot sin, in both myself and those around me. I have half a mind to report you to the pastor for a lecture—perhaps even a stern whipping or time in a pillory." He took another swig from the jug. "Next thing you know, you'll be talking like that seditious Hutchinson woman, with her heresy that any man may earn God's grace and have the Holy Spirit guide his life. Where would that leave the church, and our reliance on the pastors to interpret the Bible for us, if religion is made a personal experience?"

"Perhaps . . ." James sighed, mellowed by the beer and pipe.

Matthew laughed and slapped him on the back. "C'mon, sir. You will know God's intentions when you finish your studies, and then you shall be the pastor in our new town. We will build you a mighty church, and faith will be the strength of our streets. There we shall live in harmony and Christian brotherhood."

"It might be a while before we can find wives to complete the requirements for a town-building permit, Mister Jefferson. The pickings are slim here, and migration has slowed since the civil war started in England."

"Ah, there also I have a plan, sir. Our pilgrim cousins down at Plymouth share many of our values and—though they be less prosperous and less committed to the big designs we value—I am certain there will be a daughter or three we may preach to."

James smiled. "Maybe, but I don't know that I'm ready to settle down. Indeed, I think in my heart it is adventure I seek."

"What are you saying, sir? A new town is an adventure."

James shook his head as he stood up and stretched his legs.

"Best I return to the house. The mistress will want to pray with me before she retires." He turned and walked down the hill, leaving Matthew to lie in the grass with his pipe.

Most of the house lanterns had been dimmed, though Jemima was still washing up in the kitchen. When he walked in, she grabbed him by the arm and pulled his face close to sniff his breath.

"Mister James!" she scolded as she pushed him toward the wash-up bucket. Just as James knew she would—she always did—Jemima lathered her hands in the soap and, with one hand gripping his chin, thrust her soapy fingers into his mouth. She rubbed them across his tongue and around the inside of his cheeks. He could only hold steadfast and try not to gag.

"What'd I warn you about smokin'?" She took another handful of suds and pushed them into his mouth. "Don't you dare let the mistress smell that vile vice upon you. I have half a mind to whack you myself." She handed him a ladle of water, which he swished about his mouth and spat out the open window. Jemima took another sniff and placed her hands on his shoulders to get a good look at him. "There now, that's better. Now go help the mistress with her prayers. It's well past her bedtime and she will remind you that with her cane."

"Jem?" James said.

"Mmmm?"

He leaned against the bench as she went back to her washing. "Do you believe in God?"

"Don't you be talkin' to me about God and religion," she said without looking up. "That be for you white folks—for people who don't want to go to hell."

"But—"

Jemima held up a hand and listened to the noises of the house. James heard only silence, but he knew Jemima could tell exactly where the mistress was and what she was doing. She pulled James out the back door and down onto the step beside her.

"What's this all about, Mister James?"

James let out a sigh and slumped to rest his elbows on his knees, his face in his hands. Instinctively he reached for the comfort of the pipe in his vest pocket.

Jemima smacked him on the chest and then held out her hand. Reluctantly he pulled out the pipe and handed it to her. Her hand remained extended until he reached into his other pocket and pulled out his pouch of tobacco. Jemima's scowl softened, then turned into a friendly grin. She snickered. "Go get the lantern from above my bench."

She had already stuffed the pipe when he returned to the stoop. She leaned down to the flame and puffed on the pipe till it glowed. Then, resting her back against the wall, she stared up into the sky.

"There be somethin' up there, but I don't know what," she said, almost to herself. "Otherwise, why'd I be here?"

She handed the pipe to James, and he drew on it.

"I don't feel like I belong here, Jem," he said at last.

"You don't, Mister James! No more than me. But we are here, and if you white folks' God is part of that, then that's how it is. We all got to believe in somethin' to help us through—to make sense of things."

James took another puff before Jemima snatched the pipe away and slipped it between her teeth.

"I believe in God," James said. "And I know He will always be part of my life. I just don't think my life is here, being the one to tell others what He says. I want to know this country He has given us. I want adventure."

Jemima stared for several minutes at the night sky, the smoke from the pipe curling about her head.

"I know you got your eye on Captain McMasters' tall ships, and I got no doubt you will one day journey upon them, but you got to take it slow, Mister James. You got to let yourself live and see the adventure in each day. And if you don't want to be a preacher like the mistress wishes, well, handling that will be a part of your adventure."

"What do you think I should do, Jem?"

"You can always return to Mulberry Island, Mister James, and work your pa's farm."

James's thoughts turned dark, and he squinted. "No. Since pa was killed in the attack Mister Abraham Johnson and his twelve boys have been attending to the acreage. They have more need of it than I."

Jemima wrapped an arm around his shoulders and pulled him close.

"Well then, I think you should finish your studies so you know what you believe. Then you will know what road to walk."

P.J. Parker

The Day of Trouble is Near (1676 AD)

Clement stood behind the pulpit exactly where his father, James, had once stood. He pressed his hands against the leather family Bible opened to the Book of Romans, but he did not need to read its handwritten copperplate, as the words were part of his every thought.

"For I am convinced that neither death nor life, neither angels nor demons, neither the present nor the future, nor any powers, neither height nor depth, nor anything else in all creation, will be able to separate us from the love of God that is in Christ Jesus our Lord."

A thoughtful smile creased his face. The congregation in the small First Baptist Meetinghouse sat intently, listening. Children daydreamed out the glassless window, but he did not mind, as he knew they heard His words, and strength was building within them. The meetinghouse was of plain construction, with no adornment other than a wooden cross upon the wall, unlike the vulgar churches of their Puritan kin in Boston to the north. The doors at the front were open wide, for stragglers as well as to let the words of God filter out to those upon the steps and grassy slope. A group of natives stood beneath an oak outside—intent on hearing the word under the shade of God's creation. Clement's view out the front door reached down through the streets of Providence to where the Woonasquatucket and Moshassuck rivers converged. Tall ships were moored along the length of the Plantation docks. He hoped some of the bondsmen would come to the meetinghouse for his afternoon sermon. If not, he would visit them this evening and give them guidance through their indenture.

"We are blessed indeed to reside within the Colony of Rhode Island and Providence Plantations. The charter signed by our King Charles ensures religious freedom to those within its borders. No matter our judgments or consciences in matters of religion, this is the only settlement where we will remain unmolested for differences of opinion. I trust only that my reading of this book"—he held the Bible above his head— "will help you find your own way, on your private road to salvation." Clement hesitated. Usually a cool, steady breeze blew through the meetinghouse from the river, but today the air was hot and still. A plume of dark smoke rose from deep in the wood on the far side of the river. "But despite our own freedom, we must not forget our kindred to the north and the armageddon they now face."

He clasped his hands together, closed his eyes, and bowed his head.

"Our God, it has oft been said that the Day of Trouble is near. I fear it is now upon us. Though we have fled the puritanical doctrines stifling our cousins in the Bay Colonies, they are still our brethren and so we pray you watch over them. Their continued incursions into the red man's territories have caused much upset and bloodshed. Now the tide has turned, and it is our cousins and their families being slaughtered. God, help them. *Amen.*"

* * * *

The inside of the docks warehouse was dingy, but it was the only building in Providence large enough for the group to gather. Even so, men and boys leaned in through the windows to be a part of the proceedings. The room was crammed with English freemen and bondsmen, respected elders from the surrounding native tribes, several Dutch who had fled to Rhode Island after England's taking of New Amsterdam, and a handful of refugees from the north. There were no Negroes, no women.

Barrels, crates, hay bales, and sorting tables had been pushed to the side, with the younger men sitting cross-legged on top of them. Lanterns hung from the ceiling, burning with a black soot that darkened the overhead beams and drifted about the room.

"We should have nothing to fear from the native coalition that attacks the towns of New England," said Mister Brown, a respected leader of Providence. "Per our charter we have settled only land the local tribes have willingly given, with suitable recompense."

"That is true," said Chief Pageacoag. "You are our allies and we will fight at your side if those from the north encroach on either of our lands. The messengers who run the trails from the other confederacies have informed us the Wampanoag leader, Metacom—you white men call him King Philip—has a rage within him no longer quieted around a council fire. The past decades of troubled peace, and the Puritans' and Pilgrims' continual expansion from the coastal plains has incensed him, as his people have been pushed farther and farther from their ancestral hunting grounds. He has vowed to rid every pasture, woodland, and swamp of the white invader, and he has formed alliance with other tribes of similar mind." The chief wrinkled his brow. "The surrounding confederacies confirm he is making good on his promise. He has already slaughtered at least one third of all whites who inhabit this land, and many of my own brothers who have found kindred with yours."

The chief stood tall and showed no reaction at all as the warehouse filled with a roar.

"The Bay Colony cities are fortified to ward off such an attack. We are not," said someone in the crowd.

"Boston is said to be building a stronger stockade," said another.

Clement held up a hand for silence. "Chief Pageacoag, is there more information your scouts have secured?"

The chief nodded, stepping to the front of the room. His deerskin vest and pants were painted and fringed, resplendent against the dull, simple clothing of the white men.

"Within the last three seasons, entire tribes have been decimated," he said. "They exist no more. It was not enough that the Puritans brought their red spots and deadly hacking coughs to this land. When they could not use subterfuge to steal valleys and mountains and streams, they chose force. I can well understand why Metacom is angry." The chief glanced down at the dirt floor, rubbing at the back of his hand.

"I once had family who lived under the sovereign authority of the Narragansett tribal government. They were a peaceful nation. They educated their children in the ways of the land, cared for their sick and aged, and fished in the bays. But the white men to the north exacerbated their feud with another tribe by furnishing weapons and supplies to the enemy of those whose land they coveted." The chief straightened his back and took a deep breath through flared nostrils. "Most, including my own parents, grandparents, and four of my sisters, were killed outright. Those who were not were enslaved and sent away in the tall ships. The northern white man was victorious and he had his land."

None in the room seemed to dare even to breathe.

"We, too, are only farmers and fishermen," said one of the plantation hands.

"I know." The chief nodded toward Clement and Mister Brown. "I see what Metacom cannot. I see that you are my brethren."

Mister Brown placed his hand upon Chief Pageacoag's shoulder as he stepped forward to speak.

"King Philip, er . . . Metacom," he added, "has organized the forces of several tribes. The Wampanoags, Nipmucks, Pocumtucks, and Abenakis have converged with some remnant tribes to attack the towns across the full width of New England. Trappers, scouts, and refugees bring reports of unadulterated butchery and destruction. Without doubt, it appears that every English settlement west of Concord has been or will be wiped from existence. Indeed the whole of the Massachusetts Bay Colony may be destroyed outright."

"How is it Metacom's men can so easily subdue our own soldiers," Clement asked.

Chief Pageacoag held up his rifle. "The white men have mostly matchlock pistols and muskets that are slow to recharge. They rely on a constantly lit match to explode the gunpowder—a match that gives away a soldier's position in the dark of night, and which is made useless with rain. Metacom's men, like my own, have not only bows and arrows but flintlock firearms through our trade lines. Both are fast, accurate, and deadly."

Clement pressed his bible a little tighter against his chest.

At a sudden commotion outside, everyone turned toward the large double doors as a native ran into the warehouse. He was athletic and sinewy, wearing only the skin apron of a runner, but he was slicked with sweat as he pushed through the crowd. His chest was heaving as he gulped for breath, and reported to Chief Pageacoag in the chopped language of his people—a staccato of words that made the chiefs stiffen and grip their weapons.

Chief Pageacoag's brow furrowed as he sought the English words for translation. "Mister Brown, there is no time left to establish defenses for this town. I can recommend only that you abandon Providence immediately."

"What?" Mister Brown asked. "What did your scout say?"

"No white man's town or plantation exists for the full length and width of the upper Connecticut River Valley. All have been razed, their people slain by hatchet, arrow, and buckshot. Metacom's alliance has now swung across lower Massachusetts and entered your Colony of Rhode Island."

"But our charter—"

"—is no more than a piece of bark with magic symbols they do not recognize or respect. They know only that you are white and you do not understand the soil beneath your feet."

The messenger leaned toward the chief and spoke again, quickly and quietly. When he was finished, the chief turned back toward the crowd.

"Your town of Central Falls," the chief said.

"That's less than a day's walk north!" Clement shouted, his eyes wide.

The chief nodded. "It has just been attacked. A group of Metacom's warriors are now heading toward Rehoboth on the far side of the river. They will undoubtedly burn the docks, buildings, and meetinghouses of Providence within two nightfalls. If you stay here, you will die."

* * * *

Clement kneeled amongst the headstones scattered though the wood behind the First Baptist Meetinghouse. Knowing it was his last chance to pay his respects, he placed his hand on the stone that marked his family's grave and wiped at the cobwebs covering the epitaph reading simply: *James, Verity, and Prudence—loving father, mother, and sister of Clement.*

It had been nine years since their deaths—Verity's in childbirth with Prudence, and James's of a broken heart soon after. Still, hot tears stung Clement's eyes and wet his cheeks.

A spider crawled from the tombstone onto Clement's finger. With care, he turned his hand until it crept back onto the stone and began to repair its web.

He looked down upon an abandoned Providence. Families had fled with their native brethren to the islands in the south. The docks were deserted, the last of the tall ships, in full sail, only just visible in the haze far down Providence River. The authorities rode their mounts from street to street, lane to lane, house to house to ensure all were empty. Across the waterway, the woods and bayous were smothered in a thick, black canopy of smoke—the sooty remnants of the township of Rehoboth. It smelled acrid, sharpened by the stench of burnt flesh.

The whoop and holler of Metacom's warriors was fearsome as they crossed the river in makeshift canoes. It pumped a streak of uncertainty, of ungodly terror, through Clement's heart. He had little time left. He ran into the meetinghouse and fetched his Bible and a small treasured gift from his father. He shoved both into the inside pocket of his overcoat and secured the button. With a nod toward the cross, he hurried out to his horse and wagon, overflowing with the possessions of his neighbors.

And then the plantation docks exploded.

Fire coursed along the wharves and leapt high into the air above warehouses and stores.

Clement stood on the apron of the wagon, scanning the town—his town—to determine his best route. Alliance warriors were running the lower streets, touching torches to buildings as they went. Markets, churches, stables, barns, and homes flared up, one after another, until Providence was delineated in flames.

An authority rode past Clement at full gallop. "Make haste, Pastor," he yelled.

Flintlocks fired into the air with whoops of victory in a language Clement was unfamiliar with. It echoed less than two lanes distant. He dropped down onto the wagon's bench and urged his horse forward, the wagon lurching and jolting across the ruts of the curb and onto the lane.

Arrows and shot sang through the air around him.

A single flaming arrow thwacked into a bag of grain on his load.

Then a second.

He dared not look over his shoulder. He could not bear to see the meetinghouse his father had built aflame.

Clement flicked the reigns hard and bellowed at his horse. She took off as fast as the load would allow, the wagon rattling and creaking as it pitched side to side on their way toward the outskirts of Providence.

Behind him the once-serene streetscape sparked and flamed. Black smoke plumed and churned into the sky with an escalating thunder. Even at a distance, Clement could feel the heat reaching toward him, willing to consume all in its path.

He passed a barn just as it ignited. Flames blasted out the open doors with a horrendous roar. Clement's horse recoiled, disobeying the whip. She turned to gallop haphazardly down a side alley—barely wide enough for the wagon. The vehicle lurched on the turn as it struck into the narrow gap. Clement held the reigns tight as the wheel hubs scraped against the planking on either side, ripping a façade from the posts and flinging it across the cobbles behind. The fire coursed down the lane behind them, much faster than the horse's frantic stride. It licked every timber of their route, but still the horse ran, her rump foamed and bloody from the whip.

Clement urged the horse into a broader lane that led away from the city center, but alliance warriors jumped out from the shadows— buck naked, save for skin aprons and stiff belts loaded with arrows, tomahawks, and guns. They were heavily tattooed, the top halves of their faces painted blood red. One had the shape of a blackened hand imprinted across his mouth and cheeks. They stood without fear, taunting, lifting their weapons toward Clement and his transport. There was no other way but straight through them.

Clement cracked his whip and the horse screamed as she galloped at full speed—much faster than the wagon and its wheels were built to withstand. Jumping from the bench, Clement pushed himself flat against the floor, praying the front apron—and God— would protect him from the warriors' weapons.

Several shots fired at once, loud and terrible, followed by an onslaught of arrows. Some shattered against the bench while the rest struck the wagon's apron and cargo. None hit the horse, and Clement thanked God.

Searing pain abruptly cut along the length of Clement's arm. The agony pulled the breath from his lungs, made him lightheaded, constricted his throat into a gagging convulsion. But he flexed and stretched the torn limb, drenched in blood, to whip the horse and urge her on.

"Faster! Faster!" he screamed through clenched teeth.

They passed through the group of warriors, and they scattered.

He caught a glimpse of the flintlocks trained upon him, and again the deafening screech of shot passed close to his ear. The ache in his shoulder increased tenfold and blood splattered across his face. His horse shrieked in terror.

Clement's last memory of Providence was his face slamming into the front apron as his transport careened out onto the open southern road.

* * * *

The spring and summer were spent on Aquidneck Island, south of the colony. Skirmishes with the enemy kept to the rocky north and eastern shoreline—a ways from the stockaded village shared by native and colonial families. Though healed, Clement's arm was weak, his hand unable to grip anything smaller than an apple. The forest became his meetinghouse to share scripture. He read his Bible to those who wished to hear it, and when he was alone he read it silently, determined to find any passage that might comfort those in the makeshift village.

Some of the men had returned to Providence to rebuild and fortify after its destruction. Nonetheless, Clement had chosen to stay to support those who sought refuge on Aquidneck as the war continued across New England.

He had lost weight, food was scarce; his overcoat hung from slim shoulders. Crops had long been burned or gone untended as fighting continued, the bodies of the slain from both sides—men, women, and children—left scattered across the deserted fields or hastily buried in shallow graves amongst the ashes of the Three Sisters.

Clement looked up from his Bible as Chief Pageacoag sat down beside him on the grass.

"Does your book help you understand this?"

Clement nodded as the chief handed him some pemmican. Their fingers touched, and Clement was reminded of the loving grip of his own father's hand when he'd given him the family Bible.

"Eat slowly, my brother. There is little remaining in our stores."

The pemmican was good on an otherwise empty stomach. It tasted of bison and chokecherry.

"Is there any news from the north, Chief Pageacoag?"

"Our messengers run between here and our allies across the northeast. We know the smaller towns and plantations have been abandoned as the colonials retreat to their fortified cities, and that my own brothers and sisters have retreated as well." He sighed and attempted to rub the weariness from his eyes. "Metacom's alliance, however, still evokes much bloodshed on both sides—the grief augmented as food becomes less available."

Clement closed his bible and placed it in his lap.

"A handful of the walled towns along the lower Connecticut River Valley have survived," the chief said, "but their workforce is detained to provide security. They are unable to produce even what food they need within their own stockades." He picked up Clement's Bible and opened it to a page he could not read. He studied the black marks etched across the parchment before returning his attention to Clement. "Your own king from across the blue pond ignores his people's plight. If I were him, I would have sent food in the tall ships. Food and guns."

Clement nodded slowly. "It is a war of attrition."

"Yes. He who does not starve will win."

Kack-kack-kack-kack, came the call of a duck hawk.

Chief Pageacoag rose to his feet as the cry echoed through the forest canopy. He walked to the edge of the clearing, held his hand to his cheek, and whistled the song of the thrush. Clement listened for an answer, and the *kack-kack-kack-kack* echoed once more. The chief stared into the undergrowth, waiting. Then the pad of swift feet came near, with the messenger, Praying Sakunk.

The chief spoke with the messenger, and though Clement listened he understood neither their words nor hand symbols. In the end, the chief appeared relieved as he placed his hand on Sakunk's shoulder and led him over to Clement.

"Metacom—King Philip—is dead. Our mutual enemy has been beheaded, drawn, and quartered—his hands taken to Boston, his head to Plymouth Bay for display."

The blood drained from Clement's face. He pressed his Bible against his heart.

"And his followers?"

"They are dispersing," said the chief. "Heading to the northern lands. They will without doubt avoid the hunting grounds of the *Haudenosaunee* who have long been the enemy of any warring tribe."

* * * *

Clement journeyed alone toward Virginia. He had given his mare to Chief Pageacoag and walked the trails with nothing but his Bible, a gifted flintlock, and the thoughts of bloodshed that consumed him. A large proportion of the colonial population had been annihilated, but five times as many natives. Whether by starvation, disease, or execution, complete tribes and family lines had ceased to exist. Though he could not reconcile the useless loss of life, he was comforted to some small degree by the words of Ecclesiastes: "A time to love, and a time to hate; a time for war, and a time for peace." Yes, a time for peace—as fragile as it might be.

He spent most nights alone by a campfire but was gladdened when finally he joined with others—a lone family of the Delaware who shared with him their food and stories. They camped on the palisades overlooking the River that Flows Two Ways.

The fire cracked and spat, recalling memories of Providence. Bobcat meat lay charred amongst the stones, its mottled skin hanging from a tree. Across the broad waterway, the hilly, forested, autumn-colored island of Mannahatta was twinkling with tribal and colonial fires. To the south, where the tip of the island struck into a bay, the larger bonfires of Fort James, New York, glowed beneath the comfort of the deep-blue night sky.

"Do you think this is the end of the fighting," asked one of the Delaware children as he cuddled under a blanket.

"I do not know."

Clement slept close to the fire with the warmth of the family surrounding him, refusing to rouse until a chattering groundhog called for him to wake.

* * * *

Clement could see the smoke hanging above Jamestowne from more than a day's journey away. He should have slowed his pace at the thought of what lay ahead, but instead his stride and heartbeat quickened. The scorched remains of an Indian settlement smoldered before the thin, soggy isthmus leading out to the swampy island of the city.

Muskets boomed, and he struck through the blackened bog, wary of traveling the open road. Great trees had toppled in a recent inferno—even now, many still glowed white and red. The closer he got to Jamestowne, the more evident its devastation. Stockades, barracks, barns, corrals, homes, and stores—even the daubed church, nearly seventy years old—were piles of debris and ash scattered across the rutted slope. The shoreline and marshy forest flared as shot after shot resounded. The repetitive clatter of flintlocks, the explosion and puff of musket fire, the broken scream of men who'd not yet succumbed to their wounds—they were all that was left to signify this place had once been alive.

Two merchant ships were anchored in the river, their cannon aimed ashore.

Clement threw himself down behind a log, and its smoldering stench caught in his throat. He looked around, frantic.

Several hundred men were scattered around the clearing that was once Jamestowne. Those still alive hid behind logs, or the crumbling stone remains of furnace chimneys, or hillocks of toppled brickwork. White men and Negroes in the rags of indenture huddled with colonials, loading their weapons, rising from their hiding places to take their shots, then hunkering down once more. At least three tribes of natives had bows and arrows and flintlocks in hand. Down the slope, behind what used to be a storehouse at the head of the burned-out wharf, were men of means, their clothing muddy and torn, with natives and bondsmen, plantation hands, mariners, and a handful of young boys, all armed.

A merchant's cannon discharged, and smoke billowed as the ball careened over the water to crash into the bank.

Clement pulled the powder horn from his jacket and prepped his flintlock. Then he rested it on the singed remnants of the log and sighted down the shot tube, turning it slowly in an arc, uncertain where to shoot. His Bible dug into his side as he set his finger firmly against the trigger.

He didn't understand. There was no way he could know which side he was supposed to be on. He swung the flintlock from the log and crouched behind it once more.

"Cease this insidious play for power, Mister Bacon," called someone from the foreshore.

Clement peered around the log, and another man yelled angrily from amongst the crowd of bondsmen and Negroes.

"What? So we can continue under your weak leadership? You have done nothing to stop the natives' attacks against our plantations. You sit in your chair in the House of Burgesses, weakening our economy, levying unfair taxes, appointing your friends to power. But you do nothing for the safety of the common Virginian."

A single musket fired, followed by an interminable silence.

Then the man at the water spoke again. "And you, sir, are nothing but a murderer. You buy your buckskin brigade with brandy, incite them to disorder, and kill the very tribes that have ensured our continued existence during this trying year. You desire rebellion for rebellion's sake, Mister Nathanial Bacon—no more than a vendetta for personal gain."

Around the other side of the log, Clement saw an indentured Negro stand and take aim. He jolted back when his musket discharged, and there was a guttural yell from down by the wharf, followed by several retaliatory shots.

The dialogue continued until sundown, the fusillade diminishing, and by the end of it Clement had decided which side to join.

When the moonlight skidded across the river and the bondsmen, both white and Negro, clustered around their fires, Clement scuttled down the slope, among the friendly natives to the men by the wharf. They were climbing into boats sent ashore by the merchants, and he helped push one of the vessels, sloshing through the water and rolling himself over the gunwale to tumble into the hull. He explained his circumstance to those aboard as they rowed toward the waiting ships.

The gentleman who had volleyed with Mister Bacon was introduced to Clement as Governor Berkley. Berkley stared across the water toward the remnants of Jamestowne, looking beaten and pallid gray.

The river slapped repeatedly into the side of their craft.

"There is not enough land, or women, for these insurgents to be freed of their covenants. They cannot be trusted and will certainly rise again at the first opportunity."

Someone muttered something that Clement did not catch.

"Yes, yes, you are correct," Governor Berkley said. "The Negroes, we can handle."

The Ship (1700 AD)

Mister Clement —
c/o One Hundred Oaks
Mulberry Island, via Jamestowne
Colony of Virginia, British America
March 1, 1700

Dearest Mama and Papa,

I was much relieved to receive your letter before the Henrietta sailed from New York Harbor. I trust you are both well. Please give my love to Thaddeus, Eli, and Clementine.

Your news of the Johnson Family has filled me with an anger I know you both share. We have often discussed the deporting of free black men and their families throughout Virginia. But I thought the Abraham Johnson family was above such unforgivable harshness. They have been productive members of the Mulberry Island community for over seventy years, their mill the largest in the region. To forcibly send them from their duly gained property to some Godforsaken Caribbean island fills me with a dread I cannot place into words.

They have already suffered so under the reprehensible law of '61, under which the contracts of all indentured Negroes increased from seven years to life. And then burdening all offspring with their mother's status. I am disgusted, and despite what is written in the Old Testament, I see this act as nothing more than racial oppression in this modern day and age.

Indenture may be key to colonial growth, and our land could not flourish without it. But it is villainous to take away entirely a freedom that has been earned, without any hope of redemption.

I have had many misgivings about my service on the Henrietta, but of course it is too late as the Gulf Stream has flung us far out into the Atlantic toward England. I will see through my contract, but I fear the journey ahead, as my thoughts on indenture and slavery have more than muddied my original intentions for adventure on the high seas.

The only saving grace—as bleak as any future may be—is that you were able to secure ownership of the enslaved remnants of the Johnson family. Under your mastership, they will continue to live with dignity not afforded on many other plantations. I am eternally grateful you have saved Theodosia Johnson from deportation or sale. Regardless of her status and all its inherent difficulties, she is the one I love, with whom I intend to sow a future upon my return.

March 7, 1700

This week, our northeasterly sail has been quite mild. The few squalls—most usually at sunset—have been met with a flurry of activity aboard our vessel. A deckhand named Mister Jack Barker has told me stories of merchants lying dormant in the middle of the ocean, their canvasses ripped to shreds, their supplies dwindling, their crew resorting to cannibalism. I know not whether his stories are true, but they send shivers down my spine over a shared pipe and our daily quota of rum.

My chief duty is to ensure the continued condition of the cargo below decks. The hold is filled to the brim with tobacco and hemp, and they make my nose itch as I stay most all hours in the dark to safeguard against leaks in the hull that might cause damage. The tobac ferments and takes on the sweet smell of the rum—the previous contents of the barrels now used. It is much to my liking—smoother and more fragrant in the pipe than the unfermented leaf.

The captain says we will arrive in Bristol within the week. There we will unload our cargo and take on a full hull of copper, cloth, guns, ammunition, beads, ironware, and rum for bartering at the next port of call. We have been promised a full hour to explore Bristol before we sail on to Africa and then back to the Americas.

I will send this letter from Bristol Harbor, England. We shall see if it makes it to your hands before I myself return in three to four months' time.

With best love, &c.,
I am affectionately your son,

Jethro

* * * *

Mister Clement —
c/o One Hundred Oaks
Mulberry Island, via Jamestowne
Colony of Virginia, British America
April 15, 1700

Dearest Papa,

You must swear on your heart you will never divulge the contents of this letter to Mama. My heart

*would break were she to know. Even now I cannot
believe what Mister Jack Barker has disclosed to me,
but as the Henrietta skims along the African Coast I
know in my gut what he speaks is truth.*

    *Sincerely I do not think I will send this letter.
More likely I will confide to you my experience in the
back paddock of One Hundred Oaks, where we may sob
upon one another's shoulders.*

    *We must love our slaves, Papa. We must love
them as hard as we are able. We must give them the
respect they deserve.*

    The Henrietta . . .

A bead of sweat dripped from Jethro's nose onto the parchment. He looked up as a mighty gust filled the mainsail and foresail. The jib at the front of the vessel was flapping erratically in the stiffening breeze as Mister Jack Barker and another deckhand struggled to secure it. The *Henrietta* coursed through the choppy sea, spray blasting over the prow to drench the men clinging to the sprit. The creaks and groans of the ship intensified as she pulled in closer to the shoreline, where a lush mountain range rose from the sea, cut by bays and cavernous gorges.

Shirtless in the stifling heat, with breeches and moccasins that had seen better days, Jethro ran across the deck and jumped down into the hold. He secured his papers, ink, and quill in the niche above his hammock before running back through the cargo. Steadying himself against the bulkhead, he swayed as the *Henrietta* lunged side to side, waves crashing into the hull and the keel, tossing her up and slapping her back down again.

There was a deep, grating rumble, and Jethro ran toward the sound and placed his ear against the groaning wood. The hull was damp against his cheek—it always was—but the planks were bulging inward. The *Henrietta* suddenly surged to port. The bulge lessened, but water came spraying through the cracks along with loosened wadding and tar.

Jethro stuck his head up through the hatch and yelled, "Mister Barker!" before scurrying for the barrel of pitch and heap of rags. Jack came to his side, drenched by sea spray but no wetter than Jethro, who was covered in a briny sweat from the confines below deck. Quickly they pushed rags into the cracks and slathered them with tar. Another bung came loose, and sea water gushed into the hold. Jethro stuffed it with wadding and Jack smeared it with a thick layer of the black pitch. Then they stood in silence for over an hour, listening to the *Henrietta*, inspecting their work, and pressing their fingers along the planks to ensure all was secure.

"The old girl is fine," Jack finally said. He clapped Jethro on the back.

The ship's bell struck four times.

"We'll hit port before the bell rings five," Jack said as the two of them hoisted themselves up through the hatch into the afternoon sun.

The *Henrietta* passed several majestic forested promontories, populated by screeching noises Jethro could not identify. A throng of biting insects hung in the air with an intolerable buzz, and strange, colorful birds flew overhead. A cragged cliff face pulled back to reveal a broad curving bay, its sandy rim crashed by breakers. Slavers were moored in the calmer waters at its center with British flags flying.

Jethro gulped back the vomit rising in his throat. He felt the blood drain from his face and, despite his tanned skin, he knew he was suddenly very pale—like a booger.

From the shoreline all the way out to the undertow were hundreds of dead bodies—naked black carcasses bobbing and dipping in the water. Some had putrefied beyond recognition as human. Twoscore or more eddied in a miserable clump. Some had been mauled by carnivorous fish—raw pink flesh exposed against dark skin.

The wind shifted.

The stench was excruciating.

Jethro ran to the gunwale and vomited into the surge.

The *Henrietta* skimmed forward, her sails full, nudging carcasses aside. Jethro shuddered and retched as bodies caught on the ship's barnacles to be dragged in her wake. He turned when he felt a comforting hand press upon his back, and Jack was there, holding a ladle to his lips. After Jethro had a sip, Jack dipped it in the bucket again and threw the water across Jethro's face.

Jack gave a single nod of understanding, his countenance stony but his eyes watering in empathy. He tied a wet kerchief about his lower face then dipped another in the water bucket, pressed it to Jethro's nose and mouth, and knotted it at the back of his head. He lifted Jethro to his feet, turned him to lean against the gunwale, and wrapped an arm around his trembling shoulders as the *Henrietta* drew in beside the flotilla of slavers.

The other ships' crews stared at them without emotion, their lips pursed, their faces tight, as if to stop any sentiment rising from their own thoughts.

The captain barked his orders and the longboats were readied to be lowered.

"Come on," Jack said, urging Jethro toward the large grilled hatch in the middle of the main deck. He lifted the grating and he and Jethro jumped into the hold.

"You okay?"

Jethro nodded.

The two men stared at one another but uttered no more.

Three more hands jumped into the hold. They formed a chain and passed the cargo up onto the deck, where others passed it into the longboats. They hauled crate after crate of guns and ammunition, followed by reams of cloth and baskets of beads. Ropes were flung into the hold to heave the heavy barrels of rum. Jethro wrapped a rope around a barrel and passed it to another hand who tied it into a slip knot.

"They're not human, you know—if that helps." The deck hand snickered.

Jethro's eyes went wide, his thoughts on Theodosia. Anger consumed him and he pulled his arm back and threw his fist into the deckhand's face. Then he lunged over the barrel and tackled him, his arms swinging wild, punching as hard as he could.

"Jethro!" yelled Jack from the far end of the hold.

But Jethro continued to pummel the deckhand. They grabbed at each other, fists bloody and bruising. An elbow crunched into Jethro's cheek followed by the back of a scabby fist. His vision blurred as he heard his jaw crack and then was manhandled roughly against the hull.

"Jethro!" Jack yelled again.

A blow to the face twisted his neck and another knocked the wind from him. When he landed on the ground, a foot cracked against his chest and groin—again and again. His body was numb with pain, his eyelids swelling to blind him.

"Theo," he gasped as the last of his breath was kicked from his lungs.

* * * *

By the captain's order, Jethro was manacled to the foremast and thrashed. The whip left two dozen deep gashes in his back that cut to the rib. He hung limply from the cuffs—the iron slicing into swollen and bleeding wrists. His back and legs were caked in sticky blood; his chest, breeches, and bare feet in his own vomit. Flies buzzed and bit. He felt as if his arms would be pulled from their sockets yet he had no energy to stand. When saltwater was thrown across the wounds, Jethro twisted in agony, but he refused to scream. One of his molars shattered from clenching his jaw so tight.

* * * *

Jethro awoke to the rocking of the *Henrietta* and the new day's sun burning into the slits of his eyes. The ship was quiet, but he was unable to turn his head to see whether the deck was empty. His mouth tasted of dried blood and vomit. The stench of the bay cut into his nostrils and he convulsed, but his aching stomach was empty. From the corner of his eye he saw the water churn, and a great gray fish jettisoned from the waves, its dorsal glistening, a broken black corpse in its bloody mouth. The monster turned and rolled back into the surf with its catch.

His head hung limp for hours before he finally raised his face toward the shore.

The captains and their shipmates clustered before a wooden corral filled with chained Negroes, indiscriminate of gender or age.

The captain of the *Henrietta*, resplendent in vermillion, leaned against the palings, poking a stick into the corral, waving furiously and yelling loud words that echoed across the water. He motioned toward the cargo his men had brought ashore then climbed over the fence in amongst the terrified produce.

Outside the corral were forty or so naked, emaciated Negroes chained together at the neck. The iron chain was as thick as a forearm—meant to hold the weight of an anchor. Three in the middle of the fettering were dead, one of them a woman. The rest dragged their burden as a shipmate came at them with a whip, slashing them, thumping them with the butt, shooing them away—diseased, useless, no future but starvation and death on the sand, of no value to anyone.

A melancholy spectacle reminiscent of hell, Jethro thought.

The captain of the *Henrietta* urged several Negroes out of the corral. The remnants of any clothes were ripped from their bodies so they could be closely inspected. With whips they were made to dance, to display their flexibility and wellbeing, their masculine and feminine attributes. One Negro, who Jethro guessed was about the same age as himself, limped on his left foot, though even from a distance he could tell the young man was strikingly handsome and virile. Jethro's entire body tensed as the captain pulled his pistol from his belt and shot the injured man point-blank in the face. The others jumped and danced higher.

The selection of cargo continued throughout the day. Those traded for stowage on the *Henrietta* were chained and dragged, wailing, into the longboats. Their fear cut through Jethro, and his whole body quaked as he wiped angry tears from his cheeks.

The ship's surgeon climbed back aboard, followed by the first mate, who held a logbook, and the second who stoked the fire box and grabbed up the branding iron.

"Number 1," the surgeon said. "Healthy male Negro. About twenty years of age."

The first mate made a note in the logbook. The second lifted his iron and burned a number 1 into the slave's shoulder. The man shook violently, his mouth wide and gulping frantically for air, his eyes rolling back into his head. He was prodded across the deck and down into the hold by several deckhands.

"Number 2: healthy male Negro, ten years of age."

The boy was logged and branded. His high-pitched scream and incoherent pleading caught in Jethro's throat.

"Number 3: healthy female Negro, late teens." Touched. Logged. Branded.

The *Henrietta* was smothered in the stench of burning flesh and vomit, the pitiful moans as her hold was slowly packed.

The first mate finally closed his log on number 162, a powerful black man of determined and proud countenance. He held the surgeon's gaze as the dark flesh of his bicep puckered open and cauterized under the red-hot iron. He was thrown toward the hold; his demeanor never faltered.

The sun set a dark, bloody red.

Then the wind filled the *Henrietta's* sails and she pulled away from the bay out into the open sea.

* * * *

"You're lucky the cap'n didn't leave you in irons for the rest of your contract."

Jethro winced as saltwater was splashed across his wounds. His two deepest lash cuts needed cauterizing by the same iron used on the cargo.

Jack pulled him close to whisper in confidence. "You need to do your job, sir, or you will never see land again."

Jethro nodded.

The *Henrietta* coursed through the surge, her sails seeking the trade winds that would thrust her across the middle passage back to British America.

With a chunk of rock-hard bread and both his and Jack's quotas of rum in his gut, Jethro went below deck to do his duty—inspect the cargo and ensure its viability during the crossing. He lowered himself into the hold with dread as the darkness and stink squeezed him tight. The air was putrid—the heat and moaning oppressive. His eyes watered, and he held his damp kerchief against his mouth and nose. The men and boys had been packed into the tight shelving that lined both sides of the hull. The central aisle of the *Henrietta's* hold showed only row above row of naked feet and ankles bound together by heavy chains and irons.

Jethro trod slowly, peering into the narrow shelving as feces, bile, and urine squished between his toes. The cargo was secure, unable to turn in its confinement, flesh pressed firmly against wood and other flesh. It howled and sobbed. It yelled in different languages. He stopped next to a pair of feet. Though the ankles were black, the soles were as pink as his own. Without thought, he reached up to touch the rosy flesh. His fingers had hardly tapped it when it recoiled in fear, with a loud sob from the shelf.

Jethro cringed. He wanted to apologize, but was unable to with the tightness of his throat. He felt ashamed.

The women and younger children were held in a bay close to the crew's quarters, which could only lead to trouble on the journey ahead. As he entered the space, the cargo crouched in the dark, pressed themselves against the side of the hold, and scuttled away from him. He held out a hand, but the panic and crying grew louder, and so he let them be.

He stepped out swiftly into the crew quarters and closed the door behind him, then leaned against the door and took several deep breaths. He closed his eyes and hit the back of his head against the wood that separated him from the hold. He started to pray but the words felt hollow, so he just sobbed.

* * * *

The hull held tight during the crossing—no sign of leakage— and for that Jethro was grateful. He regularly went above deck to pull up a bucket of seawater, which he carried down into the hold to pitch into the crammed shelving. It not only washed the filth of confinement into the central aisle where he could dispose of it, but also cooled the freight from the stifling heat. The women and children were allowed above deck for most of the daylight hours, but the men were allowed out of the hold only one bay at a time, for a few minutes' exercise and the same inedible bread the crew ate. Though the men were chained, weak, and uncertain on their feet, all deckhands aimed their loaded flintlocks. Jethro could not see how they posed any real threat.

But he was wrong.

A wild screaming came from the main deck, and he dropped his bucket and scrambled up from the hold. The sun was harsh and burning, the sails full, the *Henrietta* creaking loud on the fourteenth day of the crossing. Number 37 was running in a frantic circle. The side he had been laying on for weeks was covered in bruises and boils. He yanked at the chain that secured him to four others—including the giant number 162. The first mate yelled and fired a warning shot up toward the sky, but still 37 jerked at the chain, struggling to throw himself overboard into the foam. He jabbered and screamed in an indiscernible language.

Another warning shot.

The ship pitched sideways and the entire chain gang fell awkwardly to their knees. Using the slack in the chain, 37 launched himself over the gunwale. His weight yanked the chain tight, pulling everyone in the gang toward the edge. Number 162 slammed into a wooden capstan and grabbed it with all his strength to halt the fall. The first mate fired his pistol again, but none of the crew dared to move.

Jethro ran to 162, pressed his shoulder against the Negro's, and grappled with the chain. They pulled at the fetter, its links thumping as they were wrenched one by one over the rail. Jethro and 162 leaned over and grabbed 37 by the arms and hauled him back onto the deck where he collapsed in a miserable, howling heap. His flesh had been ripped and torn by the *Henrietta's* barnacles, and his arm was broken and twisted at a strange angle.

The first mate strode over and shot the unviable cargo in the chest, then a deckhand unlocked the shackles and hoisted the broken, dead body of 37 into the water.

"Good work, Jethro." The first mate motioned with his pistol toward 162. "That one is valuable."

"But what about . . ." Jethro gazed blankly toward the churning gray waters.

"No concern. The insurance company will cover the loss of 37."

* * * *

Despite several quarrels and disturbances both below and above deck, the *Henrietta* lost only thirty-five of her freight on the two-month crossing. All were for reasons covered by insurance, which kept the captain satisfied and in high spirits. He studied his logbook each night, calculating and recalculating the value stowed below.

When the coastline of the colonies appeared on the leeward, Jethro felt like less than what he once was. He dreaded seeing his parents. He dreaded his first touch with Theodosia Johnson. He dreaded himself and his "adventure."

Within two days of making Virginia, each slave was brought above deck and inspected by the surgeon. The skin and flesh of the elbows, hips, and shoulders of numbers 12, 63, and 101 had been entirely rubbed off by the motion of the ship, leaving their bones bare. Boiling, black tar was slathered over the wounds to disguise them. Numbers 54, 77, 104, and 132 displayed the bloody discharge of dysentery. They were plugged with hemp, the surgeon certain they would survive at least until being purchased on the Virginia docks.

Jethro slouched against a mast, unable to look away from the horror that was now, irrevocably, part of his history.

"How can you do this, Mister Barker?" he muttered. "Again and again?"

Jack's face softened, but Jethro detected an underlying resolve in the gray of his eyes. Mister Barker patted the pouch of coins at his waist then turned and walked away.

Jethro continued to gaze at the cargo through tear-blurred vision as it was unloaded.

He hoped—he *prayed*—they would find some small happiness in their days ahead, though he did not know how it would be possible after what they had experienced on the *Henrietta*.

He thought of his own family's slaves on One Hundred Oaks . . . of his intended future with Theodosia and their hoped-for children, burdened by the curse of slavery. His gut twisted.

"*We must love our slaves, Papa*," he'd written. "*We must love them as hard as we are able.*"

The Sleepin' Fox Catches No Poultry; The Great Awakenin' (1738 AD)

Zachariah woke long before the autumn sun had risen. It would be a while before it would pierce the gaps in the planks of the cabin he shared with his two youngest brothers, three others belonging to One Hundred Oaks, and their overseer, Mister Grymes.

He rolled over on the threadbare blanket and scratched at his side through the coarse material of his vest. His brothers, Hannibal and Amos, were spread-eagle beside him—a puzzle of black arms and legs—wearing the same rough Negro cloth of slavery. Amos was nearly twenty years old, the youngest of ten sons and three daughters of their much loved and departed Ma Theo and Pa Jethro. But still he showed no sign of the stubble that his male brethren shared.

Zachariah yawned and sat up, the ache of sleep slow to leave him. Cuffee and Cudjo were huddled in a corner, clinging tight to each other. They twitched and jerked in their sleep—consumed, Zachariah knew, by the regular nightmare of their journey to One Hundred Oaks from some far-off land just three year ago. He stepped over his brothers toward the two, and placed his hands gently on their shoulders until they settled. The tips of his fingers caressed the scabby, puckering numbers seared into their flesh: 74 and 212.

Mister Grymes shuffled in his chair by the door, arms crossed over his broad stomach, a straw hat covering his face. The hat's frayed rim fluttered with each loud snore and whistle. Zachariah smiled, thinking, as usual, that he'd need to wake him soon enough so the whole cabin wouldn't be chastised for being late.

He stopped when he saw that Mouse was not in his corner. But no sooner had his worry flinched than the red man crawled through the window with a passel of fish and a toothy grin. Zachariah held his finger to his lips and motioned for Mouse to follow him out to the porch. The lane in front of the cabin meandered down the side of the hill, hidden from the main house by a hillock and three barns, and ended where a brook escaped from the wood. Sixteen split-log cabins were scattered along its way. Rickety fences surrounded vegetable patches; hogs grunted as they pushed their snouts into garbage heaps; two buzzards flapped down from the roof of the farthest structure. Sharp beaks and claws pulled the remnants of a rabbit carcass from a pile of debris.

"You need t' be careful sneakin' out alone at night, Mouse," Zachariah said.

The red man chuckled. "Them patrols will never catch this one."

"Still, you be owned, just like me, and if they'd catch you off One Hundred Oaks they have every right t' shoot you dead."

Mouse poked a stick into the fragments of their fire. He placed some kindling around the hottest embers, scraped the fish with his blade, and hung them above the coals.

Zachariah loved Mouse as a brother and friend. He had the strongest back in the field, he worked longer and harder than most, and he was the first to ensure all in his cabin were well fed. They sat in silence, holding their hands toward the flames. The fish smelled good and it wasn't long before Mister Grymes hunkered down beside them, sticking his nose close to their breakfast and taking a sniff. The lane was still dark, but a few more fires had been stoked to cast the stretching shadows of waking slaves upon their homes.

"We'll be workin' in the bottom field t'day and most the week t' finish the harvest," Mister Grymes said as he accepted a chunk of fish from Mouse. "No bread?"

Mouse ran off down the lane and returned with a still-hot half loaf from Aunty's oven. Mister Grymes ripped it into seven chunks and popped his portion into his mouth with the fish. He chewed loud and continued talking through his food.

"Prob'ly have t' raise our hours t' near eighteen a day t' get it all done in time. Darn'd cotton. It'll be near midnight afore you can go stealin' off t' your fishin' hole." He threw Mouse and Zachariah a wink. "This Sat'day evenin' though, we'll be workin' on the house raisin' for Mistress Clementine. The mistress says she'll need your skill as a sawyer." He nodded at Zachariah. "She got plans for two wooden columns for the big house's entrance porch—maybe nine feet tall. It'll be the gran'est plantation house on all Mulb'ry Island—maybe in all Virginia for all I knows." He picked at his nose, then flicked something toward the fire. He squinted toward the horizon. "Best t' rustle those rascals from their blankets and feed 'em up. We gots t' be in the field and well at it afore the sun hits the Ches'peake."

Near on eighty slaves were soon stooped between the rows of cotton shrubs, pulling at the bolls and shoving the cotton into sacks or woven baskets. The men wore straw hats they had made themselves, and the women wore turbans fashioned from the same rough cloth as their long dresses. The heat of day and the sweat of hard work stained them all.

Zachariah grabbed a stem in his calloused hands, twisted off a boll, and plucked the fluffy white fiber from amongst its dried leaves. He shoved the cotton into his sack and grabbed at the next boll, swift, but not so fast as Mouse, who was three bushes ahead.

"Don' you go shovin' rocks in your sack t' up the weight," Mister Grymes called to Cuffee.

"I ain' dun that, massa," Cuffee protested.

"He dun did it. I seen him," Cudjo muttered to himself with a snicker.

Hannibal and Amos were at the far end of the field, where the muddy waters of the James River eddied. Zachariah kept an eye on them to ensure no mischief.

When a scream cut through the shrubs, all ears pricked and heads turned.

"Sojourner," Zachariah said to Mister Grymes, and both ran for the edge of the cotton field.

"She ben with baby," Cudjo said, running after them.

Zachariah and Mister Grymes reached Sojourner and the women clustered around her. She lay in the dirt beneath an oak, surrounded by tobacco plants—the remnants of crops from long ago. Her belly was large, her hands stained from the morning's work, her basket of cotton overturned beside her.

"Git her up t' the cabins," Mister Grymes said to the women and one of the overseers.

One woman shook her head. "Baby be here now."

And the men stood back as a new life was pushed into the dirt.

Zachariah smiled when Sojourner's husband skidded to her side. He caught the man's gaze and nodded, but as he turned away, his smile wavered at the troubling thoughts of the newborn's future, which could be no better than any of theirs.

The sun shone down on the field as the slaves got back to work. All but one of the women picked up their baskets and left Sojourner and her baby. The husband dared stay to cuddle them both for several minutes before running back into the paddock.

Back in the field, Zachariah lifted his hat and wiped his forearm across his brow. Strands of straight brown hair fell into his eyes. He was determined to reach the end of the row before Mouse, who was now five bushes ahead. He sped up, even though his fingers were cut and bleeding. Mouse, who toiled shirtless in the heat, smirked at him and worked even harder to stay at the front.

It was dark, almost too dark to see their hands, when the workers left the field. They trudged up toward the lantern-lit lane, the brighter glow of the big house just over the hill.

"Time for fishin'," Mouse whispered after they'd eaten their meager supper.

Zachariah nodded. "Sure is." He squinted back toward their cabin. Hannibal, Amos, Cuffee, and Cudjo sat with Mister Grymes, listening to his stories around the fire.

It was much cooler out in the forest. Trees towered over the trail, and grass was thick beneath their bare feet. When they approached the boundary of One Hundred Oaks, they stopped to listen for any sign of patrol. Then Mouse laid a hand on Zachariah's arm and again they snuck through the undergrowth, scuttling under bushes and down a steep ravine to their secret spot. Mouse lit his small lantern and set it by the water. It cast a glow but would not be seen up on the main trails.

They squatted in the grass, threaded some worms, and threw their lines into the water.

"I ben thinkin' of leavin'," Mouse whispered.

Zachariah had heard this many times at their secret spot. He twitched his rod so the line slipped across the water.

"Go'n to sneak in the woods till I pass the great wagon road that hugs the eastern foothills of the Appalachians. Go'n run till this one is beyond the Alleghenies."

"The land of the red men."

Mouse held up his arm to display his red skin. "That's where I belong."

The two men cast their thoughts into the water. Then Mouse flipped his rod, and a white crappie flew over their heads to flounder on the bank. Mouse cast his line again without even peeking at the catch.

"What 'bout you, Zachariah?"

"I am a slave. There's nowhere for me to run. Nowhere I could hide."

Mouse stared at him, thoughtful. "But you're mulatto. Only half Negro, and your features are those of a white man." Mouse turned his head from side to side, studying Zachariah's nose. His brow furrowed and he ran his finger down the curve of his own nose. "Your skin's no darker than any white man who has spent his life in the fields. Even Mister Overseer is more tanned than you." He yanked another crappie from the water.

"Maybe so, but I can't leave Hannibal and Amos. They are without doubt our mother's children. The color of their skin keeps 'em firmly on One Hundred Oaks." Zachariah's line tugged but then went still. "Mistress Clementine, she pull me aside several times though. She is the last of my father's brothers and sisters, and she's held the burden for this plantation alone much longer'n any woman should suffer to. Despite bein' past child-rearin' age, she has many suitors that would gladly assist with her burden. But she'll have none of it unless they respect One Hundred Oaks and the slaves as much as she do."

"Why she pull you aside?"

"She promise me she'll find a free white girl afore she die, to love me for who I is and not *what* I is." Zachariah's line twitched again, and he flung a crappie up on the bank. "But she also made me promise to her." He narrowed his eyes, and his mouth turned down. "That if she were to die afore settlin' things on the plantation, that I were to run like the wind, to where no one knew my name, or the color of my ma."

Mouse sat up. "Then you come with me. I'll wait."

Both men flicked their rods to pull up two more crappies onto the grass.

Mouse froze, his eyes scanning left and right, his nostrils twitching. He held up his hand for Zachariah to be silent. His head jerked to the right and he inclined his ear.

"You hear dat?" he whispered.

Zachariah shook his head.

Mouse crawled across the grass, pulled the fish into a pile, hooked them onto the end of his line, then blew out the lantern. They were in pitch darkness with no moon and no stars. The wooded ravine rose steep behind them. Mouse tugged at Zachariah's vest then started to crawl up the embankment. Near the top he peered out from under the bushes. Zachariah came up beside him, their shoulders touching.

"Der it is agin."

Zachariah listened to the night. He could just make out a far-off moaning.

Out in the wood, farther than they'd ever been, the moan grew louder. The men turned to each other in fear.

"A boogeyman!" Mouse whispered.

They scrambled from beneath the bush and ran toward One Hundred Oaks as quick as they could.

* * * *

"You not s'posed t' do it that way," Cuffee said. He slapped Cudjo's hand.

"I cain' hep it," Cudjo whimpered. "I like t' be dead from tired afore the Sabbath."

"Shut your mouf or we both get whupped."

A sack was overturned with cotton spilled out onto the dirt, along with several rocks. Zachariah glared at them, and they scrambled to refill the sack. Cuffee kicked the rocks away.

"Quick, afore Mister Grymes walk over here," Zachariah said before going back to the bush he'd been plucking. He could understand—he was tired, too. He doubted anyone on the lane had had more than but a few hours' sleep the previous night, and it was going to be more eighteen-hour days in the field for the rest of the week. Lanterns were lined up, ready to be lit when the sky got too dark to see.

His arms and legs felt heavy from lack of sleep. He had to push his eyelids open as he trudged through the dirt, grabbing, twisting, plucking the cotton, and shoving it into his sack. Mouse, too, was not so fast as usual.

Sojourner was already back in the field, with the slight bundle of her newborn tied to her back. She wasn't complaining. Zachariah wondered whether she'd be able to fill even half of her sack, but he knew those around her would assist.

He ripped a boll from the bush. Mouse gave him a tired smile.

"Looks like you too tired to go fishin' tonight," Zachariah said.

Mouse straightened. "Not this one."

"You not afraid of the boogeyman in the wood?"

The Indian smirked. "I seen your skinny mulatto legs kickin' pretty fast through dem trees."

Zachariah chuckled and stuffed the cotton into his sack.

Mister Grymes huffed past them toward the top of the field, where Mistress Clementine stood holding a parasol. She was with the other overseers and a man in a fur hat. When Mister Grymes reached them, they all turned to the man in the fur hat, intent on whatever he was saying. Two overseers shook their heads, but the rest nodded in some kind of agreement. The fur hat man led Mistress Clementine and her parasol toward the big house while the overseers huddled and scratched their heads. The sun bore down from directly overhead by the time Mister Grymes strolled back down to the field. He stopped just a moment to see how Zachariah's gang's bags were filling up.

Mister Grymes lifted his chin in the direction of the big house. "That man want One Hundred Oaks to go back to tobacco next season. Promised his company will buy it all up for years to come."

"I may not be schooled like my pa and gran'pa, but ain' it said that Britain's already overloaded with tobac from these parts?" Zachariah asked.

"He didn' talk like the soldiers of King George. Said he were from a place called France. I think that'd be past Charlotte. Or maybe up north of Boston." Mister Grymes shrugged. "Either way, I don't know that the dirt here is strong enough for more tobac." He raised his eyebrows and wandered off toward the shade.

* * * *

Mouse and Zachariah squatted low under a bush, fishing poles held tight, surrounded by the black of the wood. The patrol rode by on horseback and stopped where Zachariah could have reached out to touch a hoof. He peered up through the brambles at the patrolmen in dark hats and overcoats hanging down to their ankles. Each had a star on his lapel which, though Zachariah could not read it, was inscribed *RUNAWAY SLAVE PATROL*. With sticks and whips and pistols at their hips, they stayed right there above their hiding place, listening. One of them fumbled in his coat for his pipe. He lifted a lantern to his face, and it shone bright against the bushes. Mouse sank against the ground, his arm pulling Zachariah close. The patrolman passed the pipe around and muttered something before nudging the horses along the trail. Mouse and Zachariah stayed still long after they could no longer hear the patrol. The Indian turned to Zachariah then pointed out into the wood.

Zachariah turned his ear, and a soft moaning drifted toward them. He raised an eyebrow and Mouse nodded, his eyes wide. They crept from their place and trod quietly toward the noise, skirting tree and shrub in the almost pitch black. They stopped at a mulberry tree, and Mouse was so close Zachariah could feel the tremble in his friend's body. They peered around the mulberry toward the moaning. It sent a shiver down Zachariah's spine.

A shaft of palest moonlight struck into a clearing.

Halfway up a tall oak hung a cage not big enough for a child, but in it was a full-grown Negro man, twisted and squashed into its tight metal confines, one leg dangling through the bars.

The oak's branches were covered with large birds of prey, fluttering about, attempting to perch on the cage.

Zachariah ran into the clearing, waving to scare them away, but not daring to shout. They took flight with a shriek only to settle close by to keep an eye on their prey.

Mouse came to his side and together they approached. The vultures had pecked out the man's eyes, and his cheeks were ripped open, his legs and arms lacerated by hungry beaks. Blood dripped through the cage and saturated the ground beneath. The Negro flinched, a guttural moan coming from the remnants of his face. "The birds, the birds. Aaah me!"

Zachariah and Mouse recoiled in terror but were too afraid to move.

With the vultures at a distance, a hoard of insects moved in— swarming to feed on the man's ragged flesh. He made garbled whimpering noises amongst the buzzing.

"I think he need water," Mouse said.

Zachariah ran over to a small stream, cupped his hands in the flow, and came back. He held his hands up high toward that terrible face, closing his eyes as the Negro pushed his mouth into his hands and slurped. The frayed tongue rubbed against his fingers.

"Tanke you. Tanke you." The Negro shook with a hard sob. "Put some poison, white man, and give me."

The two friends turned to one another then back to the man in the cage.

"How long you ben hangin' in this tree?" Zachariah asked.

"A week, and I don' die."

Zachariah shuddered.

"We cain' tell no one or they know we ben out here," Mouse whispered. "Why you in this cage, slave?"

The Negro erupted in a fit of coughing that made the insects rise, buzzing even louder, before settling back down for their feed.

"I lift a hand against my overseer," he said. "I kill 'im."

The man started to cry. Zachariah felt tears burning his own eyes.

"Why you dun that?" he asked.

"All my sons die of a pox. Overseer refuse to let us powder the dried toad for them. They all die."

"Did he call for the barber to bleed 'em?" Zachariah waved at the insects to shoo them away.

The man sobbed again. "Put some poison and give me."

The buzzards flapped their wings, impatient.

Zachariah held his hands to his face. It was too late to go fishing now, and when the sun came up they'd be missed.

"Wait here," he whispered to Mouse. "Keep them birds away."

He felt his way through the wood back to the stream where the broad leaves of a mayapple drooped in the shadows. He pulled a leaf from the shrub then dug a stick into the ground to get at its roots. The roots were tough, and he had to yank from different directions, falling onto his haunches when they finally came loose. As quick as he could, he smashed them with a rock into a shredded, sick-smelling mush. He wrapped the pulp in the leaf, scrubbed his hands in the stream, then ran back to the clearing.

He was almost there when he was jerked to the side and thrown to the ground. Mouse rolled beside him and clapped a hand over Zachariah's mouth.

"Them patrolmen," Mouse said.

Zachariah strained to hear. The patrolmen were with the man in the cage. Their horses chomped and trod about while their talk and laughter rang through the wood.

"Light soon," Mouse said. "We come back tomorrow."

Zachariah scrunched up the leaf of poison and placed it under a bush. They crept silently away from the patrolmen, away from the man in the cage, back to One Hundred Oaks.

* * * *

"Ain' no fishin' for you men tonight, or tomorrow!"

Mister Grymes was angry because there'd been no fish for breakfast—just some bread and leftover rabbit, but Mister Grymes didn't much like rabbit. "There ben reports of slaves in the woods that shouldn' be there. You boys get me whupped if the patrol find out it were you."

He walked ahead of his gang down toward the cotton field, spitting into the dirt every two or three steps. "Leave it a couple of days—till after the house raisin'. Should be safe by then."

Zachariah bent his back into the work.

"We gots to kill that Negro," he muttered to Mouse. "We gots to give mercy."

The Indian nodded.

*   *   *   *

The house raising started at noon on the day before the Sabbath. Masters, their wives and children, and their choice of strongest slaves arrived by wagon, horse, and foot from the surrounding plantations of Mulberry Island. The sun was hot and the flies buzzed, but all were in high spirits. A pig was stretched over a fire pit and lent a honeyed sweetness to the air. The women got busy with a quilting bee under one of the oak trees, a hundred of which lined the drive from the house down to the main island trail—all said to have been planted by Mister Clement and his young sons Thaddeus, Eli, and Jethro near fifty years ago.

The new house was being built right before the old one, now little more than a dilapidated wreck of clapboards. Already the front and back walls had been constructed of a dark red brick, one story high but going higher. A large hole in the middle of the front wall was where the door would be, and on either side were two more for windows. The new door, washed a bright white, leaned against a tree next to a wagon that carried the windows—handcrafted, much-admired, with dozens of squares of real glass in each. A score of men kneeled between the brickwork, placing floorboards and hammering nails. A score more assembled the wall frames on the ground, banging and talking loudly.

Zachariah worked with another slave on the columns that would hold the front porch high above that grand door.

"You Clementine's boy?" said a gruff man in an accent Zachariah had never heard before.

Zachariah looked up, confused. His aunt, Mistress Clementine, caught his gaze from under a nearby oak. She nodded at him, a dozen times real quick.

Standing, Zachariah accepted the man's outstretched hand and shook it—something he had never done before. The man was tall and wide with white skin and red hair. Zachariah couldn't help staring.

"MacDonald," the man said in his strange, thick accent. He flicked his head, and Zachariah followed him over to the corral behind the barn. The stranger studied the mares running around the enclosure. "Clementine said you'd be good for our wagon train. What say you?"

Zachariah was speechless.

MacDonald snorted, a grin spreading across his face. "I've already seen you're a good worker, lad, handy with the sawyering." He pulled a flask from his pocket, took a chug, and offered it to Zachariah. A quick tip of the bottle and Zachariah coughed as the liquid burned down his throat like fire. His cheeks and tongue went numb. "We'll 'ave plenty o' work for you with homesteads and fences where we're going. Plenty of strong Scot lasses as well." He gave a hearty wink and took another gulp from his flask.

"You're not from Mulberry Island?" Zachariah asked at last.

MacDonald guffawed. "Too many British around here for my liking. The farther from them, the better. We're just passing through toward the Ohio frontier, but are more than willing to lend our hand to the house raising for a belly-full of that pig roast. Perhaps some stories of the road ahead and the acquiring of some strong young lads like yourself." He knocked Zachariah's shoulder with his elbow.

"And Mistress—um—Ma Clementine said I could go?"

MacDonald nodded.

"And my brothers?"

"Clementine said you were an only son." He turned his head, scrunching his brow.

"Oh." Zachariah swallowed, heavy. He dreaded the thought of leaving Hannibal and Amos, but he knew deep in his gut that he must follow the trail delivered to him by the Almighty.

"Good, it's settled. We'll spend tonight in yonder field and start the journey west at sunup."

Zachariah's head was spinning. He needed to talk with Mistress Clementine; he needed to talk with Hannibal and Amos, with Mouse. He needed to do something about the man in the cage—he couldn't live with himself if he didn't.

When he returned to his work, his confusion had not lessened. MacDonald slapped him on the back and Mistress Clementine smiled beneath her quilting. He lifted another log into the lathe and gazed up at the field MacDonald had indicated. There were several covered wagons loaded with goods, but now another group of wagons were coming up the drive, under the canopy of the oaks. Mistress Clementine went to welcome her unexpected guests, fanning her hand against her breast often as she spoke to a man with a white collar and a black hat. She motioned for Mister Grymes and the other overseers to join her, and once they'd heard what she had to say, they scuttled up the drive to converse with the overseers and masters of the other plantations. Horses were pulled to and mounted with the overseers taking off down the drive.

Zachariah knew things were changing around him as he cut into the log. The walls were pulled high and secured, then the hammers were laid down, the whites consumed their pig, and the MacDonalds brought out a barrel and all drank with an unusual joviality. Pipes were lit.

The columns were completed and triple-checked against one another. Zachariah was proud of them, knowing they would hold a porch that would see the arrival of many at One Hundred Oaks for generations to come.

A Negro child delivered a torn bit of bread with a chunk of pork, twice the size it should have been. Zachariah devoured it. Mistress Clementine kept looking over at him and smiling more than he had ever seen her do. He smiled back with an appreciation that almost made him burst. Tears welled at the back of his eyes and he had to keep blinking, until his eyes were red and he could hardly breathe.

Then, almost all the workmen and slaves from One Hundred Oaks and the surrounding plantations came strolling up toward the house, a sight Zachariah never thought possible. They walked around the fields and up the drive like they owned the place. But then he saw the overseers herding them from behind, past the house and up into the pasture near the wagons of the MacDonalds and later arrivals. The mistress rose with the man in the white collar and black hat as well as all her guests, and they went to the wagons on the hill, Zachariah following in their wake and settling amongst the slaves beside Mouse, Hannibal, Amos, and Mister Grymes in the dirt.

The man with the white collar climbed onto a wagon. He took off his hat and smoothed back his mess of gray hair with a comb before lifting his hands to the heavens. His words were simple, but full of meaning. He spoke of God, and of mankind.

"Bruvvah, I tink he talkin' to us," Cuffee whispered to Cudjo.

And Zachariah knew it was true.

Emotion rippled across the field. This wasn't about sinners in the hands of an angry God. This was about true hope. About love and forgiveness.

The man's magnificent voice boomed, and what resonated within Zachariah more than anything was that he had a direct line to God—a personal line no other could cut. No overseer, no master or mistress, no governor and no king. No, not even the blessed King George, who allowed them to continue in their existence—an existence no God would approve of. Did this God not speak to him directly on this hillside? Did not this God reach right into his heart and squeeze it until it felt the warmth of love and charity—of respect for his fellow man?

Zachariah looked up to heaven and prayed. He prayed hard to the God that was around him and within him. He prayed till he knew in his heart that he had been forgiven.

But even as he prayed, he wondered about the Negro in the cage, in the wood, in ungodly pain.

And he knew, without hesitation, what he had to do.

*   *   *   *

Mister Grymes was asleep in his chair, Cudjo and Cuffee huddled quiet in the corner, twitching in their dreams. Hannibal and Amos grinned from ear to ear at Zachariah's whispered words and hugs, and then Zachariah and Mouse snuck out the window into the night.

The day had been long and there was no time for fishing—only time for the men to do what they needed to before Zachariah joined the MacDonalds' wagon train.

Mouse led the way through the pitch-black wood, but Zachariah could see his smile shining in the dark.

"I be leavin' tonight," the Indian said. "No more cotton or cabin or bedbugs for this one." He threw his arm around Zachariah. "I be followin' your shadow in the wood. I be watchin' you and that wagon train all the way past the Alleghenies." He snickered.

They slowed as they approached the clearing, wary of the patrol. The Negro was still in his cage. He had gotten one arm through the bars and it dangled by his left leg. Both were scabbed and bloody and torn. Zachariah thought he might be dead, but then the man shivered and moaned. He scuttled over to the bush where he'd hidden the poison, searching in the shadows with his hands. He returned to Mouse with the leaf in his hand, but just then they saw a light bobbing in the distance amongst the trees.

"Patrol," Zachariah whispered as the sound of horses came loud and clear through the trees. Mouse and Zachariah ran to the edge of the clearing and crawled into a log.

But it wasn't the slave patrol.

The men on horseback wore long white breeches and black boots. Black hats curved atop their heads, and their scarlet-red coats were trimmed in gold. White bands cut across their chests like an X, and their rifles were much thinner and longer than Zachariah had ever seen on One Hundred Oaks.

Zachariah pressed in hard against the inside of the log to spy at the men in the red coats through a hole. They were stiff in their saddles and spoke eloquently as they pulled into the clearing. Zachariah clenched the poison in his hand, waiting.

One of the men nudged his horse close to the cage. He lifted his weapon, and Zachariah's heart thumped in his chest. "May God be with you," the man said, and a shudder of relief coursed through Zachariah.

A single resolute shot resounded throughout the clearing.

P.J. Parker

The Forks of the Ohio; Not Yet a Nation (1763 AD)

Robert leaned over the wooden stockade atop the steep earthen walls of Fort Pitt, his rifle firmly in his grip. Full from the May rains, the Monongahela and Allegheny rivers roared on either side of the fort into the broad Ohio. Robert's jacket caught on a splinter, but the wood was old and weathered. He pulled the stiff blue fabric free then took a sniff of his underarm and winced. He hadn't bathed in several weeks. Despite the rivers' anger, Robert could think of nothing better than shucking off his militia blues and jumping into the surge—even for just a few minutes to get rid of the stink.

Fort Pitt was the farthest point of the Pennsylvanian frontier, the very edge of civilization. Westward was nothing bar the red men and perhaps a few lonely French fur trappers. Robert spat dust from his mouth and wiped his sleeve across his brow as he surveyed the other militiamen standing at their posts around the upper bulwarks. No other fort came close in size or strength. Pentagonal in shape with five bastions reaching out from its corners, two acres lay within its walls, with eighteen more in the outworks. Several barracks, a church, and a hospital clustered around the central open parade ground. The British flag flapped atop its pole as the soldiers of King George did their marching drills. Their weapons clattered over the authoritative voice of their drill sergeant, their red coats stained dark crimson by dust and sweat. And stink. Robert cleared his throat and spat again before lifting his rifle onto the stockade and peering along its length toward the escarpment on the far side of the Monongahela.

No sign of injuns.

Outside the fort's protective ramparts were the log cabins and clapboard buildings of Pittsborough. The sawmill where Robert's pa worked as a sawyer was the tallest building in the borough. Beyond that was the tanyard with its ever-present sickening stench. Most of the land was covered with muddy trails, swaying fields of spelt, corn, and hay, and paddocks of cattle and horses. At last count the population was six hundred and twelve, but the number was growing daily as babies were born and new settlers arrived, ready for the next leg of their journey westward down the flow of the Ohio.

Directly below his station, Robert could just make out the remnant outline of the French Fort Duquesne. Burnt to the ground before the French fled north from the British advance, the fort was now no more than a black outline in the dirt. Gravestones huddled at its far edge, and he stared at them, refusing to let his face crinkle in a grief he knew would never leave him.

The strong hand of Captain William Trent gripped his shoulder.

"They were good men, your brothers. Every single one of them," he said. "It was men like them who drove the French from this valley. God only knows what would have happened if that empire had been successful in building and holding their forts from New France in the north all the way down to Louisiana." He gazed upriver, muttering.

"They wanted the native fur trade," Robert said. "Still do."

The captain nodded. "Their alliance is strong with the red men who also want nothing but trade, even if it means killing every British settler that dares set foot in this valley." A column of smoke rose from the far escarpment. "I doubt the French will push back again. We need only hold fast against the savages."

"Didn't you once champion them, Cap'n? Trade with them?" Robert asked.

Trent studied the smoke. "And perhaps that time will come again. But for now, we must ensure the safety of our own as our colonies expand."

Robert was proud to follow in his brother's footsteps and serve under Captain Trent in the local militia. Assigned by Captain Ecuyer of the Royal American Regiment, Trent had gathered a troop of lads of firearm-bearing age alongside the Redcoats, then fought bravely, shoulder to shoulder with Robert's elder brothers before placing the stones on their graves with passionate and tear-filled words to God.

A sharp whistle cut across the fort from the bastion beside the front gate.

Captain Trent jerked his head. "Come," he said, and Robert followed him down the embankment. The Redcoats, finished with their drills, stood in the shade by the horse troughs, dunking their heads in the water to cool off. Captain Ecuyer, singularly bathed and pristine in his uniform, strode out of his cabin to meet Trent in the middle of the dirt. Robert stood at a distance.

Two militiamen came galloping in through the front gates, stirring up the dust. Ecuyer stepped back, pressing a kerchief over his lower face, and the militiamen jumped from their mounts in front of Captain Trent.

"Cap'n," said one of them, removing his hat. "Them savages have taken up the hatchet in the north. We cain't be certain, but some reports say Fort D'Troit is under siege an' Fort Niagara is surrounded by an uncountable number of red men all painted up 'n' fierce. One messenger of a friendly tribe stated that D'Troit is no more."

Trent and Ecuyer glanced at one another, brows wrinkled and lips pursed. A third horseman rode in and joined the huddle. Wearing the dusty blue coat of the militia, but with fringed buckskin pants and a single feather in his long, graying hair, he lifted his leg across his saddleless mount and leapt to the ground. It was Mouse, who had been a friend of Robert's pa for longer than he knew. Mouse gave Robert a nod, but his face was hard as he turned to the two captains.

"Which tribes?" Captain Trent asked.

"The Ottowas, Potawatomies, and Hurons attack the northern forts," Mouse said carefully with the slight clip of an almost Philadelphian accent, diluted by the many languages he had mastered over his long life. Since boyhood, Robert had been intrigued by this red man's adventurous history with his pa. Some stories he would tell again and again, but Robert was schooled enough by his grandma, ma, and sisters to notice many years of Mouse's and his Pa's lives were never mentioned.

"Pontiac, the chief of the Ottowas, leads the bloodbath. They refuse to listen to the wisdom of their women." Mouse pulled a rifle from his saddle and stepped beside Robert. "Not far up the Allegheny, the warriors of the Delaware, Mingo, Shawnee, and Wyandot gather in council. They, too, will soon push all white invaders back toward the rising sun—beyond the ridge of the Appalachians."

* * * *

The captains spent the afternoon in Ecuyer's cabin before Robert, Mouse, and Sergeant Wilmore were called in. A great table dominated the room with papers and maps spread across it. Captain Ecuyer scribbled circles and X's on a map, periodically wiping at his brow with his kerchief. Beyond the table was a cot, its gray blankets pulled tight, and a low barrel bath that was the envy of all the troops in the fort. A fire burned in the corner, making the room stifling hot.

"My officers will cover the countryside and alert townsfolk and farmers to move into the fort," Ecuyer said, and Trent nodded. "You take the militia"—Ecuyer slashed his pen across the map— "and destroy these premises. This one, this one, and this one"—three circles across the map— "will be dismantled and reassembled within the fort grounds."

Captain Ecuyer paced over to the fire and held his hands toward the flame, shivering. The other men waited in quiet as he fidgeted, then suddenly turned to face them.

"Sergeant Wilmore, send several messengers via different trails to Colonel Henry Bouquet in Philadelphia. With the men we have, we can hold Fort Pitt for several weeks, but will require assistance to route the enemy if they lay siege."

Sergeant Wilmore ran from the room to brief his men. Mouse grabbed Robert's arm as they, too, strode out of the cabin.

"You start the burning, Robert, under Captain Trent. I will make sure your ma an' pa, an' smaller bothers an' sisters are made safe. They will be at the fort afore sundown." Mouse jumped onto his horse and galloped out the fort's gate.

* * * *

The taverns and churches and homesteads of Pittsborough were soon burned to the ground. The sawmill with its dust and machinery exploded in the early dusk of the third evening. The tanyard glowed and cracked, its warehouse refusing to fall. Robert directed horses and ropes to pull it down into the dirt so it could afford no hiding place to the approaching savages. Some two hundred huts and cabins between Fort Pitt and Grant Hill were no more than smoldering heaps of debris.

The weakest sections of the fort were shored up with barrels of dirt. Beaver traps and spiked crows feet were laid in ditches dug from river to river.

The people of the borough gathered fast within the fort with wagons piled high, their animals herded along behind them, running wild amongst a growing chaos. Cartloads of planks and timbers were ripped from the sides of barns, hauled into the fort, and dumped on the parade ground. Regiment, militia, merchants, farmers, and their families worked together day and night to reconstruct makeshift shelters beside the barracks and behind the fort's church.

Barrels of water lined the inside of the fort, and women and children were trained how to use the fire buckets to extinguish the expected onslaught of flaming arrows.

The men were given tomahawks and guns, and briefings were held each morning and night. Captain Ecuyer with his articulate Swiss clip and bright red coat would relay the news of the north, but it was Militia Captain Trent and the pastors who the townsfolk paid the most heed.

The news of the destruction of Fort D'Troit, with all its occupants slain and scalped, had everyone worried, though not all messengers agreed on its truth.

On the Sabbath, a man galloped into the fort with his wife and three small children, their faces drained of color, the man able only to stutter incoherently. When at last he did speak, those who listened held their families close.

* * * *

Robert was on the ramparts when they came.

The sun skimmed above the mountains in the east and, with aching bones and bleary eyes, he cocked his gun.

They appeared over Grant's Hill—several hundred warriors painted garish colors. Some rode on horses—bareback—their steeds coated in colors that summoned thoughts of the devil.

Placing dirty fingers to his mouth, Robert let out a shrill whistle that none in the Fort could mistake. Militiamen scattered around the stockade, repeating the whistle. The Redcoats came barreling out of their barracks, pulling on their jackets, hiking up their breeches, and rattling their rifles to join the men in blue already on the walls. Ecuyer and Trent came to a stop beside Robert where they surveyed the fort's landward side.

Mouse came scooting up the hill from the western side of the fort. "There are more," he panted, pointing across the Monongahela.

Hundreds of warriors stood in horrific splendor atop the escarpment overshadowing Fort Pitt, painted different colors than the tribe cresting Grant's Hill.

"Will their fire arrows reach across the river?" Ecuyer asked.

Mouse frowned, and Ecuyer seemed to have his answer.

A shrill call went up from Grant's Hill and was taken up by all the warriors. Rifles and bows and hatchets were waved. Shots rang out. Robert shuddered with fear—a tremor through his scalp. He peered down into the fort, searching for his family. His pa pressed his back against the door of one of the barracks, rifle held in both hands, his finger on the trigger. His ma and young siblings would be safe inside, he knew. He hoped. His pa gave him a determined nod.

The screaming stopped, the echoes of war diminishing, replaced by an eerie stillness.

Five Indians on horseback proceeded down the hill toward the fort.

"Mouse, we will need you to interpret," Captain Trent said. "Robert, pack four rifles in your saddle and come with me." His face turned white, then red.

Ecuyer, Trent, Mouse, and Robert rode out into the open field and stopped less than a dozen paces from the mounted Indians. The lingering stench of burnt homesteads and the pungent smell of turnips and recently turned soil surrounded them.

Mouse pulled his horse in front of the two captains.

A painted Indian spoke, much larger, brawnier, and younger than Mouse. To Robert, he sounded pained, as if he did not wish war. He raised his rifle to the sky to punctuate his words, then pointed it at Mouse's chest.

Robert and the two captains raised their own rifles, but Mouse held up a hand. He spoke in the Indian's tongue, then turned his back to the rifle still aimed at him. The painted Indian laughed and lowered his weapon.

Robert furrowed his brow in confusion.

"His name is the Turtle's Heart," Mouse said. "He says all settlements north of Fort Pitt have been razed, their people slaughtered and scalped."

The painted Indian lifted a ropey tangle of bloody black, red, brown, and blonde hair—still attached to hacked slithers of scalp. He held the prize high and a great whooping enveloped the valley. Robert stiffened, the rifle in his grip bruising the aching flesh of his fingers.

When all was quiet, Mouse continued. "We—*you*—are the only white men still alive west of the Appalachian highlands. The Turtle's Heart would welcome a small trading post here, but not the King's garrison or the other invaders and their animals. He will trade beaver and raccoon skins with you as he once traded with the French, but nothing more. He warns there are a great number of warriors approaching to kill you, but the Turtle's Heart has prevailed on the nations to hold off—to give you time to go east of the mountains and never return to this valley. He desires you to leave before the setting of the sun."

The two captains leaned in close to whisper. Then Captain Ecuyer and Mouse rode several steps closer to the painted Indian, who again raised his rifle. He spat into the dirt alongside his painted horse.

Captain Ecuyer bowed his head. "Thank you, the Turtle's Heart, for your kind consideration." He looked to Mouse, who translated. "We have everything we require within the walls of our fort and need not trade with you—not even one beaver pelt. Here we will stay, to be joined by the army of King George, which is far larger and mightier than any band of savages. We can defend ourselves against the Indians in the wood, who should take care to protect their own before it is too late. Moreover, I tell you, if any of you return to this fort I will throw bombshells, which will burst and blow you to atoms. I will fire cannon loaded with whole bags of bullets. Therefore, take care, for I don't wish to hurt you. Go to your chiefs and tell them what I say, in the name of the glorious King George and the British Empire on which the sun *never* sets."

Robert could see Mouse was taking great pains to translate the speech exactly.

The painted Indian pulled himself higher on his horse. He glared at Ecuyer, then at Mouse. Then he spoke, his words low and clipped with anger.

Mouse turned to Ecuyer. "The Turtle's Heart hears you. He will keep fast the chain of friendship and speak with the other chiefs."

The Turtle's Heart nudged his horse forward, leaned over to slap Mouse on the shoulder, and then returned to his men, a few paces distant.

Mouse looked over his shoulder at Robert. "Do not move. Take no action. Return to your family." His face was tight and drained of color.

The painted Indian lifted his rifle and pulled the trigger. Mouse's blue militia coat and the flesh beneath it were blown apart. He toppled from his horse to the ground.

Robert's eyes went wide, his body shivering uncontrollably. His gut and throat twisted. The painted Indian and his men turned and galloped back to the top of Grant's Hill.

That evening, flaming arrows shot through the moonlight and set ablaze the fields of corn and spelt surrounding Fort Pitt. Thick, dark smoke enveloped the fort in a choking haze.

For seven days and seven nights, the painted Indians attacked, but their blazing darts were quickly extinguished within the fort. The Redcoats and militia shot their rifles sparingly and instead launched hand grenades at the attackers crouched behind the river banks. The Indians made it near the front gates, but could not get past the defenses.

The second week, the red men stood their ground on Grant's Hill and the escarpment. They made no further attack, but their singing and chanting and drumming went on unabated, bringing dread to all inside the fort.

On the seventeenth day, a dozen wagons slewed around the hill and stopped within spitting distance of the barricaded gates. Robert awoke to the Redcoats drumming, and he ran to the top of the stockade. The wagons were loaded with sacks, barrels, crates of guns, and cages of chickens. A sad-looking cow was tethered to the last wagon.

Robert gulped, the pressure in his head making it ache. Painted Indians rode upon the horses pulling the wagons. White men, women, and children lay slumped on the benches of each wagon—dead, scalped, mutilated.

The painted Indians loosed the horses from the wagons and with much shrieking, gripped their manes and rode back up to their camps.

Robert scurried down the embankment toward Ecuyer's cabin just as he and Trent opened the door. "A wagon train, Captains. All are dead, but with their loads left at the gate. Some guns, sacks of grain and other provisions."

"A ruse," Captain Trent muttered.

Ecuyer nodded. "We must leave them."

"But Cap'n, there's families, what's left of them, sprawled across the benches, something terrible. We can't jus' leave them there in plain sight of the lookouts."

Captain Trent stared at Robert, but he seemed to peer right through him. He bit at his lower lip, which was already chapped and bloody. "The moon will be near full this evening. We cannot retrieve the bodies and chance the lives of our men." He sighed heavily and Ecuyer fidgeted at his side. "Maybe in a week, when the moon has waned."

Robert stood atop the stockade and kept his attention on the painted men and their movements. His heart sank whenever flocks of dark birds descended on the remains of the wagon train. The spring rains had started again, making sentry duty miserable, but Robert hoped it would only grow stronger, thankful when the gathering clouds where thick enough to blot out all light of the moon at night.

The gate was hauled open amidst the cover of night, the slosh of mud, and the roar of a mighty downpour. Several militia and a score of Redcoats crept out into the dark toward the wagons. Robert was pulling the bodies of two children into his arms when the first arrow thwacked into the mud at his feet. Then another, and another. The mud was halfway up his boots and he stumbled twice but refused to let go of his charge. Beside him, other men carried or dragged the remnants of families. Fire arrows arced through the air—sizzling amongst the raindrops. Robert heard horse hooves pounding and the whoops of the painted men. A fusillade of shots erupted from the fort. Grenades exploded with deafening booms, troops yelling as they grew frantic.

Robert's thigh jerked, a searing pain cutting through it, but still he ran. A Redcoat fell to the mud beside him, an arrow in his back. Lurching sideways, Robert grabbed at the soldier's jacket and pulled him through the muck toward the gate. The arrow dug deep in the muscle of Robert's leg, and he crawled across the last threescore feet of mire. "Goddamned heathen savages," he muttered through clenched teeth as the pain rendered his leg useless. Still he made it through the gate and handed off the bodies of the children to another. He settled the dead Redcoat against the inside of the barricade before hobbling toward the gate once more.

A pair of hands grabbed him and pulled him to the ground. "Stay!" someone yelled, and the gate of Fort Pitt was pushed shut.

* * * *

His pa broke the arrow in two and pushed it out the front of his leg. Robert jerked in agony, his cry mangled behind gritted teeth. His ma slathered the wounds with a poultice then wrapped his leg up good and tight. The leg was stiff and pained him, but still he drew himself back up onto the stockade to do his duty.

* * * *

The siege continued for weeks. Supplies were dwindling. All the pigs had been eaten. Good milking cows had to be shot for their meat—a couple of horses, too, and some of the dogs. Morale was sinking, and there were worries that the pox amongst the patients in the small hospital might spread throughout the fort.

And the painted men played stickball.

"How does your leg fare, Robert?" Captain Trent asked as he eyed the ripped and bloody breeches.

Robert replied with a tight smile that fell immediately.

They leaned against the stockade, shoulder to shoulder, rifles in hand. They could have easily picked off a few of the Indians scampering across the field, wielding their strange netted sticks and wooden ball.

"They show no fear," Robert said.

"They have little reason to," Trent said. "They far outnumber us and are willing to wait for us to starve. Their women and children gather on the far side of the Allegheny—waiting for us to open our gate and bend our heads to be scalped."

A commotion went up amongst the painted men as their wooden ball shot up into the sky. Robert and Captain Trent followed its trajectory over their heads, and it came to rest near the flag pole inside the fort.

The painted Indians approached, holding up their hands in question.

"That might have worked up north, but not here, you heathens," Captain Trent yelled.

They seemed to understand and started laughing. One by one the painted Indians touched the gate, smirking up at the armed sentries before returning to their game with another ball.

"We, too, can play devious games," Captain Trent muttered. He settled his gaze on Robert. "Take care with what I am about to order."

Robert cocked his head, uncertain.

"Go to the hospital and have the blankets and kerchiefs of Smith, Jenkins, and Todd folded up all handsome like."

Robert recoiled. "But they got the pox, Cap'n."

"Like I said, best you be careful."

Robert nodded then lowered his gaze to the dirt. He fingered the bloody hole in his breeches.

* * * *

Robert couldn't stick his right foot into the stirrup without tongue-biting and swear words, so he let the stiff leg hang down the side of his mount. On the saddle behind him lay the blankets and linens, wrapped tight in a cow hide and a British flag.

"A nice little present—all red, white, and blue—for the Turtle's Heart and his men," Trent had said.

And their families.

Robert had felt the cramped stomach of deceit but had filled it quick with a chunk of bread and rancid lard. He sat tall now in his saddle beside the two captains. Their uniforms were a tattered contrast of red and blue—even Ecuyer had succumbed to the dirt and stench of their situation, as all water was conserved for drinking, and none dared use the rivers which were heavy with silt from the rains.

The sun was high as they trotted into the field. The Turtle's Heart and a posse of his happy, healthy men, on freshly fed and watered mounts, weaved their way down the incline toward them. The Turtle's Heart was painted a muddy green, with a blood-red handprint over his heart.

"Welcome, my friends," the Turtle's Heart said in English. "No traitor to help you speak a more noble tongue?"

"We have come to strengthen the bonds of our friendship," said Captain Trent.

Robert eyed the painted Indian, noting the upturn of his lip as he made hand signals to his men. Their hands slid close to their rifles.

"A parting gift, before you leave the Ohio?" the Turtle's Heart asked.

Captain Trent lifted his chin. "Robert," he said.

Robert kept a finger on the trigger of his rifle as he reached behind him and loosed the flag-covered hide from his saddle. He pulled it onto his lap and dared not breathe, lest the disease creep through the leather and up his nostrils. He nudged his mount forward a step, and the Turtle's Heart came to meet him. The painted Indian reached out to slap Robert on the shoulder, but Robert pulled back, tossed the package toward him, then leaned forward and slapped the Turtle's Heart's shoulder instead. The Turtle's Heart stared, incredulous, then chuckled. He clutched the package, still snickering as he pulled on his horse's mane and nudged her around the other way.

Robert's finger itched against the trigger and he wished he could shoot the chief right then—shoot him and kill him dead, watch him fall into the blood-smudged dirt where Mouse had fallen. He caressed the curve of metal as he watched the chief throw the gift to another. His own lip curled.

* * * *

"Half a crate of ammunition left. Just a little powder," a militiaman reported to Robert.

Captain Trent arrived at his side, his face gray with worry.

"The last few attacks have nearly wiped out our cache, Cap'n," Robert said. "Might be enough for one more cannon ball. Some shot to kill maybe six more Indians."

They surveyed the surrounding hills and escarpment. Over a thousand painted Indians lounged under the trees, tending their horses, checking their rifles, grabbing at sweet morsels from baskets held by their women. The echoing sounds of laugher were interspersed with hacking coughs. Neither Robert nor Trent could bring themselves to smile—not even a little.

"We have our hatchets, and the Redcoats have the daggers on the ends of their rifles. If we must die, then it will be honorably, with just as many redskins lying beside our corpses."

The third moon of the siege rose above the mountains—a thin curved slither of silver.

When the sun rose again, it seemed to Robert that many on Grant's Hill had gone—no sign of their women and children. But still the painted Indians far outnumbered the force within Fort Pitt.

The next day, there were fewer still. And the day after, the hill was barren, a few unattended fires smoldering.

Robert and Captain Trent stood side by side for the next three days and nights. Robert had barely any fingernails left.

"Ha!" Captain Trent finally exclaimed, and Robert saw a smile he had not seen for many months. He looked to where the captain pointed and he, too, let out a whoop.

Coming down the trail between Grant's Hill and the Allegheny was a long line of mounted troops. Royal Americans and the Highland Regiments.

"Distant cousins of yours no doubt, young man," Captain Trent bellowed as he clapped his arm around Robert's shoulders.

"God bless King George!" Robert yelled. He grinned wide enough to make his cheeks ache, and then he grinned some more.

P.J. Parker

A Matter of Hats and Tea (1773 AD)

"How can any man bend his knee to King George when he gives away land that has cost us all family members and friends? An arbitrary line drawn along the ridge of the Appalachians, by a man who has never seen them or the bloodshed in their shadows! My father, Zachariah, was right to proclaim there is only one true King—God!"

David lifted his mug of ale, took a hefty draft and slammed it down onto the table. He wasn't drunk, but he was angry.

"I lost several brothers in the Ohio and still my remaining eldest, Robert, limps from an arrow that went clear through his leg." David's face darkened as his fury grew.

Benjamin lowered his copy of *Poor Richard's Almanac* and squinted at his friend.

"You talk like a Son of Liberty, sir. Best you be quiet in case a Redcoat enters this establishment."

David looked around the dark, oil-lit, stonewalled tavern. The barkeep's head was low as he washed mugs, but his ears pricked. Behind him was a long plank of wood carved with the majestic buildings around Boston Harbor. David looked out the window to see if the rendering was true, but the glass was too dirty to see, and smudged by falling snow.

"Humph." He stared into his mug.

Benjamin flicked his newspaper and adjusted his eyeglasses. "It has been suggested that the colonies should follow the same form of unity as the Iroquois Confederacy."

"*Injuns*?" David asked.

"Their union is strong and has maintained their civility for many centuries, before we bothered with this land."

"But no two of our colonies are alike. We all have different laws, interests, religions, governments, and manners. We are too different, with only our contracts to the home country in common. Barkeep!" David lifted his empty mug.

"And yet we are the same. Here we have no aristocracy, no kings, no bishops, and no great luxuries. The rich and poor are not so far removed from one another—not as they are in Europe and Britain. Here a man, by his own good works, may lift himself from rags to riches well within his lifetime. We are a melting pot, and perhaps that potential in itself makes us stronger."

David didn't know whether Benjamin's words were his own or from the paper he read. "I have my own print shop," he said, thinking about what Benjamin had said.

"You do."

"And it was but a handful of years ago I was only a journeyman in Philadelphia under Mister Ben Franklin."

"Without a doubt, you have found your ground."

The barkeep approached with a mug of ale, but David ushered him away with a few shillings.

David and Benjamin left the tavern, pulling their collars high against the inclement weather. Drifts of snow gathered at the edges of the lane. They jumped the gutter and walked across the cobbles, dirty sludge rutted by wagons and horses. Large flakes wafted about as they rounded the corner into Leverett's Lane.

"I know that I talk so, but surely we could not survive without England," David said.

Benjamin kept up the pace as they walked. "With her taxes on this and that, hats, molasses and whatnot to pay for the Indian wars, the breach between us grows wider and more difficult to heal. Of course, we love her as our mother, and perhaps the King, too, when we are represented and treated fairly. However, I am of a mind that Britain can grow no stronger without us, but without her we would become a mightier people—tenfold mightier! Already we have over two million inhabitants—greater than a third of the population back home."

David shuffled on, lifting his face to the snow. It felt good against his skin. "The King did strike down the stamp tax on paper," he said. "That certainly lifted a burden at the print shop."

"But only after the good work of the Sons of Liberty," Benjamin countered.

David nodded. He ran his tongue across the front of his teeth. He could still taste the tavern's grimy stew and ale.

They came to a stop in front of David's shop—a two-story stone edifice with an attic window that was always open, no matter the weather.

"Mug of rum?"

Benjamin tipped his hat and followed David through the door and up the stairs to his parlor, where they settled into two overstuffed chairs by the fire.

"Perhaps we no longer owe our allegiance to Britain," David said. "There are so many Germans, Irish, Dutch, Italians, and God knows what else walking the streets and setting up farms and shops."

"Your words are traitorous, David, but it is as I said—a melting pot. And one cannot ignore the Africans, whose own cultures pervade."

David held his mug with both hands, staring into the fire. It warmed him until his brow was slicked with sweat. He took a sip of rum. "What next then, where do we go from here?"

"As a free adult male, you may vote. But I wholeheartedly believe we must be doers of good—right the wrongs and create a better society. And that, my friend, brings us back to the Iroquois."

David scrunched up his face. "How so?"

"In that confederacy all are equal and free—even the women. There is an untamable spirit of independence, and a personal attitude of dignity in their every action. They have no soldiers or police, no nobility or kings. There is only freedom, equality and fraternity, all working together toward the good of the whole."

" 'We, the people,' " David quoted.

"Exactly."

They sat in each other's silent company, listening to the crack of the fire, sipping their rum. They lit pipes and perhaps even dozed a bit. David finally muttered, unaware whether his friend was asleep or awake, "Still, the King has his men guarding us, parading around with their rifles and their red coats as if we are not free."

"And we pay for the pleasure, if not through taxes, then by duties. There should be no taxation of any type without representation." Benjamin's eyes were closed, his pipe balancing on the arm of his chair.

"The duties are minimal, and tea is still very cheap with them. Do you even drink tea, Ben?"

Benjamin smirked, holding up his mug to be refilled. "That is beside the point, sir. Why should we pay any duties to hold an army we do not ask for? We have our own militia; we do not need the King's."

David stepped over to his half-asleep friend and filled his mug. "Perhaps, then, you will meet me at the docks tomorrow night with some of my . . . um . . . friends."

* * * *

A dozen or so Sons of Liberty and possibly a handful of tea-smugglers crouched behind the barrels on the Boston docks. Two ships of the East India Company were moored on the far wharf. Sails were furled, all lanterns extinguished, no crew to be seen. The lap of water below the planks was the only sound.

"The seeds of slavery," Benjamin muttered, pointing to the crates of tea that lined the wharf and the decks of the ships. "With any luck we should have them all thrown into the harbor before the moon rises."

David, resplendent in buckskin and with chicken feathers stuck in his hair, patted his hand against his mouth and whispered, "Woo-woo-woo! Do I look like an Injun?"

Benjamin smiled and pushed David's shoulder. "You'll do."

David crouched beside Benjamin, peering at the ships and crates. His face softened. "I mean no disrespect, for without doubt I feel more kinship with our native brothers than I do with the English."

"No apology necessary. I understand. I also have some of that noble blood coursing through my veins." The water below them lapped and churned. "Can you swim?"

"I guess we'll find out."

P.J. Parker

West Point—The Key to the Continent and Independence (1780 AD)

Bartley paddled like a dog in the middle of the Hudson River, between Constitution Island and West Point. The tight, shallow S-bend in the mighty waterway surged between the two fortified headlands. The water was cold, but not so freezing as when the ice floe came down in winter. A rope tied around his chest was stretched tight to the gunboat that skimmed a few yards upstream. He waved at the oarsmen, and Levi Atkinson leaned around the cannon and gave the rope some slack. Bartley took several deep breaths and then dived down under the muddy waters. He pulled himself along the submerged chain that crossed the waterway, running his hands over the full curve of each link to ensure it was intact before moving on to the next. He couldn't see them in the murk but, having smithed many himself, he knew them by feel. They were large enough to stick his head through, but he would never dare, in case the current should suddenly swirl and drag him under.

* * * *

Bartley had been at West Point for over a year now, with his older brothers, David and Robert, and some three thousand soldiers of the Continental Army.

He had snuck away from the farm to join the force in 1776, when he was nineteen and sick of working the soil that could be taken away at any moment. Under the command of General George Washington, he had dug trenches and fortifications at Kips Bay, Manhattan, with thousands of other untrained volunteers. He'd seen the forty-five British men-of-war pull into New York Harbor and set anchor off Staten Island. Their presence only made him more determined in his work. He was still digging in those trenches on the 4th of July, when an officer stood upon the hill and read the declared words of independence.

"We hold these truths to be self-evident, that all men are created equal, that they are endowed by their Creator with certain unalienable Rights, that among these are Life, Liberty and the pursuit of Happiness."

The men had cheered and then gone on digging.

A week later, the first British cannonballs careened into New York City.

Within a month, the flotilla was joined by over four hundred more men-of-war. Their Union Jacks fluttered above the canvasses. The battle ships of King George were massive, each holding hundreds of soldiers and at least sixty cannon. They slid in close to Kip's Bay—so close Bartley could read their names. The closest to his outpost was the *Phoenix*. He could have hit it with a rock.

* * * *

Bartley kicked to the surface of the Hudson for air. He waved to ensure Levi saw him, and then he dived back under.

* * * *

It had been a dull September morning when the fusillade escalated, tenfold, from the river east of Manhattan. There must have been at least two thousand cannonballs fired into Kip's Bay within a single hour. The balls smashed the defenses. Dirt, planks, limbs, and screams were thrown into the air. When thousands of Redcoats came ashore in their longboats, Bartley had no musket or rifle—only his shovel. He used it to good order, its edge sharp from his digging, until the word for orderly retreat was passed along the trenches.

* * * *

Bartley neared a pontoon, where two of the West Point chain links were all but broken. He ran his hands around them to determine the degree of damage—perhaps a tumbled log had caused it, or the twisting of the pontoon in the Hudson's current. He untied the rope about him and hauled himself up onto the wooden raft of the pontoon. He collapsed onto the planks to rest, his head dizzy from holding his breath.

* * * *

Perhaps eighteen hundred Continentals were still alive after the initial attack at Kip's Bay—Bartley amongst them, with his shovel, but also with a rifle he had pulled from the grip of a dead soldier.

They followed the broad way—an Indian trail that cut diagonally up the island of Manhattan to the northwest—and dug in at the top of Harlem Heights. More than five thousand Redcoats came marching through the woods and across the wheat fields, their bugles sounding "Gone Away," the song of the fox hunt.

"I'll be damned if we're running from those lobsterbacks," Bartley heard one of the officers say to General Washington nearby. Bartley swung his rifle onto a boulder and took aim at the approaching troops.

Despite the Redcoats' methodical approach—step, drop, shoot, step, drop, shoot, directed by their mounted officers who trotted behind them—the battlefield quickly turned to turmoil. The Continentals irreverently flanked the British, throwing their form into disarray. Bartley found himself in the worst of it, amongst the abandoned, blood-splattered sheaves of wheat. Shots fired beneath gusting clouds of smoke, and he slammed headlong into a Redcoat. They grappled, and the Redcoat sliced his bayonet through Bartley's forehead and cheek—clear to his chin. Though his sight was bloody, he was not blind. He spun the butt of his rifle around, and the Redcoat's face crunched under the force of it. He fell to the ground in a lifeless heap.

* * * *

Bartley smiled as he lay on his back, crinkling the scar down the side of his face. The pontoon bobbed in the Hudson's current as the gunboat pulled up alongside him to take him back to shore.

"How does the chain fare?" Levi asked, holding out his hand to yank Bartley aboard.

"Two links below this pontoon are badly damaged. In all, five need replacement."

"General Arnold won't be happy to hear that."

Bartley rolled his eyes.

The boatswain raised his brows in question. "To West Point, or over to Beverly to tell the general?"

"Let's head back to the barracks first—I'm famished." Bartley extended his pinky and affected a British accent. "The general is probably busy, anyway, taking tea and sandwiches on the best British chinaware with his lovely wife, Peggy."

Levi broke into laugher.

The gunboat pulled into West Point docks, a short walk down the slope from the ramparts and redoubts of Fort Arnold.

"Hey." Levi nudged Bartley in the arm as they headed across the parade grounds. "Ain't that the general's wife coming from the prison house?"

"Sure is." Bartley maintained his pace across the field but kept peeking at her out the corner of his eye.

Mrs. Arnold seemed flustered, uncertain which way to turn. "Just some sandwiches for the poor wretches," she said, striding past them as fast as she could.

"She talkin' to us?"

Bartley shrugged, took a good long look at the prison and then back at the general's wife scurrying down toward the dock.

"How many prisoners in there?"

"Two Redcoats—one soldier, one officer."

Bartley scrunched up his face but kept walking.

On the far slope were hundreds of tents for those not yet housed in permanent barracks. Though made of canvas, each had a brick chimney to keep out the cold. The fire engine stood alongside one, its men spraying the hose onto a canvas that had caught fire. One side was a smoldering hole.

"Fifth one this week," Bartley said.

Levi nodded. "It will be better once all the barracks have been built. Can't have one of them fires spread to an arsenal. All hell would break loose." Levi stopped by the trail that lead down to gallows hollow and caught Bartley's arm. "You know, you shouldn't mock General Arnold. He is our leader, and a hero. Without the battles he's won, we wouldn't be winning this war against the British. Indeed, we might have lost it long ago without him. Some have stolen his bravery and glory, but even General Washington acknowledges his service to our cause."

Bartley pulled his arm free and pursed his lips. "I know, I know. Somethin' just doesn't feel right. Somethin' in my gut I cain't explain. Why would he want the commission here at West Point if he's so valued on the battlefield?"

"You know well the value of West Point, Bartley. The British have New York at the mouth of the Hudson, and they battle down the rivers from the Great Lakes in the north. If the Redcoats were to take West Point, they'd have the Hudson Valley, and our continent would be cut clear in half. The colonies of New England would be unable to coordinate with those to the west and south. We'd lose the war quick."

"You're right." Bartley shook his head. "I'm hungry, you?"

Bartley changed into a dry uniform and the two soldiers settled down onto the grass, under the shade of a boulder with a couple hundred others. The ramparts of Fort Putnam rose above them.

Bartley reached into his sack and ripped off a chunk of bread and a good portion of pork. The bread was chewy. The pork was fatty and pink—just how he liked it. He took a sip of rum, and winced. "Not the good stuff. We'll have to hurry up and become officers before this war is over."

Levi took a sip and grimaced, too. Then he smiled. "I heard General Arnold was key in a battle up in the Great Lakes to capture Quebec, before they even knew there was a war happening. He was leading troops of men that knew absolutely nuthin'."

The pig tasted good. Bartley crunched on a bit of crackling. The soldiers next to them played marbles as they ate.

"Then the British started building ships for the lake and so did General Arnold," Levi said. "They could see each other on either side of the lake, hacking and sawyering and nailing and building. When the ships were built, they attacked t'other. Now the general, being the only one who knew anything about ships, worked his men hard, and when they were all dead, he sailed and manned the cannons himself and pushed the British back to where they belonged. That makes him a hero in my mind." Levi licked his lips and took another swig of rum.

Bartley lay down in the grass. He hiccupped and burped loudly. "Still, look around, Levi."

Levi looked. "What?"

"My brother, Robert, is a sawyer and should be here building barracks. But where is he? And several hundred other soldiers?"

Levi stared at him.

"They've been out in the wood for weeks, gatherin' wood."

"Well, don't they need it to build?" Levi asked.

Bartley pointed with exasperation at the fenced field where immense piles of planks and trunks had been stored for the construction and coming winter fires. There was more than enough to build twoscore of barracks. "Then there's my brother, David. He was brung here from Boston to print pamphlets and maps and orders. And where is he now?"

"Where?" Levi asked.

"Out in the woods gatherin' kindling."

Levi's face pinched in confusion. "If General Arnold ordered it, then it must be for some reason. We are not privy to what he has been asked by General Washington."

"Still . . ."

Bartley let the conversation lapse. He ran his tongue over his teeth and looked into the sky. When the fire engine rolled past, toward yet another fire, he jumped to his feet. "Best we go to Beverly and tell the general our good news."

Bartley pulled on his military jacket, and they packed their gear and ran down to the dock. As they skimmed the gunboat across the water from West Point to Constitution Island, Bartley made notes in his log of exactly which links needed replacement. Levi manned the tiller, sliding the boat nice and easy onto the pebbled eastern shoreline.

The Robinson House, or Beverly as the general and his wife called it, was up a steep incline, past fortifications and set deep in a densely forested spot. A wooden house lined with brick, Beverly was not as imposing as the three-story, four-chimney folly—the Red House—used by Washington as headquarters over at West Point, but still it looked comfortable.

And isolated from most of the troops, Bartley mused.

They stepped up onto the porch and dusted off one another's uniforms before knocking. The guard beside the door yawned and ignored them. Mrs. Arnold opened it and ushered them into the hallway. She left them for the general's small study, leaving the door ajar, and Bartley had a plain view of the room through the gap.

Major General Benedict Arnold sat at his desk, dipping his pen into an inkwell and scrawling across a parchment. He held up a hand for his wife to be silent as he finished. With keen eyes, Bartley could just make out the correspondence—unusual lines of numbers, dots, and dashes, one after the other the full length of the page. The general seemed to be copying it from another scrap of paper, but as the ink dried, it vanished.

He looked up and saw the door ajar, and his face flushed red, his brow drawn hard over his eyes. He strode around his desk and slammed the door shut with a bang that made Levi jump. There were some heated words behind the thick, paneled oak, and then it was yanked open again. Mrs. Arnold ran out, pushing a note into her décolletage without even a glance at the soldiers.

"Come!" the general barked. His scowl remained, and Bartley noted a sheen of sweat on his cheeks. "Report!"

Bartley handed over his journal, and the general's fat finger, still oily with lard from the unfinished luncheon on the desk, traced down the ledger.

"Five links, you say?"

"Yes, sir."

General Arnold slumped back into his chair. A tight smile cut beneath his scowl, and he tapped his fingers against the desktop.

"Will the chain hold till winter?"

"It might, but I recommend duplicating the sections between three of the pontoons, then removing the damaged ones."

The general sat still, his eyes going cloudy as if lost in some deep thought. "Perhaps we should pull the chain from the river."

"Sir, that would leave the waterway and West Point exposed. The ice floe and burgs aren't expected for two months or more."

General Arnold was thinking hard. His face twisted and he sucked on his knuckle before breathing heavy out his nostrils.

"Could a British man-of-war break through the chain as it currently stands?"

"I do not know, sir. Perhaps with a full-on wind from the south."

The general leaned forward over Bartley's journal, going over the items again. He signed the last entry, then placed the journal in his drawer.

"I will give your recommendations due consideration," he said, looking up from his desk. "That is all."

The men dashed out of the office and down the incline toward the gunboat. They were just pulling out when the general's guard came huffing down the trail.

"The general wants you and your boat here at sundown." The guard crouched over in a wheeze and then turned around to start the climb back up to Beverly.

* * * *

They were true to the order, standing on Constitution Island dock as the sun fell. But it wasn't until the river bend was in absolute darkness that General Benedict Arnold came limping toward them, favoring the leg shattered at Saratoga.

"South," he muttered as he climbed into the gunboat.

Levi lifted the sails and took the tiller, and the small boat skimmed between two of the pontoons, over the sunken chain, and followed the flow downstream.

"Been a long time since I've been fishing," the general muttered to himself before crawling astern to sit near the men. Bartley took a surreptitious side-glance at Levi.

"You're Private Levi Atkinson, aren't you, son?" He ignored Bartley who pulled at some rigging.

"Yes, sir."

"You were at Valley Forge with Washington in '77?"

"Yes, sir, I were."

"Must have been young." The general made a gruff cackling noise.

"I were fourteen, sir, but nothin' could've kept me away. I still got the scars where I was inoculated against the pox." He pulled up his sleeve to reveal the three puckered lines across his upper arm.

They lapsed into silence until the boat glided close to the shore. "Keep going, son. I'll tell you when to stop." They passed a glade where the frogs were croaking loudly. The general turned to Levi again. "What did you learn there, during and after that winter?"

Levi was thoughtful for a minute. "I learnt attitude, sir. And I learnt how to fight—how to protect my country."

The general nodded. "Under Washington and Von Steuben."

"Yes, sir. We were trained in the rifles of frontiersmen that can shoot twice as far as the British muskets. We learnt the tactics of Indian woodland warriors—stealth, speed, and surprise. But we also learnt"—Levi ducked his head to miss a low-hanging willow branch— "we learnt to kill the British officers first. Without them ones that sit back on their horses, the regulars are leaderless. They don't know the orders or the tactics. A sniper who can take out a general or such is worth his weight in a hundred cavalrymen."

"Quite ungentlemanly of you, Private Levi," the general bellowed, his face crinkling in mirth. He turned to Bartley. "You have done well, private. 'Always choose companions that are your better,' my mother used to say." General Arnold turned suddenly toward the front of the boat, craning his head back and forth. "Pull in here, coxswain."

Levi turned the boat ashore, and Bartley jumped into the shallows to push the prow up onto the beach.

"Stand guard here," said the general. "I will return in two hours."

Bartley and Levi sat in the boat, in the dark, amongst the weeping branches of a willow.

"What's all this about?" Bartley asked.

Levi shrugged. "General stuff. Perhaps General Washington is hereabouts."

"No, he's not due back at West Point for a few days."

"As far as we know." Levi gave an exaggerated wink.

The frogs stopped croaking.

The moan of a hull and the lap of water against it echoed up the river and through the willows. Both Bartley's and Levi's eyes went wide at the dark shadow of a British sloop-of-war slipping up the middle of the Hudson. Its ripples made their small gunboat rock. The ship was all dark, no sign of lantern, but Bartley could discern men standing silently on its deck—not even a whisper. Bartley thought of the *Phoenix* at Kip's Bay, the ship that had been within a stone's throw. This one was even closer.

The *Vulture*.

Bartley and Levi sat within the shadow of the enormous vessel, its gun ports all open with cannons sticking out into the night.

"We got to warn General Arnold," Levi uttered, almost without breath.

Bartley shook his head. "We wait here. He told us to wait here." He held his finger to his lips and whispered. "We've got to be quiet or they'll hear us."

Suddenly the screech of rope and the flap of canvas echoed across the water. The *Vulture's* sails billowed and it drifted out into the current and turned. It disappeared downstream within a thumping beat of Bartley's heart.

The men let out their breath, eyeing each other nervously beneath the willows.

It was at least another hour before General Arnold returned to the gunboat. They told him of the *Vulture*, and he only nodded gravely and ordered them to secrecy for the good of the Continental Army. Then he directed them to return him to Beverly.

A few days later—the day General Washington was set to arrive—Bartley and Levi were called back to Constitution Island to discuss the chain with General Arnold. They were just stepping across the gunwale of their boat when the general came scrambling down the slope faster than Bartley had ever seen him run. He held tight to his Saratoga leg, but it didn't slow him down one bit.

"Take me downriver!" he barked.

"But, General—"

"Now, or I will have you arrested!" He pulled his pistol from his belt and jumped into the gunboat. Levi ran to the tiller and Bartley hoisted the sail.

"General?" Bartley asked.

"No questions. Utmost secrecy," General Benedict Arnold said. "All the sails, hurry."

"Yes, sir."

The gunboat shot downstream at full mast.

"Where to?" Bartley asked, but then a slow, grim scowl spread over the general's face.

They were but a mile from West Point when they saw the *Vulture*. It appeared much larger in the daylight. Its sails were full and it bore rapidly toward them.

Bartley reached for his pistol, but the general barked at him, "Stay. Pull alongside the ship." Bartley was incredulous as a ladder was thrown down from the British sloop-of-war, and General Benedict Arnold climbed up it faster than any man on a battlefield. At the same instant, Redcoats bent over the high gunwale of the tall ship and started shooting at them. Musket fire shattered the side of the gunboat. Water splashed, and puff after puff of smoke and shot resounded around them.

The gunboat tipped up, its cannon aiming uselessly at the sky above.

Bartley pulled Levi with him—"Deep Breath!"—into and under the water. The Hudson was muddy, and Bartley held tight to Levi's arm, kicking and reaching forward. His head was soon buzzing from lack of breath and he felt Levi go limp behind him, but still he held tight to his friend. He kicked hard toward where he thought the side of the Hudson might be. He clutched at mud and pulled himself and Levi into the shallows, the slender branches of willows throwing them into a dark dappled shadow. The *Vulture* was a hundred yards upstream, its Redcoats still shooting into the murky surge. Bartley pulled Levi into his side, but the private was lifeless. There was no blood—he hadn't been shot. Bartley stuck his fingers in Levi's mouth and scooped out a sludgy chunk of mud. He shook him, slapped him across the face, then took a deep breath and blew it into Levi's mouth.

Levi shuddered, coughing and spewing mud, and Bartley pulled him close and held a hand over his friend's face as he came to.

"Shhh." Bartley's voice was hoarse and cracked.

They sat low in the water, with only their noses and eyes above it, as the *Vulture* drifted to make its turn in the Hudson, then headed downstream toward British-held New York.

* * * *

"Whom can we trust now?" Bartley asked after word had spread of General Benedict Arnold's traitorous actions.

"Colonel Kościuszko said Arnold was trying to sell the plans for West Point so the British could take it!" Levi said.

Bartley said nothing further as he held his journal close to his chest.

He had a chain to fix.

P.J. Parker

From Sea to Shining Sea; An Empire of Liberty (1805 AD)

Monday, February 11, 1805

My pappy and uncles Robert and David always told me I was boarn [sic born] *at the exact instant President* [sic General] *Washington fired the last shot of the war at Yorktown, Virginia, in 1781. He said I took my first breaths as the Redcoats scampered away, their tails between their legs. True or not, I have grown up military. I have proudly served in the U.S. Army at Fort C* [Clinton], *West Point, and then Fort P.* [Pitt?], *Pennsylvania, since I was old enough to muck out a stable and saddle a horse. Being assigned as a private to the Corps of Discovery under Capt. Meriwether Lewis and Capt.* [sic Lieutenant] *William Clark is an honor. More so since Capt. Lewis determined I was schooled and requested me to keep a jrnl* [sic journal] *for the remainder of our travel*[s] *through the Louisiana Purchase. That we are going out into the vast unknown, to* [illegible] *and reach the Pacific Ocean, at times seems beyond comprehension—as if President Jefferson requested we go to the very moon and back. A daunting enterprise with unknown dangers. The forty or so members of our team, military men—including a few good Kentucky boys—and some French trappers, never cease to be excited by the vast west horizon and what it may deliver to our future.*

Day, clear, but could [sic cold].

AMERICA Túwaqachi

The Frenchman's sqar [sic squaw], *Sacagawea,*
had a child this evening. A boy.

—Unpublished fragment of a Corps of Discovery Field
Journal in the name of Pvt. Peter [illegible], Mansfield
Library Collection, University of Montana.

* * * *

Peter climbed the rise with Captain Lewis, through tall grasses
up to their waists. The officer's Newfoundland ran at their heels, tail
wagging, a dead squirrel clenched in its mouth. Behind them, to the
south, the Missouri plaited across the prairie, running almost clear. The
expedition boats were pulled up onto a pebbled bar, just above the fast-
moving riffle that had taken a full day of back-breaking rowing to
traverse. Oars leaned against the gunwales. Exhausted soldiers sat at
the water's edge with their lines, hoping to catch trout or grayling.
Others followed the trappers out onto the plain to shoot some venison.

"Cap'n, this must be the biggest sky in the whole darned
world."

"Impossibly big, private."

There wasn't a cloud in sight. Just blue. No matter which
direction, the horizon was not quite flat, but there was no telling how
far away it truly was. Tens of thousands—maybe hundreds of
thousands—of bison meandered across the grassy plain. Wooded
groves followed the Missouri and curled off to where the sun would
later set. Peter could make out two brown bears sitting in the water a
couple of miles upstream. He hoped they'd stay there.

"Only God himself knows how far the legendary Rockies are
ahead of us."

Peter grinned. "And all of it, now part of the United States of
America for three cents an acre."

The captain chuckled. "Yes, God bless our president's
foresight in purchasing it from the French. Though I expect the
Spanish are none too pleased."

Two years previous, the first leg of the corps' journey from
Fort Pitt down the Ohio River to the Mississippi had been punctuated

by friendly settlers, handsome small towns, and gala balls and picnics. The first winter months and drifts of snow had settled them on the Moon River just north of St. Louis. Once the French had officially handed over Louisiana and the corps had started up the Missouri, there had been little in the way of actual civilization as Peter recognized it. A few settlers—*Americans,* he thought with pride—were scattered along the waterway. A lone Frenchman occasionally passed—his canoe overloaded with pelts.

Now a herd of antelope stood less than a hundred feet away, ears twitching. Captain Lewis raised his U.S. Army Model 1803 rifle and sighted down the barrel.

"It seems the animals here are only too willing to keep us fed. As if they think it their duty."

He squeezed the trigger and the rifle jolted with a crack. A doe dropped to the ground. The rest of her herd scattered.

"Perhaps they aren't used to man and don't see us as a threat." Peter pulled up his own rifle and squinted along its length. The herd had stopped as if uncertain whether the danger was gone. His rifle popped and a buck tumbled into the grass.

"The natives must have passed through these parts for many generations—they would have hunted."

"You think them Indians been around that long?" Peter asked. "They don't even have no towns, just some stick tents—*tepees.*"

Captain Lewis pressed his fingers to his lips and let out a whistle down to the boats. York, his slave, came scampering across the beachhead and up the rise. The captain pointed to where the two antelopes lay dead.

"Yes, massa, I sees them." York backed away from his owner, his head lowered, then turned to go handle the meat.

"Let's see if we can find a beaver, private. Nothing nicer than a juicy beaver tail on the griddle."

Except maybe a fried squirrel, Peter thought.

They slid down a grassy embankment and trod along a tributary that cut into the prairie almost perpendicular to the Missouri.

"While you and the men were training at Dubois that first winter, I was down across the Miss'ippi from St. Louis with the postmaster at Cahokia. There are mounds and hills there along the river that defy explanation. I suspect they are of Indian construction."

"You don't think floodwater just eroded 'em that way?" Peter asked.

"Doubtful. There appears to be symmetry amongst them."

"And you think it was some Indian fort or something? Or maybe the Spanish. They've been around a while."

Captain Lewis shrugged. "We may never know."

"Truthfully, sir, I expected we'd be fighting Indians all the way to the western ocean. All the stories I ever heard said the land was possessed by powerful and warlike red savages. Gigantic, fierce, treacherous, and cruel. The ones we've met have been amiable, willing to trade and show us how to follow the river and cross the mountains. There were only those small incidents with the Kickapoo and the Sioux, and a few of our horses missing, but even they were amicably handled with some trinkets." Peter grasped the Jefferson Peace Medal that hung around his neck. He gave it a rub with his thumb for good luck then stared up the rise to where York was gutting the antelopes. Their four-hooved brothers munched on the grass only a few yards away; they, too, were amiable. Peter looked down the end of his nose toward the Model 1803 in his grip. Then he shook off his thoughts and raised his chin toward a bend in the stream where a beaver's dam blocked the course. "Looks like we goin' t' have some tail tonight, Cap'n."

"Seaman!" The captain gave a whistle for his dog, who was up on the rise with York. "Stupid animal. Seaman!" The dog came bounding down along the stream's edge. "I should've sold you to those redskins that wanted you." He kneeled and grasped the dog's ears then smiled and rubbed his cheek against Seaman's. The dog licked him furiously, and the captain jerked his head back. "Whew! Squirrel breath!"

Peter clambered ahead, across the dam of sticks. His foot became wedged, but he yanked it free and tumbled to the far bank, taking care to keep his finger off the trigger of his rifle. He looked down and noted another rip in his breeches. "Damn." He seemed to spend more time sewing up his clothes than being a soldier. There weren't even any Indians that wanted to fight out here on the plains.

His pa had killed Redcoats. His uncle Robert had killed red men. Perhaps the killing times were over.

Seaman jumped onto the dam of wood and mud and dived down a hole. Peter hunkered at the side of the dam, his gun aimed at another exit. Then Seaman yelped and howled, and the captain scrambled over the dam and lowered his torso into the hole. He came up all bloody, yanking at Seaman's hind leg, and the dog twisted and a spray of blood shot across the captain's jacket. The dog had been bit—the beaver likely nicked an artery. Peter crawled over, pulled the bandana from his neck, and tied it tight around Seaman's rear leg. The captain drew the dog into his arms and they ran back along the stream's edge, down the Missouri and into the camp.

Captain Lewis fixed up the dog before supper time, and Peter went back and got that damned beaver. The captain seemed appreciative as he bit into the grilled tail. He gave a morsel to Seaman, scratching the dog's hairy jaw after his fingers had been licked clean.

* * * *

On their journey west toward the Rockies, Peter came to endure endless teasing about his apparent "bear problem." It seemed whenever he snuck away from the other men to do his business in the grass, a bear would sniff him out without fail. The soldiers had enjoyed great belly-laughs as Peter had lifted his knees, high as he could across a field, with a bear scooting on his tail. They were more than happy to wait until he fell on his face before firing some warning shots into the air.

One particular day, a small yellow bear had crept up behind him and growled so fierce that Peter had nearly ripped his breeches in two as he'd pulled them up again. Though he tried, the other men would not let him forget the incident.

When finally they reached the Great Falls of Missouri, it was a sight to behold just as Sacagawea, the Frenchman's squaw, had said it would be. The spray rose above the plain like a column of smoke, and Peter and the other privates and sergeants pulled hard on their oars, guiding the boats up the Missouri toward the increasing roar that soon drowned out all orders. They pulled the boats to the side of the river, and Peter's heart seemed to catch in his throat as he gazed at the falls above. Water jettisoned over the bluff—three hundred yards wide—to crash more than eighty feet onto rocks and boulders. A great foam roiled below, and a mist lifted into the sky, cut by crystalline rainbows. The men were awestruck.

It was early the next morning when a small crew of Peter and another private, the Frenchman and Sacagawea, Lewis and Clark, and two sergeants strode up the path that veered around the side of the majestic falls. Peter made notes in his journal that they would need to pull the boats up this trail, easily two hundred feet and quite steep.

They reached the crest of the falls, and Peter could see he had vastly underestimated the effort needed to get their boats past this point in the Missouri. The sergeant beside him chewed on his lip as he stared upstream, dumbfounded.

The others returned to the lower camp to stow the gear and ready the boats, but Peter and Captain Lewis trudged almost four hours up alongside the Missouri. They were met with falls after falls—each one more grand than the last. The captain named them Crooked, Great Falls, Beautiful Cascade and, finally, Upper Pitch, which seemed to be the last one. It was some twenty-six feet high. Below it, where the water appeared still, was a handsome island with a cottonwood growing at its center. Both men gasped when a large black eagle soared over the falls and through the mist to land on its nest at the top of the cottonwood.

"No words in our ledgers could do justice to this sublime beauty," Captain Lewis said. "The expedition should have brought a *camera obscura*."

Peter wasn't familiar with the words, but no matter. He knew he was part of something magnificent—something greater than himself or the Corps of Discovery. And he knew what it was.

It was America.

And it was beautiful.

* * * *

Peter stood alone, calculating the height of the Upper Pitch, what he thought of as the Black Eagle Falls, to determine the best route

267

of portage around them. By his reckoning, it would take the best part of a month to get the boats into the upper river to continue on their way toward the Rockies.

It was then the grizzly attacked.

It came barreling out of the cottonwood and across the field. This time Peter had his pants pulled high and his belt tight, and his feet were running before he even knew it was a grizzly. Out of the corner of his eye he saw only large and brown and teeth and claws. Peter was over six feet tall, but still he felt small before the bear towering over him. A large paw swiped at him, claws ripping through his military jacket and the flesh of his chest. He would have screamed from the pain, but the air was knocked from his lungs and he suddenly found himself flying out over the edge of the falls, plummeting through the mist, past the height of the Black Eagle's cottonwood nest and into the roiling waters of the Missouri.

And just like with the dog, Captain Lewis fixed Peter up after dragging him back into the camp. Four deep claw marks slashed across Peter's chest, and the captain crushed dried rattler between his finger and thumb and pushed it into the wounds. He then slathered the incisions with Missouri mud and wrapped Peter's chest and shoulder nice and tight.

"You won't be doing no rowing for a while, private."

During the weeks it took to haul the boats around the falls, Peter helped the captain with his duties. He carried the thermometer that measured water and air temperatures—calling out readings to be logged in his book. He took interest in Captain Lewis's use of the octant and sextant and, quick to learn the basic geometry and patterns of stars, he attempted some readings himself to calculate the latitude and longitude of the falls. He felt a surge of pride whenever Captain Lewis nodded and patted him on the back.

Finally the boats were slipped into the water, and they paddled off toward the Rockies that rose in the far distance, perfectly covered in snow. Range after range climbed higher and higher still, to where the highest peaks were cloaked in cloud. Peter thought the mountains were near, but day after day after day they rowed up the Missouri and still they came no closer.

"The Appalachians are but foothills compared to these mighty peaks," Lewis said.

The river led them away from the prairies of bison and antelope, and after a month had passed Sacagawea pointed to a high plain—a point that looked to Peter like a beaver's head. The Frenchman translated that it was Sacagawea's home, that above it was a passage through the Rockies to the rivers that fell to the Pacific Ocean. Her people, the Salmon Eaters, would lead them. Peter couldn't help smirking. With the other men in his troop, he would be one of the first to travel clear across this new nation.

They harbored the boats in a tight creek off the side of the Missouri, packed their stores, and loaded them onto their shoulders. Then they started up a trail toward the higher ground. Peter's pack pulled at his wound, and he touched his jacket where a few spots of fresh blood bloomed. Luckily, the injury hardly pained him anymore. Without losing pace, he undid some of his buttons and pulled down the blue lapel to air the wound.

The corps had walked no more than five miles when it stopped amidst a cloud of dust. Peter craned his neck to see Captain Lewis up ahead, and beyond him an Indian on a horse, dressed like none they'd yet come across. He held a bow and quiver of arrows. There was no saddle upon his magnificent horse, though Peter could just spy a thin rope leading from the horse's jaw to the Indian's clasped hand.

Captain Lewis lifted a blanket and threw it into the air as a sign of friendship. The blanket unfurled and landed on the ground at his feet.

The Indian sat motionless. The captain threw the blanket a second time.

"He does not appear to share the symbols and language of those on the plains," Peter muttered to the sergeant beside him.

The mounted Indian turned his horse and galloped away, up into the range.

The captain was none too happy that evening after the failed welcome.

The next day, Peter marched up near the front of the column behind the captain. They carried trinkets and peace medals, ready to give to anyone they encountered. At midday they spotted a man and two women surrounded by dogs, about a mile up the plain. But they, too, ran off before the corps could reach them. The trail cut through deep-eroded ravines, and as they stepped from a rift they came across a group of native women no more than a few paces ahead. The women dropped to their knees in fright.

Captain Lewis held out a flag and laid it upon the ground. Then he rolled his sleeves, up above the lines of his tan so the women could see his skin was white. Peter, his jacket half-undone anyway, nudged the rest of his buttons open to fully expose his chest and abdomen— an almost brilliant white under the harsh light of noon.

"Cap'n," Peter whispered, stepping forward tentatively with a pewter looking glass and a tin of vermillion paint.

The captain took the hand of the oldest woman and helped her to her feet. Then he took the looking glass from Peter and held it before her face. He pushed a finger into the tin Peter held and smeared bright vermillion paint across the curve of the woman's cheek. "The color of peace," Peter recalled the Frenchman translating for Sacagawea.

The women seemed settled in the corps' company and urged the soldiers to follow them through the ravines. Captain Lewis pulled Peter to his side. "Leave your jacket unbuttoned, private. We cannot be far from others of this tribe who will need to see who we are. Charbonneau!" The captain waved to the Frenchman. "You and your squaw should walk at my side."

No sooner had the captain spoken than an uncountable number of painted warriors came riding in at full speed. Peter feared they would be trampled, but the horses stopped in a cloud of dust, and the warriors jumped to the ground between the women and the soldiers. Captain Lewis held up the flag. There was some chatter between the men and the women, and before Peter knew what was happening the warriors lunged at them. An Indian threw his arm around Peter and slapped him on the back with great affection. He pressed his cheek against Peter's and yelled, "Ah-hi-e, ah-hi-e!" Peter threw his own arm around the Indian to return the strange, unexpected embrace.

"I am much pleased. I am much rejoiced," the Frenchman said in translation.

The Indian pulled back and gripped Peter's shoulders. He raised his eyebrows and spoke—*a melodic language*, Peter thought.

The Indian placed a hand on Peter's naked chest, measuring the span of his fingers against the raw marks of the claw.

The Frenchman leaned in. "He says you are a brother of the bear; that the grizzly has left his mark to ensure you never forget who you are, and the land and heritage you belong to."

Peter gazed at the red hand pressed against the white flesh of his chest, then up at the painted face of the one who embraced him so heartily.

He nodded. "I understand."

P.J. Parker

A Letter from Monticello (1807 AD)

"I understand your predicament, Lieutenant." Peter shrugged the heavy blue jacket from his shoulders and hung it over the back of the chair. The symbols of his rank were still new and shiny gold against the dull blue cotton—a little dusty from the afternoon trot from St. Louis up to Fort Belle Fontaine. The room over the barracks was washed white with a window open to the Mississippi. The ramparts of the fort cascaded down through the wilderness to the water's edge.

"Thank you, Captain." Lieutenant Zebulon Montgomery Pike sat stiffly across the table.

Peter settled into his chair and pulled a letter from his breast pocket. His hand lingered at his chest before he placed the envelope onto the oak table and opened the flap. "This letter is from Monticello. It is confirmation in the president's own hand that your mission was intended only for exploration of the southern Louisiana Purchase. Just as Captain Lewis and Lieutenant Clark explored the northern regions of this new land, you were to explore the south. Do you understand?"

"Yes, sir."

"It confirms the story that you and your corps became lost. Do you understand?" Peter asked.

"Yes, sir."

"It also reiterates to the Spanish Government that you are not a spy—that there was never any intention for you to be a spy. You were a corps of discovery, and you became lost and crossed the border into New Spain without knowing it. Do you understand?"

"Yes, Captain."

"The United States government will reimburse the Spanish for the time you were—er—their *guest* in Chihuahua. You will publish what you recall of your exploration. You will state that you got lost. You will state you were not a spy. Do you understand?"

"Yes, sir. Fully."

Peter folded the letter, reinserted it into the envelope, and handed it to the sergeant behind him to deliver. When he and Lieutenant Pike were alone, Peter's lip curled. He leaned across the table and said in a low voice, "Well done, Lieutenant. You have served our country well. Now, tell me all you saw of the Spanish military and their defenses—the locations and sizes of villages, presidios and missions you encountered, any other details of interest on your trek from the Rio Grande to Chihuahua and back through Texas Province to Louisiana and, finally, any indication of insurgency or rebellion amongst the colonials against Spain. President Jefferson wishes to know everything you observed on his behalf."

"Yes, Captain."

P.J. Parker

The Shrine of Texas Liberty (1836 AD)

The twins galloped across a Texas valley that was covered in bristlegrass and sprangletop. At twenty-five years of age and just shy of six-foot-four, they were their father's sons in almost every way—handsome, broad of shoulder, blue of eye—though with the prairie-colored skin of their mother, Concepción. Their father had been killed in the war of eighteen-twelve, but they wore his memory on the flesh that covered their hearts—identical tattoos clawing across the skin.

"¡Viva México!" Daniel shouted as they pulled up onto a ridge. The range spread before them. He leaned over and slapped Christopher on the back.

Both brothers grinned.

"No regrets on leaving the United States?"

"Why should there be? Back in Louisiana and the rest of the Union, land is expensive—not to mention the fraudsters and humbugs that sell land that is not even theirs to give." Christopher let out a satisfied chuckle. "Here in Texas Province we can gain a thousandfold through hard work and determination. Perhaps even more with a bit of gambling." He winked.

They trotted down the slope toward a wide, boulder-strewn river and dismounted. The men and their horses bowed to the water and slurped it up. Daniel filled his hat to the brim and poured it over his head then ran his fingers through his dark, wayward curls.

"Dang, that's good." He settled down into the grass to lay on his back, content listening to Christopher splashing out into the stream with the horses. "Don't get the packs and rifles wet, mister."

A few minutes later, Christopher fell into the grass beside him.

"I expect it will take more than just hard work to gain our stake in this land."

"That's why we got our rifles." Daniel twisted a stalk of grass from the ground to pick at his teeth. "It's not been long since Mexico gained its independence from Spain, and I reckon before the season is over the Tejanos and Texians will declare their own. If not to be their own country, then perhaps to join the Union."

Christopher nodded and pulled his hat over his eyes. "Do you think Ma and Sis will come down once we have things put right?"

"Who knows? They got their heart set on taking one of them steamboats up the river all the ways from St. Louis to Pittsburgh. Maybe even go on to Chicago to be with the rest of Pa's family. That's enough adventure for any lifetime."

"I s'pose." Christopher scratched at the hair on his belly. "Tarnation, I could do with a jug of whiskey and some time with an adventuress."

Daniel laughed. "You and me both, brother. I'm sure we'll find plenty of all we're hankering for in San Antonio."

The twins continued along the trail through some of the most beautiful wilderness and pasture they had seen west of the Mississippi.

"Prime cattle land," Christopher said more than once as they clopped along.

They passed a few grand homesteads. Spanish longhorns roamed the open range and tired-looking Negroes built fences and swept verandas.

"I thought Mexico outlawed slavery."

"They been turnin' a blind eye for the Texians. Someone got to do the menial work for these filibusters."

"Well, it won't be that way on our acreage. No, sir. It will be our own blood and sweat that will create a future for our family."

They followed the undulating course of the Rio de San Antonio.

"Plenty of land here. We should be able to lay claim to a valley or six within spitting distance of the settlement." Christopher patted the pouch of card winnings at his side.

San Antonio was small compared to their birth town of St. Louis. Daniel guessed its population at around two thousand. A couple of streets within a loop of the river linked scattered limestone and mudbrick buildings, plus some wooden shanties and canvas tents. To the west was a massive church, and on the eastern side of the water was a little stone fort.

"We'll have to become Catholics before they take our money and give us land."

They kept on riding past the creaking sign of the empresario's land office in search of a saloon, and they soon found one. A rough plank building with swinging doors and an upstairs window or two promised to meet their needs. The twins hitched their horses to the rail and stepped up onto the boardwalk.

* * * *

Within a handful of weeks they were sleeping under the stars on their own dirt and grass. The twins' skill at the saloon's smoky backroom table had gained them twice the acreage they'd envisioned, and enough to secure three hundred yearlings from the Cortina Ranch up the range. Their days were spent felling lumber to build corrals ready for the cattle; their evenings sitting around the campfire dreaming of the future. It smelled and tasted good. Owning dirt would do that to any good man. Saturdays were spent training with the local militia down at the Alamo. And Saturday nights—well, they were pretty darn good, too.

Christopher leaned against a split-rail fence, staring off into the distance. Daniel sat on the top rail beside him and clapped Christopher's shoulder with a firm, gloved hand.

"Ain't it a huckleberry above a persimmon, Chris?"

"I reckon, Dan." He thumbed the brim of his hat up a little higher.

They squinted when they saw someone riding up the valley.

"Looks like Jimmy."

The youngster followed the course of the river, crossed at the ford, then moseyed up the way to them. He waved his hat and the twins waved back.

"Howdy, boys. Lieutenant Colonel Travis requests for all the militia to gather. Somethin's up."

"Did he say what?"

Jimmy shook his head. "Just that you need to bring all your guns and ammunition."

* * * *

Wagonloads of settlers rolled down the northern trail out of town as the twins approached from the foothills. One wagon carried Miss Kitty and Miss Eleanor from the saloon.

"Dang, it must be serious," Christopher muttered beneath his breath.

They kicked into a gallop, stirring up the dust as they entered San Antonio and then crossed the river toward the Alamo. Most of the militia was already there. The old mission buildings were heavily fortified, thanks to the work of Colonel Bowie. The chapel itself had seen better days and was in need of a roof, but the convent had been fixed up as a serviceable barracks, and the large plaza was walled by limestone blocks more than three feet thick. The river snuck into the fort through a grill in the southern wall near the main gate. Some seventeen cannons pointed out in all directions from the tops of the walls.

Lieutenant Colonel William Travis was mid-speech when they arrived. He spoke like a book, standing on a wood platform before the straight blue lines of a hundred military troops. Alongside the troops stood an almost equal number of militia, a mixture of Texians and Tejanos in buckskins and broad-brimmed hats, rifles ready.

Daniel nudged Christopher's shoulder and pointed through the crowd toward their militia leader. "Colonel James Bowie." They tied their horses and walked in amongst the men.

"What's Travis sayin'?" Daniel asked a militiaman.

"Sayin' that the Mexican General Santa Anna is coming with all his dragoons."

"Has Texas declared independence?"

"Dunno, but the Mexican general seems determined it ain't gon' happen. Says we're illegals in their land."

The brothers caught one another's gaze.

"Travis says we all need to stay here at the Alamo an' be ready. He already sent a messenger southeast to Colonel Fannin in Goliad for reinforcements."

"Colonel Bowie don't seem none too happy."

"He ain't. Still cain't stand Travis, but he cooled off some since Colonel Crockett arrived."

"Davy Crockett? He's here? I read all about him in the St. Louis papers!"

The militiaman indicated with a jerk of his head, and over near the old mission chapel yard was Davy Crockett—coon hat, fiddle, and all—standing with a dozen buckskins holding longrifles.

"They come all the way from Tennessee."

Daniel leaned into his brother. "Colonel Bowie crushed the last Mexican attempt to take back San Antonio and the Alamo. And now with Davy Crockett fightin' with us there ain't no way we can lose. We got Santa Anna sockdolagered!" He punched his fist into his open palm.

*　*　*　*

Daniel was positioned with a Bluecoat up in the San Fernando Church bell tower—the highest point in the middle of the town, where they could see clear in every direction. They took it in turns to keep watch while the other rested on the creaking boards around the bell. It was sunny for the most part, but clouds and sleet crept up on the hills. Daniel could tell a chill in the air was coming. San Antonio was near deserted, though some folks were still packing their belongings into wagons, ready to flee the approaching army.

A scout came galloping in from the southwest, shooting his gun and yelling wildly. Daniel and the Bluecoat took up the signal and rang the bell. It was deafening, and in the streets below, Texians sped up as they herded cattle and horses through the town, across the river, and up into the Alamo. Others drove wagonloads of supplies and vittles, scrounged from abandoned homesteads, stores, and the saloon.

The Mexican Army had advanced to the middle of San Antonio by the time Daniel and the Bluecoat scurried down the bell tower's ladders. They rode toward the fort, straight through a corps of dragoons.

By sunset, more than fifteen hundred of General Santa Anna's troops were scattered around the Alamo, a circle of great guns being aimed at the small stone fort.

Daniel stood not far from Colonels Bowie and Crockett on the Alamo's western wall. Crockett lifted *Betsy*, his rifle, to his shoulder and peered along her barrel for sight of the Mexican general. Christopher was on the far rampart, hunkered over his own rifle.

"Come and get it, *El Presidente*," Crockett muttered.

A blood-red flag was hoisted from the church's bell tower across the river.

"No quarter," Colonel Bowie said. "They consider us no more than pirates on their land—illegals to be reviled and killed. Humph." He followed with a hacking cough, and the back of his hand was spotted by saliva and blood before he wiped it against his breeches. "I like to think we'd be of a more welcoming mind if their people wanted to settle in the Union."

The largest cannon in the Alamo went off with a boom. A puff of smoke billowed as the cannonball flew over the river toward the Mexican Army. It bounced along the main street of San Antonio to settle near the church doors without damage.

"Dang blast that Travis. Dang fool!" Colonel Bowie stormed off toward where Travis stood near the cannon.

Daniel watched the heated argument without hearing it. Then Davy Crockett let out a deep sigh and scurried toward the dispute.

Santa Anna's troops were setting up camps beyond the range of rifle and cannon. They were orderly, disciplined, marching in straight lines, hoisting tents in regular form, and spreading their men and guns evenly around the perimeter of the Alamo. By comparison, the inside of the fort was in disarray—a few hundred besieged by thousands.

Daniel swallowed hard.

Two horsemen galloped out the Alamo's front gate and into the center of town. Once they dismounted, they were lead to a tent near the church. They disappeared inside for no more than half an hour before they returned to the fort to join Travis, Bowie, Crockett, and several other officers. The officers signaled toward the Alamo's main cannon.

The weapon fired a second time.

The ball crashed into the side of the land office then bounced along an alley, but the Mexicans continued establishing their camp without any apparent concern. There was no retaliation at all that first night. It grew too dark to see, and in the dead quiet Colonel Crockett cut a tune on his fiddle. It drifted through the plaza and up over the walls. Christopher and Daniel leaned against the wall the whole night through without a word.

Over the next few days the Mexicans maneuvered their cannon placement without so much as a single shot or obscene gesture. Under the dark of night they inched closer and closer until their guns were only a thousand feet from the walls and the twins could clearly make out the buttons, insignias, and smiles of the dragoons.

Then the fusillade started.

Ball after lead ball smashed into the walls of the Alamo and ricocheted around the plaza. In no time, Daniel's shoulder was raw from the kick of his rifle as he fired, reloaded, aimed, and fired as fast as he was able. He could see the men he killed, lying in a heap by the day, to be removed at night and replaced with more as his bullets hit their marks the following day. He was numb, his face hot and wet from anger and fear. But his brother's shoulder pressed firmly against his own, and it kept him going.

The wall below shuddered with each cannonball. Limestone cracked and exploded, rocky portions of the barrier tumbling to the ground. Each night, after the firing had ceased, the militia rebuilt the wall, filling in the cavities, repositioning rocks and brickwork before climbing back up to the top at daybreak, only to do it all again the next night.

None could sleep. It was near impossible even to blink without being jarred awake by the careen and smash of the fight.

Colonel Bowie took sick and collapsed. He was hauled into a hospital room, and it was the last Daniel and Christopher ever saw of him.

The day after, near three hundred of the Mexican troops crossed the Rio de San Antonio, taking cover in huts closer to the fort.

A dozen men, Christopher included, ventured out and set fire to the huts. As they sparked and blazed, a bitter battle erupted of gunfire, bayonets, and fists. Finally the Mexicans retreated, dragging their wounded. Christopher made it back into the fort, heavily bruised, burnt, and bloody, but still able to hold his rifle on the wall beside his brother.

"Our land is just up yonder waiting for us, Dan."

"Yes, sir, it is. Pretty as a peach. We'll have the biggest dang homesteads around these parts, and wives so beautiful we'll have to guard them with our rifles."

"And kids, plenty of kids."

"Dozens of the rascals."

A cannonball careened close past their heads, and they ducked, each trying to cover the other.

* * * *

Exhaustion riddled the men, women, children, and slaves inside the Alamo, but all followed the orders of Travis and Crockett, determined they wouldn't be beat. Morale grew when thirty-two brave men from Gonzales charged in to join their brothers-in-arms, but even with the reinforcements, Lieutenant Colonel Travis kept sending letters for help. Three of his messengers and their horses lay dead within sight of the Alamo, and the Mexicans just left them there. It was too far and too dangerous for the militia to retrieve the bodies, even at night.

The twins sat beside the well, eating bread and sipping water. Every bone in Daniel's body ached. His trigger finger was blistered, the flesh near rubbed right off.

"You, soldier," barked an officer whose name Daniel did not know. "Follow me."

Daniel pushed himself to his feet with a glance at Christopher and then followed the Bluecoat to the Alamo's chapel. They went inside, the roofless chapel giving them a clear view of the sky above. The thunder of attack resonated within. Its walls were crumbling. Dust and smoke hung low.

Lieutenant Colonel Travis stood beside the door to the arsenal talking to an unseen soldier inside. Then he turned and approached Daniel.

"You have been recommended for your riding skills, son. I am told your horse is still alive in the corral behind the barracks."

Daniel nodded, and Travis handed him a letter.

"I have sent a number of couriers to General Fannin to no avail, but I refuse to believe the people of Texas and all Americans in the world have forgotten us."

Daniel gripped the letter tight. His hand was shaking from the fatigue of a week without sleep.

"You are to deliver this letter to General Houston at Washington-on-the-Brazos and personally place it into his hands. We have enough supplies for another month, and the general and his men could easily travel here within a few days." Travis paused to look down to the floor, then back up into Daniel's eyes. "You may wish to stay in the chapel a few moments before you leave."

Daniel stared at the letter, but his thoughts were of Christopher. For Christopher, he would get the message through the Mexican troops.

Christopher had to survive.

He sank into the dirt and looked up to where a cross should have been.

* * * *

Daniel nudged his horse out of the corral and into the plaza. He'd been unable to bring himself to say goodbye to Christopher, but he couldn't stop himself from gazing across the plaza to where his brother sat. Christopher stood, his face white and eyes wide. He took a step then stopped, removed his hat, and pressed it to his heart. Daniel pulled his lapel to the side to expose the tattoo they shared, and nodded.

"Hiya!" Daniel kicked his mount and rode low against the animal's bare back. He galloped across the plaza like greased lightning and blasted out the Alamo's front gate just as cannonballs slammed into the wall beside it. Rocks, debris, and bullets whizzed by his face.

"Hiya! Hiya!" Through a cloud of smoke, over a ditch, and they were amongst the Mexican dragoons.

The first bullet hit him in the calf. The second in his thigh. But he was thankful it was he who'd taken the shot and not the horse. She kept up her pace.

The third and fourth bullets shattered his upper arm and shoulder.

Daniel pressed himself lower, his cheek hard against the neck of his mount. His legs and arms were almost numb, his eyes blinded by tears, but still he dug in his knees and yelled in his horse's twitching ear.

"Hiya! Hiya!"

* * * *

General Houston rode into the settlement of Gonzales with his troops.

Daniel rode at the rear.

Word spread through the column of men of what had occurred in San Antonio.

Everyone at the Alamo was dead, their bodies piled up and burned to ashes.

P.J. Parker

The Trail of Tears: Nu Na Da Ul Tsun Yi (1838 AD)

Daniel slumped half asleep on the back of his horse, racked by memories and the pain of his bad leg and arm. The horse ambled north, never more than a few miles a day. Some days she just stood in the shade of a tree, nibbling at the grass, her master too weak from lack of food and emotion to dismount.

Daniel didn't care how long the journey would take. He didn't care about the acreage he'd left behind in Texas. He didn't care that Santa Anna had surrendered to Houston's army or that Texas was independent.

He needed to be with his family. And that meant going to Chicago.

Sometimes he would wake with a start, head throbbing, eyes swollen, and throat raw from crying in his sleep, to another valley he had never seen before and never would again.

The weather turned bitter, and drifts of snow made travel difficult. His clothes were threadbare, his feet naked and numb.

The cold sun was sinking to the horizon when the horse stopped on a bluff overlooking a river. Chunks of ice tumbled in the surge. It might have been the Mississippi. Perhaps it was the Missouri. The sky and river were a faded purple, and lightning flashed in the distance. Down by the river on a swampy plain shone the lights and fires of a wagon train.

Daniel's stomach growled and he leaned over to dry retch. The horse carried him down the slope toward the train, past the naked, dead body of a woman—Indian he reckoned, by the color of her skin and length of her hair. Then he passed the frail corpse of a tattooed warrior, his breechcloth little more than a rag, his thin flesh stretched over his ribcage. He passed another, and another—without really seeing them through the rawness of his own thoughts. Perhaps he was better off dead, too.

The horse brought him to the westernmost wagons. Soldiers in new uniforms with bright shiny buttons looked up from their fires and pewter plates piled high with meat, gravy, and biscuits. They must have seen the star on his jacket, for they waved for him to join them.

He stared at them as his horse kept on toward the river, and the wagons became fewer and more tattered. Indians lay in the dirt around fires—thousands of them. They were barefoot and wore rags, surrounded by mounds of snow, sharing meager bowls of a yellowy-brown stew.

His horse stopped before an old Indian, his face long, his eyes sad. He was all but naked in the freezing cold, and he held up his bowl toward Daniel. Daniel manhandled his right leg over the horse, fell to the ground, and crawled toward the fire. The Indian tipped the bowl to his lips, using his fingers to push the stew into Daniel's mouth. He was silent as Daniel chewed and swallowed, then tilted the bowl again.

When he'd had enough, Daniel stared into the flames, feeling the icy heat of the old man beside him.

"What is the name of your horse?" the old man asked.

Daniel cleared his throat and coughed. "It's . . . It's Sammy, sir."

The old man nodded. "I can see you are my brother. We follow the same trail, though we travel in opposite directions."

Daniel wiped at this mouth with the back of his hand. He shuffled to sit up properly. "How so, sir?"

"We both know death. But whereas my people are driven toward it, your journey will take you from it—toward life."

The wrinkles in the old man's face were deep, but so were his eyes, which held the story of his people. Daniel looked along the trail of campfires weaving their way to the river's edge, the frigid night air cut by crying and singing that wrapped around his heart and froze it to ice.

The old man held out his thin arms, and Daniel curled up and rested his head on the ancient lap and cried. The old man pressed his hand against the exposed mark of the bear on Daniel's chest, and

Daniel shuddered. Through the flicker of the flame he could see the stars. They were sharp and true.

"Do not fret, my brother, my child. For the buffalo will roam the plains once more."

* * * *

The sign read, "Hannibal, Missouri," but Sammy trotted past at such a pace that Daniel didn't catch it. It was a little town of no more than a handful of plank houses and a church, stuck to a bend in the mighty Mississippi where the fragrance of locust blossoms filled the air. He passed a pump where white kids played with mulatto and colored kids, in the cloth of slavery, filling up pails and getting up to audacious mischief and laughing all the while. They set down their buckets and marbles to stare, wide-eyed, as Daniel rode down the main street. A young girl stood amongst pansies behind a picket fence. She was beautiful—all plaited yellow hair and blue eyes—wearing embroidered pantalettes and a white summer frock. She waved before returning her attention to the posy she was picking. Somehow the simple gesture lifted Daniel's heart from the darkness that had followed his trail.

Up ahead, a kid in a straw hat sat on a barrel under the shade of a mulberry, dangling his legs and munching on an apple. Nearby, another kid was whitewashing a fence, pleasantly chubby and seemingly happy, whistling a tune Daniel was unfamiliar with. He didn't recall ever seeing anyone so happy doing work. Except maybe Christopher and himself, building their corral.

Daniel pulled on Sammy's reins and stopped beneath the mulberry.

"Well-a-well, what's all this truck?" he asked.

"Geeminy, mister, this ain't no work," said the boy in the hat. "You don't get to whitewash a fence every day."

"No, sir, you don't."

Daniel dismounted, spying the bucket of whitewash and a long-handled brush. The fence was near thirty yards long and nine feet high, and there was no way the chubby kid would be able to reach the top. It had been almost two years since Daniel had done anything that could be called *work*. He was thoughtful for a moment, rubbing at his sore arm.

"I could help you with the top."

The boy on the barrel looked up. "Well, see, my aunt is particular about this fence—bein' in the front of her house and all. I cain't trust just anyone to do it how it's got to be done." He pulled his dirty feet up onto the barrel and wrapped his arms around his knees, then jerked his head toward the fortune beside his bandaged big toe: a tin soldier, a doorknob, a few bits of orange peel, and a dead rat tied to a string. "Perhaps I can be persuaded."

Daniel fumbled in his pocket for his own family treasure that grandpa Bartley had given him, but he kept it in his pocket when he caught the kid staring at his lapel.

He ripped the metal star from his jacket and handed it over. "Would you like this, kid?"

"By jingo!" The kid took the star then waved toward the bucket and brush.

Daniel grabbed the brush, dipped it in the wash, and drew it across the uppermost plank with vigor. He swept it back and forth, stopping now and then to check his work. He sweated in the sun, but it lifted his spirits, and soon he was whistling a tune and applying a second coat. The fence shone in the afternoon light, and other kids started helping, too, after increasing the wealth on the barrel. All the while, the kid in the straw hat sat munching on his apple core, inspecting his big toe, seeming awfully pleased with himself.

Daniel spent that night lying in the grass beside the Mississippi with Sammy beneath a nearby tree. A steamboat whistled in the distance. The water churned and surged toward unknown adventures.

With the morning sun and a tranquil heart, Daniel galloped north toward Chicago.

P.J. Parker

Br'er Rabbit and the Fox
(1861–1865 AD)

Chicago.

Big and dirty and wonderful.

Buildings along the lakeside—six and seven stories high—scrape the sky. Hundreds of factories spew smoke into the air. Slaughterhouses, mills, and lumberyards jostle for space, running day and night, loading their products onto ships bound for New York via the Erie Canal. Steam trains blast their whistles, impatient to start their passage west. Horse-drawn trollies carry fashionably dressed men and women to ornate hotels to discuss abolitionism, the importance of Miss Stowe's *Uncle Tom's Cabin*, and the policies of Chicago's own son, President Abraham Lincoln.

Montgomery slung his squirrel gun over his shoulder and gave one last wave to his ma and pa. They looked small on the porch of their homestead, his ma with her hand to her bosom, his pa pulling her in tight to his side with his good arm. The hulk of an old steamer towered behind the homestead, in the river in his pa's salvage and construction yard. Montgomery's younger twin brothers, Chris and Daniel Junior, signaled from the scaffolding around the rusted smoke stack. They were jealous, but he knew once they talked ma and pa into it, they wouldn't be far behind him. He nudged his knees into Polly's flanks and headed toward the south side of town, urging the mare into a gallop across the rail tracks when the approaching steam engine blasted its horn in warning. Some fellow up yonder was not as fast and got flung by the cowcatcher—an everyday occurrence that could not stop the power of industry.

When Montgomery arrived at the recruitment center, the street out front was crowded full with young men. This section of Chicago was still swampy lowland. A few three-storied warehouses at the end of the street were jacked up on logs, ready for new dirt to be pushed beneath them and the new road to be cobbled several feet above the waterline.

Truly a city of the industrial age, Montgomery marveled. *An engineering phenomenon.*

He dismounted, tied Polly to a rail, and joined the gathering.

He made fast friends with Henry and Joseph, men of color who vigorously shook his hand with excited smiles. They vowed to stick together as they signed their contracts under the watchful eye of military blue.

"You boys born in these parts?" Montgomery asked.

"No, sir. We skedaddled from Tennessee when we got word of the Confederates' hostilities at Fort Sumter."

"An' now we're headin' back into the thick of it. Goin' to make good for all our brothers and sisters."

Soon they were quick on a steamer chockfull of new recruits—many as young as fourteen—chugging and tooting down the smooth stretch of the Michigan Illinois Canal toward the inland rivers. Their vessel dragged a barge carrying the oddest-looking contraption.

"Looks likely to be a gigantic bullet," Joseph said.

Montgomery leaned against the rear balustrade. "It's a submarine. It sneaks under the water to attach torpedoes to enemy ships. Some folks were buildin' one at my pa's dock. Leastways they were tryin' to. Weren't havin' much luck. It kept sinkin'."

Henry shuddered. "I sure wouldn't like to be in dat bucket. Don't like bein' underwater."

The steamer was halfway down the Illinois River when the clouds came in and it started to pour, hard. The men huddled on the deck, their coats pulled over their heads.

"My old massa sure did hate dat Mister Lincoln," Joseph confided, flicking raindrops from his face. "He said it was every state's right to have slaves or not. Didn' the Union let Texas and Missouri in with their slaves? Anyhow, he sure was glad when the Confederacy split off."

"How'd you get gone from him?" Montgomery asked.

Joseph and Henry got fidgety, and Montgomery didn't push for an answer.

It was still dark when the steamer turned in to the docks at Cairo, Illinois—where the Ohio hit the Mississippi. Montgomery was jolted awake by the suffocating rabble of stink and noise. In the morning light, Cairo was a rough-looking place, with barracks and tents and derelict sheds scattered across a muddy headland. Plank boardwalks lay askew in the muck, offering no real thoroughfare between buildings. A steam engine was smoking into town, and he wondered if Polly was in one of its freight cars, on her own journey to join the cavalry.

They were fed hardtack biscuits and thick coffee then marched up through the sludge to Mound City. It wasn't much better as far as stink, but they settled into the tents pitched amongst the strange grass-covered mounds and dried their clothes by the fireplace.

In the dark of five o'clock the next morning, the bugles played. Montgomery was fast to pull on his boots and loop the buttons of his new blue military jacket. He ran out the front of the tent, Joseph and Henry tight on his heels. *At least it's stopped raining*, he thought as he sank halfway up his calves in the mud.

Officers stood on the tray of a wagon, their uniforms pristine from the knees up.

"Soldiers!" bellowed the officer with the most gold on his shoulders. "You have been assigned to the Union Army's Western Gunboat Fleet. You will be questioned and allocated by your captains before breakfast."

Henry leaned over. "I'm afeared to go in one of dem underwater buckets."

Montgomery filled his lungs and pressed his lips together, wondering how long he could hold his breath. Not for very long.

After the questioning and the biscuits and coffee, he marched down to the docks with Joseph and Henry in a troop of a hundred and seventy men. They passed two submarines, and Henry let out an audible sigh, before they stopped in front of an ironclad.

A sign on the dock read, "United States Ship Cairo." Below the text someone had scratched into the wood, "Pook Turtle."

The ironclad, one of three along the rickety docks, looked nearly two hundred feet long and fifty feet wide. It sat low in the water, its exposed sides sloping in toward the top and covered in sheets of thick charcoal iron. Gunports were opened all around the turtle-like shell with massive smoothbore and rifled guns protruding. Behind the smokestacks of the ship an iron barrel encased the upper swing of the paddled spider wheel. As they boarded the modern marvel, they each were handed their weapons: a mighty fine rifle, an M1851 naval pistol, an 1860 naval cutlass sword, and a boarding axe. Montgomery ran his hand along the barrel of his new rifle. *Yes, sir*, he thought. *I'll be able to shoot down a lot of those Confederates with this beauty.*

Inside the ironclad, hammocks hung from the beams between cannons, and Montgomery and his two friends laid claim to three of them, one above the next, then secured their weapons. They'd be bumping shoulders at night with three firemen who were already swinging and snickering in their hammocks beside them.

While the firemen went to coal the furnace, check the boilers, and grease the wheels, the soldiers' first duty was to clean the ship of all the mud tracked through by the new crew. They sloshed buckets of water and mopped the debris across the deck and out into the river. Hours of scrubbing and aching knees later, the *Cairo* blew her horn, the wheels started turning, and she swung out into the main current. Montgomery would have liked to have been up on deck, but a crowd had beaten him to it and there was little room left. He contented himself lying on a cannon and sticking his head out a porthole, grinning and whooping as the riverbank slid past.

For almost a week the *Cairo* chugged back and forth along the Ohio and Mississippi, turning this way, then that—sometimes surging forward at five and half knots.

"Le Commandant Bryant getting a feel for how she pulls," said a Frenchman.

Montgomery stood on the main deck with Henry and Joseph and several others. A German was showing them how to use the rifle and pistol. Montgomery took aim and shot at a tree on the riverbank, and the pistol jerked high. He changed his grip and the German said, "*Ja*," and nodded. Joseph had never touched a rifle before, but he was the quickest to learn and he had good aim. Montgomery leaned the barrel of his rifle on the gunwale and trained it on a bird. The rifle popped, and the bird dropped from its perch.

"Much better than my ol' squirrel gun."

Montgomery was polishing his sword when the *Cairo's* horn blasted and she swung wide to head up the Ohio. Henry, who had been snooping about the boilers with the firemen, came running.

"Trainin's over, boys! We goin' into battle! The chief fireman says the pilot makin' a course for the Tennessee, then Cumberland rivers. Some kind of rail bridge at Clarkesville we goin' to secure." He grabbed his rifle and started cleaning it, his cheeks purple with excitement.

The *Cairo* steamed up the rivers with another ironclad alongside, slowing as they approached Clarkesville. Willows hung from the banks, and church bells echoed in the distance.

"Tarnation." Montgomery spat as the ironclad surged around the bend and pulled in close to the bank. White flags flapped on either side of the river. "I was all set to wake the snakes with those rebels."

Up on the bend the railroad bridge smoked, and a score of Union soldiers were batting down the flames with blankets and buckets of water.

"Cap'n says the rebels and all the townsfolk have plum pulled foot from this here town—they done gone," Henry said, disappointed. He shielded his eyes from the sun to see the bridge. "At least we saved the rail for the Union trains." He smiled and slapped Joseph and Montgomery on the backs.

The men were fired up again—*itching* was the word Henry used—when the ironclad plowed full-steam toward Nashville. But again, the rebels had run, leaving the little state capital as easy pickings for the Union. The mockingbirds made more of a ruckus than any of the Bluecoats had a reason to. *Ain't we ever goin' to see the elephant?* Montgomery wondered.

He spent the afternoon practicing with one of the forty-two pound cannons, and blew an onshore outhouse to smithereens. "Yeehaw!"

The *Cairo* moored at the Nashville docks for several weeks, where the men continued with cleaning and gun practice, until ordered up the Tennessee to Savannah. Montgomery stood proud at attention—his buttons and rifle shining—as the ironclad passed the Cherry Mansion where General Grant saluted them from the colonnaded veranda. A dozen photographers stood on the lawn, their bulbs flashing a blinding white.

On they went, south, bound for Eastport, Mississippi to support Brigadier General Sherman and his troops.

* * * *

Montgomery was swinging in his hammock, half asleep, Henry above him and Joseph below. The firemen snored beside them, and the stink of men, feet, and fart hung in the damp, confined space.

The *Cairo's* horn sounded, a deep resonance within the iron shell.

Two hundred bare feet hit the deck and a hundred hammocks rolled as one. The soldiers were dressed and at their stations, weapons at the ready, in just three minutes, horn blasting all the while.

The guns boomed from the *Cairo's* portside and smoke filled the ship. Then they were charged and fired again.

But there was no returned fire.

"I guess our ship is enough to make any Confederate afeared," Montgomery said, sticking his head out beside a smoothbore. It was hot near his cheek. No sign of rebels in the woods or on the banks of the river. A few coloreds stood by the water, fishing poles neglected, eyes and grins wide, their cheeks set to burst. They danced about on the grass and returned the soldiers' whoops.

The *Cairo* returned to base at Mound City, then headed for Memphis, Tennessee, full steam ahead.

Montgomery was on deck when the ship sent up a flare that curved across the sky—the signal for battle. He hunkered down on his knee, his rifle tight into his shoulder, as the *Cairo* swung around Plum Point Bend, just north of the Confederate Fort Pillow. The unwieldy motorboats and their large cannons skimmed in their wake.

This was the battle Montgomery had been waiting for—had been prepared for since he'd stood in line in Chicago. It was his chance to do what he thought was right—to fight for the rights of men and women, no matter their color. He was already sweating, the pits of his jacket saturated.

The Union ironclads *Cincinnati* and *Mound City* pulled alongside the *Cairo*, and the high staccato scream of the rebel yell greeted them. To Montgomery it sounded like jackrabbits caught in traps—thousands of them shrieking in a struggle to survive. His heart beat fast at the sight of Confederate ships in the river ahead—fancy old wooden sidewheel paddleboats, outfitted with cannon. Rebel soldiers stood along the balconies, yelping, but their rifles did the talking as soon as the Union ships were within reach.

The *Cairo* screeched and vibrated as she loosed her weapons, great puffs of smoke accompanying the volley of cannon fire. A dozen or more of the *Cairo's* cannonballs splintered the upper decks of a Confederate steamer, and rebels were flung into the surge. Montgomery fired his rifle again and again, the ironclad reverberating as its cannons kept up the fusillade. The ships were slow— cumbersome even—as they turned sluggishly in the brown churn of the river. They were so close Montgomery could have touched the foot of a rebel, but instead he fired his rifle, then his pistol, toward the men in gray uniforms who looked just like him—scared and determined.

A Confederate ship was mere yards away when it fired a cannon toward the *Cairo*. The ball clanged against the iron an arm's length from Montgomery, then ricocheted onto the riverbank. Another cannonball hit the Union's *Mound City*, careening through a gunport and splintering through the ship. The echoing scream of men made Montgomery shudder, but he kept loading his pistol and firing. From the corner of his shooting eye he saw the *Mound City* was taking on water quick. The *Cincinnati* was, too. They lilted in the river, their cannons and men still firing—hell-bent for leather. The captain barked, the horns blasted, and the three ironclads pulled into shallow water, where the deeper-keeled Confederate ships could not approach.

Still, cannons fired unrelenting from both sides, and a rebel ship exploded—a rapid set of detonations that flung splintered wood and dead soldiers every which way. Thick black smoke spewed and tumbled across the river. Another rebel ship blew its whistle and the Confederate steamers turned askew and chugged down river away from the battle—zigzagging like a Virginian fence. The staccato yell faded into the distance, but still it sent a shiver down Montgomery's spine.

He rolled onto his side, plum tuckered, his shoulder and hands numb and bruised from shooting. Men jumped into the shallows as the *Cincinnati* sank near the shore. The *Mound City* grounded herself on a sandbar with a low creak. It would take weeks before the soldiers could salvage and refloat them.

Henry pulled Montgomery to his feet. "Those graybacks are nothin' but parlor soldiers. It's time to show those kids how to toe the mark."

The *Cairo* and the motorboats left the two damaged ironclads and followed the rebels to Fort Pillow—cannons discharging the entire route. They bombarded the Confederates for seven weeks straight, until the rebels finally set fire to the fort and skedaddled overland. Montgomery stood on the deck as the fort blazed, the buildings and surrounding cottonwoods flaming like Hades. The early morning sky was an incandescent red long before the sun rose.

"Now we take Memphis," he yelled, loud and strong, in unison with the hundreds of Union soldiers standing upon the surrounding ships. "Memphis! Memphis! Memphis!"

Within hours the *Cairo* was blasting the city—its stores and homesteads, warehouses and saloons—in a spectacle Montgomery could never have imagined in his worst nightmare. Handsome buildings flamed, covering the city in a thick gray smoke. Union and Confederate gunboats turned amongst each other, lining up cannon and firing their arsenals point blank. But the battle lasted only two days. In the end, the crew of the *Cairo*, along with six other Union ships and a tug, whooped and hollered in victory. Montgomery knew they had done good, the buttons on his jacket stretching with pride. He caught the gazes of Henry and Joseph and smiled.

* * * *

Henry and Joseph were reassigned to the newly formed African-American corps to train freed slaves to fight against their previous owners. They couldn't have been more excited, and they promised to meet up with Montgomery back in Chicago once the war was done.

Montgomery stayed with the *Cairo* when it was transferred to the U.S. Navy and Commander Selfridge took over the captaincy.

But there were whispers through the ironclad. "I heard every ship he's touched has sunk." Montgomery was reticent, but he would follow orders—would do whatever was needed to end slavery in the South and reunite the States.

He sat on the prow, the waterline a few feet beneath his boots as the *Cairo* paddled up the Yazoo River, the ironclad *Pittsburg* and the ram *Queen of the West* in her wake. The tinclads *Marmora* and *Signal* were dead ahead, the latter lifting a Confederate torpedo from the water. To Montgomery the bomb looked like a glass jar floating just below the water—a jar full of explosive powder. He kept a keen eye and a well-aimed rifle on the riverbank for Confederates; a single rebel bullet could blow the torpedo and two tinclads to smithereens in an instant.

After the torpedo had been lifted without incident, he went below deck and crept amongst sleeping soldiers toward his hammock. He was unrolling the canvas when he heard the clang of shot fire. He rushed to a gunport with his rifle. The ship's horn blasted and men ran to their stations. Heavy rebel guns on the bluff opened fire, and two of the ironclad's cannons took shot, shattering explosions amongst the trees. The *Cairo* was drifting close to the bank, and the paddlewheels groaned to a stop, then screeched as they reversed. As the ironclad surged back into the current, an almighty explosion ripped through the rear of the vessel. The far end of the hold lit up in flames.

The *Cairo* tipped slantindicular, throwing Montgomery onto his stomach. He slid across the splintering deck and slammed into the hull, gashing his chin and biting through his lower lip. Water rushed into the hold, and cannons went skidding. Chest deep in water and sludge, Montgomery pulled himself along the length of the *Cairo*, taking hold of a seaman he reckoned was unconscious. Cannon tumbled past them, the current roiling within the ship. Montgomery tripped and was pulled beneath the surge but was quick to find his footing. He breasted the surface near a hatch, pushing the seaman up to the deck before hoisting himself through the opening. Two soldiers gripped him and tossed him onto the deck of the *Queen of the West*, just as her paddle wheel screeched to a stop and reversed to send her back down the Yazoo away from the gunfire. Lying on the deck, coughing up a half gallon of the Yazoo, Montgomery watched the *Cairo* dip beneath the surface of the river, only her stacks remaining above the waterline.

*　*　*　*

"Damn stupid Negroes! I'll be damned if they aren't better off being slaves anyways. If it weren't for them, I'd be back in Chicago with my puss and our kids."

Montgomery turned quick, his eyes wide. "What are you saying, sir?"

The Mound City barracks went suddenly quiet as soldiers turned away and hunched over their breakfasts.

"You heard me, mulatto!"

Montgomery leaned back on his bench. "I am white, sir."

The soldier sneered, his nose a veiny red against a pudgy white face. "Yeah, you keep telling yourself that, Mulatto!" He shoved a spoonful of gruel into his mouth.

Montgomery clenched his fists and started to rise, but then he spotted the gold on the soldier's jacket—he was an officer of rank. High rank. Montgomery ground his teeth in attempt to still his anger. He rubbed furiously at the bandage around his chin.

The officer elbowed past him on his way toward the barracks door.

"We will win this war," Montgomery muttered to himself.

P.J. Parker

The White City (1893 AD)

Bromley gripped the calloused colored hand of the foreman and climbed from the ladder onto the top girder of the construction site, sixteen stories above the noisy Chicago streets. A web of iron beams, ladders, and scaffolding rose from the rutted mud of Van Buren and State Streets to the bottom of his boots. Load-bearing masonry walls crept up the outside—an unadorned brown-purple brick.

"Thanks, Tobey." Bromley tipped his hat and balanced across a few yards of iron to lean against a post. He unfolded one of the architect's drawings and checked it against the construction. The wind whistled, and he ducked as a bucket of glowing red-hot rivets swung past him on a chain. A youngster with tongs, his skinny white legs dangling either side of an iron girder, gripped one of the rivets from the bucket. He leaned back as far as he could beneath the two Skywalkers that stood over him. They bore the unmistakable bone structure and coloring of their Native American Indian heritage and were able to work with confidence at the dizzying heights of the building. Sledgehammers clanged and sparks flew as Bromley calculated the number of bricks still needed to finish the outer walls. He made some notes with his graphite pencil, then peered through the bay window casements that overlooked the squalid landscape south of the river—rambling streets of low-rise buildings, little more than an unsympathetic attempt to house the homeless after the Great Fire two decades ago. Bromley certainly was glad the slums were being torn down to make way for the new Chicago. And he was heartened with the formal beauty of the new suburbs being built just outside the city. He liked that word—*suburb*. It was fresh and exhilarating.

He squinted into the distance. Not far to the west, a little bit north, he was building his own family home that would soon be finished. The design was by a bright, young architect—a Mister Frank

Lloyd Wright—and it excited him almost as much as the building he stood upon now.

"Yes, sir, Pop Montgomery," he whispered to himself. "We sure have come a long ways since granddaddy's construction and salvage yard."

He leaned against the parapet and looked out over the mud. Very few had been in a building so tall before and he knew them all by name, as most of them worked for his family's company on this very building—the tallest in the world. It made Bromley's chest swell with pride, not just for his family, but for Chicago.

"We have truly scraped the sky. Much more impressive and modern than that little Gothic bridge from Manhattan to Brooklyn." He spat out into the heavens, smiling as he followed the course of the spittle toward the ground. He couldn't be certain, but it might have landed atop the trolley that was *ding-ding-ding*ing around the loop, heading back to the center of town.

* * * *

"Bromley, can we go to the fair, tomorrow?"

Eight-year-old Berton squeezed up into the overstuffed chair next to his big brother.

"No, not tomorrow. We'll all go on Thursday." He kept his attention on his newspaper as the fire crackled in the fireplace.

"But I heard there's going to be free watermelon tomorrow. I heard it."

Bromley stretched out his arms and Berton squirmed up onto his lap. He flicked the paper out flat and read. "It appears they finally caught that Dalton Gang, down in Kansas. The authorities believe they were influenced by Jesse James and his brother."

"Confederate guerillas, the lot of them. That's what Papa used to say," Gertrude called from across the parlor, and Bromley smiled.

"Watermelon," Berton whispered.

"We cannot go to the fair tomorrow, Bertie. It's, um ..." Bromley attempted to catch the gaze of his sisters, Gertrude and Nora. They kept their heads down, embroidering by lantern light. Nora's lips were pursed in anger.

Bromley let out a sigh. "We cannot go to the fair tomorrow because it's colored folks' day."

"But I like watermelon."

"Yes, and so do colored folks."

Nora threw down her needlework. "Why don't you just say it, Bromley? Go on, say it."

Bromley's cheeks grew warm, and Berton turned in his arms to peer at him.

Nora rolled her eyes. "The free watermelon is incentive, Bertie—a way to entice the coloreds to the fair so they can see how great the White City and our white culture are."

"Nora, Bertie is too young to understand."

Berton looked back and forth between his older brother and sister.

"He will only understand what we show him. And what we are showing him is something that I cannot reconcile. We are a family of value. *You* know men of means and power and yet you do nothing to change how things are."

Bromley held up a hand. "All of our construction sites have gangs of coloreds working with the whites. We have coloreds in our head office."

"But they don't work together—they keep to their own gangs and never mix. And I hardly call a colored cleaning the lavatory or driving the elevator as working at the head office." Nora paced the room. "When was the last time you walked across the street with a colored, Bromley?"

"It's the law, Nora. Separate and equal."

"Let him be," Gertrude said. "You know he does what he can. Change takes time."

"You give a glass of water to a man on fire when you own a fire engine? This unjust law should be out of print." Nora ran out of the parlor, her hand over her heart.

Bromley knew she was right, but for the life of him could not think of what he could do. Integration seemed inconceivable. Frustration welled within him, and he tightened his face to keep it from surfacing. He dropped the newspaper and smoothed Berton's hair, pressing his lips to his little brother's head. "We'll go to the fair on

Thursday, Bertie. And on Friday and Saturday, too. Just not tomorrow. Is that ok?"

Berton snuggled into Bromley and nodded.

The parlor stayed silent as the clock struck eight, and then eight-thirty. The broadsheet lay crumpled on Bromley's lap as he stared, numb, into the flames of the fireplace. He was thinking, hard, but his mind was blank.

At nine o'clock, Nora stepped quietly back into the room and over to Bromley. She pressed her cheek to his, and they caught one another's red-rimmed gazes. They nodded their understanding.

"Please read more from the *Tribune* for me," she said as she returned to her embroidery.

Bromley cleared his throat and attempted to straighten his back beneath the heavy weight of his sleeping little brother. "Experts estimate less than two thousand bison remain in the wild—down from what was likely a few million."

"White man's legacy," Nora said with a sniff.

Bromley flicked and folded the paper, squinting. "There've been further skirmishes with the red men, but none as bad as Wounded Knee. Since they've been recognized as people, it is now compulsory for them to send their children to school."

"Well, at least that should lead to some good."

Bromley nodded, scanning the columns for anything else of note.

Gertrude shifted in her chair. "I took the carriage out to River Forest this morning. It appears your new home will be ready by spring. I must say, it is very modern and striking. Unlike anything else in the area. I spent a lovely hour having tea and sandwiches with Mister Wright—quite a personable young man."

Bromley smiled, thinking of the house.

She cleared her throat conspicuously. "Speaking of your house . . . I have requested Miss Agnes Abbington accompany us to the Chicago Fair on Thursday. Thirty years old is high time for you to procure a bride, my dear brother, and no man could do better than Miss Agnes Abbington. It would be a pleasure to visit her at the River Forest house when it is complete." With that, Gertrude and Nora snuffed out their lantern and retired to bed.

Bromley cuddled his young brother tight. "Thursday will be a wonderful day at the fair, Bertie."

* * * *

"Hold still." Gertrude tied the bright green bowtie around Bromley's neck and pulled it tight, expertly dimpling its knot. "There, now." She licked her fingers and smoothed an errant curl of brown hair down flat against his head.

"Aw, sis, come on."

"You want to look nice, and I want Miss Abbington as my sister-in-law."

Bromley smirked and glanced sideways at Berton, who was dressed in the same striped shirt and blazer but with a blue bowtie.

"It's up to you, and Bertie in a few years"—she nodded at their young sibling—"to carry on the family name."

She looked to the two wicker buggies in the front hall, one of which held her daughter, Ethel, and the other Nora's daughter, Florence. Nora leaned over them, tucking in the baby blue blankets as the babies snoozed amongst the profusion of flannel and lace. They were such quiet little girls—unlike their mothers. Bromley smiled in fondness of all the women who surrounded him.

"I thought Willie and Charlie were coming with us." Bromley peered down the corridor, hoping for the backup of his brothers-in-law.

"They'll meet us at Mister Ferris's wheel at noon."

"The wheel, the wheel!" Berton jumped up and down before running to the front door and pulling it open. Bromley donned his light brown derby then followed his sisters and their buggies out onto the front porch.

The morning was bright, the breeze sweet with honeysuckle. They strolled through the front gate and to the trolley stop down the street.

"A charming day." Gertrude looked Bromley up and down, presumably to confirm his readiness for Miss Abbington. "Yes, charming."

A chestnut horse pulled the trolley around the corner with a *clang-clang-clang*. Miss Agnes Abbington stepped down onto the walk—a vision in a magenta walking dress, her hair coifed luxuriantly high. Bromley's heart skipped a beat, and he tipped his hat and offered her his arm. "Miss Abbington."

It was a pleasant walk to the fairgrounds at Jackson Park.

"Is this your first trip to the Chicago Columbian Exhibition, Miss Abbington?" Bromley asked.

"Please, call me Agnes."

Gertrude slowed her pace so as to miss none of the conversation.

"My uncle and aunt have brought me here on a number of occasions," Agnes said. "They say there's no better education than a stroll through the pavilions. Indeed it is exciting to see the exhibits of the cities and states of this great nation—as well the advances in the sciences—but merely being here is wonderful. We once spent an entire day sitting by the lake in the Court of Honor, admiring the space and the buildings surrounding it."

"Yes, they are beautiful," Bromley said, gazing into her eyes. "It is how urban spaces should be designed. The White City is the city of the future." He shook his head to stop himself staring at her. "Is there any exhibit in particular you'd like to see today, Agnes?"

She smiled—a brilliant curve of the mouth and puff of the cheek that made Bromley blush. "I've heard of a horseless carriage—and I must admit I brought an extra thirty cents so I might treat you all to a ride on the moving walkway."

"Such an extravagance, Miss Abbington!" Gertrude feigned shock, but it quickly dissipated as excitement crept into her eyes. "Then you must let Bromley escort you onto Mister Ferris's wheel."

"What about me?" Berton stomped his foot into the dirt.

Bromley pulled his little brother into his side and said, without taking his gaze from Agnes, "You can come too, Bertie."

They ambled amongst the hoard of fairgoers into the Court of Honor, and even Bromley gasped at its magnificence. The Beaux-Arts exhibition halls surrounding it were blinding white and several stories high—their grandeur uncommon outside the cities of the old world he'd only ever seen in picture books. A reflection pool stretched the length of the court, and replicas of Columbus's caravels sailed in the morning breeze—canvases pluming toward the breathtaking gilded statue of the Golden Lady. Elaborate fountains sent water spraying high above Venetian gondolas and Indian canoes. Agnes's grip on Bromley's forearm tightened, and he dared to place his hand upon hers. It felt right.

The Machinery Hall at the end of the court was already beyond capacity, the noise of steam engines and electric dynamos deafening but exhilarating. They strolled through the court's peristyle toward the parkland and pier, exhibits and merchants spread out along either side of their route. They reached the moving walkway, which stretched from the lake promenade onto the pier, and Bromley stood back as Agnes counted out her coins for each of them—five cents each. He felt an unexpected rush of pleasure watching a woman so confidently handling money. He took her hand once more as they stepped onto the moving walkway. Berton ran back and forth, and Nora and Gertrude settled on the benches, their knuckles white gripping the handles of their buggies. They were conveyed along the pier and back at a speed as fast as they could have walked—perhaps a bit slower, but so much more exciting than walking. They were all breathless when they stepped back onto solid ground.

For luncheon they settled on the New England Clam Bake restaurant for chowder, Boston baked beans, pumpkin pie, and carbonated water—which they all agreed was innovative and refreshing.

It was almost noon when they entered the midway. Their stroll was slow at first, after the chowder, but Gertrude's stride suddenly quickened as they passed the Street in Cairo with its hootchy-kootchy belly dancers. She said they needed to hurry up to meet Charlie and Willie at the wheel.

Mister Ferris's wheel was by far the largest attraction, soaring over two hundred and sixty feet high. It dominated the landscape of white-washed buildings, ornate gardens, and scientific wonders.

"Oh, my," Agnes said, retrieving her fan from her bag to cool her excitement.

Bromley held her hand tight. "A magnificent structure—taller even than our Van Buren Street building."

"Is it safe?"

Bromley nodded, wondering if he could convince the engineers to increase his building's height by another four stories to rival this edifice. The structural steel could handle the height, just not the outer brick walls. If only there were a lighter material—or perhaps if it were all windows with no actual wall. Bromley almost chuckled as he pushed the ludicrous idea from his mind—for later analysis—to concentrate on Agnes.

Agnes's hair shone, and a loose blonde curl fell against her cheek. He longed to touch it, but Berton was pulling at his coattails.

"Charlie! Willie!" Gertrude called. Bromley turned to see his brothers-in-law idling near the hootchy-kootchy before joining the family at the wheel. Gertrude narrowed her eyes as she pulled her husband to her side.

The great wheel rotated above them, thirty-six cars around the enormous steel spider. Gertrude pushed her buggy forward and snatched at Berton's sticky hand. "We'll take this car, Nora." She waved her family on ahead. "Oh dear, it appears this one is full, Bromley. You and Agnes will have to take the next one." She yanked Berton and her husband and smiled as the steel-framed glass door closed behind them. Bromley tipped his hat as his siblings were lifted up and away.

He escorted Agnes into the next car, to one of the forty revolving seats, and the capsule was soon filled with over sixty people. The doors closed and the gondola lurched up into the air amid gasps and laughter. Agnes gripped her chair, her face flushed and grinning. The fairgrounds opened up below as they rose to the full height of the wheel in intermittent jerks that made the gondola swing.

"Why, we can see to the very edge of Chicago!" Agnes yelled amongst the thrilled din inside the car.

Bromley pointed north into the misty haze. "I dare say that's Canada." He threw her a cheeky grin.

Agnes pressed her nose to the glass before turning and nodding. Still she held that smile and Bromley's hand with a warmth that made all of Gertrude's promises true.

"Hold tight, Agnes," he said, joining her on the edge of her seat. He rested an arm along the back of her chair, and she leaned into his shoulder. The car pitched forward as the wheel lowered them toward the ground and then back up into the air with a breathtaking swoop. Laughter and enthusiastic screams filled the car, but all Bromley could feel was Agnes's grip tightening on his forearm. He couldn't have been happier.

The family was waiting for them as they exited onto the platform. Gertrude's neck looked near to breaking as she craned to see them amongst the crowd. When she saw Bromley and Agnes walking arm in arm, she smiled.

"Coloreds!" Berton screamed at the top of his voice. "What are they doing here?"

A troop of black-faced minstrels were readying their instruments on a stage.

"Bertie!" Gertrude shouted.

"But they got no right to be here! It isn't colored persons' day!"

Bromley closed his eyes and pinched the bridge of his nose.

Gertrude wrangled Berton and gave him a slap on his backside. Nora glared at Bromley. Agnes slipped her hand from Bromley's arm.

"But Gertie, they're black. Bromley said—"

Another thwack to the backside and Berton's words escalated into a squeal.

"Please forgive him, Miss Abbington," Gertrude said, her face beet-red. "He's young. He doesn't understand. Too much pie and excitement."

Agnes nodded, but uncertainty had shattered her smile.

Gertrude took a deep breath. "Please, why don't the two of you continue through the fair? It's high time we got this youngster home." Without waiting for a response, she pushed the buggy into the crowd and the rest of the family dutifully followed in her wake.

"I am so sorry, Agnes," Bromley said. "I assure you Bertie's tantrum does not reflect the thoughts of our family."

Agnes nodded slowly, her brow crinkling. "We live in a complicated society, Bromley—one that is changing and which does indeed need to change. But do you not think any change must begin within our own family gathering?"

Bromley pressed his lips together and nodded.

Agnes replaced her hand on Bromley's forearm. Her face softened, and a glimmer of that smile returned. "Come, we'll view the moving pictures and try some of Mister Wrigley's new gum before the Court of Honor lighting ceremony. Perhaps we'll have time to see the horseless carriage. Then, if you like, we can watch the football game—Uncle will be there. He said Chicago will play against West Point."

"Football in the dark?" Bromley asked, incredulous, realizing even more why Miss Agnes Abbington could be nothing but loved.

"Electric lights, my dear Bromley. Electric lights!" she shouted as she pulled him into the crowd.

P.J. Parker

Jazz Hot, Baby—The Crash (1929 AD)

Ralph turned the breezer down a side street and into an alley. The convertible slunk through the darkness, as the warm, meaty stink of Chicago eddied in doorways and dead ends. His girlfriend, Edith, was buzzed and leaning into his side, eyes half open and a silly grin on her face.

Ralph was feeling mighty pleased with himself as he idled the car in a pool of light cast by an electric streetlamp. That afternoon he'd signed on several hundred thousand acres of useless land at a steal. Useless, that was, until his new partner extended the rail line to it. Ralph licked his lips, mentally calculating the money the new suburb would make for the family construction business.

"We're gonna be billionaires, bunny," he said, nudging Edith. "You and me and little Mildred."

"Pos-i-lute-ly," Edith muttered.

"And how!" Ralph revved the convertible's engine and flashed its lights. A garage door screeched open and he pulled the car into a warehouse. Dozens of Lincolns, Chevrolets, and Chryslers—all black—filled the space like a million bucks. "C'mon, baby. I need you hitting on all sixes when we meet these fellas."

"Oh, daddy!" Edith let out a sigh. "Light a ciggy for me?"

Ralph grinned, lit a cigarette, and took a deep drag before popping it into Edith's mouth. She shifted in the plush leather and blew a smoke ring that floated into the heights of the warehouse.

"What kind of juice joint is this place, anyway, Ralphy?"

"The kind that makes us connections and money, babe." He let his gaze wander down past the pearls slung across her chest, to her tight skirt. He placed a hand on her thigh and leaned in to kiss her neck.

Edith laughed then smoothed a garish red lipstick around the curve of her lips. "All ready."

The speakeasy was at the back of the garage, down a flight of stairs, and through a heavy wooden door with a peephole. Once inside, Ralph had to unholster and check both his Colt 45 sidearms. The rush of smoke, jazz, and liquor embraced them as they stepped down into a cavernous basement. Big timers and flappers, gangsters and molls lounged in the dim light, drink in one hand, cigarette in the other. A couple of neckers were tangled in each other's arms near the door to the john, and a rumpled-looking guy lay in the corridor at the stair, unconscious, a crooked smile on his face. Ralph and Edith stepped over him.

A four-piece band of New Negroes on the stage mixed smoke and whispers with the soft notes of jazz. Ralph reckoned their song might have been a take on Gershwin, but wasn't sure. *Not really my thing*, he thought.

A man in a booth waved him over, and he and Edith sidled past a drunken couple attempting to dance.

"Hey, Ralphy, isn't that your little brother over there?"

Ralph followed Edith's pointing finger through the fog of smoke, and there was Harrison, hanging off a sailor, his other arm thrown around a flapper, his mouth pressed against hers.

Ralph nodded to the man in the booth, held up a finger to excuse himself, and then strode through the crowd toward Harrison.

"What the devil are you doing here, Harrison? Drinking's illegal at your age."

Harrison laughed. "Drinking's illegal at any age."

Ralph pulled his brother into his arms and manhandled him down the corridor into the john. Edith followed, peeking in to make sure it was empty before stepping inside.

Harrison immediately doubled over and threw up on the floor.

Edith grimaced and turned away.

Ralph rolled his eyes. "I said, what in the blazes are you doing here?"

"Havin' fun."

"Damn you, Harrison." Ralph thrust his brother's head into the sink and turned on the faucet. Harrison kicked and flailed as Ralph held his head under the freezing water. "You could ruin everything by being here tonight."

Harrison jerked and fell against the wall, gulping for air. The spark in his eyes showed the drunkenness had been shocked out of him. "What'd you do that for?" He threw a punch, but Ralph caught his fist and twisted his arm up behind his back.

"You do as I tell you, kid. You got no right to be here. Now scram!" He slammed Harrison into the door. "You've always been trouble—just like Uncle Bertie."

Harrison licked his lip, cut and bloody. "Leave Uncle Bertie outta this. You're the one who doesn't care about our family. You don't feel for nothin' but money." His eyes darkened, and he spat on the floor. "I've always hated you, big brother!"

Ralph shook his clenched fist in Harrison's face.

"All right, all right, I'm blowin'." Harrison turned and gave Edith a sheepish smile. "Sorry, Edith," he said and scuttled out the door.

"Poor kid," Edith said.

"He always was sweet on you."

Ralph grabbed her by the pearls and pressed her to the tiles, his lips hard against hers, until she squirmed for breath and pushed him away. Still he held firm and licked along the edge of her ear. "And don't ever let me catch you smoochin' around with him, or it will be poor Edith, too."

Edith nodded, eyes glazed.

"Now, clean up your makeup. We got business to do."

* * * *

Ralph kept his eye on Edith from the darkened booth as she danced the Charleston across the dance floor. She'd done her bit, been the arm candy he needed at the introductions, and then been bum-rushed out of earshot with a group of flappers. He talked out the side of his mouth with his host, at all times ensuring Edith never split off with any single man. He decided she was happy. Of course she was. She had him.

Over the course of the evening, hands were shaken, cigarettes lit, and bootleg slurped. Ralph nodded attentively—once for each million bucks that filled his head.

A light flashed on the wall by the door, and the band stopped playing. Everyone went quiet, listening. A leaky drip echoed through the basement from the john.

Outside, through layers of concrete and wood, Ralph heard the wail of a siren. It grew louder until it must surely have been in the street just outside, but then it screeched off into the distance.

The light on the wall flashed again, and the band picked up their tune.

*   *   *   *

Edith puffed on a cig as Ralph sped from the city, through the suburbs, toward River Forest. She was snoring by the time he parked alongside the curb in front of their low-slung ranch home. He lit a cigarette of his own, content to watch the first rays of the new day dapple through the trees of the gravel avenue. He smiled and pulled Edith into his side. She was a doll. Just like their daughter. Maybe one day he would make an honest woman out of her.

"C'mon, bunny. Time to go to bed."

When she didn't respond, he chuckled and lifted her over his shoulder. He carried her across the lawn and pushed open the front door with his foot—it was always unlocked.

"Ralph, that you?" Agnes called from the kitchen.

"Just a minute, Ma."

Feeling suddenly angry, he ground his molars and deposited Edith onto their bed before sneaking back through the house. He peered into Harrison's room—a University of Chicago banner draped from the picture rail, and model airplanes hung from the ceiling. The bed was still made, but Harrison was sprawled across it, clothes disheveled, smeared lipstick and drunken drool covering his unshaven chin.

"Splifficated sap," he muttered, then joined his ma in the kitchen.

Agnes was in her housecoat, face unmade, graying hair tied back in a bun. She cuddled a cup of coffee while Uncle Bertie, in his pajamas, leaned over the breakfast table, studying the company ledger.

"What've you done, Ralph?" his ma asked, her voice raw. "Mister Braendel from the Federal came by last night with our passbooks. All the money, Ralph . . . You took all the money?"

Bertie looked up from the ledger, and Ralph stared at them. *Pathetic*, he thought, smiling as he strolled over to the coffee pot. "I done what I needed to do to put us all on top," he said, pouring a mug.

Bertie leaned across the table. "You don't have no right to spend company money without your ma's approval."

"Shut up, Bertie. I'll be thirty come next March, and I should be making all the decisions. I'm the one with the goods and the connections."

"Agnes has been running the company just fine. Done a mighty good job, too—quadrupled the size of our holding since your pa died." Bertie made to stand, his face red, but Agnes put a hand on his shoulder and he sank back onto the bench.

"I invested the funds, Ma—enough to see our family set for generations. Everything's gonna be jake. I bought up a whole swath of land across north Cook County, clear up the lake to Fort Sheridan."

"Wilderness?" Agnes asked, wide-eyed.

"There isn't a train there!" Bertie shouted. "No highway! Even Chicagoans with cars can't get there without a highway!"

Agnes knit her brow. "I don't like speculation, Ralph. We've been right to build homes for folks as they need them—*where* they need them."

"Give it a few months, Ma. This deal ain't no bull. We'll be richer than you or pa ever imagined."

Agnes shook her head and stared at the swirl of coffee grounds at the bottom of her cup, drumming her fingers against the table. "Go get me the documents you signed."

"I'm wasted, Ma. I'll bring 'em home tomorrow."

Agnes stood and slammed her fist down onto the table. "Now!"

* * * *

"They don't know from nothin'," Ralph slurred, slouching in a chair at the back of a gin mill. Hair of the dog and a cigar in one hand, he wrapped his other arm around some skirt, hopped up on who knows what. "Nothin', I tell ya." He took a swig from his flask and winced. "Give me some cash, baby doll." He puckered up and leaned in, tasting the remnants of dope on her upper lip.

Ralph had driven straight to the Green Mill instead of doing his mother's bidding. The place was still jumping from the night before, all the flappers well and truly over the edge—just how he liked them. A Negress sang at the piano.

"A thirty-eight point drop!" someone yelled in alarm from the far side of the mill.

Ralph turned to peer over his shoulder. Several men huddled in the corner around a radio. Two of them grabbed their fedoras and darted for the door, their trench coats flying back to give full view of their tommy-guns beneath.

Ralph shrugged and sank back down into the chair with his debutant. He took another swig from his flask.

It was a dozen hours—and flasks—later that Ralph abruptly awoke. The singing had stopped. The debutant lay unconscious beside him. It was dark outside, as no light shone through the cracks around the boarded-up windows. A full day had passed and that made him happy. *Won't ma be angry?*

He smirked and staggered over to a group of men still hovering around the radio. "What's up, fellas?"

They ignored him, intent on a faint chatter from the wireless, so he leaned in to listen.

" . . . and hundreds have thrown themselves from buildings . . . investors and stockbrokers lying dead along the length of Wall Street . . ."

Ralph shook his head to clear it of the boozy fog.

" . . . twenty-three percent wiped from all stocks . . . an unprecedented financial crash . . ."

"What?" Ralph slurred.

One of the men shot him a glance. "Get with it, buddy."

Ralph stood, dazed, as the words from the radio pulled him into numb understanding. The blood drained from his head, and he stumbled out into the foyer, searching for a phone. A crowd of men surrounded it, the one using it slamming the receiver against the table. "The line's clogged!" the man shouted.

Ralph shoved through the crowd, but he was pushed back and knocked to the floor.

"Scram, ya dewdropper," one of them said.

Sprawled on the floor, Ralph trembled, completely sober. Vomit surged at the base of his throat. The market had crashed. The rail line would never be built. The useless land would remain just that—useless. More than useless—no value at all.

He ran out of the mill and jumped into the breezer. The rear wheels screeched as he stomped the accelerator to the floor and sped toward home.

* * * *

His fear turned to anger as the breezer jumped the curb and ripped across the grass, the front crunching into the granite base of the family ranch home. He ran up the steps and into the house, his blood pumping hard, thumping through his skull. His eyeballs ached and his mouth tasted like a curse.

Agnes was sitting in her chair at the window, frail as a corpse. She didn't move.

"It's gone, Ma. It's all gone."

But Ralph knew that she knew.

Hate welled up inside him.

From the corner of his eye, he caught a glimpse of Harrison and Edith in the hallway, looking nervous and fidgety. Edith was gripping tight to his brother's bicep.

"*What did I tell you*?" he screamed, launching himself at them. He knocked Edith to the rug with a fist to her face and then jabbed his elbow into his brother's chest. He grabbed at Harrison's flannel shirt and threw him across the corridor, but the unexpected smash of a returned fist to his own jaw sent him staggering. The brothers tripped and stumbled into the main room, delivering blow after blow.

"Ralph! Harrison!" Agnes screeched, and Uncle Bertie came running from the kitchen, stricken with horror.

Ralph slammed Harrison into the fireplace, and he landed on the hearth with a grunt, soot pluming around him. The elder was quick on top of him, paying no mind to the raw, bleeding pain in his knuckles as he punched his little brother again and again.

"Ralph! Ralph! Stop it! You'll kill him!"

A punch cracked against Ralph's jaw, and he rolled his tongue and pushed two teeth from his gums. He spat blood, and then he unholstered one of his Colts. Harrison lunged at him, smashing the top of his head into Ralph's chin.

The gun blasted.

Harrison was thrown across the rug, his face white and eyes terrified, his chest and abdomen saturated in blood.

Ralph could only stare at his little brother, crumpled on the floor. And then all went black.

* * * *

Someone screamed. It must have been Edith, but Harrison couldn't tell through the pain filling his entire body. Then his ma's hands were on him, pulling him to his feet. She yanked the gun from his hands.

"Go clean yourself up, Harrison. Quick! Give your clothes to Bertie."

Agnes ran across the room, taking care to sidestep the growing puddle of blood. She bent over Ralph, but there were no tears. They had all been used up many years ago.

"Bertie, take the kids into the city," she said. "None of you were here—do you understand me? I will handle this."

The family did as they were told and scuttled down the corridor.

"We will blame the crash." Her lips moved without giving breath to the words.

Agnes brushed a hand across the forehead of her dead son. Then she placed the gun in his, turned the barrel to his temple, and fired it a second time.

P.J. Parker

Over There (1941 AD)

Harrison slid into the over-cushioned wicker chair that smelled of perfume. He pressed a glass of whisky, straight up, to his lips and gazed along the lantern-lit, flagstoned colonnade of the El Mirador Hotel. Military personnel mingled with Hollywood glitterati in various states of conversation and conviviality. Laughter kissed the dry desert air of Palm Springs, and through the open French doors came the sounds of Mister Miller's big band trumpets. Hundreds of GIs swing-danced with pretty young starlets. Amongst them the flair of handsome cowboys and tuxedoed legends of the silver screen sashayed across the floor with women whose beauty and glamor was adored in every Main Street USA movie house. Harrison had even danced with Dorothy Lamour—one of the biggest stars any fella could ever hope to meet. She had held him tight, as tight as a military man needed to be held. She had touched his cheek and asked about his black eye. When he'd told her it was from a football game at boot camp, she had thrown her head back and laughed a vibrant laugh. It had made him feel good and proud to be serving his country.

He whistled and took another slug of whiskey as he sank further into the cushions.

The famous yell of Tarzan undulated across the hotel's grassy courtyard, and several nubile ingénues, wearing little more than the star-studded cover of darkness, jumped into the Olympic-sized swimming pool. The cinematic ape man himself finished his jungle call then leapt from a high dive to splash into the water. On the far side of the pool, the hotel's tall Renaissance tower was silhouetted against the snowcapped heights of San Jacinto—the mountain defined by the decadent glow of L.A. to the west. Search-lights from the center of Palm Springs village, the ones in front of The Plaza Theatre down on Palm Canyon Drive, arced across the night sky.

"Well, hi-de-ho! I thought I'd find you out here, flyboy."

Harrison lifted his glass. "Sarge."

United States Army Air Corps Sergeant Sawyer dropped into the lounge beside him. He pulled a pack of cigarettes from his jacket and offered one, but Harrison shook his head. A match flared.

"You not on active duty tonight?" The sergeant jerked his chin toward the Malibu-tanned, silk-draped view.

"Nah, Sarge, you know I'm hitched to my honey."

"Right, Edith! Of course."

Harrison thumbed in his pocket for his wallet then flipped it open and handed it to the sarge. A photo of Edith and little Mildred—pretty at thirteen—in Central Park. The twins, Franklin and Tommy at nine years old, posed in front of them in homemade superhero capes.

"You're one lucky guy. New York?"

"Yep. Once the twins came along, Edith wanted to be closer to her mom and pop in Manhattan."

Sergeant Sawyer nodded. "I heard your family owned a lot of acreage up Chicago way. That would have bought a nice chunk of the Upper East Side—several blocks of Central Park views, most likely." He smirked.

Harrison stared into his whisky, swirling the liquor around the glass. "Actually, Ma had to sell most all of that for peanuts—less than peanuts. She didn't want anyone in the company riding the rails to find a job, or losing their homes and families during the depression because of . . ." He pressed his lips tight together. "She felt responsible. We all did."

Harrison didn't mention his great-grandpappy Daniel's land down near San Antonio. Per his ma's last letter, in the last few weeks it had sprouted more oil towers than it ever had trees. He wondered what it would come to, if anything at all.

Comedians Bob Hope and Mickey Rooney waltzed out of the ballroom, serious scowls on their faces, to slide and twirl down the full length of the colonnade, laughter and cheers cascading in their wake. Sergeant Sawyer, a big man—made even bigger by the sharpness of his uniform—snickered and puffed his cigarette.

"Listen, Sarge." Harrison lowered his voice and leaned in close. "Do you think we'll ever be pulled into this war?"

Sawyer was quiet for a time, and then he shrugged. "Germany and Italy sure are some long ways a way, and from what I can tell, Japan is prob'ly just as far in the other direction. None would ever dare to declare war, let alone attack the US of A. I don't think it's of much concern to us." He stubbed out his cigarette. "Sure, we'll ferry some planes and ammo over to Britain and China, even Australia, to help, but I doubt we'll ever see our own boys' boots on foreign soil. Not our soil, not our fight, as far as I see it."

Harrison looked thoughtfully into his whisky glass. "I heard the Iroquois Confederacy is already at war with Germany—declared it back in the Great War and never made peace. Their warriors are signing up in droves to fight the Krauts," he said. "What if the British and Chinese empires lose?"

The sergeant shrugged again.

A squeal of laughter rippled from the pool. Harrison bit at his thumbnail as he gazed at the picture of Edith and the kids, all smiles. "Yeah, I guess you're right—as long as it all stays over there." He closed his wallet and pushed it into his pocket.

The first bullets of sunlight ricocheted across the windblown dunes of the Coachella Valley as the military vehicles drove north out of Palm Springs into the desert. The convoy thudded over the rail tracks. Some of the men were boisterous—singing and laughing about their conquests. Others leaned against their brothers to share sleepy conversations. There were accounts of first, second, and third base. One cadet proclaimed a home run with a blonde bombshell, but no one believed him for a moment. Well, maybe they did.

Harrison was content, holding the steering wheel steady as he skidded around a clump of Joshua trees and onto the dirt track that led behind the Little San Bernardino Mountains into the Mojave Desert. The camp was a dog-awful place—a handful of curved, corrugated-steel huts edging a dusty airfield. Beyond the perimeter fence was nothing but rattlers, coyotes, roadrunners, and bomb-blasted sand dunes. Dried-up date palms clustered in shallow arroyos. The noses of six Douglas C-47s, Dakotas, poked from wide steel hangars. As he drove beside the airstrip a towplane was lifting off from the field, pulling a sun-bleached wooden glider behind it. They curved up and over the Mojave, circling high above the camp and desert. The tie was released, and the engineless craft dipped and turned with the score of gliders already riding the air currents. They soared like mythical thunderbirds.

The heat in the barracks was oppressive despite the early morning hour. Harrison peeled off his uniform, wrapped a towel around his waist, and walked barefooted across the planks to the shower hut. The steam-shrouded corrals were all full, so he waited on the bench outside. Another flyboy, Airman Woodfield, leaned against the wall beside him. He was skinny, short, tattooed, and butt-naked except for a standard-issue towel draped over his forearm—after all, there were no women for at least ten miles. Harrison had often thought about getting a tattoo, and maybe one day he would, but he couldn't for the life of him think what he'd want needled into his skin. His ma had once mentioned that his great-grandpappy Daniel had had some kind of ink on his chest, but she had never seen it, nor known what it was. Maybe Uncle Bertie knew—he had a small collection of letters and treasures handed down through the generations.

"I thought your pass lasted until eighteen hundred hours, Harry?"

Harrison stretched and yawned and scratched at the hair on his chest. "I wanted to get some work done on *Betty*'s right engine. She spluttered a bit yesterday. Did you score with a starlet last night, or what?"

The airman's lip curled—a toothy Southern-California grin. "Palm Springs has a lot more to offer than just beautiful women."

Harrison held up a hand but didn't bother suppressing a smile. "Yeah, I know, buddy. It's the magnificent scenery and wildlife."

Both men laughed.

"I could help you with *Betty*, if you like." Airman Woodfield shielded his eyes against the sun, to see the gliders circling high in the deepening blue of the desert sky, mere pinpricks above the clouds. "DeRego and Stephens have the cadets up in the air for the whole day. I don't have to lecture them again till noon tomorrow."

"Thanks, Woody, I'd appreciate that."

The showers were fed by springs that bubbled up at the edge of the salt-flats. That the hot water—*Agua Caliente*—was a direct link to more than two thousand years of Native American Indian spiritually was not lost on Harrison. It was earthy-smelling, naturally warm, and made him feel cleaner than any water he had ever known—as if he were somehow part of nature itself.

The showers were where officers and regulars were equal, where they could be themselves, joke around, and talk about sports and the sweethearts they'd left at home. It was far removed from the possibility of a war that lay not so far beyond the horizon.

After scrubbing up, Harrison grabbed a couple hours' shuteye and then wandered over to the hangar where his Dakota was housed. The silver bird was majestic, reflecting the full sun streaming in through the hangar doors. A hand-painted Betty Grable stretched luxuriantly along the front side of the fuselage, a cheeky but innocent smile that left a hopeful lump in your throat. Woody was already up a ladder, bent into the engine casing, covered in sweat and grease.

Harrison pulled himself up onto the trestle beside him. "Anything?"

Woody straightened, wiping the back of his hand over his forehead, smearing grease across his brow. It made him look like a raccoon. "What you grinnin' at?"

Harrison slapped his friend on the back. "Nothin', pal."

Airman Woodfield stuck his head back inside the engine housing. "Found a stripped bolt. Just checking the others to confirm all okay." He fumbled in the pocket of his overalls for the bolt then held it out to Harrison without turning from his work. Harrison squinted and ran his finger along its length.

"Hairline fractures. The last thing we want is for a couple of these to shear off during flight."

"Yeah, I figured. You think we should just replace them all, especially with the long-haul flight scheduled for tonight?"

Harrison raised his eyebrows. "Flight?"

"Sergeant Sawyer received the order 'bout an hour ago. Couple hundred Navy'll be bussed up from San Diego after dark. All the Dakotas'll be taking off tonight at balls o'clock."

"Where we taking them?"

"Gosh darned middle of the Pacific—Pearl Harbor. Sarge reckons we'll be stationed at Hickam airfield by the Navy base there till at least after Christmas."

"Then we better strip this baby while we have the chance—make sure she's all nice and sweet." Harrison threw a wink to Betty on the fuselage.

They switched out the bolts, their grunts echoing through the hanger as they wrenched the nuts as tight as they would go. When *Betty* was as snug as she was ever going to be and the engines fired up and sounded all lulu, Harrison and Woody lay on the cool concrete beneath her belly, leaning against a wheel and sipping colas.

A roadrunner dashed past the front of the hangar.

Harrison let out a heavy sigh. "You know, sometimes I wonder if I'm doing enough."

"What d'you mean?"

"I mean we're out here in the desert and the most meaningful thing I can do is fix an engine. It's hardly something to write home about, or tell the kids to impress them when I get home. When I was little, my Uncle Bertie would tell me stories of our family. Great men and women doing things you'd only ever read about in history books, achieving something in their own way that made our country stronger. That helped it evolve into what it is today. And yet here I am grappling with a monkey wrench and drinking a coke, with no prospects except going to some forsaken island in the middle of the Pacific—far from where I can make a difference, from my family, from where anything is ever gonna happen."

"Careful what you wish for, Harry." Airman Woodfield set down his cola and pulled off a boot to scratch at the bottom of his foot. "The stories that make up our history, that make America what it is, aren't just the ones in history lessons and books. From where I sit, they're just a glamorous handful of the hundreds of millions of stories, most of which are prob'ly never told far from a family's own fireside. And who's to say what's significant in the making of a country—its values, its strengths? My great-grandma makes the best danged apple pie this side of the Appalachians. That recipe has brought more happiness and strength to generations of my family than anything ever achieved in Washington. My Uncle Pete's tomatoes have won blue ribbons at the L.A. County Fair for as long as I can recall. And Mama . . . Mama brought up ten kids on her own and I reckon she did a mighty fine job. These are important things, Harry, and to me they're the things that make our country what it is. And then there's you." He picked up his coke bottle and clinked it against Harrison's. "You're my best bud. Ever since we signed up and swore allegiance at the foot of Lady Liberty in New York Harbor, I knew you accepted me for who I am, that you had my back and I could trust you. You and I may never do anything they'll write about in history books, but we have our families, and our own stories, and they're important in their own way." Woody nudged Harrison's shoulder. "We each live our lives as good as we can, in the best country to live 'em in. To me, that's a pretty good tale to tell."

Harrison's face softened into a smile. He nodded and took a swig of coke.

A jeep skidded around the road, swung into the hangar, and came to a stop under the Dakota's nose. Sergeant Sawyer stood up, waving. "Come on, boys, get spruced up quick. One last trip into town before our passes expire."

"What is it, Sarge?" Harrison asked as he and Woody jumped to their feet.

"That Tarzan guy and Esther Williams are in the pool at the Desert Inn. Photoshoot for some kind of Madison Avenue spread. Their agents reckon the pics would be better with some military in the crowd—shame to waste an opportunity to see a pretty young starlet in her bathing suit!"

"What are we waiting for, let's go!"

* * * *

They had run no more than a few yards across the Hickam airfield when Woody was struck by gunfire from a low-flying Japanese fighter. The bullets tore through his shoulder, and he hit the tarmac with his face. Harrison rolled to the ground as the plane zoomed overhead, the engine growl earsplitting. The aircraft tilted its wings, clipped the fronds of a coconut palm and turned to skim the waves of Pearl Harbor.

"Snafu!" Harrison grunted through gritted teeth. He scurried sideways on his hands and knees toward Woody. The airman's face was smeared by the blood that soaked his jacket, his jaw locked, his cheeks tensed in pain. He was gasping for breath, his eyes rolling up under spasming eyelids.

Harrison grabbed him by the collar. "Get up, airman! Get up!" He wrestled Woody to his feet and they stumbled toward the flight line. The planes at Hickam Airfield were lined up wingtip to wingtip alongside the tarmac, but that first wave of attack had blown several to smithereens, and fire leapt from fuselage to fuselage, explosions erupting down the line toward the hangars and munition stores.

A hoard of enemy fighters darkened the sky like a curling black dragon, hundreds of planes converging on the harbor and airfields from both the open ocean and the cloud-shrouded mountain passes of central Oahu. Harrison recognized the dense droning sound of dive bombers. He couldn't see them, but he knew they were up there—somewhere near the twelve-thousand-foot mark.

The horizontal bombers had made one devastating pass of the airfield and were turning across Honolulu for a second strike at the prone craft. Directly south of Hickam, a swarm of torpedo bombers lifted from sea-level and tore over the headland, then back down to the waves in the harbor. Repeated, low-pitched, thudding detonations, the resounding screech of ripping metal, and the unmistakable smell of burning gasoline and flesh spewed from the Pearl Harbor naval base, only hinting at the horror Harrison was unable to see.

He scooted under the wing of an aircraft with a dozen other airmen who had run from the barracks. The craft beside it was blazing—soon it would explode. Woody kicked the wheel chocks out of the way, and the men threw their shoulders into the craft to push it out of line. One of them was still in his pajama shorts, others in khakis. No one had been prepared. Harrison had quickly pulled on his Aloha shirt over football shoulder pads with the first blast that had shaken the barracks—they were supposed to play against West Point that morning. And Woody, well, Woody was a bloody mess.

They ran to push a second plane in the opposite direction out of the single line of enemy fire, Harrison and Woody side by side as they rammed their shoulders against the hard metal of the craft. Woody's mouth twisted in pain, but Harrison held his gaze, willing him on.

"We gotta get *Betty* into the air," Harrison said. "It's the safest place for her."

Woody nodded.

A mass of Japanese aircraft, the red sun emblazoned on their wings, shot across the fields. At no more than twenty feet above ground they spewed bullets, shattering the U.S. fighters into flame and shrapnel that fragmented across the base. Woody and Harrison went flat against the tar, pistols drawn, firing toward the red insignias that zoomed at close quarters. They emptied four rounds each and still the Japanese planes continued to pass over their heads.

"C'mon, Harry, let's get our girl to safety. She's gonna be needed after all this is done."

Airman Woodfield was a quarter of the way across the airstrip while Harrison fired off his last slug then sprinted after his bloody copilot.

Betty was squeezed between two other birds, one pouring smoke from shattered windows, the other turned askew, its fuselage and wings riddled by bullets and shrapnel. The airmen climbed into *Betty*'s hold, their girl's perfume of leather and hydraulic fluid giving them some semblance of comfort. They slid into their seats, and Harrison yanked off his Hawaiian shirt and ripped through the print of Hula dancers and palm trees with his teeth and wound the shreds around Woody's shoulder, pulling it tight enough to make his copilot wince.

"You're doin' great, pal," Harrison said. "And you do know that was my favorite shirt, right?"

Woody almost choked on his laugh.

Propellers whirred as *Betty* rolled out into the center of the runway. An almighty explosion shredded across the harbor to the west, but Harrison clenched his jaw and kept his gaze straight ahead, caressing the throttle as the Dakota bore down the strip and lifted up over the Pacific.

"Hang!" Woody shouted, indicating straight ahead and above.

A dozen fighters coiled out of formation toward the Dakota. There was little to no cloud cover over the water to hide in, and there was no way *Betty* would be able to outrun them. Harrison turned her sharp. "Is there an airfield through the pass?" A heavy layer of cumulus hung above the Koʻolau Range.

Woody flicked through the maps and pulled one open on his lap, his fingers leaving smears of blood across Waikiki and Diamond Head. "Over Nuʻuanu Pali then into Kaneʻohe—if it's still there." Woody's face was grave. "If not, we'll swing her west and take our chances landing in Kahana Valley."

Betty shot straight through the carnage of Pearl Harbor.

Ford Island and its airstrip was a surging mass of fire and plumes of black smoke. Arcs of electricity crisscrossed the island, from what could only be exploding transformers. Two enormous battleships were already sinking, their hulks listing, one of their prows underwater. Thousands of men paddled in the bomb and bullet-riddled surge. The green Hawaiian water was now purple with flaming gasoline. And American blood.

Harrison's anger swelled and he slammed his fist into the console. He hadn't felt this kind of fury since Ralph had betrayed the family. But this was so much more than that. He stared into *Betty*'s hold but there were no arms, no bombs, no artillery, nothing he could do—just an empty void to convey troops, jeeps, and heavy guns. He slammed his fist again, splitting the skin on his knuckles. Woody grabbed his hand to hold it still.

"One battle at a time, my brother."

The two pilots gripped the flight control yoke together, urging the Dakota up into the clouds above Pearl Harbor. Neither saw the fighters in their wake, but they felt *Betty* shudder as the spray of bullets ripped through her wings and fuselage.

The drone of her propellers waned and then stopped.

The dials swung erratically then froze.

Wind whistled through the bullet holes along both sides. And *Betty* dropped—unseen mountains surrounding her, hidden by clouds.

Harrison caught a glimpse of cliff face and swallowed hard, bringing to mind all he knew about gliding. He'd done it a hundred times in an actual glider. Only twice in a Dakota, and that had been in the bright clear light of the Mojave, not in a subterfuge of clouds, through a pass with uplifts and downdrafts he had no knowledge of.

He turned to his copilot. "You're the expert at this, Woody. I trust your instincts."

Airman Woodfield took the controls and held them steady, his gaze flicking left and right, up and down to get some kind of bearing within the cumulus.

But they could see only each other's reflections in the windows, the pallor of the clouds obscuring any view around them.

"I've got your back, buddy," Harrison said. "And no matter what happens, I know you've got mine."

A Time Comes When Silence is Betrayal (1967 AD)

Tommy was naked and stretched across the crumpled cotton sheets, staring at the whitewashed ceiling of his West Village warehouse loft. It had been more than a decade since his dad and "Uncle" Woody had helped him paint the old beams and planks, when his parents had given him the two-thousand-square-foot apartment as a present for his twenty-fifth birthday. It needed repainting. His twin brother, Franklin, would never help him—he knew that much for sure. Tommy rolled and breathed in the remnant smell of pungent smoke, Southern Comfort, and sweat from his pillow. He reached out with an open hand to the other side of the mattress—now empty, but still warm. He stroked the indentation, fingers quivering, doubting that it would ever be truly filled because of the way things were. He hated the way things were. Perhaps he even hated himself.

The LP record on the high-fidelity player skipped on a scratch in the vinyl, a line from the Mamas and the Papas on repeat. The words filled the apartment, seeming to define the rut of Tommy's life, to underscore that so much needed to change. He wondered if it ever would.

He got up out of bed and lifted the needle to the next song on the groove, smiling and shaking his head with the new melody and intrinsic lyrics. "Jeez, Mama Cass, you've got my life nailed." Tommy's heart swelled as Cass Elliot assured him that, despite the pain caused by others' hang-ups, the song in own heart was worth singing, too.

He grabbed his blue jeans, T-shirt, and treads from off the floor and pulled them on. The leather jacket eased on nice and smooth over his arms, heavily tatted with symbols of a proud heritage—ink his twin shared. He greased back his hair, nudged shades onto the bridge of his nose and went out to find his friends and a breakfast with a bottomless cup of joe. It was cold outside, the April breeze skimming off the Hudson, up Christopher Street, and into lower Manhattan. He hurried along the sidewalk, bracing himself against the chill, rubbing his hands up and down his torso to keep warm.

Officers O'Flaherty and O'Toole stood in front of the Stonewall Inn, and he thought it best to keep his distance. They knew who Tommy was—*what* Tommy was; he had the "accidental" baton bruises to bear witness to that.

He jogged down past Sheridan Square. Hershey and Arnie were sitting in the window of the diner on Sixth Avenue, and Tommy sidled in.

"Well, now, if we don't finally have the whole *Miss Marmelstein* gang," the waitress called from behind the counter.

Tommy winked then slid into the plush velveteen booth. "I'll have the usual, Hazel, thanks. You guys ready for the Mobe?" he asked his friends.

"I reckon half the city has been waiting for this mobilization since Doctor King's speech," Arnie said, finishing off a stack of pancakes.

Hazel placed a large helping of cornbread, hash browns, bacon, and eggs in front of Tommy, and poured a mug of coffee to the brim. "I thought you fellas had enough of a fight without getting involved in the war protest."

Tommy blew on his coffee. "Hazel, equal rights for guys like us, or even basic acceptance, is far from anyone's agenda. I doubt any of us will see it in our lifetime." He squirted ketchup over his hash. "The rights of African Americans and the poor are another story. That is a fight that has gone on openly for centuries and it is one that can be won quick if we put our shoulders into it. The tide has turned. Doctor King and others made massive headway but this blasted war in Vietnam turned the attention from civil rights to a useless conflict half a world away."

"But ain't it our responsibility to help out and to stop the Commies?"

Tommy's brow furrowed and he dug his fork into the sunny-side-ups. He'd had this argument a dozen times with his brother, and neither had been able to gain the upper hand. He squeezed more ketchup onto his plate and swilled his yoke through it.

"Hazel, I'll clue you in," Hershey said. "Uncle Sam is sending kids six thousand miles away to fight for rights those same kids don't have here in their own country. The ghettoizing of city blocks ensures negroes and the poor have inadequate schools, markets, and facilities. It also guarantees they're the first to be sent to die in bunkers on some foreign hillside."

The waitress fidgeted with her apron. "That doesn't seem right."

"No, Hazel, it don't," Tommy said. "And on top of that, the direction of the war has tipped outta control. To some degree we've become the enemy of the people we intended to help." He stopped and stared at his reflection in the diner window. It was the same face as his dad's. "Folks sit at home, eating apple pie and watching *I Dream of Jeannie*, when kids are killing kids in some foreign rice field for no good reason." He pulled his attention from the reflection. "As my uncle says, 'One battle at a time.' And the first is to get this war over and done with. Get Americans out of that godforsaken jungle and back home where they belong. Then we can concentrate on our own people's civil rights."

"Meanwhile, back at the ranch . . ." Arnie fingered his watch.

Tommy nodded and shoveled the last of his breakfast into his mouth. "Time to percolate!" He grinned and pushed a couple of quarters across the counter before the three of them headed uptown to Central Park on the A Line.

"This is the scene!" Arnie shouted, standing high on his toes to see over the crowd, a colorful sea of like-minded people who had had enough: tweeds, socials, greasers, tools, bikers and jocks, busloads of parents with their kids, businessmen, secretaries, groupies, hippies, and regular folks.

"What's happening?" Tommy asked a guy in sandals and a tie-dye, holding a cardboard sign above a dubious cloud of smoke.

"Everything's everything, man," the guy said.

They passed hippies with placards that read, "BURN YOUR DRAFT CARDS." It appeared many men had done just that, as fires licked from trashcans along the way. Tommy had not received a card—probably something to do with his family's connections—but he had no doubt that if he did, he would burn it as soon as look at it. He thought of his twin brother, and a sad, unsympathetic taste filled his mouth. He spat into the gutter.

"Where we headed?" Tommy asked as the crowd moved out of the park and past the Plaza Hotel.

"The United Nations," Arnie finally confirmed with a cool-looking chick who reminded Tommy of Janis Joplin.

In the next couple of hours, the Mobe advanced down the avenues and along the streets to the East River. Crowds cheered from the windows of buildings along the way, and the traffic on 42nd Street came to a standstill in front of Grand Central Terminal. Tommy linked arms with an African American man as they marched and sang "We Shall Overcome," sharing a brotherhood he'd listened to his dad talk about, though he never understood until now.

The crowd poured into the plaza in front of the UN. Some cops stepped back into uncertain lines, and others gave reassuring nods to the ranks of the Mobe.

From the steps of the building, Doctor King's speech made Tommy's eyes sting on that cold, April afternoon. There was a freedom within the crowd—a freedom that might come for some but, he knew, might never come for him and his friends. It was still a freedom worth fighting for.

He turned to his newfound friend and saw a man who shared his interests, his goals, his need for acceptance and integration. Their grip on each other tightened as they gazed past Doctor King and down the long, but hopeful road that still lay ahead of them all.

* * * *

Bomb Saigon Now!
Bomb Hanoi Now!
Bomb Disneyland Now!
Bomb Everything!

The four stickers crossed the front of Franklin's helmet, right above where he'd scratched the word *Hippie* into the gray metal. He hunkered down in the back of the Cobra, his machine gun resting across his thigh, his finger caressing the trigger. He chewed his gum with his mouth open. The chopper lifted off from amongst the tall elephant grass, the *thwack-thwack-thwack* of blades drowning out the sound of all hell that constantly surrounded them.

Franklin clenched the strap on the bulkhead above and leaned out the open cargo door. His nostrils flared with the sharp stench of napalm. The rice fields below were bloody, uncountable corpses lying half-submerged in the rushes. Most of them were men—most of them. He saw movement near one of the muddy walkways and squeezed the trigger, sending a round into the grass. No more movement.

He blew a bubble with his gum and popped it.

There was a resounding clang of metal—bullet against helmet—followed by an instant of star-spangled bloody vision. Franklin was flung into the guts of the Cobra, a carcass splayed amongst loose ammunition.

* * * *

He woke up screaming, loud and guttural, drenched in sweat. He pressed his hands to his head, gulping for air, looking around fast to determine where he was. Dorothy ran into the bedroom, her hair in rollers.

"It's okay, Frankie. You're okay, darlin'." She sat on the edge of the bed and wrapped her arms around her husband. Franklin pressed his face into her hair, angry tears blinding his good eye when he felt his wife trembling. He caught the silhouette of Carmine standing nervously at the door. Franklin stretched out an arm toward him.

"Come here, son. Daddy's okay. C'mon, buddy. Daddy was just having a bad dream."

Carmine approached slowly, wiping tears from his cheek with his pajama sleeve. He crawled up onto the bed and into his father's arms without a word.

Franklin held tight to his wife and son, squeezing his eye shut so he wouldn't see his reflection in the bureau mirror—the deep,

331

crisscrossed scar over his right temple and cheek, the vacant stare of his right eye.

"My God, how I love you both," he whispered, kissing his wife on the cheek and his son on the top of the head. He could feel the tears surfacing, but kept it in check. He hated the way things were. Perhaps he even hated himself.

But then a happy thought burst into his mind, and he smiled.

"Isn't it somebody's birthday today? Let me think. Whose could it be?"

"It's mine! It's my birthday!" Carmine shouted, forgetting his grief.

"Why, so it is." Franklin stood and tightened the drawstring of his pants before stooping to reach far under the bed. "What have we here?"

Franklin handed Carmine the box, papered in the smiling blue face of Huckleberry Hound. Then he snuggled into Dorothy's side as they watched their son tear open the package. Carmine leapt off the bed and ran around the room holding his new space glider toy and making swishing spaceship noises. Franklin grinned wider than he had in an awfully long time, and Dorothy caressed his cheek and touched her head to his. Her smile almost made him cry, and he pressed his lips to hers.

"We need to be at your mom and dad's by five for the party." Dorothy hesitated, biting her lower lip. "I invited Tommy."

Franklin's eyes darkened. For a moment, he stared at some distant memory within the tattoos that swept across his skin. Then he gave a curt nod and turned back to watch his son zooming from the moon toward Mars.

* * * *

His parents' townhouse on the Upper East Side was much larger than Franklin and Dorothy's Brooklyn brownstone. Franklin held open the door of the town car as his wife and son stepped out onto the sidewalk. Carmine was all decked out in a suit his great-grandmother Agnes had bought him for Christmas. Franklin looked up at his childhood home. He and Tommy had had the complete run of the fifth floor as kids. They weren't allowed to enter the reception rooms on the lower floors without an adult, but up there on the fifth they could do whatever they wanted.

He wondered what had gone wrong—how he and Tommy could have turned out so different. They were, after all, the same man split in two at birth. Franklin shook the thought from his head, trying to remember who had told him that story. It seemed so very long ago. It might have been Great-Uncle Bertie, God rest his soul.

They went inside and climbed the grand, curved stair to the reception room on the second floor. Its double doors were flung open wide for the special occasion. Carmine was seven—practically a man. He held the space glider high above his head as he ran ahead of his parents into the room festooned with helium balloons.

"Granddad!" Carmine yelled, jumping up into Harrison's arms.

"Hi, dad." Franklin gripped hands and pressed cheeks with his old man. "Where's mom?"

"Still icing the cake. She's been baking up a storm all day— won't let me anywhere near her."

Dorothy gave Harrison a peck on the cheek. "I'll go help Edith. Keep an eye on the birthday boy—make sure he doesn't break anything."

Franklin loved this room, from the family photographs and memorabilia that covered the walls to the enormous grizzly bear skin stretching in front of the fireplace. The earliest photo was from 1807— some relative standing stiffly in a cavalry captain's blue uniform, a bear head mounted on the wall behind him. Franklin's favorite was of the twins in Texas, sitting proudly on their horses, clasping a title deed for the valleys that formed the backdrop. They had always looked a bit Hispanic to Franklin, but he guessed he could see the family resemblance. The largest photo on the wall was four feet wide—one of those strange-looking metal ships from the Civil War, with more than a hundred crew members on its deck. If he turned his head and squinted, he could just make out which one might have been his ancestor. Above the mantle, between an antique squirrel gun and a cutlass, was a hand-painted photograph of Franklin's grandmother and grandfather at some fair. *Agnes was a total babe*, Franklin thought whenever he saw it. Some of the photos were framed, modern prints: Tommy and Franklin as teenagers climbing the ruins of Mesa Verde; searching for arrowheads at some ginormous ancient pueblo in New Mexico; laughing their heads off on the teacup ride at Disneyland. Even Franklin couldn't tell who was who in that teacup. They were both just so damned happy.

He placed his hand on the ancient family Bible, its leather cover tattered, soiled, and partially burnt. His eyes were stinging, and he blinked away tears for the second time that day.

"Bourbon?" Harrison poured two whiskeys, straight up, and opened a bottle of pop for Carmine. Harrison settled into a chair by the bay window and Franklin sank into the chair opposite.

"How's the, um . . ." Harrison touched his finger to his temple.

"I have my days. Some better than others."

His father nodded, and Franklin knew he could see the physical injury but only guess at the mental damage beneath. He himself had lost too many buddies to bombs, bullets, and depression. He'd witnessed friends being blown to bits in the Pacific, and still others in Korea. He'd cradled men he loved as the life drained from them, into the bloody soil of foreign lands.

But his son was alive, and for that, Franklin knew, his father was grateful.

Franklin and Harrison stood when Agnes entered. At ninety-three, she walked with a stick but still cut a fine figure.

"Granny!" Carmine ran the full length of the room toward his great-grandmother.

"Careful, Carmine," Franklin said. His son stopped short of Agnes and gave the deepest of bows—a bow his granny had taught him to show women his respect and love.

Agnes ruffled the boy's hair. "Over there, Carmine—your present is by the fireplace." She smiled and went to sit in her chair. "A construction set," she whispered to Franklin as he kissed her hand. "He can build buildings like my dear Bromley. Watch out; there are a lot of pieces in that box." Agnes cackled and pointed a gnarled finger toward the gin. "Where's Tommy?"

"Probably in jail again," Franklin muttered, pouring her a glass.

Agnes took a sip before she settled her gaze on her grandson. "Does it make you think less of him?"

"Well, of course it does," Franklin said with a bitter laugh.

Agnes rubbed her chin. "Strange. I couldn't be more proud of him because of it."

Franklin pressed his lips tight, wishing the birthday cake would come out soon.

"I have known men, and women, jailed for the color of their skin, the scriptures of their religion, or their wish to be accepted as equals." Agnes placed her gin carefully on the side table. "Did you know I was jailed back in '17 with my suffragette sisters? Several times, in fact!"

Franklin shook his head.

"Have you talked to Tommy? Do you know why he was jailed?"

"Because he's a coward and a f—"

"Franklin!" Harrison shouted. "I will not have you talk about your brother that way."

Agnes glared at her grandson, and he shrank back into his chair.

They all turned at the sound of footfalls on the stair, and Tommy walked in carrying a large, flat box, covered in Huckleberry Hound wrapping paper.

Franklin swigged the contents of his glass and turned to peer out the window, listening to the squeals of his son—and of Tommy— as they unwrapped the gift together. In the window he could see the reflection of some kind of race car set. A twinge of regret cut through him when Carmine hugged and kissed his Uncle Tommy. Tommy said his hellos, gave Agnes a gentle hug, then sat on the footstool at her side without acknowledging Franklin. Other than Carmine's excited commotion, the party sat in an uncomfortable silence.

"How are things down at your garage, Tommy?" Agnes finally asked.

"They're pretty sweet gran'. A couple of classics from the twenties arrived this week. It will be hard to find parts, but I'm sure we'll be able to restore them. One of them is a breezer—just like the one rusting in your back yard in Chicago when we were kids." He smiled and Agnes ran her finger around the rim of her gin glass.

"Playin' with cars while the whole world is going to hell," Franklin muttered.

Tommy's face flushed red. "Would you rather I go over to Nam and kill the ones you missed, Frankie?"

"At least I'm willing to fight for my country. I ain't no coward."

Tommy rose from the footstool and stepped toward his brother. "Go to hell!"

"Well, it's obvious *you'll* be there."

"Frankie, hush now," Harrison said, jerking his head toward Carmine.

"No. It's gotta be said." Franklin squeezed his fists tight. "I don't want my kid around some guy without the guts to do what's right."

"What the hell do you think I've been doing?"

Franklin grabbed Tommy's lapel, and Tommy grabbed his.

"No!" Agnes cried. "No, Ralph! Not again!"

The twins released each other to look at their grandmother, confused. Neither of them had ever even met their uncle Ralph. He'd died long before they were born.

"I'll handle this, Ma." Harrison glared at his sons until they stepped away from each other. Then he pointed to the photos covering the walls. "Do you see these people?" he yelled, and even Carmine went silent. "In one way or another, all of them had a fight on their hands—whether it was with Indians, the British, the Spanish, the French, or just the damn elements. For some it was against other Americans—religious persecutors, unadulterated bigots." His gaze flicked to Tommy. "Now, I ain't no preacher, like the ones who first owned our family Bible, but I've got a pretty good handle on what's right and what's wrong. Both you boys know I've seen war across the world, but I've also seen war right here on our own dirt—for God knows fighting for Civil Rights or against any type of hatred is a war that can be just as heartbreaking, just as dangerous, just as deadly. The casualty rate is most prob'ly higher."

Harrison stared at Carmine crouching over the race car set, then looked back at his sons.

"I can see myself clear in both you boys, though it seems you've each taken a part of me and made it your own fight. Tommy, why did Frankie go to war? Was it to kill people?"

"Well . . ." Tommy sighed. "No, of course not."

"Then why?"

"I guess it was to help. Because our country has a responsibility, given our size and power. It's something a big brother does." Tommy looked up at Franklin who was, by at least three minutes, the elder.

Harrison nodded. "And this particular war might have gone to hell, but sometimes war is needed to make things right when diplomacy and communication have failed. Frankie, why was Tommy jailed?"

Franklin shrugged.

"Well, ask him!"

Franklin turned to his twin. "Why?"

"The first time was at a peace sit-in at JFK, when cargo planes were unloading crate after crate of dead soldiers from Nam. The authorities didn't like the size and color of the crowd, or that I was holding hands with an African American woman who was inconsolable. All four of her sons were in boxes. They broke my hand to teach me a lesson—that's why it's kinda twisted now. I spent the week in jail before I was able to get it plastered up."

Franklin stared at his brother's hand, his forehead creasing as he recognized the damage.

"The second time was when I was with my friends. Some of them don't fit the stereotype of the all-American male. We were just being ourselves, just having a beer at the Stonewall."

"Just having a drink," Franklin echoed. "The land of the free and the home of the brave," he said, almost inaudibly.

Harrison placed his hands on his sons' shoulders. "Those words aren't true because they're in an anthem. They're true because we fight to keep them true—to make them true—each of us in our own way. I have watched you boys grow into men, choose your own battles, and fight where you thought you could make a difference. And I couldn't be more proud. There is no doubt that the wars are far from finished, but they still have to be fought if we're ever gonna get to the end."

He looked around at the photos. "Somewhere, sometime, someone told me we are all one, all connected. We are part of the same world, the same destiny. No matter our color, religion, hopes, or dreams."

Agnes stood up beside her son and rested her hand on his forearm. "We are *all* of the same family. We always have been and always will be."

The twins looked at each other, at themselves, at the face that was so familiar but unrecognized until now, seeing each other for the first time in many years. They stepped close and threw their arms around one another in a heartfelt embrace, a bear-hug rocking from side to side, their cheeks pressed together, glued by tears.

"Ah-hi-e, ah-hi-e!" the twins called at each other's ear.

"I am much pleased; I am much rejoiced," Harrison mouthed.

Carmine ran toward the huddle of his father and uncle. Laughing and throwing his arms around their legs, he stared up at the twins.

"A bright morning sun lit a cloudless blue sky." (2001 AD)

He stared up at the twins.

They soared a hundred and ten stories into the cloudless blue sky, aluminum and steel reflecting the bright morning sun.

Carmine held Destiny in his arms as his wife, Aisha, gripped tight to Austin's and Tyler's hands.

He checked his watch. 8:26 AM.

The plaza at the base of the World Trade Center towers was humming with thousands of people. Businesspeople hurried across the pavement, juggling briefcases, laptops, and coffees. Tourists sat on the benches around the Sphere, eating breakfast burritos and panning with their video cameras, waiting for the observation deck to open.

"Daddy, is this where you work?" Tyler asked.

Carmine smiled. "Sure is. Right up there." He squatted beside his son and pointed up at Tower One.

Austin jumped up and down, clapping his hands.

"We'll go get some bagels and meet you up there, okay?" Aisha said.

"Sounds like a plan. I need to handle a few things before we head down to the museum." Carmine stood, with Destiny cuddled close to his heart, as Aisha and the boys headed off across the plaza. "Hey, honey?" he called after them.

Aisha turned with an arch of her eyebrows.

"I love you!" Carmine shouted, so everyone within earshot knew it.

Aisha grinned and mouthed, "I love you, too," before heading off with the boys in tow.

8:29 AM.

The crowd waiting for the elevators wasn't as bad as Carmine had thought. It was only a minute before he stepped onto the express to the 78th floor Sky Lobby. The elevator smelled of freshly dry-cleaned suits, aftershave, and perfume. The confinement of people ascending floor after floor, faster than the beating of their own hearts, felt somehow relaxing to Carmine. All individuals with their own thoughts, hopes, and desires—all following the song in their heart. Carmine smiled, and Destiny gurgled. With the change to the local floor elevators, conversations picked up.

Carmine stepped out on the ninety-third floor and walked to his office in the southwest corner.

8:37 AM.

"Morning, Stella," he said.

The receptionist glanced up from her computer with a welcoming smile. "Morning." She checked her notes. "The Smithsonian Museum of the American Indian has confirmed your ten o'clock. A Mister Solomon, of the Lakota tribe, will meet you and your family in the rotunda of the museum."

Carmine checked his watch and nodded. "Aisha and the kids will be up in a minute. Just send them on through to my office. Thanks!"

He passed the glass-walled conference room and stepped into his office. One wall was covered in photographs of his recent construction projects: a resort in the Caribbean; luxury condos on Central Park West; office towers in New York, Chicago, London, and Dubai. The office had a clear view from the Verrazano Bridge in the east, across New York Harbor, Ellis and Liberty Islands and out over Jersey City. Scores of passenger jets circled the sky, ready to descend into Newark, LaGuardia, or JFK.

8:42 AM.

Aisha and the kids would be in the Sky Lobby by now, Carmine thought after checking his watch again. With one arm cradling his baby daughter, Carmine spun the combination lock of the wall safe and swung open the fireproof door. He reached in to extract a small box. Its contents was the reason for his visit to the Smithsonian. It was the greatest treasure his family owned, and it needed to be shared. He sat down at his desk and opened the box.

It was beautiful, shimmering, obsidian.

8:44 AM.

Pressing his lips to Destiny's cheek, he held up the blade of the Great White Bear. It was a glassy dark blue, almost black, reflecting the movement of cloud and shadow out the window behind him. It was mesmerizing.

Still sharp enough to cut, it nicked the pad of Carmine's thumb. A trickle of blood slipped from the fresh cut, down the face of the obsidian.

8:46 AM.

Do you still not recognize me?

The fire was extinguished.

Másaw slumped against the great oak at his back. Numb, he stared at the rubble of embers.

He pushed himself to his feet and walked across the glade and through the forest of swamp white oaks. Squirrels scurried around trunks, and birds chirped in the highest branches.

The canopy opened above him, and he stepped onto the pavement surrounding the two memorial fountains—deep footprints where the Twin Towers once stood. Water cascaded into the ponds of reflection, pulling his thoughts with it. He touched the bronze parapet surrounding the pool before him, trembling fingers caressing the names closest to his heart.

He knew every one of the almost three thousand names inscribed, felt every broken heart, and knew every story that needed to be told. Thousands of family sagas converged at this one sacred place.

"Is that the end of the story?"

Másaw turned from watery memories. With weary, gray eyes, the storyteller listened to the melody of his own heart song once more. He looked through the pages of time and into the eyes of the one who dared to ask the question.

"No, my child. What I have told you is only the beginning. Now you must live, and when you are ready, you will tell me your chapter."

Hereditary Line

Chapter and birth dates are translated to the Gregorian calendar equivalent.

All pre-Columbian dates are open to conjecture and controversy dependent upon the most recent schools of scientific or ecclesiastical thought, archeological finds, and dating methods. For our family, the author simply counted the number of pictograms on the history skins, or correlated the stories with the speculated time periods of the flora and fauna described in the stories handed down through the generations. Future archeological digs or major theological events may prove these times to vary from those currently hypothesized.

Ancestral line from previous worlds not documented

16,024 BC Great White Bear and Rainbow Cloud (twin sons of the previous world)
16,007 BC First Light (son of Great White Bear and Little Pebble)

Fourth Morning of the Seventh Moon (16,000 BC)
First Light (7 Thaws)

Do you not recognize me?
Másaw (*unknown*)

Túwaqachi, the World Complete (15,999 BC)
First Light (8 Thaws)
Great White Bear (25 Thaws)
Rainbow Cloud (25 Thaws)
Little Pebble (23 Thaws)

P.J. Parker

15,990 BC Rearing Mammoth (son of First Light and White Cloud)
15,981 BC Tusk (second son of First Light and White Cloud)

Glacial Horizons (15,976 BC)
Rearing Mammoth (14 Thaws)
Tusk (5 Thaws)
White Cloud (31 Thaws)
Sundance (*unknown*)
Red Star (*unknown*)

15,973 BC Dancing Bird (son of Rearing Mammoth and Many Caribou)

Ice (15,958 BC)
Dancing Bird (15 Thaws)
Tusk (23 Thaws)
Like Blue Skies (18 Thaws)
Musk Ox (*unknown*)
Bear (*unknown*).

[Recall section: Rearing Mammoth (16 Thaws), Tusk (7 Thaws)]

| (unknown generations)
15,398 BC Distant Thunder (son of Coyote and Clever One)

Vision Quest (15,383 BC)
Distant Thunder (15 summers)

| (unknown generations)
14,209 BC Beaver (son of the Running Stream and Happiness)

The story of Beaver (14,194 BC)
Beaver (15 summers)

| (unknown generations)
12,516 BC Blazing Sun (son of Crow and Pretty Fox)

Fluted Stone (12,500 BC)

AMERICA Túwaqachi

Blazing Sun (16 summers)
Dark Moon (*unknown*)
Fluted Stone (*unknown*)
Beautiful Leaf (*unknown*)

| (unknown generations)
8152 BC Many Hands (son of Courageous Hunter and Flowers in the Stream)

Many Hands (8135 BC)
Many Hands (17 summers)
Dusk Runner (*unknown*)
One-Tree Rock (*unknown*)
Black-Footed Crow (*unknown*)

| (unknown generations)
1321 BC Bright Eyes stolen from the Clan of the Great White Bear.
1319 BC Moon River (son of Bright Eyes and Healing Water)

**Do you understand the meaning of the soil beneath your feet?
(1302 BC)**
Moon River (17 summers)
Hope (16 summers)
Faith (1 summer)

| (unknown generations)
269 BC Darkwater (elder brother of Hohokam)
267 BC Hohokam (son of Butterfly Drinking Dew on a Leaf and unknown)

The Three Sisters (250 BC)
Hohokam (17)
Darkwater (19)

| (unknown generations)
810 AD Chaco (son of Woven Basket and Place Where People Meet)

The Great House made of Dawn (828 AD)
Chaco (18)
Friend of the Snake (18)
Rain Shadow (18)

| (unknown generations)
1190 AD Hopituh Shi-nu-mu "Hopi" (son of unknown and unknown)
1192 AD Fox Walks Well (brother of Hopi)
1196 AD Yellow Snake Who Rattles (sister of Hopi)

Creators of Tall Buildings; Ancestors of the Peaceful People (1209 AD)
Hopituh Shi-nu-mu "Hopi" (19)
Fox Walks Well (17)
Yellow Snake Who Rattles (13)
Spirit Warrior (*unknown*)
White-Tailed Deer (*unknown*)
Gentle Stream (*unknown*)

1211 AD Wind that Dances (daughter of Hopituh Shi-nu-mu and unknown)
1235 AD Pleasant Rain (daughter of Wind that Dances and unknown)
| (unknown generations)

City of the Sun (1322 AD)

| (unknown generations)
1521 AD Cahokia (12 generations removed from Pleasant Rain and unknown)

The Child of the Sun; The Silent Enemy (1541 AD)
Cahokia (20)
Sky Full of Stars (15)
Creek (19)
No Man Hunting (*unknown*)

AMERICA Túwaqachi

Tallahassee (7)
Trail Runner (*unknown*)
Sweet Flower (*unknown*)
Jackrabbit (*unknown*)
"Child of the Sun" (45)

1542 AD Handsome Stream (son of Sky Full of Stars and unspeakable)

We the People . . . The People of the Longhouse (1562 AD)
Handsome Stream (20)
Sky Full of Stars (36)
Genesee (16)
Autumn Moon Shadow (*unknown*)
Chief Yellow Corn (*unknown*)
Coyote is Dancing (19)
Moose in the Water (*unknown*)
Morning Star Blackbird (22)
Atotarho (*unknown*)
Chief Broken Tree (*unknown*)

1564 AD River Maker (second son of Handsome Stream and Genesee)

Trade (1584 AD)
River Maker (20)
Algernon (*unknown*)

1587 AD Arrow Feather (son of River Maker and Leaves Rustling in the Breeze)

Powhatan . . . A Chance of Brotherhood (1607 AD)
Arrow Feather (20)
Blossom of Black Cherry (18)
Paramount Chief Powhatan (*unknown*)
Chief Opechancanough (*unknown*)
Matoaka (Pocahontas) (11)

1608 AD Chauco "John" (son of Arrow Feather and Blossom of Black Cherry)
1626 AD James (son of Chauco "John" and Matilda)

Built on Smoke (1628 AD)
Chauco "John" (20)
Matilda (17)
James (2)
Abraham Johnson (18)
Captain McMasters (28)

A Model of Christian Charity (1647 AD)
James (21)
Jemima (*unknown*)
Mistress McMasters (45)
Matthew and Tobias Jefferson (22)

1655 AD Clement (son of James and Verity)
1667 AD Prudence (daughter of James and Verity)

The Day of Trouble is Near (1676 AD)
Clement (21)
Chief Pageacoag (*unknown*)
Metacom (King Philip) (37)
Praying Sakunk (16)
Governor Berkeley (70)
Nathaniel Bacon (29)

1677 AD Thaddeus (first son of Clement and Sofia)
1678 AD Eli (second son of Clement and Sofia)
1679 AD Jethro (third son of Clement and Sofia)
1681 AD Clementine (daughter of Clement and Sofia)

The Ship (1700 AD)
Jethro (21)
Jack Barker (23)

| (Seven sons and three daughters of Jethro and Theodosia [née Johnson] not documented)
1716 AD Zachariah (eighth son of Jethro and Theodosia)
1717 AD Hannibal (ninth son of Jethro and Theodosia)
1718 AD Amos (tenth son of Jethro and Theodosia)

The Sleepin' Fox Catches No Poultry; The Great Awakenin' (1738 AD)
Zachariah (22)
Hannibal (21)
Amos (20)
Cuffee (*unknown*)
Cudjo (*unknown*)
Mouse (*unknown*)
Mister Grymes (*unknown*)
Mistress Clementine (57)

1740 AD Robert (first son of Zachariah and Katherine [née MacDonald])
1750 AD David (sixth son of Zachariah and Katherine)
1757 AD Bartley (ninth son of Zachariah and Katherine)
| (Six sons and six daughters of Zachariah and Katherine not documented)

The Forks of the Ohio; Not Yet a Nation (1763 AD)
Robert (23)
Captain William Trent (48)
Captain Simeon Ecuyer (*unknown*)
Mouse (*unknown*)
The Turtle's Heart (*unknown*)

A Matter of Hats and Tea (1773 AD)
David (23)
Benjamin (23)

P.J. Parker

West Point—The Key to the Continent and Independence (1780 AD)

Bartley (23)
David (30)
Robert (40)
Levi Atkinson (17)
Peggy Arnold (20)
Major General Benedict Arnold (39)

1782 AD Peter (only son of Bartley and Sarah [née Matthews])
| (Thirteen daughters of Bartley and Sarah not documented in this work, for whom a mere footnote would not do justice to their names. Suffice to say, their contribution to the history of our country deserves its own extensive investigation and dissertation.

From Sea to Shining Sea; An Empire of Liberty (1805 AD)

Peter (23)
Captain Meriwether Lewis (32)
Second Lieutenant William Clark (36)
Charbonneau (38)
Sacagawea (17)
York (35)

A Letter from Monticello (1807 AD)

Peter (25)
Lieutenant Zebulon Montgomery Pike (28)

1811 AD Daniel and Christopher (twin sons of Peter and Concepción [née Clara] Tomasa)
1813 AD Clarisa (daughter of Peter and Concepción)

The Shrine of Texas Liberty (1836 AD)

Daniel (25)
Christopher (25)
Jimmy (18)
Lieutenant Colonel William Travis (27)
Colonel James Bowie (40)

Colonel David "Davy" Crockett (50)
General Samuel Houston (43)
General Antonio López de Santa Anna (42)

The Trail of Tears (1838 AD)
Daniel (27)
An old man (*unknown*)
A kid in a straw hat (*unknown*)

1838 AD Montgomery (son of Daniel and Laura [née Stevens])
1845 AD Christopher Jr. and Daniel Jr. (twin sons of Daniel and Laura)
| (Fifteen sons and daughters of Daniel and Laura not documented in this work)

Br'er Rabbit and the Fox (1861–1865 AD)
Montgomery (23–27)
Henry (*early 20s*)
Joseph (*early 20s*)

1865 AD Bromley (first son of Montgomery and Ada)
1869 AD Laura (first daughter of Montgomery and Ada)
1872 AD Gertrude (second daughter of Montgomery and Ada)
1873 AD Nora (third daughter of Montgomery and Ada)
1885 AD Berton "Bertie" (second son of Montgomery and Ada)

The White City (1893 AD)
Bromley (28)
Miss Agnes Abbington (19)
Gertrude Molloy (23)
Charlie Molloy (24)
Florence Molloy (2)
Nora Denman (22)
Willie Denman (25)
Ethel Denman (1)
Berton "Bertie" (8)

1900 AD Ralph (son of Bromley and Agnes [née Abbington])
1911 AD Harrison (second son of Bromley and Agnes)
1928 AD Mildred (daughter of Ralph and Edith Jacobson)

Jazz Hot, Baby—The Crash (1929 AD)
Ralph (29)
Edith Jacobson (18)
Mildred (1)
Harrison (18)
Agnes (55)
Berton "Bertie" (44)

1932 AD Franklin and Tommy (twin sons of Harrison and Edith [née Jacobson])

Over There (1941 AD)
Harrison (30)
Edith (30)
Mildred (13)
Franklin (9)
Tommy (9)
Airman Woodfield (29)
Sergeant Sawyer (37)

1960 AD Carmine (son of Franklin and Dorothy [née Edwards])

A Time Comes When Silence is Betrayal (1967 AD)
Agnes (93)
Harrison (56)
Edith (56)
Tommy (35)
Franklin (35)
Dorothy (26)
Carmine (7)

1996 AD Austin (son of Carmine and Aisha [née Hussein])
1997 AD Tyler (son of Carmine and Aisha)

AMERICA Túwaqachi

2000 AD Destiny (daughter of Carmine and Aisha)

"A bright morning sun lit a cloudless blue sky." (2001 AD)
Carmine (41)
Aisha (35)
Austin (5)
Tyler (4)
Destiny (1)

Do you still not recognize me?
Másaw (*unknown*)

353

P.J. Parker

Acknowledgements

This work has been the song in my heart for much longer than I ever expected. Its research and writing stretched over a decade—with too many interim years spent ignoring it, even forcibly forgetting it altogether, relegating it to the scrapheap with a writer's broken heart. Authors can be overly dramatic like that. During the time I was writing *America Túwaqachi: The Saga of an American Family*, I released two other works of fiction. One specifically, *Fire on the Water: A Companion to Mary Shelley's Frankenstein*, was written purely as an escape from the demanding research of 18,000[1] years of "American" history—a vacation in pure imagination with minimal research requirements, fed by my love of Shelley's wretch.

The research for *America Túwaqachi* was extensive, calling on not just intensive reading and listening, but living a life open to others' points of view. Due to the nature of the work, it was not unusual for me to read thousands of pages of dry archeological thesis to write one sentence or paragraph that was palatable, if not exciting. I steered clear of the romanticized Hollywood versions of history and attempted, as best I could, to follow source material. Where such was inadequate or nonexistent, then Native American Indian written and verbal history and mythology took precedence over the interpretations of those who followed and conjectured. *America Túwaqachi* was never meant as an historic document, but rather a catalyst that might urge readers to follow through with their own interests and discoveries to determine what might be true.

---

[1] The research and first draft of this work actually started with the Big Bang, a lot longer than 18,000 years.

I would in particular like to call out the following sources and inspirations:

Smithsonian Institution

The National Museum of the American Indian (Smithsonian Institution)

The Native Americans: An Illustrated History (1993) (David Hurst Thomas, Jay Miller, Richard White, Peter Nabokov, Alvin M. Josephy Jr.)

500 Nations: An Illustrated History of North American Indians (1994) (Alvin M. Josephy Jr.)

Various works on the Myths and Legends of Native American Indians

Portraits from North American Indian Life (1972) (Edward S. Curtis, A. D. Coleman, T. C. McLuhan) (photographs bound in a book gifted to me by the beautiful Lynne Fitzek)

A Biography of America (The Annenberg Foundation)

The Journals of Captain John Smith

The Letters of J. Hector St. John de Crèvecoeur

The Journals of the Lewis and Clark Expedition

The Journals of the Zebulon Pike Expedition

Ansel Adams

The Bible

The life of Samuel Clemens (Mark Twain—*Tom Sawyer*)

The works of *The Mamas and the Papas* (Cass Elliot, John Phillips, Denny Doherty, Michelle Phillips)

Though the creation of this work was at times quite lonely, it was done with a passion bolstered by the friendship of others (many whose idiosyncrasies and/or namesakes are within these pages). In particular, I would like to recognize those closest friends who have been directly impacted by my distraction and obsession: Keiko and Chris and Stephen, but most of all, Steven, who has long suffered my passion for writing.

Second to last, I would like to thank the editors who have helped me grow throughout my career as a writer: Doug Watts and Hayley German Fisher. An exemplary thank you to Hayley for her brilliant editing on this work.

And last, but in no way least, this work is the direct result of a love of reading instilled in me by a woman of profound and unconditional love: my great-aunty, Aileen Bernice Cecily (née Dennes) Hardaker.

P.J. Parker

About the Author

P.J. Parker was born and raised in rural Australia. With a Bachelor of Science Architecture Degree from the University of New South Wales he has travelled and lived extensively around the world—intrigued by cultures of historic interest and buildings of architectural significance. An avid reader and researcher, P.J.'s writing is undertaken with a passionate and exacting degree of attention to detail. *Roxelana and Suleyman* was P.J.'s debut novel and was quickly followed up by the internationally acclaimed *Fire on the Water: A Companion to Mary Shelley's Frankenstein.*

Also by P.J. Parker

Roxelana and Suleyman

"A magnificent rich pageant of historical fiction. Lush, dramatic and so very, very readable."

"Aleksandra is a great main character: strong, determined, and definitely intriguing. She's one you can't help but love and follow on her journey.... The start is intense and sets the stage well for what is to come."

Fire on the Water: A Companion to Mary Shelley's Frankenstein

"Fire on the Water by P.J. Parker appears to take on a monumental task when it attempts to weave the iconic story of Mary Shelley's Frankenstein with a more modern tale of a young American biographer named Rachel. This book is full of the potential to revitalize a classic tale but it could also have turned into a colossal disaster. Fortunately for readers P.J. Parker is enormously talented and Fire on the Water is a tremendous read!"